Praise for the Sweetpea series:

'Think *Bridget Jones* meets *Killing Eve* – only
with better jokes. This darkly comic novel has
the potential to become a cult classic'
Daily Mail

'Makes Hannibal Lecter look like Mary Poppins.
Dark, depraved and devilishly delicious'
John Marrs

'Not for the squeamish or the faint-hearted.
Think *Bridget Jones* meets *American Psycho*'
RED

'Brilliantly written characters, original
and engaging. It's so good!'
BA Paris

'Filthy and funny . . . a compulsive read'
Sunday Times

'You MUST read this book especially if you like your
anti-heroes dirty-mouthed and deadly dark. I adored it'
Fiona Cummins

'Pitch dark, laugh-out-loud hilarious – the
Sweetpea series is pure genius escapism'
Susi Holliday

CJ Skuse was born in 1980 in Weston-super-Mare. She has two First Class degrees in Creative Writing and Writing for Young People, and aside from being a novelist works as a Senior Lecturer at Bath Spa University.

Also by CJ Skuse
The Alibi Girl

Sweetpea series:
Sweetpea
In Bloom
Dead Head
Thorn In My Side
The Bad Seeds

For Young Adults:
Pretty Bad Things
Rockoholic
Dead Romantic
Monster
The Deviants

THE
BAD
SEEDS

C.J. SKUSE

ONE PLACE. MANY STORIES

HQ
An imprint of HarperCollins*Publishers* Ltd
1 London Bridge Street
London SE1 9GF

www.harpercollins.co.uk

HarperCollins*Publishers*
Macken House, 39/40 Mayor Street Upper,
Dublin 1, D01 C9W8, Ireland

1
First published in Great Britain by
HQ, an imprint of HarperCollins*Publishers* Ltd 2024

ISBN: 978-0-00-860839-2

Set in Sabon LT Std by HarperCollins*Publishers* India

Printed and bound in the UK using 100% Renewable
Electricity at CPI Group (UK) Ltd

For Ted and Bill

'A true friend stabs you in the front'
ATTRIBUTED TO OSCAR WILDE

Part 1: Aftermath

18 October 2021

Raf was on top of me. We lay there, surrounded by shouting and chaos and boxes of Pop Tarts falling from shelves and glass breaking and cans rolling, my back was pressed to the coldness. I looked over and the guy in the blue shirt – the deputy manager, Luiz – lay an arm's length away, not breaking his stare. The front of his blue shirt bloomed red. He was gone. I turned my head, my face smothered by Raf's hair. He wasn't moving.

'Raf?'

I couldn't say it again – I couldn't breathe; he was too heavy on top of me. Too still. I tried to push him off but he was a dead weight. I tried to wake him up, pull his shirt, slap his face, but he wouldn't respond. Both my hands were covered in warm red wet. I'd never been so scared of a dead man in my life.

'Come on, get up, spic lover!' Mama Fratelli shouted again, still coming at us with her gun. Her face was bruised where I'd caught her with the can weeks before in this same supermarket. Now she had shot my husband. I deserved this. I deserved to die too. 'Get up and face me! Not so tough now, are you, bitch?'

The warmth of Raf's blood brought me screaming back to

reality, and with all the strength I could muster, I heaved myself out from under him and scrambled to my feet. I fixed on her as she waddled and stamped down the cereal aisle, crunching over spilled boxes of Cap'n Crunch and Lucky Charms and smashed jars of jam and honey. My hands were red. My heart thumped. My anger surged through me like a gasoline fire.

'Where's your muscle man, huh?' Mama Fratelli shrieked. 'What you gonna do now?!'

I didn't think. I tilted forwards and ran at her with everything I had; crunching over Fruit Loops and Frosted Flakes, full-thrust rugby tackle, roaring my head off – a sound that came from deep within my soul.

'AAAARRRRRGGGHHHHHHH! FUCKING BIIIIIIITTCCCHHHH!'

BOOF! Down she went, the gun clattering to the hard floor and skittering off along a side aisle. She'd taken the one thing in this rotten life that was worth breathing for; worth leaving everything I knew for. Taken it all in three gunshots. Everyone else in the place had scattered.

Nothing was going to stop me now. Nothing could.

That molten feeling was back as I straddled her colossal form. That urge and the wetness between my thighs as I strangled her with my hands still covered in Raf's blood. This Goonie-looking freakshow who'd killed my husband. The rippling, crippling can't-do-anything-else-but-kill thrill sizzled through me the way it had so many times before. Oh, how I wanted her. So badly. Just like all the rest of them.

But there had been a shift. Because this wasn't paradise anymore. I'd known paradise with him. And now he was gone. And this was hell.

'AAAAARRRGGHHHHHHHH!' I screamed, gripping her neck as tight as I could, smashing her head against the stone tile, again and again and again.

'AAAARRRGGH! YOU FUCKING PIG YOU FUCKING BITCH CUNT PIG YOU KILLED HIM YOU KILLED HIM YOU FUCKING KILLED HIIIIIMMMMMMMMMM!'

After a while, she stopped struggling. Blood pooled behind her head and the knocking sound her skull had made on the floor had become a wet splat. I let go of her and scrambled off. All I could hear were my own short breaths and my heart thumping in my ears.

As I stood up, the supermarket slowly came back to life around me. Glass tinkled. A CB radio crackled and echoed from the tin walls.

'Shots fired at the Food and Home, repeat, shots fired at the Food and Home store on the corner of Marshall and Palm. Repeat . . .'

Someone was crying, hunkered down in the Coffee, Tea and Baked Goods section. Heavy breathing from behind the pharmacy counter. Two guys were crouched beneath a stack of reduced-price Fancy Feast cat food. The sound system cut through my thoughts – Billie Eilish, 'When the Party's Over'. So crushingly appropriate. The slap-slap of rubber soles on tile as someone ran out, or in, broke into my thoughts.

Outside, groups of people had gathered in the parking lot, some talking to uniformed cops, standing around in the sunlight wearing masks. A couple of old women were crying and handing out tissues to other rubberneckers with bulging bags of groceries at their feet. Two police cars sped in.

Inside, the CB radio crackled with static again – it was coming from Luiz's belt.

'We're gonna need more ambulances, all you got, man, all you got!'

'. . . one active shooter . . . I think she's down, shooter's down . . .'

'Ambulances rolling, they're coming, man, just hold on . . .'

I walked back towards Luiz, kneeling beside his head and checking for a pulse I knew wasn't there. I don't know why I bothered – his eyes were still wide open. I didn't want to look back at Raf but I didn't want him on his own either. I would stay with him, I decided. Until they zipped up his body bag, I would stay.

'Suspect is down, repeat, suspect is down, wearing blue jersey, red pants and black boots, mid-fifties. No movement, repeat, no movement from suspect. Weapon is disengaged . . .'

I choked down my fright and fury and lay back down next to Raf. He was still warm. I turned his cheek towards me, held his heavy head. Kissed his mouth.

'Thank you for loving me.'

This was a crime scene and I was crying all over it but I didn't care. I didn't care if I died right here next to him.

Time was I thought love was that feeling I got after a kill, cutting through the layers of skin and flesh to the bone beneath. The anxious knot in my chest disappearing, the electrification of my limbs. But I knew now that had been lust. Smashing Mama Fratelli's head to the floor – lust. Strangling her red neck – lust. Anything I'd ever done before I met Raf. But with him, this was love. And I couldn't fucking believe it was gone.

There were voices inside the store now, shouting, coming closer.

'Suspect down. Suspect down,' one yelled.

'Weapon's here—'

'Over here!' cried a voice somewhere behind me. 'Please hurry!'

'It's okay,' I whispered into Raf's ear, cuddling him closer to me. 'I won't leave you.' My hands shook as I held him. I should have kissed him more. I should have held him for longer. A lifetime was never going to be enough for us, I knew it.

'I'm sorry,' I whispered again, my forehead to his neck. 'I'm so sorry.' His neck was so warm. And then . . . a twitch.

I reeled back to look at him – the muscles in his neck spasmed. His right eye flickered, ever so slightly. Or was I imagining it?

'Raf?'

Please, God or whoever, please tell me I wasn't imagining it.

I pressed my fingers to his neck again – and then I felt it. Ever so slightly, like the fluttering of a tiny, trapped butterfly.

A pulse.

We're losing him . . .

Pressure's dropping . . .
No visible exit wounds . . .

I can't lose mi joya, no, not
my baby!

He's not gonna die, Mom. Raf
survived Afghanistan – he's
not gonna be taken out in a
cereal aisle.

If he needs any blood, tell
the doctors we're all here.

Padre nuestro, que estás en
el cielo. Santificado sea tu
nombre . . .

Pressure's dropped again . . .

She shouldn't be here. Esta
loca, te lo advierto ahora!

Ariela, she's his wife . . .

I don't care! She is a devil.
Billy, get her out of here.

There's no point eatin' her
head off, the girl's in pieces.
She nearly strangled the
gunman to death . . .

Gunwoman. She was in
her sixties, the cops said.

Radial pulse is strong . . .

It was the same woman
she attacked weeks ago.

*She caused this. Raf could
die cos of her!*

*She was defending Raf!
Ophelia? Come on, let's get a
cuppa while we're waitin' for
news, eh?*

*Raf's a warrior. He'll be all
right.*

But what if he's not?

*Then we'll do what we've
done before. We'll get
stronger. And we'll be strong
for Ophelia too. Right?
RIGHT?*

The San Diego Union-Tribune

Woman shoots Food 'n' Home staff over face mask

Reuters
Monday, October 18, 2021, 01:58

A MANAGER of a Los Abrazos grocery store was shot dead and a store assistant wounded when a customer pulled out a gun and opened fire after she was told to wear a face mask inside on Sunday.

Andrea Smith-Lansing, of La Mesa, had gotten into an argument with staff at the Food 'n' Home in Los Abrazos on Sunday over their mask policy. The 62-year-old appeared to leave the store after the argument, returning moments later holding a handgun, according to a police spokesman.

Smith-Lansing first shot at store assistant Rafael Arroyo-Carranza, 36, before aiming at his colleague Luiz da Silva, 41. The store's security guard Manny Ortiz, managed to fire back twice, causing the woman to drop her gun.

Store manager da Silva was pronounced dead at the scene. He leaves behind a wife, Natalia, 34, who is pregnant, and their four-year-old son, Ángel. His mother Miriam said last night: "It is not fair. He died a hero, doing a job he loved and protecting his staff, but I can't believe he has gone."

Following an operation, Arroyo-Carranza is said to be in a stable condition at Scripps Mercy Hospital.

A witness, identified as 47-year-old Cathy Pearson, said Smith-Lansing has caused trouble in the store before. "She's always coming in here and shouting at the staff. I've seen her lick food and put it back, just to cause trouble."

Pearson saw the moment Smith-Lansing pulled out her gun.

"She was aiming it at this young woman and this guy flew in to protect her. He took most of the bullets. Then another guy got shot and that's when the younger woman got up and ran at her, knocking her flat and just strangling her. I thought she was gonna kill her. Then the security guy took over and made a citizen's arrest."

The San Diego County Sheriff's Department said the shooter has been charged with first-degree premeditated murder, attempted murder, gun charges and violating the executive order that mandates shoppers to wear masks.

Monday, 18 October – Scripps Mercy Hospital, San Diego (late evening)

1. *TikTok accounts that don't edit their military homecoming videos. Open the damn door already.*
2. *People on TikTok who don't greet the dog during videoed reunions.*
3. *People who film themselves crying on TikTok – oh my god, guys, I just crashed my car and broke my neck. Can you call me an ambulance? Hit the comments if you wanna see my foot facing the wrong way.*
4. *People who use their phone on speaker in a public place.*
5. *Andi Smith-Lansing – who almost killed the love of my life.*

The TV warbled on in the corner of the family room – *Sounds of the Nineties*. Bryan Adams, '(Everything I Do) I Do It for You'. Just when I thought things couldn't get any fucking worse.

My entire head throbbed all over. Liv's punch didn't hurt that much – it was her acrylics that almost tore out my scalp. She and Nico's wife Ariela both went to town on me when they'd arrived at the hospital, screaming and raining blows until Nico and Billy pulled them away. I stayed there on the floor of the family room, curled up in a ball. I didn't want to fight back. I think I wanted them to kill me.

I lay there for hours on that carpet where a thousand grief-stricken soles had trod, staring at a scuff mark on the skirting board of the piss-yellow wall. There was a leaflet just out of reach that had fallen from the rack above. 'Diseases of the Heart: The Number 1 Killer of San Diego Residents'.

Until I came along, that is.

I reached across and slid the leaflet towards me. There was a form on the back you could fill in if you wanted more advice on how to eat 'Heart Healthy' and 'Limit Your Tobacco Use'. The shots rang through my mind; a never-ending nightmare loop, accompanied by the echo of my screams as Rafael lunged towards me, knocked me to the floor and saved my fucking life.

'Come on, missis, up you get,' said an Irish accent as the door swung shut. 'I've got you another tea, nice and sugary.'

It was Billy, Raf's best mate. I wanted Nico, my brother-in-law, or Bianca, my pseudo mum. I wanted them to scoop me up and hold me between them, stroke my hair and tell me everything was going to be okay. But they wouldn't do that, would they? They were in another room down the hall, seeing if my sisters-in-law of no mercy, Liv and Ariela, had broken a nail while slapping me back to factory reset. Seeing if either of *them* needed a cuddle so warm you could fall asleep in it.

Billy switched off *Sounds of the Nineties* and chucked the remote into the toy basket. 'At least get up and wipe your nose. Yer lookin' manky as fuck.'

'I don't care.'

The sound of chair legs being dragged across carpet accompanied movement on the fringes of my view as Billy came over to sit beside me. He was still trying to offer me the plastic cup of tea. I didn't take it. He reached over to the TV unit and grabbed the box of tissues. 'Take one.'

I didn't reach out.

A big sigh. 'Right, I'm not having this; come on, up now.'

Billy heaved me to my feet before dragging me towards a chair and plonking me down on it, like a pissed-off puppeteer. For a man with fake legs below the knee, he wasn't half strong, but then he was an ex-soldier too, like Raf was. He pinched out some tissues from the box and wiped my nose for me. The tissues came away red. I was covered in it anyway – I looked down at my hands – Raf's blood had dried on them now. It was still on my top and my jeans as well – Jackie Onassis for Banana Republic. Billy had gone back to the Food and Home and collected my rucksack for me once the police had finished clearing the scene but I hadn't changed my clothes. I *wanted* his blood on me. I never wanted to wash it off.

'What a mess, eh?' I felt his hands in my hair, redoing my ponytail from where it had come loose.

'I'm going to lose him, aren't I? He's going to die.'

'No, he's not – he's in a bad way but he's going to pull through.'

'He won't.'

'He *will*.'

The 'will' faltered on his tongue – he didn't know for sure either. Some doctor with too big hair and Fuck Me shoes on had minced in half an hour ago and said they'd done a chest x-ray, then an abdominal exploration which revealed

14

three small injuries and one large intestinal one. They were operating on him now.

'He's not going to wake up.' I sniffed. 'I've seen *Grey's Anatomy*, I know how this goes down – they open them up and it's only then they find he's bleeding internally somewhere and they can't get a clamp to it and then they start overacting and shit.'

'You've got to be more positive, Rhiannon.'

'What's the point? Everything's fucked.' My voice was all husky like that actress in the film with the talking kids. Billy attempted to pass me the plastic cup of tea again and this time held it to my lips. I puckered up meekly and took a sip. 'Ugh. That's sugary as shit.'

'It's meant to be. It's for shock.'

'I'm not *in* shock. I'm in realisation. I did this to him. May as well have pulled that trigger myself.'

'Don't talk shite.'

'I can't be here. It's like when I gave birth to Ivy. I knew I loved her and that's why I couldn't be with her. People I love get hurt around me, Billy. Even when I don't want them to. He's alive for now. And he needs to stay that way. He needs to stay the hell away from me.'

'Don't talk like this.' He took my hand but I shook it away.

'I don't want to see him. I don't deserve to. His family need to see him.' I could barely get the words out before the tears came.

'You don't mean a word of that. That's why you're bawling. When he wakes up, he'll want to see you more than any one of us. Does your wrist ache? Here.' He fumbled in my rucksack for my brace and strapped it on my forearm for me. The relief was immediate.

'He knows who I am,' I said, barely able to see Billy's face through water. 'He's known for about a year. And he doesn't care.'

Billy's eyebrows shot up. 'Raf *knows* about Sweetpea?'

'He knows everything. He read the biography.'

Billy blew out some air while he digested the facts. 'He knew? Fuckin' hell. He knew who you were, and he *still* took three bullets for you?'

'We were booked on a flight to Mexico last night. We were running away.'

'Is someone onto you?'

The flood of memory almost drowned me. I sat with my head in my hands. 'Oh god it's such a mess. That kid we rescued in San Francisco – River Goffey – he's doing an interview in the next week or so.'

'So?'

'So? He'll tell the world what we did – how I broke into the apartment, how Raf killed Elliot Mansur. How we saved him. He'll have given police a photofit description of us already. We need to get away before the whole country knows who we are. You know what true-crime sleuths are like – they'll be like a pack of wolves on our scent.'

'You don't know that,' said Billy. He was the only other person who not only knew who I was, but also what Raf and I had done on our honeymoon – saved an eleven-year-old boy from a predatory paedophile who'd abducted him three years before. It was massive news but up until now, his liberators were just shadowy avengers. But it was only a matter of time.

'Anyway, why would River grass on you? You saved him – he owes you.'

'He's a kid. A kid in the spotlight, and a traumatised one

at that. He won't be thinking about protecting us – he'll just want to get his story out there. And even if he *doesn't* grass, there's too much heat. I went into a Starbucks before I entered Mansur's apartment. There'll be CCTV footage. Someone will recognise me.'

'Maybe not?' Billy mewed.

I glared at him. 'You don't think Ariela or Liv will go to the cops as soon as they see that footage?' I gestured to my split lip, possible nose break and eyebrow cut.

'No, I don't. You saved Liv, remember? You got her out of the shit when you disposed of her abusive old fella. She won't say fuck all about you. And Ariela's too shit-scared of Nico going to jail to land you in the brown stuff after what you did for him. They won't say nuthin' about you. And neither of them would dare do anything to hurt Rafael, would they?'

'Then why did they attack me?'

'Cos they're scared. They thought Raf was gonna die and they were lookin' for someone to lash out at – and they couldn't get to the bitch who shot him, so you had to do. They'll come round.'

'That kid's gonna do a world exclusive sit-down interview in the coming weeks. And he *will* give us away – he'll be asked what he remembers about us and he'll say, "She was British, he was Mexican, and I heard her call him Raf." Everyone will know then. If it's not one of the family, it'll be someone from my work. And then how long will it be before it *all* comes out? Before people link the British female vigilante who saved a boy in San Fran to the British female vigilante who's *not* in that grave in Vermont? They're exhuming the body as I speak, Billy. The net's closing in.'

'Christ. So that's why you're going to Mexico? To hide out?'

I shook my head. 'Not anymore. Another complication has come up in the meantime. Always does, doesn't it? My bad luck never comes in ones – it's always threes, fours or ninety-eights.'

'Oh god, what now?'

'I got a call from my sister when I was packing. I haven't heard from her in weeks, so I knew something was up. She didn't even text me on my wedding day. Anyway, she had a bomb to drop of her own: Ivy's dying.'

'WHAT?'

'She's got leukaemia, and she needs a stem cell transplant or she's going to die. I shit you not.'

'No.' Billy's skin went at least two shades paler as the news sank in.

I nodded. 'Seren's in the UK now, getting tests done. But she isn't a match for her. I would be though, wouldn't I? Being her biological mother.'

Billy's face was doing some serious smell-the-fart acting. 'You're not thinking about going back to the UK, are ya? Not *now*?'

'Raf said we could. He was going to come with me. We were just headed out to quit his job when that . . . cunt witch opened fire.'

Billy sat beside me in perfect silence. In the few weeks I had known him, he hadn't been able to stay silent for any length of time, but the cogs were clearly whirring. 'You can't leave Rafael like this though.'

'He can't come with me now, can he? And Ivy needs me. Her cancer is spreading – the sooner she gets a transplant the better. I *have* to go.'

'They'll arrest you the second you land. It'd be like walking straight into the police's arms. You *can't* go back to the UK, Rhiannon.'

'Maybe that's what Fate's trying to tell me. That I *should* go and help her and . . . hand myself in. Save her. Save Raf. Save everyone.'

Billy took a quick glance at the doorway before leaning in. 'Listen to me – you've had a big shock. *Two* big shocks, including Ivy. You're not in any fit state to make decisions, are ya? Raf would not want you to do this alone. And anyway, are you even sure your sister's not lying to yous about Ivy being sick?'

'Why would she lie?'

'To get you back to the UK, of course. To get you *arrested*. Maybe she's in cahoots with that sexy detective woman.'

'Géricault's not even on my case anymore.'

'She sure talks about you enough on the telly.'

'Exactly. She wouldn't be allowed to do that if she was, would she? Hang on, you find Géricault sexy?'

'Yeah, big time. I mean I can't stand her either cos she won't leave you alone but yeah, she's got that ice queen thing going on. Keep thinking about her handcuffing me and pinning me to a wall, woof.'

'Ugh.'

Billy shook his head. 'Nah, it's gotta be a trap. Well, it's a bit out of the blue, isn't it? First Géricault finds those two bodies at Honey Cottage that your dad buried. Then that family start talking about digging that grave in Vermont that you may or may not be in . . .'

'I'm not.'

'Obviously. And now this? It seems dodgy as fuck, like.'

'Seren wouldn't lie about this. If I was arrested, *she'd* be arrested too for lying about killing me in the first place. Believe me – it's in her interests to keep me buried. She would not survive jail.'

'But you can't go back, you just *can't*. That'd be it for you. For you and Raf. For Sweetpea.'

'Some people think that would be for the best.'

'What people?'

'Ariela and Liv, for a start. And the British police.'

'What about the Bad Seeds? Your fans? Your *legacy*? The people who believe in you?'

'Digital nobodies.'

'No, they're humans who look up to you. Who you inspire. And there's *thousands* of us.' He opened his denim jacket to reveal the black tear-shaped badge with a gold crack through the middle pinned to the inside – the mark of a true Rhiannon Lewis stan. 'You're a symbol of empowerment. If you're arrested, it'll break our hearts.'

'Who the fuck do you think I am, Katpiss Evergreen? I ain't no symbol. And anyway, they all think I'm dead – why is it worse to be arrested than dead?'

'The real die-hard Bad Seeds never thought you were dead. And there's been rumours it's not you in that grave in Vermont since the start. They prefer to think you're still out there somewhere, killing pervs, stalking weirdos, doing your thing. The fandom's crazy for it. You're like an enigma. Nobody knows for sure, and they like it that way.'

'They'll all join another fandom before long. Some overrated YA fantasy novel. Tom Daley's knitting needles. Bernie Sanders's left mitten.'

'You *can't* get caught. It'd be like Batman getting caught.'

'You mean The Joker. I don't want to be that pointy-eared prick with a costume and a trust fund.'

'Whatever, Rhiannon. Just think about this.'

'What else can I do, Billy? I've no other ideas, so bring 'em on. I've got a dying husband in there having his spleen removed and a baby across the Atlantic who will die without my help. What would *you* do?'

Billy had no answers either. I kind of felt sorry for him – he didn't have Raf's knack of dealing with my outbursts and he couldn't hug properly either. I needed a Mexican hug. I needed *my* Mexican's hug. It was all I wanted.

A doctor came in, an average-height curly-haired woman with a nose shaped like a miniature ski slope and green eyes like mine – acid green. She said a lot of words and medical terminology and spoke more to Billy than me, but the upshot of the shoot-up was that Raf had 'an injury to his colon which they hadn't noticed on x-ray'. They'd removed all the bullets and had him on antibiotics. Now they were just waiting for him to wake up. She said I could see him if I wanted to. Billy thanked her and she left.

'Have you ever been shot?' I asked as he sat back down.

'I've been blown up, that was bad enough,' he replied, clanking his titanium legs together beneath his cargo pants.

'No, but have you been *shot*? Like bullets going in you?'

'I've taken four hits. I was wearing body armour but it still hurt like a motherfucker. I didn't have to have operations for those – they were just surface wounds. Got sewn up by the duty medic. One time I broke a couple of ribs when a bullet hit the armour plate of my carrier. That was like being hit by a sledgehammer. Couldn't catch my breath. Scary as fuck.'

'Christ.'

'But I'm still here. I survived, and so will Raf. You heard what she said . . .'

'I didn't hear anything beyond "We're waiting for him to wake up".'

'Nothing hit an artery. They missed all his vitals. He's gonna be fine.'

'He hasn't woken up though.'

'He will, give him chance.'

I sniffed. 'He once told me he'd die for me. We were playing Morticia and Gomez. That's what he said. "I'd die for you, Morticia." And I said, "I'd kill for you, Gomez." He fucking *meant* it.'

'So did you,' said Billy.

'I'm not used to this kind of love, Billy. It's better if I leave.'

'No, it's not.'

'I have to go. Ivy dies if I don't. If I was put on this earth for a reason, it was to save her. I have to.'

Billy knew he was not going to win me round this time. Not even he could argue with the pros and cons of saving a two-year-old child from certain death. It was a complete no-brainer.

'When?'

'Soon as possible. There's a flight to the UK at . . .' I stared up at the wall clock – it was almost seven o'clock. '. . . ten p.m. I could get that one. If I went to the airport now—'

'What, covered in three types of blood? Yeah, I doubt security would even notice. You're not thinking straight. Fuckin' hell, come on, you gotta snap out of this.'

'I don't need to snap out of it. I need to go.' I patted my back pocket for my phone – opened up my flights app. 'There's some seats left on the morning flight. I could go home, get a shower, grab my passport and—'

'You might not be able to,' said Billy, and I followed his gaze towards the porthole window in the door. Two faces had appeared. They came in one after the other – navy-blue suits. A tall blond that looked like he'd failed the audition for *Home and Away*, and a tall moustachioed one with an accent.

'Detectives Ismael Vargas and Allen Brogan from SDPD, Mrs Arroyo-Carranza,' said Vargas, aka Moustachio. 'We're sorry to trouble you—'

'But you will anyway.'

I barely remembered to mask up and affect my all-American girl accent, which had become habit when conversing with strangers – especially strangers who might want to arrest me. They sat at the table. Billy dragged my chair over for me and took it as his cue to leave.

'I'll be just outside, Ophelia.'

Vargas opened his notepad. 'Who was that?'

'Billy O'Shea. He was in the army with my husband. Got injured out. They're good friends.'

Home and Away piped up. He wasn't Australian, annoyingly. His accent was Texan with a dash of *Can you just fucking not* so I didn't push my luck. 'We thought now might be a good time to talk, Ophelia – that all right?'

'Fine.'

In fact it went through my mind to tell them everything right there – that Ophelia was *not* my name. That my real name was Rhiannon Lewis, serial killer of this parish, wanted internationally on murder charges and equally adored and reviled depending on which social media thread you scrolled. But I didn't. I just nodded and waited for him to say something else.

'What can you tell us about the incident?'

'What else is there to say? My husband and his colleague were shot by an unhinged Goonie-looking hick. There, didn't take long, did it?' I got up briefly to sling my scrunch of bloody tissues in the bin – they missed.

'The gunwoman in question, Andrea Smith-Lansing, do you know her?'

'You *know* I know her. You also know she's a racist piece of shit and they've had trouble with her there before.'

'The security footage suggests she was targeting *you*.' It wasn't a question from Vargas, more of an accusation.

'She was. We'd had a couple of heated exchanges previously.'

'Why was that?' asked Home and Away.

'I told you – she's a racist piece of shit. Rafael was helping her put her groceries in her car one time and she was rude to him. I told her off, she told *me* off. I told her I'd rip off her head and shit down the stump or something. You know, the usual. A couple of weeks ago, we had another run-in.'

Home and Away checked his notes. 'You threw the can at her head?'

'Nine hundred thousand likes on TikTok and counting.'

Vargas stared at my blood-stained hands. 'Rafael is a very brave man.'

More than you could possibly know, I thought. 'Does Luiz's wife know he's dead?' My question was met with two hard stares. 'Shit. She's pregnant.'

'Lansing's done jail time before,' said Vargas. 'Twice, both times for aggravated assault with a weapon. She's prohibited from owning a firearm.'

'Well, that's a relief. Wouldn't want her to hurt anyone, would we?'

'It means she'll be going to jail for a long time. Justice will be served. Soon as she comes out of hospital, that is . . .'

'She's still alive?' I said.

'Against all odds, yeah. But they don't expect her to wake up.'

'Are you honestly going to charge me for that? I thought she'd just killed my husband. I wasn't thinking straight – I overreacted.'

Home and Away almost-laughed. 'You broke her skull.'

'It was already fucking broken.' My English accent poked through again. I lost all track of my American one.

Vargas stared at my eyebrow. 'The cut on your face. Was that her?'

'No, that was my sister-in-law. I went in for the hug, but she lamped me. More fool me. And then I yanked her extensions out and called her a fucking bitch and then my other sister-in-law Liv smashed my face in to defend *her*, and *she* pulled my hair out as I was about to smash *her* face in. Then the first sister-in-law slammed me into the wall. That's when Billy and my husband's brother Nico pulled them both off me and I haven't seen them since. They're in a holding pen down the corridor.'

'Why are they so angry with you?'

'They think I brought this on Raf. I suppose I did. I riled Lansing up.'

'You wanna press charges?' asked Home and Away, pen poised.

'On them? No,' I said. 'They're his family.'

It was weird saying 'his family' rather than my family, like I had been saying for the past two years, but these were the pitiful facts. They'd chosen their side, and I wasn't on it.

'Tissue?' offered Vargas, holding out the box.

I hadn't noticed my nose was bleeding again and it had dripped down to my mask. He set the box down and continued to ask obvious questions to which I gave obvious answers and eventually I went into a sort of fugue state and stopped answering. They said something about asking some more questions about what I did to Lansing and that they'd 'come back when I was feeling better'. Then they left me alone with my blood loss.

As usual.

Through the corridor window, Nico was at the water cooler. He saw me, then glanced back towards the room where his wife was, presumably to check she wasn't watching him – before cheersing me with his cup to see if I wanted one. I shook my head. I missed his smile and his big hand ruffling my hair. I missed Bianca's iron-sure arms around me and her calling 'mi cielo' and making me champurrado. I missed Liv's laugh, her hair flick over her shoulder and Baby Mikey's giggle as I tickled his chin. I missed them all so much.

But that was all gone now. In three gunshots.

I don't belong in this family's embrace anymore. I am an anomaly. An interloper. I am that parasite that enters the fish's mouth, eats away what's there and lies still, pretending to be the tongue. I walked towards the window overlooking the car park and stared into the night. Luiz's pregnant wife Natalia stood beside her car, wailing into her father's shoulder. She'd just been in to identify his body.

The moon was bright – The Man was listening.

'Don't take him, *please*. Don't take Rafael as well. I'll do anything. I won't kill again. I'll leave and I won't come back.

Just keep him alive. Even if I'm not with him – just keep him safe. *Please.*'

Who the fuck was I even talking to? The Man in the Moon? I'd ditched him when I'd found the Arroyo-Carranzas as there'd always been someone to talk to. Now I needed him again. I needed someone. Anyone. No, not anyone. I needed the one person I couldn't have: Raf.

I sat on the too-small sofa in front of the TV. When I couldn't stand the sound of my own fractious breathing anymore, I did what all concerned relatives do – mindlessly scrolled the internet looking for a shred of dopamine to take my mind off it all.

I practised my Spanish on Duolingo but I'd forgotten even the most basic stuff. How am I supposed to know what time 'Juan' wanted to meet his fucking sister?

Did a BuzzFeed quiz – *How Depressed Are You?* On a scale of Sad Pug to Kurt Cobain, I scored an 88.

And after a few Twitter refreshes, Instagram lurkings and a six-minute TikTok recipe of the tiniest peanut butter and banana toastie I'd ever seen, I found one:

Rhiannon Lewis Named Serial Killer of the Century

According to subscribers to Betsy Blohard's Maniac Monthly vlog, I have officially been named Numero Uno in Crazy Town. Top Dog in Crimesville. The Miss World of Multiple Massacre.

Lucky old me. I internally practised my acceptance speech on my YouTube channel (if I had one):

'*Hi guys, well what can I say? I'm so unbelievably proud*

to accept this award on behalf of all mass murderers who've gone before me. Thanks SOOOOOO much for voting – I'm hella proud to have beaten off Bundy (though not in the way he'd have liked LOL). I dedicate my prize to all you budding killers – dream big, babiez! Smash that Like button if you want to hear the full story of the time I cut a man's cock off with a steak knife, or when I chopped up my baby daddy in a bathtub . . .

'Before I forget, guys, today's sponsor is the Magical Fit Fruit Peeler from The Slice Is Right. Are you tired of getting all messy with your fruit and veg? Bored of banana skinning? Me too! That's why I started using this – the Magical Fit Fruit Peeler – perfect for peeling with its array of different serrated steel attachments from apples to zucchini and back again.

'That's all for now. See ya, wouldn't wanna bleed ya!'

Time was, I'd have been ecstatic to win an award like that. It would have made such a difference to my self-esteem. But today it doesn't mean anything. I don't even care if those cops come back and do a double take, realising who I really am. I don't care if there's a neon sign above my head right now blazing 'I'M A SERIAL KILLER – COME AND GET ME, YOU BIG HORSE'S ASS.' Do it. End it. I. DON'T. CARE.

But they didn't. And it was another two hours before the door opened again. I looked up, expecting Billy, but it was a nurse with Don't-You-Dare-Fuck-Me shoes on and short red hair.

'Rafael's awake, Ophelia. He's asking to see you.'

Without another word, I picked up the Diseases of the Heart leaflet and a felt-tip pen from the kids' playbox and scribbled a note on the form.

There was no sign of anyone when I got to the window

outside his room. He was lying, tilted up on his bed, bolstered by a medley of pillows, abdomen wrapped in bandages, see-through tubes coming out of his nose and a little cotton wool pad taped to the top of his hand. Just like Dad in hospital. Just like Mum. Just like when I last saw Ivy in the incubator and put my hand through the hole to feel her tiny breaths against my palm. All tubes and medication and woolly hat like an egg cosy. Fingers soft as petals. Skin smooth as catmint.

I said the same now as I said then: 'You deserve better than me.'

That was the moment I knew I loved him with every fibre, both as Ophelia and Rhiannon and everyone else I've ever been in between. I felt it like a heart attack. I only wanted the best for him. And the best was not me. I could not subject him to the kind of life we would have together. The tears came again.

'I want you to be with someone who puts you at the centre of their world. Because however hard I try, I can't make you the centre of mine.'

'Hey,' said Billy, behind me. 'I told you he'd be all right. Everyone's feeling shit about the punch-up, you know. They've all agreed to wait until you've seen him first before they go in. So . . . you going in?'

'Will you feed the fish for me?'

'Huh?'

I tightened the straps of my rucksack on my back. 'I'm gonna go.'

'Rhiannon, don't do this. Don't go. You *can't*. Not now. Please . . . just talk to Rafael first . . .'

I shook my head. 'Look after him, Billy.'

'No, wait—'

'When those cops come back, I'm toast. They'll take my prints. Probably charge me with assault. Then it's over. Ivy needs me more.'

'They've charged *her*, why would they charge you? That's not gonna happen. Please, just go in—'

'Give him this for me.'

I handed him the Diseases of the Heart leaflet, folded over. The second it left my hand, I walked.

'Rhi—'

I turned before Billy could finish the name he shouldn't say and I didn't stop running until I was at the far end of the longest corridor in the world and through the electronic doors into the heat of the night. I tore off my bloody hoodie and yeeted it into a Dumpster, then hurried across the car park, dodging screaming ambulances and screeching trucks and beeping cars until I escaped out onto the street and sprinted along the sidewalk until I couldn't feel the ground beneath me anymore.

Until I couldn't feel that pain in my chest and it was all I could do to catch my breath. And then I walked, and I breathed and I cried and I breathed. And I came to the bus stop just as the one for Los Abrazos pulled into the littered kerb.

And I got on.

And I didn't look back.

Tuesday, 19 October – Somewhere over the Atlantic

1. *The writer of that crime thriller 'everyone is talking about' that I've never heard of. That could have been me . . . *side eye emoji**
2. *Travis Scott.*
3. *Bitch barista in Starbucks who threw me a snooty look when I asked for a second muffin. Yeah, I'm a fat bitch, do your job and lose the 'tude.*
4. *Zookeepers who shoot dead escaped animals.*
5. *People who piss and whine about how busy somewhere is when they are IN the busy place – aka, me in this fucking airport right now.*

Every step I take, it's a miracle nobody utters the inevitable shriek of 'IT'S HER! IT'S RHIANNON LEWIS, EVERYBODY, LOOK! IT'S SWEETPEA!' because I'm doing fuck all to hide myself. When I remember to pull up my mask or use my American accent, it's half-assed. I care about getting to England, of course I do, but I also *don't* care. Because I can't believe this is happening. I don't want to leave San Diego but I *have* to. I *have* to go to Ivy. I'm in autopilot.

I spent a fitful night trying to sleep on a hard metal seat at the airport, waiting for the British Airways check-in desk to open and wearing so much make-up I could barely frown. Liv gave me a bottle of the foundation she uses for my last birthday and it's incredible for covering any sort of blemish or bruise, even tattoos. No wonder *she* used it – must be designed for battered wives. Apart from the occasional nosebleed, I look almost like my old self. Almost. Some things just ain't for masking.

Like my temper.

Remember that halcyon sliver of time during the Lockdowns when every motherfucker stayed home? I thought there wouldn't be *that* many people on my specific night flight to Heathrow from San Diego at this time of year, but as usual, I was wrong. It was twats a-gogo. Cunts akimbo, as far as the eye could see. And every last one of them was trampolining on my tits.

Nevertheless, in the wake of Covid, it's amazing how quickly you can clear an area with a well-timed cough. And not for the first time in the last two years, that helpful little disease saved my bacon. Any time I could pull my mask up and my sunglasses down, I took it. Nobody looked at me; nobody came too close, and better still, nobody recognised me.

It also helped that most people in the world still thought I was dead, I suppose. Most people except that malodorous qweef Detective Inspector Géricault. It keeps dawning on me that if she *was* waiting for me at Terminal 5, this could be my last time ever on a plane.

My last time ever eating airplane food.

My last chance ever to buy duty-free perfume or Toblerone

or Cartier watches again (not that I bought any this time, nor any other time I've been to an airport).

I tried to focus on other things as I stepped ever closer to my doom, but all I could conjure up was that film where the plane crashes and they're stuck in the snow and have to eat each other. I'd sooner that than this. I'd eat human if I had to. I'd start before the nuts ran out.

But of course I am merely dabbing my anxious brow with humour, as per. In reality, I was terrified; an emotion that's not a familiar bedfellow for me and let me tell you, I didn't like it one bit. Raf's abuela had once told him that I would strengthen him – *Ella te fortalecerà*. She was right. But I think he had weakened me. I still had my temper – there was no shifting that – but I didn't call on it as often as I once had, and I felt emotions, like love and fear, more easily now. It put me in mind of when I'd just given birth to Ivy. I'd never felt sodding pain like it. Not the labour – leaving her. I wasn't sure if that was a good or bad thing.

There was a strong possibility that I would get arrested between here and Blighty. And if so, that jail cell door would slam behind me and never open again.

I tried to distract myself thinking about what I *wouldn't* miss about flying, like my fellow travellers. All the things that are getting on my last tit on this last journey I will ever take.

Like the prick who lost their boarding pass and held up the flight for half an hour.

And the twat in the line for security to whom the shoes-off rule simply didn't apply.

Or the knob head with the huge carry-on who insisted on cramming it into the overhead locker and threw a strop when he was told it had to go in the hold.

33

Or the asshole already in holiday mode and walking snail-pace towards every store, toilet or departure gate I needed to get to.

And the parents with ALL the kids but the control of none.

And the wanker who took root by the baggage carousel.

And the spunk-gargling buffoon in flip-flops with his feet funk stinking up the entire plane.

And that god-awful animated Peter Rabbit atrocity I've just sat through because my TV screen is stuck on one channel.

The only thing keeping me sane(ish) was my little Sylvanian pig figurine, Richard E. Grunt. 'Here we are again, Dicky. Just you and me versus the world.' He didn't respond. 'I know. You're sick of travelling too, aren't you?'

Cue the stink-eye from the stewardess as she sauntered past with two bags of salted pretzels. In another life, I'd be picking her out of my teeth right about now but somewhere between the line for security and boarding, I'd lost the will to fight. I just wanted to sleep. I tried to lose myself in imagining the torture methods I'd inflict on James Corden given half the chance, when a crab-addled bellend tapped me on my right shoulder. I looked round to see Billy's face gurning back at me.

'The fuck?'

'Well, if it isn't San Diego's biggest serial killer. Small world, eh?'

'How the hell—'

'Same as you,' he wheeze-laughed. 'Booked a ticket, caught an Uber, got felt up by a Shrek-lookin' bag of fuck posin' as a security guard and hopped aboard.'

'Where did the woman with the bunions go?'

'In the crapper. Think she's having a bit of trouble by the

sounds. I saw the empty seat, so thought I'd stop by and say hi.'

'Rafael sent you, didn't he?'

Billy made out like he was thinking hard as his face dissolved into a shit-eating grin. 'Now how did you guess that?'

There was a shift inside my chest – the anxious knot had come undone at the thought of Raf still watching over me in some way. I held Richard E. Grunt a bit too tightly in my fist for comfort and in my head he squealed. 'You couldn't have known what flight I was taking – you must have followed me.'

'Correct,' he said, sliding into the seat to clear the aisle for the trolley coming through. 'I was going back today or tomorrow anyway so it was no bother to change my flight. Awww.' He leant over to take Richard from me but I snatched him away, banging my hand on the wall of the aircraft as I did. Faces turned. I lowered my gaze and raised my mask.

Billy chuckled. 'Hey, you'll never guess what I picked up at the airport.' He reached into the top pocket of his denim jacket and pulled out a small pack of cards, holding them up to show me. 'Top Trumps Serial Killers.'

'Joy.'

'You're in here, you know.'

'No, I'm not.'

'Yeah, you are. Aren't you excited?'

'Oh yeah, I'm pissing my Poise pad. What did Raf say?'

'He said you were going to the UK to save your kid and that if he couldn't go with you, he wanted me to go instead; to keep an eye on you and stuff.'

'Knob head.' I sighed. 'How was he?'

'How do you *think* he was? He was heartbroken. And he thinks your sister's lying about Ivy being sick, which I do too by the way. Why didn't you wait? I could have gone over there first, checked things out for yous. Sure, it'd only have been a couple of days.'

'I didn't want to wait—'

'Or more like you were doing your usual self-sabotage thing, thinking you deserve to get caught.'

'You don't know me well enough to make that observation.'

'I've read the book. This is what you do, isn't it? Your world-famous "boo-boos"? I know how much you love the Arroyo-Carranzas. You'd do anything for 'em, including getting out of their way if you thought you weren't wanted.'

'I'm *not* wanted. They hate me.'

'No, they don't.'

'Raf is better off without me.'

'Ah right,' he said. 'So, you're doing the martyr thing now, are ya? Yeah, Raf said you might do this.'

'So what if I am? He doesn't deserve the sort of life I'll give him. I was bloody lucky to have found him in the first place. Meeting him was like finding a golden needle in a mountain of needle-dicked . . . twats. But some things are more important than being happy. I want *him* to be happy.'

'He *was*. With *you*. I've never seen him as happy as that and I've known the guy a long time. So you owe it to him to get back in one piece, all right?'

'Pretty bloody difficult now, isn't it?'

'Well, we'll cross that bridge when we need to piss in the stream.' He meerkatted above the seats to check for Bunion Bitch. 'No sign – poor cow. Must be egg-bound. Come on, let's play a quick game to take our mind off stuff.' He shuffled his cards and divvied them up between us.

'I don't want to,' I said, posting Dicky back inside my bag

and folding my arms. Billy dealt me a stack but they remained piled up on my tray.

'So BTK made his first kill at twenty-nine. How old were you?'

I eyerolled for a bit, then seeing no alternative entertainment, gave in to his insistences. 'Eleven.'

'*Eleven years old?* Was that your grandad?'

'Yes.'

'Fuck me!' He chuckled, handing me the Dennis Rader card. 'Okay, fair play, you won that. Number of victims? I've got Dahmer on seventeen.'

I paused for thought. 'Twenty-seven, or twenty-eight now. I think.'

'What?'

'At last count. I haven't kept score for ages.'

He dipped his head and moved closer to my ear. 'You've offed twenty-eight people?'

'Roughly, yeah.'

Whenever Raf appears at my ear like that, he kisses me and just the sound of his voice or the touch of his mouth bathes me in gold like that girl in the Klimt painting. I'm calm in seconds when he does that. God, I wish he was here, bathing me in his goldness now.

'So where you staying in the UK?' asked Colin Feral, interrupting the one happy thought I'd had in days.

'Nowhere.'

'What do you mean, "nowhere"?'

'I didn't book anything. There's no point. Soon as Claudia greets me at the door, I'll be staying at Her Majesty's Pleasure for the foreseeable. What's the point of booking a Premier Inn?'

'Gimme Claudia's address,' he said, sighing. 'I'll get an Airbnb nearby. I'll stay with you, keep an eye.'

'I don't *want* to stay with you.'

'Well, you have to sleep somewhere. Is that really what you were going to do? Just march up to her door as soon as you arrive? What if it's a hoax? And even if it's not a hoax, how were you planning to get from Heathrow to deepest Wiltshire? It's like a three-hour drive.'

I stared at him. I had no idea what to say next. It was true: I just thought I'd rock up there. No plan. No failsafe. 'But it's *not* a hoax . . .'

'You don't sound sure about that.' He read the address off my Notes app and punched it into his phone. 'There's one Airbnb nearby. Same street, almost opposite. It's vacant this week. Pricey as fuck but I'll grab it. Nice area. Dog walks, birdwatching, ancient monuments . . .'

'. . . deposition sites?'

'I can't believe you haven't thought about this.'

'I haven't thought about anything, Billy. I just grabbed the flight.' I looked at him. 'I don't know what I'm doing.'

His face changed. I couldn't read it. 'It's all right. I'll look after ya.' And he winked. A fuck-wink.

'I'm not shagging you.'

He put his phone on his tray and held up both his hands. 'Hey, I know better than to try and shag my best mate's wife, especially one who's offed twenty-eight people. I already lost both me legs – I can't afford to lose me cock as well.' He picked his phone up and continued to make the booking.

'It was only one cock,' I grumbled, sifting out the in-flight magazine from the rack in front, which I'd already read and posted my chewing gum inside an article about how tough Adele found wealth and fame.

As I read, a thought bloomed like an ink blot in water: I needed Billy. I needed a soldier. Someone who strategised, who thought things through before reacting. Someone to walk me through this, even if he didn't have real legs anymore. I am the Queen of Boo-Boos after all and this was uncharted territory. I had no plan, no clue if Seren *was* lying to me about Ivy being sick and no idea how I'd cope if she was *or* she wasn't.

I scrolled through mine and Raf's wedding album on my phone. Our first dance, surrounded by strings of fairy lights and petals all over the dancefloor in Bianca's garden. The tables heaving with food. Raf's hand in mine. Liv and me clinking glasses. Bianca giving me my first hug as her daughter-in-law. Raf's hand in mine. Me twirling with Nico's three kids to Despacito. Walking back down the aisle, smiling. Raf's hand in mine.

'Do they always shit themselves when they die?' Billy's question speared through my meandering thoughts.

'No.' I switched off my phone.

'You'll have to ditch that as soon as possible,' he said, nodding towards it. 'Flush it down the pan if need be. Just get rid. We'll get you a prepaid one.'

'Okay.'

Bunions Woman reappeared, red-cheeked and a little sweaty about the brow from her ten-minute straining session and Billy packed up his Top Trumps and went back to his seat. My distraction gone, anxiety and panic continued to churn balletically in my thorax as I clung to the phone and the thoughts of the life I'd left behind.

The closer we flew to England, the more I worried Raf and

Billy were right – maybe Ivy *wasn't* sick and maybe Seren and Géricault *had* cooked this up between them – some sort of plea deal to keep Seren out of jail and bait me into it. If that was true, I was screwed. Following breadcrumbs right into a jail cell. There was no better chance of me being caught. What if Géricault was not at Terminal 5 but at Claudia's house, waiting to slap on the cuffs?

The meal came round but my meat was practically still twitching in the dish, so I left it. I asked the air steward for a sleeping pill to knock me out but she didn't have any. Luckily, the German woman behind me felt my pain and offered two of hers. I took one and saved the other for later. You never know when you're going to need to put yourself out of your misery.

Or someone else.

We landed in Blighty just after lunchtime and got priority disembarking because of Billy's disability and him being a war hero (he laid it on thick with the airline staff). It didn't feel like coming home at all. Back in San Diego, I'd often fantasised about rainy days and driving on the left-hand side and awful customer service but now I'm here, the only place I want to be is back there, preferably eating la concha dipped in fresh coffee from our local panaderia.

Preferably sitting beside Rafael, watching him chew.

Everything at Heathrow felt small and prying. The battleship-grey walls. Masked police on every checkpoint. Litter everywhere. Parents who didn't want to come home, wailing kids who didn't want to be born at all, old dinosaurs shuffling along who wouldn't hurry up and turn into fucking oil already. We shuffled towards passport control with the others from our flight: the two gammon Karens in Skechers Arch Fit trying to contain their farts. A Leo DiCaprio–looking fuck in clothes so baggy he looked like he'd borrowed them from his obese dad. The couple who'd been together about ten years too long and were arguing over every little thing. Two red-faced twentysomethings who'd clearly been exchanging fluids in the plane toilet. A man and a preggo woman with too many clinking bottles in their bag to not be alcoholics.

Couples couples couples.

And an insufferable trio of curly-haired musical theatre students who seemed to think everyone in the line welcomed their impromptu performance of 'Defying Gravity'.

We didn't.

A ginger toddler stared me out over his dad's shoulder, and I pulled up my mask quick sticks.

Starey toddler got the green light and went through the e-barrier with his family, and the flip-flops guy, who'd been on the aisle seat opposite me on the flight, went through next, also *pas de problème*. Then Billy went ahead – green for go. When it was my turn at the e-gates, I posted my passport under the scanner like I'd been told and waited for the green. Green for pleasant English cricket pitches, British racing green and all things Robin Hood. But instead, there was an alarming *buzz* and a stark red light bulb flashed.

Fuck it.

A wrinkle in the page, maybe? I flattened it out, slid it through again. But again, angry red light. Every other e-barrier was on green except mine.

FUCK.

'Be cool. Probably just an issue with the machine,' said Billy from his safe place on the other side.

I scanned it again, frowning like I didn't know what could be wrong even though I knew exactly what was wrong: e-barriers do not like serial killers. My chest thudded and my throat tightened and the passengers behind me all huffed and puffed like they were ready to blow down my paper-thin house.

'Come on, come on, come *on*.'

I slid it through again – another red light. I was not going anywhere. The Perspex barrier remained firmly shut. Everyone was looking my way. I'd crossed the fucking Atlantic. It couldn't all end *here*.

'It's all right,' said Billy, returning to the gate. 'Be cool as a cucumber. It worked in San Diego – it'll work here.'

'Madam, would you come with me please, we need to check something.'

I didn't dare look up and meet the eyes of the woman in the burgundy uniform who had appeared to my left. Her badge read 'Shelley Cartwright, Border Force'. 'Shelley' – like the concierge at our hotel on honeymoon. Except this Shelley wasn't smiling and showing me which buttons were which on the hot tub. And the honeymoon was over. I looked back to Billy.

'Is there a problem, darlin'?' he asked her, giving it the full Irish twinkle.

'Are you travelling together, sir?'

'Yes, Ma'am, we are,' I said in my meekest American accent through gritted teeth.

'It won't take a second, we just need to check your documentation. Do you want to accompany your wife?'

'Yes,' Billy affirmed, all strong and without hesitation. He was loving it. Actually enjoying my pain. When the gate opened, he snaked a tattooed arm around my waist. The second Shelley disappeared, I removed it. Not literally.

I didn't know whether to laugh or make a run for it, through the armed police to where the rest of the passengers were merrily schlepping towards Arrivals.

But what I did was follow her, Shelley's little lamb to the slaughter. Heart a-thumping. Knees a-jellying. Even though there'd been a pretty good chance of getting arrested, I still wasn't ready for it. I thought it would happen at the hospital when I went for the tests on my stem cells. I'd be handcuffed to the bed as they read me my Mirandas and took their sample to save Ivy's life. This *couldn't* end now, I thought.

'I have to be somewhere,' I mewed. 'You don't understand. It's literally life or death. Please, *please* listen to me.'

'It won't take too long, madam. Just in here, go on through.'

Billy and I followed Shelley past two armed police officers through a Staff Only door to the left of passport control.

'Don't say anything more until they do,' he muttered. 'They only know what we allow them to know.'

'You've done this before, haven't you?'

My breath caught as she opened the door and ushered me in. There were three police officers at the back of the room. Big guys. White sleeves. Kevlar vests. Chit-chatting among themselves. The door locked automatically. I wasn't going anywhere.

Border Force Shelley directed us to the bank of seats at the back of the room. 'It won't take long,' she reaffirmed, from which I could gauge nothing. She took all Billy's documents, and mine, and disappeared through the grey door at the back, assuring us she 'won't be a tick'.

'Well, if you could crack on a bit, love, only my legs are aching terrible from being on a ten-hour flight and all.' Billy rolled up his left trouser leg and detached his prosthetic. 'This one's giving me murders.'

'Of course, sir,' said Shelley, who did move a bit faster through the door. Billy looked at me when she'd gone.

'"You have to play the system. They think you're weak? Act weak. Use their prejudices against them."'

'Where have I heard that before?'

'You said it yourself, in your diary.'

'Oh.'

'They won't want to risk an anti-disability suit. Flash your wrist brace around a bit too, that might help. We'll be out of here in no time.'

What greeted us were grey walls spackled with greasy Blu-tack marks, a flank of rusty blue lockers, a half-empty vending machine, a maddening puzzle carpet with myriad stains on it and a messy chipboard desk with a half-eaten Double Decker resting on the mouse mat. That was all England had to offer, according to this room. Go back now – you're not welcome.

The police officers glanced over at me, then Billy took my hand in his and kissed my knuckles. They carried on chatting, seemingly unable to hear us whispering behind our face masks. But the intrusive thought returned. *Fuck it, own up now. Accept the cuffs, get this over with*. I couldn't think straight. I knew this was coming but I couldn't deal with it. The room felt sweltering all of a sudden. I dropped Billy's hand like a shitty mitt.

'Maybe it's me?' he whispered.

'It was *my* passport that beeped. You were home and dry.'

'I'm the one with the criminal record. They already confiscated my shaving foam in San Diego. And did you notice how long that security guy was checking out my shoes? He didn't do that with anyone else in that line.'

'Considering who I am, trust me, your drunk and disorderliness won't scratch the card.'

Two of the officers left and one stayed behind to remove a bunch of stuff from a locker.

'It's probably a visa thing. It's aways a visa thing,' Billy said.

'You did fill out the forms properly, didn't you?'

'Yes. If in doubt, I'll trot out the old war-veteran-with-no-legs sob story again; they'll be putty in me hands.'

'This could be a holding pen for Broadmoor for all you know. Shelley's probably outside right now with the straight jacket and hockey mask.'

'Why would she?' asked Billy. 'You're *dead*, remember?'

'Not everyone here thinks so. The Bad Seeds for instance.'

'Yer panicking. Raf said to practise your breathing when you get like this. "She can't see her own reflection when the water's boiling." That's what he said.'

'That's straight out of his therapist's mouth, that is,' I spat.

'He's right though, isn't he?'

I closed my eyes and tried to clear my mind, inhaling, exhaling, thirty times over. Then ten more. *Cool the water. Cool it down. Breathe. Breeeeeeeeathe.* After the last exhalation, I took in the breath again as deeply as I could and held on to it. When I could bear it no more, I let it out.

The door at the back opened again but instead of Shelley or a rabble of besuited detectives with sack trucks and cuffs, in waddled a short, tubby guy in the baggiest grey trousers I'd ever seen, keys a-jangling on his hip. His name, according to his badge, was Ken Singh, but his role at the airport was unclear. And I didn't actually care at that moment – all that mattered were the words coming out of his moustachioed Lancashire hotpot beak.

'There's an issue wi' your name, lass.'

'What?' I barked, momentarily forgetting my American accent and going straight into *EastEnders* outrage.

'You've got documents wi' wrong name on. We got to check 'em all out.'

'What do you mean the "wrong name"?' asked Billy.

Ken sat down at the desk, eyeing up the half-eaten Double Decker. 'We've got a passport here that says Ophelia White but vaccination certificates and a passenger locator form that say Ophelia Arroyo-Carranza.'

I held my relief in check as I still couldn't believe that was the only issue. Was that all? Just the wrong name on some forms? 'Oh yeah, I got married last month.'

'Ahh, many congratulations.' Ken smiled, looking at Billy.

'No, this is his best friend. He's accompanying me on this visit. Visiting family in . . . the Cotswolds.'

I knew what the look on Ken's face meant: these two are screwing. And before I could wash his mouth out with caustic soda, Billy jumped in.

'Yeah, we got a thing going on.' He grinned, squeezing my thigh. 'We're stopping with her folks until we can sort out our extended visas. It was all a bit of a rush in the end. She ran out on her husband. He's a bit of a cunt.'

I stared at Billy, hoping the stare produced enough tiny daggers to stab him all over and cause massive blood loss.

But he didn't take the hint and looked pointedly at me. 'Ain't that right, darlin'? She'll be getting a divorce as soon as she can so we can marry instead. But for now, we're on the run, like Bonnie and Clyde.'

'Yeah,' I said, turning slowly back to Ken Singh. 'All that's missing is the bullet-riddled Ford sedan.' Billy threw another ill-timed arm around my shoulders and laughed; a little too manically to be innocent.

Ken Singh sighed. 'Well, technically you should get new forms sorted wi' your Ophelia White name on, like your passport, but if you're going back to White anyway . . .'

I give it the full *yes sir, no sir, three bags of bullshit whenever you like, sir* until he smiled at me. 'I could apply for fast-track replacements while I'm here perhaps?'

Ken tapped in something on the computer near the Double Decker, sniffed the end of it and put it back down on the mouse mat. 'Probably best to do that once you know where you're staying long term. You've got three months, but I'd suggest getting the ball rolling quickly cos there's always a hell of a backlog. We'll need to see a secondary form of ID wi' your Arroyo-Carranza name on – have you got a driving licence or your marriage certificate?'

'Oh!' I cried. 'Yes, I do!' I fumbled in my bag for my diary and removed our marriage certificate from the back where I'd posted it at the last second along with the wedding photo of me and Raf that we kept by our bed, and a generous handful of dried sweetpea flowers that we'd sent out with our invitations. I wanted it all as proof to myself that I hadn't imagined it. I handed it to Ken, sans sweetpea petals.

'You married, Ken?' asked Billy.

'Oh yes.' Ken smiled. 'Coming up forty years.'

'Seriously? Aww, congratulations, my man.'

The old funt then ventured into an interminable anecdote about the amount of snow they had on his wedding day to Saanvi and Billy did an amazing impression of someone hella interested as I fawned my way through it, trying to copy what facial expressions I could see behind his mask and dropping in the odd 'Awww bless' and 'It's a day you'll never forget' but frankly all I wanted to do was cunt-punch him into the wall. The adrenaline coursing through me at the relief of not being headlocked by the long arm of the law was too much. I was shaking all over.

The door at the back clicked open and in breezed burgundy-coat Shelley, fresh from her forty-minute 'tick'.

'Mr and Mrs Arroyo-Carranza, thank you for waiting.' She and Ken shared a brief conversation and she gazed at his screen.

'Oh no,' said Ken. 'This isn't Mr Arroyo-Carranza; this is Miss White and Mr O'Shea. These two are . . . well, how would you put it?'

'Shagging,' said Billy and he and Ken laughed openly.

'In flagrante delicto,' I suggested, and they laughed even harder with added wheezing.

Shelley smiled professionally and picked up the Double Decker and moved it to the trash. Ken's face momentarily morphed into that guy's from *Die Hard* when he's falling off the building. 'Oh I see. Well, congratulations!'

'Thanks,' said Billy. 'Yeah, me and the old ball and chain just can't get enough of each other. I stole her away from her husband, but she'll be an O'Shea as soon as I can get that ring on her finger.'

'You'll have to prize the other one off my cold dead hand first,' I muttered behind my mask.

Shelley didn't seem to hear me. 'Can I just double check where you'll be staying – it's The Hermitage, Coddleford-on-the-Fosse, is that right?'

'Yes, it's an Airbnb in the Cotswolds.'

'And how will you be getting there?'

'I've got a specially adapted VW Golf parked up in Slough so we'll get an Uber or something from here and go and pick it up, it's no bother.'

'We'll book you an Addison Lee. On us,' offered Ken. 'To save you any further inconvenience, Mr O'Shea.'

'Oh that'd be grand, Ken, thanks a million.'

I stared at Billy, unable to comprehend his luck. Also, when the hell had he booked an Airbnb? I let him do the rest of the talking while I concentrated on not looking like a serial killer. He segued headlong into his injured-war-vet schtick, complete with flash of metal calves, and I think Ken started to fall in love with Billy. At that moment, I think I did too.

'Allow me to escort you both through to where the taxis are, Mr O'Shea. And I'm sorry for the inconvenience.'

'We did it, we fucking did it!' Billy muttered as the locked door opened and allowed us back into the land of the goddamn lucky. We strode on through to Arrivals with the rest of the free world.

'I think my arse just fell out,' I said, just about catching my breath. 'I can't believe I'm through. I just . . . can't believe it.'

'Luck of the Irish rubbing off on you.' Billy winked.

'You better not rub anything off on me,' I snipped, glancing at his crotch as he rearranged his jeans. 'When did you book an Airbnb *and* a car?'

He slung his backpack onto his shoulder again and picked up mine as my wrist was hurting. 'In the line for security. And the car is mine – got it parked up at an old girlfriend's flat. It's specially adapted.'

'I didn't know you had a girlfriend.'

'It's a pretty open thing. She's got a flat with a parking space, but she doesn't drive. She doesn't mind the car though –

I know how to keep her sweet. You'll have to wait outside while I go in and . . . grab the keys.'

'Is that where she keeps them, is it?'

Billy sniggered and tightened his topknot, like he always did. It was oddly reassuring.

'Thanks,' I added. 'For organising stuff. And looking out for me.'

'Raf told me to look after you.'

'What else did he tell you to do?'

Billy thought for a second as we walked. 'He said to treat you like a Gremlin – the cute kind. You know, don't make her angry, don't feed her after midnight. He said if you get really bad, I have to put on one of your favourite films – *Sister Act* or *Rocky* or anything with Gordon Ramsay. I downloaded a few things to my phone, just in case.'

'It's *Sister Act TWO: Back in the Habit.* The first one won't cut it. And *Ramsay's Kitchen Nightmares UK* for preference. But I don't mind *Hotel Hell*.'

'Ah shit, I fucked up already.' He laughed. And despite myself, I laughed too. 'He also said that if all else fails, just give her a hug. That's all she needs.'

I couldn't think about that too much – I stared down at my phone, willing something to appear, anything, any message from Rafa. When there was signal again, they started to ping through.

Please call me.
I love you so much.
Baby, tell me where you are.
Are you with B?
I love you.

As I composed my response text, Billy put his hand over my phone.

I looked up. 'What are you doing?'

'It's too risky. Turn it off. You're still in the danger zone, remember? All the numbers in there will be investigated if you get caught.'

'*When* I get caught.'

'We just jumped a big hurdle – we're safe enough for now. But that thing is a direct line to the cops so we need to get rid of it ASAP. Gis it here.'

I didn't know much at that point, other than the fact I was jetlagged to fuck – even my autopilot needed a long lunch – and so I did as Billy asked and watched him disappear into the gents' toilets. When he returned, it had gone.

'We'll get you a pay-as-you-go one from somewhere on the way to the Airbnb. You can text him from that.'

'Whatever.'

I didn't say one more word as the Addison Lee took us to Billy's girlfriend's place in Slough. When we arrived, I parked myself in between two wheely bins at the back of the property while he went inside and did whatever he needed to do to get to his VW. It took no longer than ten minutes and he was back outside, swirling the keys around his finger, beaming with afterglow. The sex-haired old sow in the doorway looked old enough to be his grandmother.

'Jesus,' I said as he clicked the fob to unlock all the doors. 'Hardly fresh out the vadge, is she?'

He grinned. 'I like the more experienced woman. They know their way around the old man, you know what I mean?'

I blew out my cheeks with pretend vom.

'Why don't you get in the back and get some shut-eye?'

he suggested, slinging my bags in the boot. 'Sat nav says it's exactly two hours from here in current traffic.'

I didn't argue. He could have been taking me to a police station himself, I wouldn't have cared. At that moment, I just wanted to sleep. To inhale the fumes from his faded coconut Sex Wax air freshener dangling from the rear-view mirror and slip into a peaceful oblivion where none of this was happening.

CNN Breaking News

'Jesus McQuirk here: some other news for you now. In Vermont it's being reported that the woman shot dead at the home of Seren Gibson, serial killer Rhiannon Lewis's sister, in January 2020 was not Lewis at all but a doppelgänger.

'It's a quite extraordinary story, this one. The identity of the deceased woman is believed to be Kacey Carmichael, 27, a self-confessed true-crime addict besotted with Lewis, and who even went so far as to have surgery to look like her serial-killing heroine.

'Carmichael's family has been certain of Kacey's identity as the woman slain at the house in Lawford Heights ever since the story first broke. They say following extended treatment for mental health issues, Carmichael would regularly stalk the Gibson residence and send letters for Lewis's attention and this behaviour was escalating. Gibson shot her dead as an intruder in January 2020. What's not clear at this stage is why Gibson went on to identify the deceased woman as her sister Rhiannon, aka Sweetpea. Is it simply a case of mistaken identity? Or something a little more sinister? Reporter Guy Majors has the story . . .'

Cut to a reel of Majors sitting on the front porch of the house of toothless meth addict Barbara Carmichael – 'Barb' as she likes to be called. This is Kacey's mother, who in between cigarettes and teeth falling out, recalls the story of Kacey's childhood growing up among the barley fields and confederate flags.

'I don't know what happened; she and I always got along. She was my pride and my joy. A very special person. But I knew when it came on the news – I knew it was her who broke into that house because she was obsessed with this Rhiannon woman. That woman infected her life, the last couple years.'

'Obsessed with Seren or Rhiannon?' asks Majors, his three-piece navy suit hugging his lockdown-chunked frame in all the wrong places.

'Rhiannon,' says Barb, on a cough. 'Kacey idolised her. Always writing letters to Sweetpea. She weren't all there in her mind, like, I knew that when she had the surgery to look like her. First it was the tattoos – flowers on her thighs – and then that wasn't enough and she had to go under the knife. I didn't think there was much to worry about because she was still going to work and eating and stuff.'

'Why did Kacey go to Seren's house in the first place that day?'

'To be near Rhiannon, I guess. I think she just liked pretending that Serena was her sister as well. She sent her cards and little gift baskets. Nothing harmful. She wanted to be a part of their family, I think. She didn't have a daddy growing up – she had uncles but a couple of 'em weren't kind. She liked the idea of Rhiannon coming to save her and them going on the run together, like Bonnie and Clyde. Or Bonnie and Bonnie.'

Cut to Majors doing his concerned askance-nod bit, leathery face creases and all. 'You were certain she was the one killed, weren't you?'

'Oh yeah. She was always pestering that family but they wouldn't talk to her so what did they expect? She just wanted

to say hi, meet the kids and stuff. She didn't mean no harm. She wanted a friend, that's all.'

'But how did they know she meant no harm?'

'She just didn't. Yeah, she did a few bad things . . .'

'She claimed to have family on MH370, didn't she?'

'We been all through that. She was going through a tough time with her boyfriend and living in her own head too much. She saw that on the news and I think she just wanted the attention.'

'And she claimed her own father died in the Twin Towers?'

'I didn't realise she had lied about that 'til I saw her at the twentieth anniversary thing on the news. And I thought "Oh my god – that's Kacey!"'

Majors checks his notes. 'She'd done it multiple times, hadn't she?'

'Yeah, she'd see something on the news – a guy who died choking at a local diner or a shooting and she'd go to the scene to talk to the reporters, acting like she was family. She always was an attention seeker.'

'Is that because she didn't get any attention at home?'

'I can't be with her 24/7, 365, can I? What kind of mother can do that?'

Back in the studio, Dan Donovan scrolls his iPad, waiting for the hand-back. 'This all begs the question – if Sweetpea isn't buried in that grave up in Vermont, Guy, then where in the world is she?'

Majors is live on the roadside outside Seren's house now, head to toe in Ralph Lauren and probably jizz from wanking over his own mirror image. He raises his hands in mock flabbergast. 'We simply don't know, Dan, and it's all quiet at the Gibson house here in Weston, Vermont, today. Nobody's *home and it's believed that Seren Gibson herself is out of the country right now. Is she with Rhiannon right now, we may well ask? Well, a week ago I'd have said no. But now, anything is possible, Dan, anything is possible.'*

I lost myself to the car's rumbling engine as Billy drove us through pockets of rain and hail. His terrible rendition of 'If You're Getting Down, Baybeh, I Want It Now Baybeh' woke me up as we hit the B roads.

'Come on,' hollered Billy. 'You do Abs's bit and I'll do J's.'

'Fuck off, I'm trying to get some kip back here!'

'Never mind kip, this tune is a stone-cold banger!'

'I know, you've played it six fucking times.'

'Philistine.' He grinned, playing it for a seventh.

And now the thoughts came – leaving Raf brought its usual ache. Getting arrested brought another. And I kept wondering how it would be to see Ivy, my little poppy seed. To see her so ill. I wondered if she would smell like the baby she was, or all chemically. I couldn't bear the thought. I wondered if Claudia would let me across the threshold. She'd have to if she wanted Ivy to survive. She was in a lose-lose too.

That two-hour journey turned into four hours and twenty-eight minutes – an interminable traffic-laden affair in pissing rain. Billy didn't complain once. He played the radio too loud and he drove too fast but after my fitful naps, and lightning-quick sojourns for petrol, Pret, a piss and a brand-new phone for me, we arrived at our Airbnb just after eight that night.

Claudia lived in a 'chocolate box village' called Coddleford boasting a medieval bridge straddling a duck pond and the grave of some guy who'd once wiped King James's arse. You can always tell a rich area because there's loads of blackberries on the hedges – rich people don't eat for free. The Hermitage was a one-bed whitewashed cottage offering everything we needed – a sixteenth-century king-size bed, a wet room with full disabled access, a wood burner with a complimentary basket of logs.

And an unobstructed view into the sizeable back garden of Bodkin House: the hamstone manor opposite where my little girl lived.

Lived and was dying.

Billy's Airbnb was run by two crusty old simps in advanced stages of physical decay, called Philip and Dorcas Price: Coddleford residents of the last fifty years. Neither had achieved anything of note according to their Airbnb profile: a decade or two of vanilla sex then separate beds forevermore; the odd hundred quid raised for Unicef or a Best in Show marrow. Dorcas had probably contributed most of the patches on the 'Thank You NHS' quilt mouldering beside the village war memorial. And I bet neither of them had missed a week of doorstep applause.

Oh, to have been in England for *that*.

Nevertheless, they were true to their email to Billy and had left the key under the ornamental frog by the back door. On the kitchen table was a welcoming hamper of delicacies: sundry fruit and veg, Dorcas's spiced beetroot and carrot chutney, two bottles of wine – Coddleford Reserve – clotted cream fudge, shortbread biscuits, tea, gourmet coffee, loaf of bread and two small pies, all of which were either homegrown or homemade.

I didn't normally like homemade shit, unless I was the one who homemade it – I knew what went in the stuff I had crafted. This lot could be smegma pie or pube pasties as far as I knew.

A notecard with a lavender sprig was underneath the basket.

Welcome to The Hermitage, Mr and Mrs O'Shea! Do make yourself at home. The wifi code is on the back of the hub under the lounge TV!

'I wish everyone would stop assuming we're married,' I snorted, screwing up the card. 'I can't *stand* people who overuse exclamation marks. It's the mark of someone trying too hard to create a personality with punctuation.'

Billy took the card from me. 'There's something on the back. "We have stocked your fridge with the basics and if you would like a tour of the village just pop up the road to Number 28 and knock on our door! Dorcas runs a Knit and Natter group on a Weds evening and you're welcome to pop along if you're at a loose end! All best – the Prices."'

'Thanks, Dorcas! But quite frankly! I'd rather fucking die!'

Billy unpacked the hamper. 'We've landed on our fake feet here.'

I went upstairs to the one double bedroom and sat on the end of the bed. It was dark so I couldn't see much of Claudia's manor, Bodkin House, but there were lights on over there illuminating rooms behind curtains and blinds, and a single parking area to the side lit by a motion-sensor security light. Billy couldn't have found us a better spot for a stakeout.

'I did good, right?' he crowed, coming upstairs with his bag and slinging it down against the chest of drawers. 'Paid well over the odds for it but it's worth it to get such a view of the place. Now we can see what's what, when it's daylight at least.'

'How did you pay?'

'Visa but Raf's given me some money, so yer grand.'

'I'm sorry, Billy.'

'For what?'

'Dragging you into this.'

'Ahh I dragged meself. I don't mind one bit. Glad to be of service.'

'How the hell have I got to this point? How come I wasn't arrested at the airport? Ken and Shelley didn't recognise me. Why?'

'Nobody expects you to be alive, let alone back in the country, that's why. I read about this in a magazine once – it's called "inattentional blindness". People aren't looking for you, so they don't expect to see you.'

'They'll be expecting me when they find out the woman in that grave in Vermont isn't me.'

'They haven't exhumed her yet so you're all right for now.'

'And then what?'

'Right now, we just have to worry about *that*.' He pointed towards Bodkin House and sat on the bed next to me.

'I know Raf said to love me but I still ain't shagging you, Iron Man.'

He smirked. 'The sofa downstairs is a pull-out – I checked.'

'Whose are those cars over there, do you think? There's two – a red one and a silver one.'

Billy peeked out the window to see for himself as the security light illuminated a black cat striding across the shingle. 'Silver Mercedes estate by the look of it. And an Audi A5. Do you know what car that copper drives?'

'Géricault? Nope.'

'So, let's not play our hand 'til we know how the cards are

stacked, eh? Leave it for now. I'll get over there first thing, see what I can find out.'

I started to unpack my bag, taking out Richard E. Grunt and Raf's Ninja Turtles T-shirt, freshly sprayed in his cologne just before I left. I sat Dicky on my nightstand and inhaled the shirt.

'They could be watching us now. Undercover cops, scoping the street. Maybe the people you've booked this house with, who knows?'

'You're being paranoid, cos you're wrecked. Why don't you have a kip and I'll make us some grub. Come on, I'll tuck you in and bring you something up.'

'I'll tuck myself in, thanks. I want to call Raf. It'll be safe now, right?'

Raf normally tucked me in when I had a menstrual headache or just felt a bit run down. He'd wrap me up like a burrito and it would always make me laugh. I didn't want Billy doing that.

He handed me his iPhone and unlocked it for me – he had four messages, all from Raf.

Did you make it?
Did she make it through?
Dude what's going on – Im killing myself here.

I texted him back, fingers shaking on the keys.

I made it. B ditched my phone and got me this one.
How are you? I miss you endlessly, Tortuga xxx

The phone rang as soon as the message sent. Billy took his leave and went downstairs in search of food.

'Baby?'

'Yeah,' I replied. 'I made it.' His voice was exactly what I needed to hear, bathing me in gold as I snuggled down into the bed cuddling his T-shirt, and pretending he was next to me. 'We're at an Airbnb opposite Claudia's.'

'Oh my god,' he laughed, 'I can't believe you made it. Are you all right?'

'Yeah. How are you?'

'I'm still in the hospital – they're worried about peritonitis – but I'm just worried about you. I couldn't think about anything until I knew you were okay.'

'You're the one with the gunshot wounds.'

'They'll heal.'

'What's peritonitis?'

'An infection. They got me on antibiotics so it'll be all right – I just can't stand being stuck in here and not with you.'

'Just get better, okay? Promise me you'll get better.'

He laughed. 'I'm doing my best, baby. Mom and Nico haven't long since left – they feel terrible.'

'Do they?'

'Yeah. I explained everything. Mom's okay. Liv and Ariela don't know the full story but they feel pretty bad they took it out on you.'

'My scalp says apology accepted.'

'What's happening with Ivy?' he said, with a sniff.

'Billy's going over to the house, tomorrow morning. Suss it out.'

'You can trust him, you know. He won't put you wrong.'

'I know. Just wish it was you.'

'You're so far away. I can't bear it. Got this constant pain in my chest. And it's not one of my injuries.'

Hearing that made me feel better in a strange sort of way. I snuggled further down into the bed. 'Have they said when you'll be discharged?'

'Not yet. It'll be a week or so. I feel better just hearing your voice.'

'I know what you mean,' I said, nuzzling into the warmth of the marshmallowy duvet. 'I've got your Ninja Turtles T-shirt.'

'Ah well that's something.' He laughed.

'I don't want to go, Raf,' I whispered, and it all burst out of me. 'I don't want to see her like that and I don't want to give myself up. I don't want to lose my freedom cos I'll never see you again. I can't do it.'

'You'll be okay. I'm there with you. I'm in that tattoo on your hand, remember? I'm in that ring on your finger. And I'm always in your heart, don't you forget that.'

I couldn't speak. Richard E. Grunt stared at me from my nightstand. I grabbed him and held him close to my neck inside the T-shirt.

'Remember who you are, Rhiannon. You're not that little girl anymore – you're in control.' Raf cleared his throat and tried to sound upbeat but I knew that was just him trying too hard.

'First sign anything's amiss, book a new flight and get home.'

'I *can't* come home, can I? The police will want to arrest me over beating up that bitch who shot you.'

'No, they're not pressing charges.'

'Seriously?'

'Seriously. They came by yesterday looking for you – I said you'd had to go for a job interview. Didn't know what else to say.'

'What about River Goffey?'

'No word yet. Just gotta wait. Maybe we can meet up in Mexico, like we planned? Or I'll come to you.'

'You can't leave your home for me.'

'You *are* my home, Rhiannon.'

That ended me. That was the key to it all: that he knew me as Rhiannon and he wanted me back. That Rhiannon could count on someone for once. That Rhiannon would be waited for. That Rhiannon was loved. And I, Rhiannon, sobbed for the rest of the phone call.

'I'll find a way for us to be together again, all right? Trust me.'

I do, I mouthed, though he couldn't hear it.

'In the meantime, be good. And if you can't be good, be good-ish.'

'I will.' I managed to squeak out 'Bye' before the call ended and his name disappeared from the screen.

I hugged the phone close in lieu of a husband and cried myself to sleep.

Wednesday, 20 October –
The Hermitage, Coddleford-on-
the-Fosse, Cotswolds

1. *Programme makers who put 'Contains some distressing information' on true-crime docos. Oh really? I turned on this John Wayne Gacy doc expecting to learn about his love for cupcakes and origami.*
2. *Drivers on narrow roads who stop when you stop, not seeing you have nowhere to pull in but they do, so you have to wait an age for them to grow a brain and notice that fact themselves.*
3. *The contestants on* Escape to the Country – *they don't escape. They just view three houses and fuck off back to town. Waste of time.*
4. *That 'Daisy Daisy Daisy' Marc Jacobs advert.*
5. *Channel 4's afternoon programmers – the* Countdown *'banter', leathery couples buying duplexes in the sun, hapless detectives solving puzzles so easy a blind pig would beat them to the punch. Ugh. Ugh. Ugh.*

I spent the morning setting up my new shitty arsed £40 phone and putting three numbers into it: Billy's, Raf's and Seren's. I flung Seren a lightning-quick message to say this was my new number, but she didn't text back. Billy sent me a photo he'd taken on our wedding day for my wallpaper, and I was so glad to have Raf back with me in some form, even though I had to put up with Billy's dumb-fuck face photobombing in the foreground.

I still hadn't ventured over to Bodkin House – aka the only reason for being here. I was stuck between jet lag and that space between having something important to do and having no desire to do it. I ate the crackers and chutney from the hamper, which I puked up twenty minutes later, and settled into an *Escape to the Country* marathon but nothing was helping me galvanise myself into going over to Claudia's. Nothing could. So in the end, Billy said he would do his 'old schtick to see what's what'.

His 'old schtick', as it turned out, was to pretend to be a delivery driver with the householder's name and address on a hastily cobbled together parcel in order to gain an open door. Then once he was on the doorstep, he'd pretend the parcel had no return address – the householder left thinking it was a mistake and they had a free gift. Billy would pretend to have trouble with one of his legs and ask if he could sit on their step to adjust it. The householder would take pity and in that time he'd assess the lock on the downstairs windows, and if they had an alarm. Sometimes, the householder would invite him in for tea where they'd get into conversation about his war heroics. Now in his thrall, they'd lower their defences, allowing him to take a better look around for spare keys and easy access points. If he was lucky, he'd find a wall planner with details of the family's movements so he'd know when they'd be out. Then he'd bide his time and come back when the place was empty.

The plan on this occasion was just to confirm Ivy's sickness. He re-packed the hamper to pretend that was the parcel in question, and headed to Bodkin at 2.30 p.m. I just had to wait.

And wait.

And wait.

And not being the most patient piggy in the playpen, I soon got bored of pacing and took to the internet, namely TikTok. From watching potato salad recipes to deaf babies getting cochlear implants to the diary of a skin tag removal, extended footage of a dormouse eating a prawn cracker and a woman's 911 call about decapitating her own mother, it was like a dopamine soup of distraction and I guzzled it down while it was hot.

The algorithm took over and I entered #RhiannonTok, where the Bad Seeds shared their thoughts, theorems and fantasies about yours truly. I also caught a three-minute *Up at the Crack* interview with two of the PICSOs – remember them? The People I Can't Shake Off? I should change that now to the People I *Did* Shake Off Who Are Now Famous Just For Having Known Me. Imelda had become a micro-influencer on #CleanTok – Mrs Hinch for the mentally compromised. Aside from endless nails and hair extensions, she'd had some serious cosmetic surgery too since I last saw her – collagen, tits. Mind you, who was I to talk? At least my teeth didn't look like they came out of a fucking cracker.

Anni sat next to her – as naturally beautiful as ever. Bitch. She'd become a 'mumpreneur'. I couldn't be arsed to listen to the preamble about what she'd invented – some vape thing to keep toddlers quiet on long journeys. The Bad Seeds were all over it.

Ugh what a bitch! No wonder Rhiannon hated her.
That one with the teeth – she's clearly jealous Rhiannon's
so famous.
God, I hate her – wish Rhi had done her in when they
were friends.

Not that Imelda had ever been a friend to me. True friends didn't make money off you. True friends didn't organise surprise birthday parties for you and then forget to send you a sodding invite – oh yeah, true story.

Heather Wherryman, the solicitor I'd saved from certain rape and who'd handled Ivy's adoption, was nowhere to be found. Neither was Marnie, my friend from that baby group I'd momentarily joined. They hadn't released any tell-all books, no interviews, no 'shock claims' coming from them. Marnie's Instagram profile had been briefly unlocked last summer to share a picture of her new baby girl, new husband, and idyllic life kneading dough in some hilly villa in Italy. Her frown lines had vanished too. Somewhere in the depths of my broken soul, that made me feel good.

But not as good as the Bad Seeds Tumblr feed where fans of mine wrote in to tell me how I'd inspired them. How I'd changed their lives, or rather, encouraged them to change their lives. Like this one:

From 'The Bad Seeds' Tumblr

Chère Sweetpea,

I was sick of my friends having the things I do not have. My best friend, M, has everything handed to her on a silver plate and I have to make do with my sister's hand-me-downs and shitty gifts my relatives have knitted. My parents never give me enough pocket money and even if I do all the chores, I barely get enough for coffee with my friends. And then something happened at school and I found money another way.

My history teacher, Mr J, came into the art room talking to me about extra classes. He caressed my ass. I told him to stop. He said I look younger than thirteen and he offered me candy. I took it. And then he did it again. I said I would tell but he gave me fifty euros! Just for touching my ass! So I let him do it again.

The next time it happened, he came looking for me in the girls' changing rooms and said he wanted to put his head in my lap. I did not like the way it felt but he gave me another fifty euros and it meant I could buy some expensive lipstick. He asked if he could see me out of school. I said for two hundred euros. I thought he'd say no way, but he said yes!

I told M a boy was paying me to let him do stuff and she called me a whore. That made me feel dirty when I said I wasn't going to have sex with him, but she said the more you do, the more they'll *want* you to so you better '"Pea Up." Take a knife and if he tries to put it in you, threaten to chop it off.'

So I did! Three nights ago. I took a knife with me, in my satchel. He parked his car in this alley. He unzipped his fly, and I said I didn't want to. I said it lots of times, but he kept going on about how happy it would make him, and he climbed on top of me and I kept saying, 'No' but he wouldn't listen – so I slid the knife out of my satchel and . . . I CUT OFF HIS PENIS!

I only meant to threaten him but as soon as I saw him try and force his way in, I snapped. And then I screamed, and he was screaming and crying, and I ran, out of the car and all the way back home. I threw the knife in the river and now I'm worried the police will find it and knock at my door.

But it's been three days. His car is gone. He hasn't come back to school. Does it mean I've got away with it, Rhiannon? How am I meant to feel? I feel bad that I hurt him – he's the only person who's ever called me pretty – but also, in another way, not bad at all.

from G in Issy-les-Moulineaux, Paris, France

And that was just the first one I saw. There were many more along the same lines. After a life spent trying to get people to notice me, trying to get liked, loved, promoted, seen as anything other than just good old 'Sweetpea' who'll drive you home if you're pissed and makes a damn fine photocopy, it was this letter which got my arse off the sofa that afternoon. Page after page, girl after girl, woman after woman saying they'd stared out a perv on the subway or taken a self-defence class or left a bad relationship or fought a guy off because of me:

Rhiannon Lewis. Admin assistant for life. And the artist formerly known as Sweetpea.

Women standing their ground as a strange guy swore at them in the street. Young women fronting out stalkers and abusers. Schoolgirls punching out perv teachers. Mothers hunting down randoms who'd preyed on their kids. Because of me. Saying they did it *for* me.

It felt like I was being held up by a sea of hands, all guiding me towards something good; something right.

And then the back door clicked open and reality dawned, once again.

'God this feckin' rain. There can't be much more water up

there to come down. It's worse than back home.' Billy was soaking wet and still carrying the hamper. He wiped his feet on the doorstep and hung his denim jacket on the back of one of the chairs.

I ran in to the kitchen and stood on the flagstones on the tenterist of hooks. 'And?'

'Sorry – I spotted a pharmacy up the road so I went to get some shaving foam. Then this old feller keeled over in there and I waited around to see if he was all right. Christ, this is driving me mad,' he said, scratching his stubble.

'Fuck your stubble, what's going on over there? What did you see? Is Ivy sick or not?'

'Oh, nothing. She wouldn't let me in.'

'Who wouldn't?'

'Claudia. At least, I *think* it was Claudia. Short blonde hair, huge tits.'

'Yeah, that's Claudia.'

'She asked to see ID, which they don't do normally, but I said I'd left it in me van at the other end of the street. I don't think she bought it – she wouldn't take the hamper either.'

'Why not? What kind of person doesn't accept a free hamper?'

'Maybe a person expecting an escaped serial killer to pay them a visit?' He eyeballed me.

'Did you at least hear a child's voice? Any coughing? Did you see a nurse? Were there any cartoons on in the background?'

'No sign. Maybe she's at the hospital?'

'Maybe. How did Tits McGee seem?'

'Normal. Fed up. Not taking any of *my* crap, that's for sure. I pulled all the usual tricks – the wink, the lopsided smile. Nothing. She still had a face like a smacked backside.

70

One thing I *did* notice were the cars. There was no red Audi anymore, just the silver Merc estate and I noticed a blue Porsche parked around the other side of the house – number plate: Mitch 1.'

'Yeah, that would be *his* car, the paedo's.'

'Which begs the question . . .'

' Whose car was the red Audi?'

'Géricault's?'

'Maybe Seren's hire car? I don't know.'

He gave me a look I couldn't read. 'So? Are you going over?'

'Yeah. In a bit. I will . . . just . . . in a bit.'

There's not enough Ls in the world to describe how colllllllllllld it was in that cottage as I waited and watched through that window. My extremities were yellow, my nipples like light switches and all because I wasn't used to the British climate anymore and we couldn't work out the thermostat. Billy went back to bed and snored away the afternoon while I thawed myself out with a hot shower, wrapped myself in two itchy-ass throws and watched the comings and goings of Bodkin from the blanket box at the end of the bed.

Nothing happened for ages – passing glimpses. The odd upstairs window closing or a shadow behind the glass. But then a woman stepped out onto the patio at the back of the house facing the garden, wearing a pink dressing gown and lighting a cigarette.

It was Seren.

Past lunchtime and still in her pyjamas – this wasn't like my sister. I wasn't surprised she'd taken up smoking again though – she never could stick to anything, except hating me.

She looked like a dishrag in need of a boil wash – all grey and limp.

'Christ, what a sight.'

Her greasy brown hair sat on her shoulders like it couldn't be arsed either as she puffed away on her cig like she was giving it mouth to mouth. Her eyes swept the garden and at one point she looked up at my window.

'Fuck!'

She looked, for a second, like Mum. Ready to bollock me for playing with matches again. Ready to bollock me for existing at all. By the time I ventured another peek above the blanket box, she had gone back inside and it had begun to drizzle.

Still no sign of Ivy. Above the garden, an upstairs window was curtained. Was that her bedroom? Was she getting any daylight? Was she dying alone in pitch darkness?

Around an hour later, a blond man with broad shoulders and chunky calves left via the side door and crossed the shingle driveway. He had AirPods in and wore a sleeveless running vest and black shorts, and his phone was strapped to a sizeable bicep.

I recognised him at once: Mitch Silverton.

Aka the owner of the blue Porsche, aka the man I almost returned to the UK to kill.

He wasn't driving, he was out for a run – phone on his arm, all the Lycra. Strangely enough, the sight of him didn't elicit the same venom it once had. Even though he'd slept with a thirteen-year-old at a school he once taught at. Even though he was a convicted sex offender living with my daughter. At some point in the last two years my pilot light for him had gone out. He didn't matter now – only Ivy did. Maybe my priorities were finally in the right place. Or maybe I just felt too sick with anxiety to focus on any rage.

Around 4 p.m., the sky was darkening but I could still see someone else leaving, this time a blonde woman. Claudia left in a black mac carrying a clutch of empty bags for life. She'd changed since I saw her last. Her blonde hair was short – a post-chemo crop, I surmised – and her tits were noticeably pneumatic (a post-mastectomy boob job, perhaps). I zoomed in on her expression. Was this a woman who'd just fought cancer herself and was now having to be strong for a cancer-stricken child? Was this a woman desperate to get her shopping done and be back in that house to be with her ailing baby?

Why the hell was I even trying to figure it out; I can't read expressions. She drove off in the silver Merc.

It was then that I truly geared myself up to go over there. No Mitch. No Claudia. That meant it was just Seren there now. And possibly Ivy too, somewhere. Hooked up to a drip or being tended to by a live-in nurse.

That was a thought: maybe the red Audi was a carer's car? Or just a visiting friend even? In which case, no Géricault. This could all be on the level after all: Ivy *was* sick and I was the only one with the cure, so they *might* be pleased to see me. It was the tiniest of mights. Looking at the size of Bodkin House, Claudia could more than afford live-in nurses. But Ivy didn't need nurses. What she needed was me.

I should go. I should go *now*, I thought, when Billy was in the shower. There was nothing and no one stopping me.

But as much as I knew I *had* to, the longer I left it the harder it got. Just one more piece of fudge from the hamper, I kept saying, then I'll go. Just another ten minutes of *Four in a*

73

Bed, then I'll go. I'll just see Payment Day to see if it all kicks off over that piss stain in the mattress, *then* I'll go.

The truth was, I didn't want to see Ivy like that. I could watch anyone die – *anyone*, but her. But I could save her, I kept saying to myself. I could stop this. Give her what she needs to thrive. But what if I give her what she needs and it doesn't work? I'd cut off my other hand if I thought it would help but what if I'm too late? Seren said it was 'spreading fast', like Mum's did.

'Stupid bitch, stop being such a pussy!' I yelled, switching the TV off and throwing the remote across the room where it knocked my make-up bag off the drawers. I pulled on my coat and boots and to summon up a little Dutch courage, poured myself a fat glass of Coddleford Reserve from the hamper. I necked it, which somewhat calmed my nerves, and went to pour myself another when there was a resounding knock at the door.

'The fuck?' I gasped, almost jumping clean out of my epidermis but just keeping hold of my glass.

I grabbed my face mask from the table and opened the latch, easing the door open to find a smiley grey-haired string bean in head-to-toe Cath Kidston, including face mask, standing on the path.

'Hallo there! Dorcas Price.'

Ah. One of the Herm's owners. A courtesy call to ask if I'd like a 'socially distanced tour of the village'. After knocking, she'd stood back just in case Covid pole-vaulted out of my throat, through my mask, through hers and straight down her neck.

'Um, maybe later,' I drawl in my best Dolly Parton voice. 'I'm just waiting for mah husband – he's shaving.' I only

74

realised then that I hadn't put any make-up on that morning so my black eye and cut eyebrow were visible.

She frowned, looking at my eye. 'Ooh, that looks nasty. Are you all right?'

'Oh, that's nuthin'.' I laughed with a wipe of my good hand. 'You're so precious for noticin' – well, I'm such a klutz – I slipped on some bar-bee-cue sauce on the kitchen floor back home and I went down like a whore's drawers, I ain't kiddin'. But it's healin' up nicely now.'

'And did you have everything you needed in the hamper? I see you've tried our wine.' She noted the empty glass in my hand.

'Oh yeah.' I giggled. 'I just couldn't resist no longer, and I thought hey, the sun's over the yardarm so why not?'

'Why not indeed?' Dorcas nodded. The woman was so small and grey – squinty eyes, hairy neck, and the smallest feet I'd ever seen on an adult woman. It was as though I'd caught her mid-transformation into a mouse.

'I saw your husband going out this morning – I hope we didn't miss anything?' She seemed heartbroken at a potential oversight.

'Oh no, he had his shaving foam confiscated at the airport, that was all. He couldn't put up with the scratchy-scratchin' a moment longer.'

'Ah I see, well, if there's anything else you and hubby need, dear, just let us know – and if you'd like that tour, we're home all day tomorrow, putting the garden to bed for the winter, so it'd be our pleasure!'

'Why thank you so much, honey,' I said, still staring at her facial slide.

'There's a bonfire up on the green tonight about seven

o'clock for the kiddies. There'll be fireworks and soup and hotdogs to raise funds for the church. And if you and your husband want to meet us down the local, it's the monthly pub quiz tonight. Our table is Number Four by the inglenook.'

'Thanks, honey bun,' I said, having made a mental note years ago to give all British community events a swerve. The door was closing as Dorcas asked:

'Ooh, did you try the chutney yet? It's a new recipe. I made it myself . . .'

I opened the door wider. 'Oh yes, the chutney was real good.' I made an okay gesture with the same two fingers that had been reaching down the back of my throat to puke it up just an hour before.

'I'm so glad you enjoyed it. Most people think chutney's terribly complicated but it's just a case of chopping the fruit and vegetables and bringing it to the boil with some—'

I've cut this conversation short here because believe me it went on far longer than I normally allow people to talk to me when they're being unutterably yadda yadda, but it was as Dorcas recalled every single herb and spice in her chutney recipe – and where they came from – that a movement caught my eye across the road. A flurry of dust or snow. But as I watched the stuff flutter nearer, I saw that it was bubbles. From a bubble machine.

Without warning, a little girl appeared, squealing and running out of the side entrance to Bodkin House and onto the pavement, chasing the flurry of bubbles. My heart thudded in my ears – there she was. The pink jellybean I'd left in the incubator. Running and squealing happily, glittery tights and fur-lined coat. Apple cheeks and AJ's caramel curls. AJ's smile. My baby.

My Ivy.

Seren appeared seconds later, all of a flap under her grey

pashmina, grabbing the child before she ran into the road, which set off a full body tantrum with screams and kicking feet.

'NO! NO SEZZIE! I WANT MY BUBBLES!'

'Come on, Dolly Bird, let's go inside. We'll play bubbles later. You can have a bic-bic if you like.'

Seren dropped the offending bubble machine on the pavement and stooped to pick it back up, with some difficulty thanks to the scream queen.

But Ivy turned off her tantrum like a tap at the mention of biscuits.

Realisation hit me like a slow-motion punch: that was *not* a sickly child. There *was* no pallor, no grey circles, no bald head, nor any sign of the lethargy you'd expect from a kid on death's door and knocking for my stem cells.

In short: there *was* no fucking cancer.

And all the anxiety of the last week shattered like a broken window – and in poured a steady flow of burning hot lava.

Dorcas caught me looking across the road. 'Oh they're a nice family, the Silvertons. My daughter babysits for them sometimes. She's a clever little thing but goodness me, has she got a temper!'

'Yeah,' I muttered. 'Just like her mother.'

I closed the door on Dorcas as quickly as my fake politeness would allow to save her and the world at large from the inevitable volcano about to blow. But as it turned out, no lava. Way back when, I'd have trashed The Hermitage or burned the place to the ground – I am Sweetpea, after all. But if there's one thing a Sweetpea does, it's grow. There was also the small matter that I was covered in my own blood.

'What the—?' came the cry behind me. Billy stood in the kitchen doorway, Hawaiian shirt open, wet hair hanging and newly shaven with his legs on under his cargo shorts. 'What the fuck's happened?'

'That lying, cunting bitch!' I seethed.

'Rhiannon, what have you done, darlin'? You're hurt.'

I couldn't catch my breath. 'Seren *was* lying. She LIED TO ME!'

'You're *hurt*,' he repeated, pulling out one of the dining chairs and sitting me down on it. He didn't seem to be saying anything back even though I was telling him what I'd seen, who I'd seen, where I'd seen her.

'What are you doing?' I said. 'Don't you understand – Ivy's not sick!'

The fury gave way to crying, then sobbing, and the sobbing gave way to laughing. It must have been relief. Ivy *wasn't* ill. She *wasn't* going to die. I looked down – my entire hand was red and stuck all over with little fragments of glass. I'd smashed the wine glass in my fist without even realising it.

'Oh shit.'

'It's all right, you sit there, and I'll sort you out. Don't touch anything.'

Billy set about cleaning me up and removing every single shard from my skin and the floor around me. It was like the bloody thing had exploded.

'Talk to me. What's happened?' he asked when he had sat next to me, pawing at my cuts with a sanitised swab.

'She ran out, chasing bubbles. Ivy. You were right. Raf was right. My god, she's so beautiful.'

Billy rubbed his face and sat there processing it all for a second or two before positioning my arm across my chest so it was above my heart. 'Keep that there for a bit. I fucking knew it, didn't I say this could be a trap? I told you, didn't I?'

'YES!' I shouted. 'YOU REALLY NOSTRADAMUSSED THE SHIT OUT OF THIS, BILLY, WELL DONE, HAVE ANOTHER FUCKING MEDAL!'

'All right, all right, calm yerself. Listen – this is a *really* good thing. They didn't see you, did they?' I shook my head. 'Good, good. Okay, so we're gonna clear this up and then I'm gonna book you a return flight. Then I'll drive you back to Heathrow. Now we know what's what, you can go home, can't you?'

I stared at him, mutherfuckerly. 'Seren lies about my daughter having cancer to lure me here and I'm supposed to just . . . get on a *plane*?'

'What's the alternative?'

'You *know* what. She's my kid.'

'Ah come on now, Rhiannon, she's not yours, not anymore. She belongs to them and she's okay. She's safe. I promised Rafael I'd get you back home if all this was a hoax and that's clearly what it is so—'

'I'm not leaving her there.'

'What are you thinking of doing, kidnapping her?'

'Yes.'

'Ah for God's sake, don't act the maggot, think it through, would ya?!' he shouted, leaving the dustpan and brush for a second and marching over to me, his grip surprisingly strong. 'If you go over there, it's over.'

'I want my baby. I'm going to get my baby.'

'Oh right, cos stealing kids always ends well, doesn't it?'

'She's *mine*!'

'No, she's not, not anymore. Right now, you've got a

79

chance to go home and live your life. You've flown over here, against *all* odds, dodging every bullet along the way, all to do the right thing. And I think you're a savage for that. Truly amazing. But you've been thrown a lifeline here and if you go over to that house now, this entire thing comes undone.' He showed me the wallpaper on my phone – the picture of me and Raf at our wedding with him in the foreground. When I was so damn happy.

I turned the phone off. 'Why did you come here if you weren't going to help me?'

'I *am* helping you – I am doing exactly what Raf told me to do; keep you in line. She's a mother herself, isn't she, your sister Seren?'

I glared at him.

'She's got two kids – *your* nephew and niece, back in Vermont?' I glared at him harder, all evil, but he held me in place where I sat. 'If you go over there and take that kid or do anything to hurt your sister, it's over for both of yous. You'll be giving Seren away and those kids will lose their mammy. Think. About. Her. Kids.'

I deflated. He'd read the book – he knew kids were my weakness. Kids and dogs.

'How could I not tell she was lying? How did she forge those medical notes, Billy? The *picture* of Ivy, looking so . . . grey?'

'Maybe she had help?' He sighed. 'Or she can use Photoshop? Good editing software will take care of all that.'

This had Nnedi Géricault written all over it. She was a computer whiz – had degrees in it. I'd learned that much about her in the time she'd been up my arse like a particularly raw haemorrhoid. Detective Inspector Genius. I got up, my injured hand still across my chest, and looked through the diamond-leaded glass windows. No sign of police cars down the street – either obvious or undercover. No tinted glass or double antennae. But she was out there, somewhere. Hiding in shadows. Waiting for me to go over there and commit the most legendary boo-boo in my attempt to wreak revenge.

The tears overcame me again and I stood before Billy, a mess of a human being. A mess with a conscience too loud for her thoughts. 'She's in there.' I pointed back at Bodkin House. 'My baby is in there, right now, with at least one liar and a convicted paedophile.'

The pilot light for Mitch flickered back on.

'How about this,' said Billy, clapping his thighs and standing up beside me. 'I'll book you on the next flight to San Diego or Mexico or wherever it is you want to go. Then we go out to that supermarket where we bought your new phone and get Dorcas some new wine glasses to replace the one you smashed and while we're there we'll get all the stuff we need to make tacos – lettuce, tomatoes, the lot. Then we'll come back here and watch a good film and stuff ourselves silly. They won't be as good as Bianca's but—'

'I can hear Raf saying all this.'

Billy nodded. 'He told me you tended to settle your petals once you knew what the plan was. And he said Bianca's tacos sorted you out too. Never met anyone for whom spicy food makes 'em calm but I guess you're not a normal person, are you?'

'I didn't think I was,' I sniffed.

'So whadda ya think? Tacos are a little piece of home, aren't they? And pretty soon you'll be back there, with Raf and your family.'

'Say more things about home.'

He made me look him in the eyes. 'Raf needs you. Don't do *anything* to prevent yourself getting back to him. It's not worth it. What you two have is the stuff people stay alive for. Don't let it slip away. I've never talked a serial killer down before. How am I doing?' His hand was shaking.

'I feel . . . icky,' I said.

'Icky's good. Icky's not murderous. Why don't you give Raf a call while I make a start on booking your return ticket, eh?'

'I've got blood on his T-shirt.'

'We'll get some stain remover when we're out. It'll be good as new. Hey, *Look Who's Talking Now* is on one of the Sky channels later. We can get some popcorn and watch it, yeah? Raf said you liked family films and popcorn.'

'Pop *Tarts*,' I said. 'And I want to see *Sister Act 2*.'

'Okay, deffo! I can fire that up for yous, no bother!' said Billy, a little more excited than was necessary. 'Blueberry's your favourite Pop Tart, isn't it? We'll get you a couple of boxes of them, no danger.' He was talking to me like a jaguar who'd just escaped and he was trying to coax me back to my enclosure.

'You go get it all. I'll wait here. I'll be good.'

'What do you think I am, an eejit? I'm not leaving you alone. You can do this, Rhiannon. Let's just take it an hour at a time.'

Every one of those hours was torture; walking around Tesco, thinking about Ivy, texting Raf and not hearing back, Billy texting Raf and not hearing back, choosing new wine glasses, thinking about Ivy, discovering Tesco was out of Pop Tarts, checking *my* phone again, choosing mince, frying mince, thinking about Ivy, turning my phone off and on again, popping popcorn, thinking about punching Seren in the face. Failing to fire up *Sister Act 2* because Billy's iPad kept buffering. Thinking about kicking Claudia down the stairs. Thinking about Mitch's head bursting open when I smashed it with a conveniently placed lamp.

I heard a bit of Billy's voicemail to Raf when he thought I was washing my hands. '*What do I do with her? She's spoiling for a fight, dude.*'

And then there was more bad news – the next flight back to San Diego was in two days. I'd have to stay inside the cottage until then but the thought of that was unbearable. Ivy's proximity was intoxicating, like a poison, luring me, beckoning me, pulling me across the road into Bodkin House. Her little face lighting up as she saw me, knowing beyond all doubt that I was her mummy. I could hear her calling for me. Arms up. Screaming. My hands ached. My stomach lurched. I could hear the fireworks from the bonfire party she was at. Every bang was another hammer blow to my skull.

BANG!

Raf still hadn't called me or Billy back.

BANG BANG BANG!

What if his infection had got worse?

BANG BANG!

What if he'd slipped into a coma?

What if he was dead?

BANG!

Billy seemed to sense my discomfort as we settled in to wade through *Look Who's Talking Now*. I was quieter than usual – not so many snappy comebacks. Not so much piss-taking of a truly abysmal film. I didn't even care that he talked through most of it – I was lost in my quiet fury.

'Oh, I got a surprise for you,' he announced, unzipping his hoodie.

'You know what happens if it's your cock.'

'Tah-dah!' He pulled out a bag of Maoams and threw them into my lap.

'Thought it was blueberry Pop Tarts.'

'They didn't have any, did they, but I saw these instead. You like Maoams, don't you?'

'Not anymore.'

'Ah shit.' He took the bag back and tore it open. 'Hey, did you know Danny DeVito is the voice of one of the dogs?'

'No,' I said.

'Do you think he's a Scientologist too?'

'No idea.'

'I was reading up about it all. Apparently the guy who started it was—'

'Do you want to watch this fucking film or not?' I snipped.

He picked up his glass and sank the dregs of his Coddleford Reserve.

'Top up?' I asked him by way of an apology.

'Yeah, there's another, isn't there?'

I picked up our empty glasses and made for the kitchen. I settled the glasses down by the sink, stopping beside the cutlery drawer. The stainless steel called to me from inside. I thought about Raf.

Two days. I wouldn't see him for two days, at least. Longer if I caught Covid on the way back and had to quarantine. I needed him here, now, beside me. He hadn't even read my texts, let alone called me back. What drugs did they have him on that could knock him out for so long? Fuck's sake. I leant against the nearest cupboard, imagining his head leaning against mine, promising me it would be okay.

Por donde vayas, llevas mi corazon contigo, mi amor.

But the red mist was too thick – so thick I could barely remember what he looked like. What would the Bad Seeds want me to do? I thought. I scrolled my phone – clicked onto the last thread I'd been reading. Bad Seeds chiming in with their predictions as to how I'd handle a Glaswegian father and son who'd been charged with running a paedophile ring:

She'd have their guts for garters.

> *Yeah, g'wan Sweetpea. Get*
> *'em.*

God I wish she would.

> *String 'em up Sweetpea.*

Flay them.

> *Burn 'em alive!*

Live! Laugh! Love to kill perverts!

> *She wouldn't let us down.*

No way. Sharpen those Sabatiers!

> *Slay 'em, Sweetpea. Slay*
> *'em good.*

And as I was pouring our wine a WhatsApp finally *ping!*ed through. I grabbed my phone with my bandaged hand and fumbled to unlock it. I could hardly wait to see his name on my screen again, see his words of understanding, feel him closer.

But it wasn't him. It was Seren.

Got your new number. Are you on your way? Let me know your flight number. I'll give Ivy a kiss from you. You're doing the right thing.

And that was it. The hot light in my head was on again and there was no cooling it this time. I was fully locked on. The Marshmallow Man had been summoned and that, as we all know, is that. I didn't open the chat – just turned my phone off altogether.

I felt lighter on my feet all of a sudden, like I was being held up by all those thousands of Bad Seed hands and they were guiding me across a sea of doubt towards what I had to do.

Go on Rhiannon, do it, do it, do it, they chanted. *We believe in you. We love you, Rhiannon. You can do anything. Go over there. Finish this. Get your baby. Get your baby. Get your baby.*

I took each knife out of the drawer and placed them onto the work surface in height order – shortest to longest – the stark light glinting off each blade. The chef's knife would do. Strong grip. Even stronger steel. Long enough to pierce the right organs; short enough to carry unseen in my coat.

I saw myself over there already, darting into shadows, hiding behind walls as the family went about their business after dark. Maybe Mitch is coming out of the shower. He doesn't see me, but I see him properly – the sheepish mugshot from the papers; the nonchalant stare from the news bulletins. The ten-years-older version of the chalk sketch, downcast in the dock, now with a beard and grey temples.

He has the presence of mind to grab for a weapon – a can

of spray deodorant – aims it straight at me, but I'm quicker. No time to deliver any fancy parting shots like I stupidly did with upskirter Brad Pfister (yes, really).

He's on his knees, bleeding out, crying. Then comes the screaming pig noise as I slice his throat open from left to right. The *drip drip drip* of his blood on the thick bedroom carpet. And as he crouches and ducks and tries to scurry away, I plunge the knife into every area of his water-spattered skin. Back to front, to side to heart, over and over. I lose count. It's like a workout.

Pulse two three four, stick it in for four, hold it, and out for four, that's gooooooood, Mitch, work with me . . . Pump that chest! Slash those arms! Looking good now, boy, looking gooooooood.

And *I'm* looking good too. Well, good-ish.

By the time I've finished, he's more nicks and cuts than pink skin. Once his knees have buckled so he's on his front, I hop aboard and pin him with my thighs and *stab and stab and stab and stab and stab* his back. I lie on top of him, my mouth in his wet hair, and whisper . . .

'Oi, get in here!' Billy called out. 'You're missing the best bit!'

I put the knives back in the drawer and grab our drinks. On the sofa beside him was our half-full bowl of popcorn. My face was trained on *Look Who's Barking at Scientologists* but I was not watching it. My mind was already across the road. In that house. In some drawer, looking for her passport. Floating into her bedroom. Picking her up softly from her bed, wrapping her in a Peter Rabbit blanket. Creeping through the back door, placing her on the back seat of Billy's car, nestling Richard E. Grunt in beside her.

My mind was already in there – I just had to get my body in there too.

The bonfire party was due to finish around 8.30 p.m. and a quick scan of Bodkin House in darkness from my bedroom window around eight let me know they were all still out enjoying it. I don't like parties, never have. I'd rather tour an operational death camp than go to a party. It's always odds on I'll end the night shitfaced in the garden shed or throwing tennis balls for the dog. But this party was actually useful. This party was my ally.

Between farts that sounded like a door opening in a haunted house – the result of a lactose intolerant determined to have cheese on his tacos – Billy necked the Coddleford Reserve and grew more and more pissed. It was minutes before he drifted off on the sofa – aided by the one remaining sleeping pill the German woman on the plane had given me. His eyes rolled as Travolta was getting molested by his Brit bitch boss with the eyebrow in the ski lodge.

I changed into Raf's Turtles shirt and threw on my hoodie, coat and boots, then flew upstairs to pack my pockets with everything else I'd need for a quick getaway – passport, documents, Sweetpea petals, phone (turned off) and charger, money, my little woollen gatita and of course, Richard E. Grunt. Those were my only fire-grabs. I masked up and made my way silently out the front door and across the street.

The silver Merc was on the shingle drive but no Porsche. The rockets were still going up on the other side of the village where the green was. The road outside Bodkin was all but empty. The streetlights were few and far between and there was no sign of sirens or Géricault hunkered down in a red Audi, so this was my chance.

It was dark at the front and the back of the house. I tried the door handles, just in case, but of course everything was locked. The alarm didn't appear to be on either as the box wasn't blinking. The back door was one of those stable numbers that opened in two halves, but around the corner where the bins were stacked, was a window into what I could see was a utility room. There were two washing machines and a clothesline bedecked with cycling shorts, running vests and sports socks. I scanned the garden for something to throw and found half a red house brick underneath a flowerpot, so I used that. I was in no mood to unpick locks or jimmy frames. My left wrist still not entirely reliable when it came to throwing events, I yeeted the brick with my bandaged hand, and the entire pane smashed pleasingly and dropped right out.

'That's what you get for buying Grade Two Listed. Shit windows.'

I stood on the food bin and crawled up inside and along the draining board. I spied a torch on a wall charger and ripped it down, entering a sort of boot room, red floor tiles strewn with wellies, children's trikes and boxes of washing powder. I followed the flow of red tiles into the kitchen, then the lounge – an enormous cream affair with navy sofas, gold accessories and an inglenook fireplace, either side of which stood massive Jo Malone candles, Fig & Cassis on the left, Wild Berry & Bramble on the right.

'I bet she changes them according to the seasons and all,' I muttered.

There were pictures of Ivy all over the place – in ballet tutus, sitting on rocking horses, parked between Mitch and Claudia at professional photo sessions with a white background where they were looking at Ivy catching a beach ball like she'd just secured Olympic gold.

But Ivy smiled widely in all the pictures; a smile that lit up a room, just like AJ's.

There was a ride-in pink BMW with IVY 1 on the numberplate parked up next to the hearth and, next to that, a make-believe kitchen set up next to the hearth labelled IVY'S CAFÉ, with buttons that made noises and an oven that had a light inside it – a blob of dried red Play-Doh sat on a plastic plate waiting for attention. There was a mini Etch A Sketch on the counter with her scribbles on. She could write her name. I traced my finger across the screen.

She was happy here.

I crept up the thick stair carpet like Nosferatu on speed. There were so many rooms off the mezzanine – at least six, plus two bathrooms. One of the open doors revealed an office with a large desk, filing cabinet and more pictures of Ivy all over the place in gold frames. I shone the torch over a cabinet where the drawers were neatly labelled – A-F, G-M, N-S and T-Z. My hand lingered on N-S where the passports were likely to be but it was locked.

'Shit.'

. . . although the next drawer down was open and at the back, I found a shit load of cash, presumably Mitch's tip stash from personal training, stacked inside a shallow tray. At least a grand's worth. I pocketed that instead.

Across the landing was the master bedroom, the theme olive green and gold, and the sequin gold cushion on the bed had a tiny handprint on it. There were large vases in the corners, full of eucalyptus fronds, and the curtains were swagged.

There was a smaller vase with a single eucalyptus sprig in on Claudia's bedside and a heap of books about eating well after cancer. One of those air diffusers was on top of the stack. I puffed it – eucalyptus.

'What are they, bloody koalas?'

I noticed a tiny gold photo frame, shaped like an ivy leaf next to the stack and in it was another picture of my daughter, on her own, on a swing in the sunshine – beaming, curly like AJ, happy. They loved her so much.

Across from this room was a spare bedroom – there was a pair of slippers beside the bed and a badly packed suitcase on a stand by the window. I smelled my sister's smell – saw that minging pink dressing gown hanging on the back of the door. It stank of cigarettes.

And next to that was Ivy's room. Yellow and white with a bumble bee frieze around the middle. A bee and beehive dangly thing hanging from the ceiling plus every cuddly toy you could imagine stuffed into corners and crevices. I ached at the sight of her tiny sheep slippers parked neatly next to her bed and matching dressing gown draped across the duvet. The height chart by the door showed how much she'd grown this year. There was yellow chintz bunting over her tiny bed and on the walls were even more framed photos of her at various stages; with Claudia and Mitch on a beach, in a park, at some aquarium pointing at a shark thing and holding a cuddly octopus.

She loved them right back.

There was a honeypot-shaped bookcase, holding stacks of picture books and a yellow beanbag with her bottom print in the middle. Ivy couldn't wish for anything more. I sat down on one of the four chairs at her round craft table and traced my fingers across her crayon scribbles. I reached for the doll in the pink highchair with the toy milk bottle stuck in its face. I smelled the doll's hair but it just stank of plastic.

She was safe. Billy was right: I should have stayed away. I should go home and live my life. But it was too late.

There was a click downstairs and low-key chattering as the front door opened. A light flicked on in the hall, illuminating the staircase. I flicked off the torch. Someone was coming up, creeping up the stairs. I ducked behind the bedroom door as a figure entered the room and placed something heavy on the bed – Ivy, fast asleep. The figure put the nightlight on – it was Mitch, all bundled up in brown leather jacket and jeans and scarf, faintly smelling of cold air and sulphur from the fireworks. He dimmed the light and gently slipped her out of her coat and shoes, pulling down her tights.

I was ready. Behind that door – I was ready to cut his head from his shoulders if he touched her. I allowed the knife to slide down into my palm.

He reached under the pillow and pulled out Ivy's pyjamas and replaced the tights with them as well as a pair of fluffy bed socks. He did the same with her dress and jumper, replacing them with a white pyjama top. She grumbled.

'I know, Dolly; Daddy's just putting your jammies on.'

It galled me that he called himself Daddy. Her daddy was dead – I knew that because I was the one who killed him. And for some reason, this realisation cooled my fire. I pushed the knife back up my sleeve. Once she was dressed, he tucked her inside her duvet and wrapped her up like a burrito, settling the large cuddly octopus from the aquarium photo in next to her. He dimmed the light and stroked the curls from her face.

Someone else entered, also wearing a coat but no shoes and reeking of Chanel. 'She okay?'

'Yeah, she's soundo,' Mitch replied.

'She hasn't done her teeth or had her milk.'

'Do you wanna risk waking her up?'

'Maybe not.' They stared at her for a bit then left when she started snoring, pulling the door shut behind them. I listened out for their footsteps. Heard the chattering again once they were both downstairs.

It was just me and her now. In the bed, Ivy snored and I caught my breath as she turned over to sleep on her other side. I couldn't resist getting closer, kneeling down beside her. Listening to her rhythmic breaths. Her curls shone and her eyelashes were so long they looked like falsies.

'You look so much like him,' I whispered. I stroked her head. Breathed her in. My god she was beautiful. I couldn't see me in her at all – she was all AJ. And that was a very good thing.

Once upon a time, in that parallel universe, she might have opened her eyes and grabbed for me; wanted me more than anyone else. It hurt in my body in a place I can't explain. She wasn't going to do that now, and I knew it. She was so well looked after. I couldn't take that away from her.

Taking her away from her bookcase and her sheep slippers and her beanbag with the tiny dent where her bum fits, it would be like that paedophile Elliot Mansur taking River away from the Goffeys – for my own satisfaction only. And I am *not* like him. I may be all kinds of wrong, but I'm not Elliot Mansur wrong.

'You were a boo-boo, Ivy,' I whispered. 'Giving birth to you was the worst pain I've ever experienced. But giving you up was worse. You're doing okay though, I can see that. Anyway, I better go now. Fuck knows how I'm going to get out of here but it was worth it to see you. Stand your ground, okay?

Don't take any shit from anyone. This world is baffling – you're gonna need your anger, but not too much.' I breathed out, tried to remember the technique to clear the knots in my throat. 'Can I have a cuddle? Just one?'

I reached in and lifted her out of the bed under her armpits, picking her up and cuddling her against me. She grumbled but snuggled in and it felt so good as she went heavy against my chest. I kissed her head, breathing her curls in – soap, biscuits and warmth.

'Someone told me once that when a woman grows a baby inside her, some of that baby's cells stay forever, even after it's born. I'll always be with you. And if you ever need me, come and find me. I love you, Ivy.'

I took Richard E. Grunt out of my hoodie and tucked him into the bed beside the octopus.

'I stole your pink bunny that I bought you, but I think it got left in Mexico. So you can have him instead. He'll look after you.'

One of my tears landed on her forehead and she stirred. 'Mumma?'

'Yeah, I'm your Mumma.' I smiled, as she leant back to look at me. But as I palmed the curls from her cheek, along with it came a thick streak of red. My bandage had come off – I hadn't even noticed.

'Oh shit.'

My hand was red again, thick with blood, and so was Ivy. She had it on her face, in her hair, all over her clean white pyjamas. She was covered in it.

'Uh, fuck, shit, sorry . . .'

'Mumma?' Her face changed into an expression I recognised now – fear. Her soft hands became little fists that pushed and pummelled against me. She was fully awake now and shouting: 'No, I want Mumma!'

'*I'm* your Mumma, Ivy. I gave you your name. Stop struggling. Stop it, you little shit, come here!'

'NO! WANT MY MUMMA! MUMMA! MUMMA!'

And the more she struggled the more I tried to hold on to her and the more her pyjamas got covered in my blood. She was struggling so much I had to let go and she snaked down my body back onto her bed where she grabbed her octopus and cuddled it against her, wailing and backing away from me into the wall. She saw the blood on the top of her hand and screamed out again. 'MUMMAAAAAAAA!'

'SHHHHHH! Fuck!'

Outside her room, the landing and staircase were still dark. There was a light on beyond, somewhere downstairs, and the sound of a TV chittering away. I readied the knife in my sleeve and ran back down the stairs, past the kitchen but the corridor suddenly illuminated as a light flicked on – and my cheek hit the ice-cold barrel of a gun.

'I wondered when you'd turn up,' said a breathy voice, too close for comfort. Nnedi Géricault; a spattering of raindrops on the shoulders of her fur-hooded khaki mac, and a smile the like of which her face had never seen. 'Drop it.'

The knife clattered to the floor before I could stop it.

As I mentally assembled a comeback, the sounds of Claudia screaming reverberated through the corridors of the house and a punch sent me flying backwards until there was nothing but stars – stars and darkness.

When I came round, cheek a-throbbin' against a velvet cushion, I found myself lying on one of the navy sofas in the living room. My hands were cable-tied behind me and the knife was on the coffee table, more than an arm's length away. As I levered myself up, someone snatched it: Seren. She stood back by the bifold doors leading out onto the patio.

My face throbbed from where Nnedi had punched me. I prayed Billy would come in any moment and say some Irish gift-of-the-gab shit and unpick me from this knot I'd tied myself in. No luck – the combo of that sleeping tablet and the Coddleford Reserve would see him out for hours.

'She's fine,' said Mitch, coming back inside the lounge. 'Her mum's with her. She's just getting her some milk. Told her it was a bad dream.'

'*I'm* her mum,' I snapped.

Nnedi looked to Mitch. 'Go and be with them – I'll take care of this.'

But Mitch didn't move. He stood in the doorway like Big Daddy, all triceps and calves, as though expecting any minute for me to steamroller over him and kidnap my own kid. Seconds later, Claudia appeared behind him with Ivy snuggled into her in clean pyjamas and wrapped up in a fluffy pink blanket, clutching a bottle of milk. Claudia handed him my sleepy girl and stormed across the lounge towards me, lamping me one across the face on the other cheek to where Nnedi had. The force knocked me flat to the carpet.

'*That's* for AJ,' she said, spitting in my hair, before marching back towards him, extracting Ivy from his arms and disappearing up the stairs.

I was mildly impressed at Claudia's bravery in standing up to me. Previously she'd done nothing more audacious than send a passive aggressive email to HR about pension contributions. I shook out the ache in my face and wiped the back of my head on the sofa arm as I stood up. 'She's got a decent right hook for a woman in remission with knockers that big.'

Mitch stared at me with his ever-so-slightly-rapey blue eyes as blood trickled down from my nose into my mouth.

'What are you looking at, Nonceferatu?' I hissed, licking my lips clean of blood.

He could no longer make eye contact, it seemed. He walked around me like I was nuclear waste and sat on the footstool by the fire like a protein-addicted garden gnome. I glared at him until he looked at me.

'You better be the best goddamn father to that kid or I SWEAR, I will fill a butcher's window with your body parts.'

When he was sufficiently shook, I glanced at my sister Seren, waiting for an explanation.

'She threatened me with prison, Rhiannon!' she cried, tears streaming down her cheeks, beginning the case for her own defence. 'She said I'd never see my kids again. I *had* to lie to you, please believe me.'

I knew she was telling the truth now because her eyebrow was going up and down, like Elton John's at Diana's funeral.

Nnedi was a little greyer, with an extra wrinkle or two and a bit of lockdown tittage, but apart from that she was the same old Nnedi – scraped-back hair, hard stare, fur-hooded raincoat and pristine Chelsea boots. The fourth and fifth fingers on her left hand hadn't grown back either. As she came over to the sofa, she yanked me to my feet.

'Rhiannon Lewis, I am arresting you on suspicion of multiple murder. You do not have to say anything, but it may harm your defence if you do not mention when questioned something which you later rely on in court. Anything you do say may be given in evidence.'

I hocked a globule of bloody spit to the immaculate carpet. 'Finished?'

She plunged her finger-challenged hand into her coat pocket again and pulled out her phone. 'We can do this now or we can wait for backup and you'll be spit-hooded and wrestled to the ground. And *that* will hurt too.'

'What gave me away? Ring doorbell, was it?' I'd only just realised, having glanced at her phone screen and seen the app front and centre.

'We installed it a week ago, just before Seren told you about Ivy. All I had to do was wait for you to take the bait. Claudia and Mitch weren't convinced but I was. I knew you wouldn't let her down.' She tightened my cable ties and then turned her attentions to my sister. 'Seren Gibson, I am arresting *you* for aiding and abetting a murderer. You do not have to say anything but—'

'NO!' she cried breathlessly. 'You *can't* – I did what you said, I said everything you wanted me to say and it got her here!' She burst into tears. God she was weak. 'I've cooperated – YOU SAID I'D GET IMMUNITY!'

'I lied,' said Nnedi.

'You can't do this! No, please! I have two kids!'

A thought flitted through my mind all the while Seren was shrieking – *she's my sister, I should help her out here. Back her up. Blood is thicker than water and all that*. But the feeling passed. She'd built her own gallows this time. Let her hang.

'So when's backup coming?' I asked, on a backdrop of my sister's sobs, knowing Nnedi was fully out on a limb here. 'If you have the support of the Met, then they'll be on their way, right?'

I'd barely finished the sentence when Nnedi pulled out a

Taser from her other pocket and brandished it in my direction. 'I can pump you with enough volts to bring down a shire horse. Do exactly as I say or I will fry you.'

'I'll sue.'

'Try it.'

I did as she directed, even though something about this smelled fishy. Nnedi worked on cold cases – she wasn't an active detective anymore, at least not on live ops – and yet here she was with a gun, *and* a Taser, *and* as one of the bruises on my face could attest, police brutality. Also, why wasn't backup here? And why wasn't she waiting for any? Was that even allowed for the apprehension of an internationally famous serial killer? Where were all the uniforms, the flashing blue lights, the strait jacket and padded van combo?

'This is way weird,' I mumbled as she poked me in the back with the gun all the way across the shingle drive towards the hastily parked red Audi.

'Keep walking,' she ordered, shoving me forwards.

'You're going to take full credit for this, aren't you?'

She unlocked the back door and pushed me inside, leaning over and clicking on my seatbelt. I gave it the full Hannibal slither as she came closer.

'You smell nice. Sort of bacony . . .'

'Shut up,' said Nnedi, a bundle of white cloth appearing from her bottomless pockets. A chemical stench shot up my nose, sending me flying.

She'd only bloody *chloroformed* me as well. Endless bitch!

I awoke to the sounds of an engine as Nnedi Géricault's Audi wound along nondescript dark country lanes. And something else didn't make sense – it wasn't Nnedi driving her own car –

it was *Seren*. Nnedi was next to me on the backseat, eyes fixed on the passing road, handgun lowered but still trained on my person. My hands were tied at the front now and my injured palm had been cleaned up and re-bandaged – I couldn't work out why.

Rhiannon was born free but everywhere she was in chains.

'Why's Seren driving?' I croaked, my head still foggy from the chemical compress. 'Who bandaged up my hand? It stings. Where are we going? Did you chloroform me?' Nnedi sat beside me with her arms folded, handgun still poised, safety was off. 'Oh-kay.'

'It's not chloroform. Similar compound but a quicker reaction time.'

'What's it called?'

'I'm not giving you ideas,' she sneered.

My brain fog was clearing the more miles we ate up and more memories were coming back to me – Ivy. The blood. Claudia punching me in the face. I couldn't remember exactly the sequence of events that had caused things to go from bad to worse to fucked in seventy-two hours, but I was pretty sure it started with one of my infamous boo-boos.

Typical me.

'Isn't it illegal, arresting someone like this? Knocking them out, pulling a gun, getting their supposed accomplice to drive?'

'Call the police then,' said Nnedi, as Seren changed gear and we rounded a blind bend. I don't think she'd stopped crying since we'd left.

'Why have you got a gun? You wouldn't be allowed a gun, working on cold cases. You nicked it, didn't you? From a police evidence locker or summat. I bet you nicked the not-chloroform-but-similar too, didn't you?'

'Shut. Up.'

She cocked it again and I faced front. I looked outside, trying to see in the wing mirror if Billy had by some miracle followed us from Coddleford. But the road was empty – dark skies and drizzly windows and the odd car pulling out of a junction and going in the other direction. There was a buzzing noise somewhere in the car and a trilling ringtone. I'd turned my phone off so it couldn't have been mine. I felt around in my coat for it anyway – that little link to home – but it was gone.

'It's in my boot,' said Nnedi. 'Along with your sister's.'

There was a blinding orange flicker as the streetlights passed and I couldn't focus on any of the road signs. We were heading out into the sticks.

The skies might have been dark as shit but realisation was dawning. 'Which police station are you taking us to?'

We came to a junction where the road looked strangely familiar, even in the dark. We definitely didn't come this way when we drove up from Heathrow. Then we passed a road sign with some Welsh writing on it.

'Why are we in Wales? Where are you processing me, Cardiff?'

'We're not going to a police station – we're going to Ogmore,' said Nnedi.

'*Honey Cottage* Ogmore? Why? There's no police station in Ogmore.'

'She wants us to dig,' sniffed Seren from the driving seat. 'For a body.'

'What body?'

Her voice shook. 'The third lawyer.'

'How would *we* know where our dad buried some random lawyer?'

Nnedi scoffed. 'We spent a week running cadaver dogs over the place and they signalled the presence of VOCs in the woods near the farm. We believe that the third lawyer – David Micah Robinson – was buried out here along with the other two. We just don't know where.'

'What are VOCs?' Seren asked.

'Volatile organic compounds – aka human remains. Plus a forensic archaeologist matched rock type and soil deposits from the woods with those found on Tommy's shovels so we know he buried something out there. It's just a question of what. We also have a witness who says he saw David Micah Robinson with Tommy Lewis in Bridgend days before he was reported missing. Stands to reason that if Tommy was going to bury him, he had the perfect place to do it at Honey Cottage Farm.'

'Who did? What witness?'

'David's car was found in Bridgend, which is fifteen minutes from Ogmore,' said Nnedi, as Seren indicated right and slowed to make the turn onto the gravel driveway. 'He'd tried to make it look like a suicide. Left a note on the dash, but it wasn't his handwriting.'

Just then it dawned on me. 'You're not taking me in?'

'Not yet, no.'

'But this is illegal.'

Nnedi gave it the slow head turn.

'You shouldn't be doing this – you've kidnapped us, illegally drugged me with Christ-knows-what and now you want us to dig up someone else's land for a body you don't know is even there?'

Nnedi glanced from the road to me and back again. 'Yes.'

I was quite aware of the hypocrisy of what I was saying,

so was everyone else in the car, including the moth who had joined us at some point on the journey. I buzzed down my window to let it get sucked out. Lucky fucker.

We passed the horse stables and the sign for Honey Cottage. There was a 'For Sale' sign up too. 'Tommy buried the other lawyers here so it stands to reason the third is here too. And *you* are going to show me where.'

'Our dad was a *builder*,' I reminded her. 'Any number of extensions or patios could have a body underneath them.'

'I believe he is here. All evidence points to here.'

Seren pulled up outside the cottage and switched off the engine as the rain pitter-pattered on the car roof.

'Lot of memories here for you both, I imagine,' said Nnedi, unbuckling her belt. 'All those summers with your grandparents. You had a special relationship with your grandfather especially, didn't you, Seren?'

My sister's breaths were shaky and she was trembling like she was cold, despite her padded jacket. She stared through the windscreen. Of all the places in all the world, she did not want to be back here.

'How did you know about that? I never put it in the diaries.'

'I told her,' said Seren. 'She wanted to know more about this place . . . and why I hate it so much.'

The cottage had been painted since I'd seen it last when I'd strong-armed Craig into viewing it. Before everything went to shit. The wide windowsill was still there in the front where I used to watch the ponies trotting down the lane. A smell of old manure wafted up from the stables. I'd always pined for this place. Now when I looked at it, I could see the sickness inside those walls.

Nnedi got out, slamming the back door behind her. I

watched her stride round to the back of the car, changing her Chelsea boots for wellies.

'I cannot go to jail, Rhiannon,' Seren hissed at me in the rear-view mirror. 'Do something.'

'You want me to help *you*, after what you've done? You've fucked us both in the arse without lube here. I got nuthin'.'

'Géricault is the only person in the world who knows you're here. If I distract her, you run off. Just go and—'

'Go and what? Claudia and Mitch already know I'm still alive – they'll have called the *Daily Mail* by now. It's over, for BOTH of us.'

'No, it's not,' she sniffed. 'She told them to sit tight and wait for her to get in touch – they won't do anything without her say-so. They're more scared of her than I am.' Her voice lowered. 'She's doing all this outside of the law. No one else knows we're here. Come on – there's two of us. If we get rid of her, we can escape.'

'No, we can't. Game's up, Buttercup.'

'Why are you acting like there's no way out?'

'For the record, I'm not acting.'

'No, no way, we've got to do something.'

'How?' I gestured to my tied hands. 'She's stronger than both of us put together, she has a gun *and* chloroform *and* a Taser and she knows how to use all of them. She's won. Face it.' I checked the clock on the dash – 10.43 p.m.

'I've got to get back to my kids.'

'Again, how? Grab your passport when she was arresting you, did you?'

'I'll call Cody. He can fast-track me a new one or something.'

'As someone who has had her fair share of fake passports, lemme tell you that is not going to happen overnight.'

'Well, he'll know what to do,' she snipped, fumbling in her pockets.

'She took your phone too, remember? And what's your husband gonna do from Vermont? Throw his Pokéball at her? Send Fuckwit the owl with a note?'

'He's the calm one.'

'Yeah, I have one like that,' I muttered. 'And I left him because *you* said my daughter needed me. YOU fucked this so YOU fix it.'

There was a movement in my side mirror. My passenger door swung open and Nnedi thrust the gun into my side. 'Do exactly as I say.'

'You suit being a dom,' I said, batting my eyes at her. 'My safe word is "hypocrite", by the way.'

She unclicked my seatbelt – her face an inch from mine. I didn't do the Lecter impression this time – it never had the desired effect on Nnedi anyway. Like throwing stones at a rubber wall.

It was raining hard by now, the sky starless and the air strangely warm. We stood beside the car, staring across the driveway and out to where the paddock and the barn and the field beyond all lay. It was night as far as our eyes could see. Only the moon knew we were there.

Nnedi flicked the handgun equally between me and my sister. She cocked it and switched off the safety. 'If you don't find something, when I KNOW there's something in that field, I'll kill you for real, Rhiannon, and I'll make your sister bury *you* out here.'

Seren seemed too stunned to argue as Nnedi pressed the gun into her cheek. 'And if you want to see your children again, you will do what I say.'

And with that, the great detective snipped my tied hands with a small pair of nail scissors from the glove compartment and picked up one of two shovels she'd retrieved from her boot, throwing one in Seren's direction. I reached down for the other but she beat me to it and jabbed me in the side.

'Ow!'

'Back field. You lead. You next. Go.'

She kept jabbing me, all across the paddock and the field behind the barn – the place where too much happened. Seren couldn't help looking at it – her head kept turning towards it and turning away.

'You know, Dad would never bury a body in deep woodland if that's where you're taking us. We did that once before but there were so many roots it took us twice as long.'

'He cleared a section,' replied Nnedi. 'With a JCB in the days before.'

'Oh.'

'*Your* daddy thought of everything, didn't he?' she sneered.

Every now and again I stumbled and fell down in the mud but Nnedi kicked me to my feet again, lighting us with a large police-issue torch. It would be funny if it were happening to someone else. Seren just walked and sobbed.

'We did have some good memories here, Seren,' I reminded her. 'Remember horse-riding on the beach? Playing board games in the back bedroom? Midnight feasts? Seeing Lee Mead coming out of Costcutter?'

Seren didn't answer. We crossed the river where I'd watched Grandad drown – it slinked sluggishly along in the moonlight like a shoal of adders. This place is a friend as well as a foe – I remember that even if Seren doesn't.

'Remember when Grandad died? That was a laugh.'

'Shut. Up,' said Nnedi.

'Remember picking daffodils for Nan on St David's Day?' I continued. 'And helping her make the Welsh cakes and the toffee for the tourists. She had a sweet tooth, our nan. A sweet tooth and a rancid personality. Remember when we saved that lamb that had got onto the road? And Grandad delighted in telling us that's what we'd eaten in the stew the following Sunday?'

'No,' said Seren. 'I remember you sidling up to me at his funeral saying, "Let's jump out on Nanny so she'll have a heart attack as well and then we'll get the will quicker."'

'Didn't work, did it? Didn't get diddly squat out of that old cumrag. And I got a mouthful of her when we chucked her ashes into the sea. Bitch.'

'We're heading over there,' said Nnedi, pointing the torch at a cleared section of ground in front of a patch of trees on the other side of the field.

'Why do you care so much about this David Micah Robinson dude anyway?' I asked her as we were halfway across the river, slipping a foot at a time into the water to wash off the caked mud on our boots. 'Yet another police commendation medal in it, is there?'

'Not this time, no.'

'And how are we supposed to dig for a body in pitch dark?'

Nnedi didn't answer immediately. She waited until we were across the stepping stones and had arrived on the other side.

'We have a torch,' she said, dryly, clicking it on and flashing it in both our faces. 'And we have spare batteries. *That's* how we will see. We have shovels. That's how *you* will dig. And I care so much about David Micah Robinson because he was my dad.'

*

It all became screamingly clear – why Nnedi hated me so damn much. Why she'd hated my dad. Why Seren and I had been brought there as a matter of even greater urgency than getting me under lock and key.

And why she had two fingers missing on her left hand.

'Lyle Devaney was one of the most prolific paedophiles in the country in the late Nineties,' Nnedi explained as we crossed the last few yards into the dark, dark woods. 'His preference was runaways. Girls in care homes. Girls who wouldn't be believed or missed. There were rumours he procured them for gentlemen's clubs in London but this was never proved. My dad was his lawyer and because of Devaney's "friends in high places" and an oversight in Devaney's arrest procedure, Dad was confident of getting him acquitted. It was just a job. Then Tommy's detective friend Keston Hoyle informed Tommy about the case and the certainty of Devaney getting off. And my dad was a dead man walking. Devaney was top of his list and Dad was second.'

The black stillness beyond the trees provided an unsettling backdrop to the pissing rain. The adrenaline coursing through me was enough to keep me upright at least, despite how bone tired I felt underneath. Nnedi trained the gun on me, above the torch. I could barely see for blinding light.

'Killing Devaney wasn't enough,' she continued. 'Tommy didn't just want to get rid of the paedophiles but the lawyers who got them off too. When he came looking for Dad at our house, he found me instead.'

We stared at her fingerless hand. Seren said it first.

'Our dad did *that* to you?'

'I wasn't squealing like the pig I was training to be,' she replied curtly. 'I didn't tell Tommy where to find him, so he kept going, with the bolt cutters, until Keston Hoyle turned up and stopped him. Tommy was relentless. He would've killed me to get to my dad; I have no doubt.'

'Dad wouldn't have killed you,' I said.

'Wanna bet? Sometimes I think Tommy was worse than *you*. Then I remember what *you've* done.'

Her torch swept the clearing. Leftover strings of police tape fluttered on nearby gorse and much of the grass had been churned up into a muddy slick from myriad footsteps. The entire area had already been picked over by search teams and forensic archaeologists and just inside the wood stood three small red markers sticking out of the dirt.

'These three markers are where the dogs concentrated most of their time,' Nnedi explained. 'So here is where you will dig.'

'But it's real dark,' moaned Seren.

'Then dig *quickly*.'

'And my hand has a cut on it,' I added.

'You're double-bandaged and padded up – you're fine. Now *dig*.'

And so, we dug. Shovel after shovel, the mound of our toil growing larger beside us, and the rain came down with unacceptable urgency. The only benefit to the rain was that it softened the ground – otherwise it would have been too hard to dig. I'd clearly eaten too many tacos since I'd dug my last grave as my boobs had got so big they swung when I swung. I'd have to invest in some kind of sports bra at this rate.

My wrist started aching and my dig-rate grew slower. Nnedi clocked it.

'I didn't say you could stop.'

'My hand hurts.'

'So what?'

'No, not my injured one, my other one. It was amputated just over a year ago. It seizes up sometimes.'

Seren stared at me. She didn't know about that. 'Amputated?'

'Yes, amputated.' I didn't say any more, just dropped the shovel and yanked up my sleeve to show her and Nnedi the scar. 'See? I need to rest it. I usually wear a brace but I don't have it with me.'

'How did it happen?' Seren asked, digging faster as I was permitted to ease up a little.

'Mind your own beeswax.'

The hole at the first marker grew bigger beneath our feet but we unearthed little but mud and the odd rock. Nnedi ceased our operations in that spot after a while and pointed to the second marker. We climbed out of our pit and she sat on a tree stump, training the torch and gun on us at all times. I would say she was cheering us on but I don't think even she was looking forward to finding what we were digging for.

Goody Two Shovels Seren wasn't listening. 'Why didn't the police dig this?' she puffed, her giant shovel-loads dwarfing mine by some way.

'The signals the dogs were giving back weren't convincing enough to extend the search. We only get so much time and money and it wasn't thought a reasonable use of resources to keep them going. I was given all the excuses – "not in the public interest . . . Tommy is dead anyway, most of his gang are behind bars". My dad meant nothing to them, but they underestimated how much he meant to me.'

'Oh,' she said, leaning on her handle. Nnedi glared at her and she set to digging again.

'How could a man who defended nonces mean so much to

you?' I pecked. 'What kind of person would *love* a guy who did that?'

'You loved *your* dad and he hacked a woman's fingers off. You loved *your* dad and he buried a man upside down in a peat bog – alive. You loved *your* dad even though he beat an innocent man to death.'

'What "innocent man"?'

'MY FATHER!'

There was a silence between arguing and digging as the wind howled through the treetops and the mud squelched beneath our feet. Seren restarted digging first, encouraging me to do the same.

'I do think it's strange though,' said Nnedi. 'That Tommy never knew about what your granddad was capable of.'

Seren stopped again.

'Surely if he had any inkling that his own father-in-law was a predator around young girls – his own *daughter* – he wouldn't have let you two anywhere near the man.'

'He didn't *have* an inkling,' spat Seren. 'I never told anyone.'

'Except her.' Nnedi looked at me. 'And you never told a soul either.'

'She told me not to,' I said, pulling my wet hems away from my calves.

'Even your beloved dad, Tommy? Known vigilante? Scourge of all sexual predators? He could have done to your grandfather what he did to my dad.'

'*I* wanted to do it,' I replied, and they looked at me with faces I couldn't read. 'I wanted to kill Grandad. But his clogged arteries beat me to it.'

I stopped digging to flex my wrist again, expecting Nnedi to berate me but she didn't. She seemed deep in thought, even though the gun was still trained on the pair of us.

'I'm sorry I lied to you,' puffed Seren as she dug, 'but I had no other choice. She told me to get you back in the UK, at any cost.'

'Relax, Seren. If I wanted to kill you, I'd have done it the first time you told the police on me.' I turned to Nnedi. 'Miss, can I go for a piss please?'

'No.'

'I need the toilet. Have you no humanity?'

'Look who's talking,' Nnedi scoffed. But she relented and pointed the gun at my head all the way to the hedge encircling the field. There was a gap into the next field. 'Behind there. One minute. Do not test me.'

'You're da boss.' I pulled down my soaking-wet jeans and pants and let the rivers flow. I could hear Nnedi on the other side, pacing and huffing. 'Have you thought that maybe his body was dissolved, not buried?' I called out.

'What?'

'Dad used lye to dissolve remains sometimes. He'd get it from builder's merchants. Huge heavy tubs of it, enough to dissolve a corpse. Maybe that's what the dogs smelled and there is no body because he's powder?'

'Just hurry up.' She sighed.

We were digging for around forty minutes before Seren's shovel finally hit something hard by the third marker. She sprang backwards as Nnedi leapt up from her tree stump and scurried over to us. 'GET HIM OUT NOW!'

'It's been decades – chances are it's too late for CPR,' I said, jimmying the object free from its earthly clutches.

'SHIT!' shouted Nnedi, holding the gun steady with her less-than steady hand. 'Oh my god.'

But the more I dug around it, the easier it became to identify as definitely *not* body-shaped – it was smaller and squarer. The mud finally gave up its prize and I pulled out a rectangular box triple-wrapped in bin liners and yellow insulation tape, no bigger than a briefcase.

And that's exactly what it was.

Nnedi yanked it away from me and gave it to Seren. 'Open it,' she ordered at gunpoint. All eyes were on the object as my sister tore open the plastic wrapping, at least two layers of it, maybe more, finding the leather underneath. There was a faded three-letter monogram on the front – D.M.R.

David Micah Robinson.

'It's his,' said Nnedi, staring at it. She was not going to cry. She wouldn't. She'd been ready for this for years.

The lock was broken – Seren levered up the lid and pulled out nondescript papers, a small ball of blue poly rope and a squash of carrier bags, tied up roughly with it. She sniffed it, baulking away.

'Oh Jesus.' There was something dead in there.

'What is it?' said Seren, breathlessly.

'It's probably fingers,' I said. 'Your dad's might be in there. Yours too. He used to keep them and send them to people for intimidation.'

'Oh my god,' baulked Seren, resisting the urge to be sick.

Nnedi took the case and put everything back inside, clicking it shut. She sat with it on the tree stump for the longest time. 'He taught you to do that, didn't he? You cut Julia's fingers the same way he cut off mine.'

'Yeah, but I did it to Julia for fun. He did it to you to find out where your dad was. Big difference.'

'Keep digging.'

'There's nothing else here, it must be midnight . . .'

'KEEP. DIGGING.'

'My wrist is killing me,' I whined.

'I DON'T CARE,' she yelled. It was weird hearing Nnedi shout. Her voice didn't sound like hers – it was all coarse and flecks of spit flew out of her mouth as bits of hair escaped her tightest of tight buns. It would have been chilling, if I could have been chilled.

So we kept digging, as instructed, into the wee small hours, even though I knew full well there wasn't going to be anything else unearthed tonight. The blue rope had stirred a memory for me, but I pushed it aside until I could bring it to the fore. By this point, I was just running down the clock, waiting for an opportunity to smash Nnedi over the head with my shovel and make a run for it. But another hour and a half we were at it, in between pee breaks and time-outs for wrist ache and rain showers, but at all three markers, we hit nothing. Some undecipherable bone fragments, maybe, but not enough to piece together to form a human and certainly not David Micah Robinson.

'SHIT!' Nnedi shouted upwards into the sky, as she kicked the briefcase across the clearing and into the hedges.

'For what it's worth,' said a soaking-wet Seren, shoving her shovel into the dirt and leaning on the handle, breathless, 'I'm sorry.'

'Bullshit,' Nnedi spat. 'You don't care where my dad rots. As far as you two are concerned, he was just some crooked lawyer who defended perverts. But he wasn't that to me. He was my dad.'

It was the first time ever I'd seen her truly emotional and it was like her face could crack with the pressure of it. Suddenly she whipped her head round to face me, pointing her gun.

'NO!' screamed Seren.

'TELL ME WHERE HE IS!' She snatched away my shovel and threw it into the darkness in the same direction as the briefcase.

'I DON'T KNOW!' I yelled, hands in the air. 'I swear I don't know!'

'Don't give me that, you were Santa's Little Helper; you went everywhere with Tommy. Dad came here, with Tommy. Where were *you*?'

'I can't remember!'

'Dad's car was found in Bridgend. Tommy must have brought him here where he buried the others.' The gun pushed into my temple; her finger on the trigger. 'Did he dissolve him? Did he cut him up?'

'PLEASE, STOP IT, DON'T HURT HER!' I didn't know if it was rain or tears streaming down Seren's cheeks.

'SHE KNOWS WHAT TOMMY DID TO HIM. SHE WAS THERE. TELL ME NOW OR I WILL SHOOT YOU IN THE HEAD!'

'I DIDN'T SEE ANYTHING! HOW MANY MORE TIMES?!' I yelled.

'YOU DID, I KNOW YOU DID – YOU WERE ALWAYS WITH HIM, WATCHING HIM, YOU KNOW. YOU FUCKING KNOW!'

'I DON'T!'

The gun cocked. Her finger trembled. Her face streamed as her mouth howled. Her finger trembled on the trigger. And then—

'I know where he is!'

We both looked around at Seren. We waited for more but she was just crying and shaking like she had sudden-onset Parkinson's.

'Don't you lie to me as well—' hissed Nnedi.

'I'm not. I know where Dad buried David, I do. At least, I *might*.'

'Talk.'

'I was there.'

'When?'

'I-I-I came back from horse-riding one day . . . Dad told me to go inside the house. I can't remember where Rhiannon was but I don't think she was even home. I-I-I did as I was told . . . but I saw him putting a large, long object into his van. It was wrapped in bin bags and yellow tape, like the briefcase . . . he pulled out of the drive and . . . went right, towards Southerndown. When he came back later, he had sand on his boots, yes. Sand. I know he'd been to Southerndown. We had a holiday home there, at the campsite. They bought it with the proceeds from Rhiannon's TV career when she was a child.'

Nnedi looked at me – I looked at Seren. Where did she get *that* load of old clit from? She was lying her arse off. She never went riding without me, and we didn't *have* a holiday home up at the campsite. We always stayed at Honey Cottage whenever we came to Ogmore. I have to admit though, I was curious to find out where she was going with this.

'Dad probably buried him in the g-g-garden at the holiday home. We had some raised beds. I remember that summer, Dad was gonna fill them in. If David's remains are somewhere, I bet it's there.'

Nnedi threw me a look, then back to Seren. 'Where is the holiday home?'

'We don't own it anymore, but it's at Southerndown. About five minutes up the road. It's a beach with rockpools and c-ccliffs. We can break in and check the garden. It'll be empty for sure – nobody stays there in the winter.'

'Whovians call it Bad Wolf Bay. I don't know why,' I added. A bit of local colour to decorate the whopping-great porky pie Seren had baked. Nnedi stared us both out. Neither of us could be sure if she'd bought it but she eventually lowered the gun and flicked the safety back on.

'Back to the car. I'll drive.'

The clock read 2.28 a.m. when we got back to Nnedi's Audi, the treads of our trainers and boots clogged thickly with mud; our bodies exhausted and running with sweat and rain. The sky was an inky purple, verging on black. Nnedi held the gun to my head as Seren secured my hands again with a fresh cable tie from the glove compartment and strapped me into the passenger seat, like when I was little. Nnedi slammed my door and frogmarched Seren round to the other side, pushing her into the back like a sack of potatoes.

Nnedi went to close the door. 'If you're lying to me—'

'I'm not lying. If he buried him that day, that's where he'll be.'

Nnedi got in the driver's seat and slammed her door. She didn't start the engine immediately, just sat there huffing and puffing and generally looking pretty done with the pair of us. I recognised the expression as one my mum had on her face a lot.

'Come on then. Kill Site Number Two please,' I trilled.

Nnedi flicked on the engine, slamming the gearstick into reverse and gunned the accelerator fast out of the gravel driveway and onto the main road before speeding off towards Dunraven Bay (as Southerndown is known).

'Tell me where I'm going,' she ordered.

'Just keep straight,' said Seren. 'It's a straight road.'

'Can we have some music on?' I asked. 'Dad always used to put music on when we went to our holiday home.'

'Shut up.'

'Why should I?'

'Because I'm feeling pretty murderous myself right now,' she replied through teeth so gritted she could have franked steel envelopes.

'Am I going to prison after this?'

She didn't answer, just kept taking the blind bends at break-neck speed. I glanced behind at Seren – she looked, I don't know, furtive? Up to something? One hand was placed on the lock of her seatbelt but I couldn't see where her other one was. I focused on the winding road ahead.

'Can we get a Maccy D's after we've dug up your dad? As a treat for being good?'

No answer.

'I'll eat it outside so it doesn't stink up your car.'

Clenched jaw. She wasn't focusing on Seren at all.

'I'm quite looking forward to jail,' I said, wiping my nose. 'If I'm down for a full stretch, I'll kill all-comers in there, not just sex offenders. Decent people. Screws. Psychiatrists. Dinner ladies. Creative writing tutors. I won't be able to stop myself. And that'll all be on *you*.'

Still no answer. She hit fifth gear.

'Prison will be like a candy shop for me. Perhaps I'll carve your name into their butt cheeks. My new calling card. I'll use the anus to dot your i.'

'You'll be in a glass box in the bowels of the prison,' Nnedi spat. 'You won't be allowed near others. You'll be like Maudsley. Left to rot like the festering pile of shit you are.'

'He killed sex offenders, didn't he, Maudsley? Poor lamb.'

'You're insane,' she seethed.

'I could plead insanity. Get a lighter sentence, cushy hospital wing with extra privileges . . .'

'You wrote a coherent six-hundred-page manifesto describing in stark detail everything you did and why. You planned, you stalked, and you strategised. You are anything *but* insane, Rhiannon.'

Nnedi's voice was sharp and loud like my headmistress's when I was called into her office for stabbing the school gardener with his own fork.

Loud enough for Seren to get undone.

'If you put me in Haverfield with that Roxanne Peach bitch, you KNOW I'm gonna have her for breakfast, lunch and tea, don't you?'

'Who's Roxanne Peach?' asked Seren, shuffling forwards in her seat.

'You must have heard about her,' I said. 'She's been in there about ten years. Killed all those babies on a hospital ward. Oh yeah, she's *mine*.'

Nnedi rounded another bend and I scrolled the radio channels until a song came on I recognised: 'Try a Little Tenderness'. Commitments version. She didn't stop me.

'Remember this, Seren?' I asked, turning it up. 'Dad would belt this out in the car on the way here sometimes. Me and her would be bundled in the back under a blanket. Mum thought he was so embarrassing. Do you remember, Seren?'

I looked back at my sister – she had her eyes closed and she was breathing quietly, like she was in labour, or going to be sick.

I sang, hitting every note with a sledgehammer, boosting the volume the more I could hear Seren rummaging about.

'I thought *I* was a bad singer.' She laughed, but her voice was too light, like it was the last voice she had in her. Her face was different too. She was still shivering; her eyes as wide as I'd ever seen them.

'Stop looking at her!' ordered Nnedi.

I continued to sing, turning up the volume. I knew she was waiting, and indeed just anticipating, so the song seemed a fitting accompaniment. Seren teetered on the edge of her seat, belt unclicked in the chaos of my dulcet tones.

'What are you doing?' said Nnedi, flicking a look across at me and then in the rear-view at Seren, but by this point, it was too late – Seren was on her, around her, pressing her neck with her own seatbelt.

I clutched my own belt as the car swerved across the road, this way and that, Nnedi choking and spluttering as Seren squeezed her tighter. Then at once the Audi swung sharply to the right, colliding with the grass verge as we skidded off the road, down a grassy bank, smashing hard through a wooden fence and juddering along the uneven ground.

'SHITTING HELL!' I yelled as we bumped at speed through the field. The car briefly lifted up onto two wheels and I scrambled across to correct it with my still-bound hands, wrenching the steering wheel this way so we didn't tip over. We sped towards a thicket of trees and there was nothing I could do as Nnedi's scrabbling feet hit the brake as the car lunged to a stop metres away from a mighty oak. We came to a halt with a clatter and a hiss, 'Try a Little Tenderness' still blaring out, headlights on.

Nnedi was slumped against the steering wheel, unmoving. The engine had stopped but the lights were still on and the indicators blinking orange. I pushed open my door and limped around to Seren's side and opened hers.

'Oh my god!' cried Seren, holding her head where she had banged it against the window.

'You all right?'

Nnedi was coming to in the driver's seat. Without a second thought, Seren reached forwards again to yank the seatbelt back against her throat.

'Go!' she said breathlessly, pressing hard on Nnedi's windpipe.

'What are you doing?'

'RUN, RHIANNON!'

'You don't have to do this for me.'

'I'm *not* doing it . . . for you,' she heaved, pulling tighter on the belt as Nnedi gargled. 'I'm doing it . . . for my kids. I will *not* . . . go to jail for your crimes. My kids will *not* . . . lose their mom . . . Get my phone.'

'How the hell is killing her going to get you back to your kids?' I said, retrieving the nail scissors from the glove and going round to the boot to get our phones.

'I'm not thinking . . . too far ahead right now, Rhiannon. I'm just . . . doing what needs to be done . . .' she strained. 'She's in the way. She . . . has to go. Stop wasting time. Go! NOW, Rhiannon!'

I fumbled with the scissors for an age to cut my cable ties and the relief of renewed freedom was immediate. I threw off my soaked hoodie in favour of my big warm coat and got going. But then it dawned on me – where the fuck *was* I going?

'I don't know where *to* go!'

Seren glanced at me, just for a moment as Nnedi gargled and bulged.

I looked around. These were fields I knew but beyond them, nothing. In every single direction. Nothing and nowhere that wanted me. Nothing I could see. Nowhere I could go. No point. No point in running at all.

'GO!' Seren yelled, the detective still writhing and struggling and frothing at the mouth beneath her grip.

I whipped my head around – in every direction, there was just my own hot breath and black, black sky. 'Where do I go, Seren? WHERE?!'

'JUST GET OUT OF HERE. DON'T LOOK BACK! NOW!'

Thursday, 21 October –
Ogmore-by-the-Sea,
South Wales, very early morning

I ran across the field, through a thicket of trees in the rough direction of Honey Cottage – the only place I could think to go that wasn't straight into the sea. I had to stop to catch my breath but then I pushed on, further and harder than ever. And then I tripped over a tuffet and fell flat on my face with an *OOF!* in a patch of damp leaves. And then I got my boot stuck in mud and had to yank it out and then I ran again but it was no good – I was sodden through, exhausted and extremely unfit. And what was I running to, for fuck's sake? There was nowhere to go. The time was 3.04 a.m.

And then a loud bang rang out across the night, shattering the stillness into a million sparkling pieces. My chest tore in two halves, once again.

The echo resounded in every direction. I ran back in the direction I'd come – through the trees towards it. This time I didn't fall. I didn't feel the cold or the wet or the rain that continued to pelt down. And when I got back to where the trees thinned out, I saw the car, headlights dimmed, indicator light flashing, roof illuminated by a stark white moon.

I walked towards it, my fast breaths the only sounds in my ears. The back and driver's doors were wide open. Driver's belt back in place. There was a loud gasp. The rain came down, harder.

I followed the gasp to the other side of the Audi, to see my sister, still and unmoving on the grass; eyes wide open. In the blare of the headlights, I could see a clean hole in the centre of her head. Nnedi Géricault knelt beside her, breathless with sobs.

Nnedi looked up as I moved closer. The gun lay beside her on the grass but she made no attempt to grab it.

'Seren?' I don't know why I said her name – I knew she wouldn't wake up. I knelt down on the sodden ground next to her head, pulling her to a sitting position as the blood trickled down her face from the hole. 'Seren?'

Nnedi just stared.

'Seren? Oi, come on, wake up.'

It was like my mind knew it but my body didn't. I kept smacking her cheek to rouse her but nothing came back.

'SEREN!'

I kept smacking her and calling her name but she still wouldn't answer me. The feeling of her heavy head against mine was a sensation I hadn't had for years; an almost-hug that melted me. We were kids again and she was hugging me to thank me for the smelly eraser set I'd bought her with my pocket money. We were kids again, and I was lying in a hospital bed, and she was in her school uniform, running towards the bed with a Sylvanians Pony Hair Salon box, so happy I was alive. We were kids again and she was happy I was out of my wheelchair for the first time. We were kids again and she smiled at me to thank me for killing Grandad. We were kids again.

'Seren? You've got to wake up,' I said softly, like it was Christmas morning and our stockings were waiting at the foot of our beds.

Nnedi shook; her face soaked with rain. 'She was going to kill me.' As if to prove her point, she started coughing and hacking through a hoarse throat.

An amazing sense of peace had come over me – the kind of peace I only feel when I've killed someone myself. The certainty that I have them forever now if I want. That they won't ever leave me. That Seren won't get married and move out. That she won't go back to America, despite my begging. That she won't forget my birthday for the fifth year in a row even though I never forget hers or her kids'. I held her still-warm body close – I could now, forever.

'Stop it,' said Nnedi, pulling me away from her as the rain pelted down.

'Get off me,' I whispered. 'I'm staying here.'

The rain grew heavier, drenching us but washing away all traces of mud and blood the second it hit our skin. 'You'll freeze out here.'

'I'll die with my sister then, won't I?'

I wanted to hold her and put my cheek on hers like that photo of us on holiday when I was five and she was ten and we had matching pink dresses and tans and both had hair wraps in – hers on the right side, mine on the left – and Chupa Chups lollies sticking out of our mouths.

Nnedi stood up and tugged on my arm but I shook her off. As she pulled me away altogether, a new rage surged inside me from the ground up.

'GET THE FUCK OFF ME!' I spat, punching and kicking her. She stumbled away, grabbing for the open car door but I was on her then, bodily, mounting her, forcing her onto the wet grass and reaching for the handgun, somewhere behind me. As I fumbled, she pulled some police academy manoeuvre and slammed *me* onto my back instead. And once she'd proved her power over me, the fight went out of me and I lay still on the grass.

And so did she.

'What the fuck happens now?' I said to a starless sky. She didn't answer. I felt the same way I did in Birmingham when I went there to kill Wesley Parsons. My heart just wasn't in it. My blood lust had disappeared in a puff of gun smoke. But now I could reason with it – Nnedi had defended herself. Seren was killing her and she wasn't going to stop. And now Seren was dead. Killing Nnedi by proxy was not going to change a thing – the bullet hole in Seren's head said so.

The rain came down harder than ever and Seren's open eyes didn't close in reflex. I crawled over to her, trying to exhale all the poison in my chest. I suddenly felt so damn tired and I lay with my head against hers, like we had when we'd watched the Perseid meteor showers on hay bales in the fields. The sister who had helped me walk again, talk again, taught me how to roller skate and lace my shoes, who'd played Sylvanians with me, taught me how to spell *inconsequential*, and French-plait my hair. Who'd spent hours designing outfits with me on the Fashion Wheel and helped me bury the toys in the garden to save them from the charity shop. The sister who'd sobered up in time to see me and Dad coming through the kitchen door, his khaki trousers covered in her boyfriend's bloodstains; my hands covered in mud.

But she was also the sister who'd told police I was the one who should be in prison, not Craig.

And the sister who'd lied about Ivy having cancer to get me back here.

And the sister who'd left for America when I needed her the most, even though I begged her to stay.

I felt a tap on my shoulder – the handle of the gun. Nnedi was giving it to me by the barrel.

I didn't move.

She knelt down on the grass beside me. 'Take it. I'm finished.'

Past Rhiannon might have taken that gun, pistol-whipped her with it and gone to town on her remains, wiping up her wet leftovers with a slice of Hovis. But I just didn't have it in me.

'No.'

'Someone will have heard the shot. Seen the lights. I'm done for.'

'No.'

'Just finish this!'

'I can't hear anything.' I tried to wrap Seren's arm around me but it kept slipping back onto the grass.

'I'm sure I heard sirens.'

'They're in your head. I hear them all the time.'

'Go then. I'll wait here.'

I stroked the wet worms of hair away from Seren's forehead, feeling the heat from her skin disappearing beneath my fingertips. I leant down and went to kiss her but then a thought bloomed in my mind – if she were alive, she'd shake me off. She'd baulk at me touching her. Seren *hated* me with a passion – couldn't get far enough away from me. And as for trying to kill Nnedi, that was to get back to her kids. She didn't care what happened to me.

What the fuck was *I* apologising to her for?

That seemed to break the spell.

'Help me move her,' I said, and stood up. Nnedi hadn't moved from her spot beside me on the grass.

'What?'

'We need to hide her.'

'You can't be serious.'

'Worth a try, isn't it? If I'm going to prison, it will be for something *I* did, not you. Now help me move her.'

Thunder cracked in the sky, feeling like a warning from God to get a fucking move on, so we did. Nnedi turned off the headlights and helped me drag Seren into the woods where we buried her beneath a shallow pile of leaves. At first glance, you wouldn't know she was there – you'd just think *Oh neat, a big pile of leaves. Let's jump in and have a leaf fight.*

As Nnedi made her way back to the car, I reached into my pocket and pulled out my passport. In the back I'd saved a few of the Sweetpea petals from my wedding confetti. I tucked them inside Seren's still-visible hand and chucked a load more leaves over her to cover it.

'The rain's our friend,' I said, catching up to Nnedi. 'It'll wash stuff away. Gimme your keys.'

Nnedi didn't hesitate or argue like I thought she would. I got in the driver's seat. I didn't think it was going to start at first but then it fired up. She just stood in the field, getting even more soaked as the rain pelted down.

'Well?' I called out through the open door. 'Are you coming or are you going to stand out here like a sodding scarecrow all night?'

I don't know why I ordered Nnedi to come with me. I think it was the Man in the Moon, guiding my every move, lighting our way. Something told me to help her – an instinct. A gut feeling. Guilt? I'd felt this before. It was a queasy feeling, like when your tongue locates a hair in your mouth.

But for a couple of scratches and a dent to the bumper, Nnedi's red Audi didn't show any significant repercussions from our crash. Once we were out of the field and back on the main road, I sped as quickly as the country bends would allow. Nnedi Géricault, arch enemy, shivered beside me in the passenger seat. The clock on the dash ticked over to 04.00 a.m. exactly.

'Where's the gun?' I asked.

'Here,' she said, removing it from the footwell. It sat there in her lap, still loaded.

'We've got to get rid of it.'

'Where are we going?' said Nnedi, through chattering teeth.

'To. Get. Rid. Of. The. Gun,' I said slowly, like she had brain damage as well. 'Put the heater on.'

She fiddled with buttons as I drove, straight on towards the signs for Dunraven Bay, careful to turn the headlights off as we passed houses. I followed the signs for the access road to the beach, which led us snaking down to a small, deserted car park painted with white lines.

'Empty it out and give it here,' I said, putting on the leather gloves from the glovebox, and holding out my hand for the gun. She gave it to me straight away, no fuss. 'And the Taser. And that chloroform rag.' I bundled it all up with Seren's phone inside one of the car mats and tied it up tightly with a set of jump leads. 'Pray the tide's in.'

Nnedi waited in the car while I forced the door open

against the battering wind and walked down to the car park's edge. It was relentless darkness as far as the eye could see and the water below roared and crashed against the sea wall. I ran back to get the torch and shone it down below to where the tide lapped and spat. And then I hoyed the bundle down into the swirling dark liquid. I summoned the Man in the Moon while I was out there.

'Take it, please. Take it as far away as you can.'

The wind stole my breath as I said it so I knew he'd heard me. I could rely on the Man in the Moon. No point relying on God. I prayed for my school bully Julia's death every day of the week in assembly and in the end I had to do it myself. But the Man in the Moon rarely let me down.

I stood there looking out at the inky sea. I felt exactly like I did the day I left the UK on the cruise ship when I stood on the top deck of the *Flor de la Mer* as the water lapped at the sides and I was surrounded by happy, smiling faces, party lights and buffering balloons. I was as bone-cold and dog-tired then as I was now – pulling my coat tighter around me. There were no party poppers. No sequined people with glasses of champagne. No leaking tits for a baby I'd left behind. A baby who didn't want me now. But the uncertainty – the *crushing* uncertainty – of what lay ahead was almost too much to bear. I wanted to throw up.

When I got back to the car, Nnedi's eyes were on me. We sat in a less-than-companionable silence for a long moment, both freezing and shivering. I tried to remember my meditation mantra – *in for seven, out for four. I am here, I am breathing, I am loved.* But it was no use. I was there and there was purgatory. I was breathing, but my breaths were short and my heart thumped so loud I could hear it. And I was loved?

Yes, okay, I was loved. Raf loved me but he was thousands of miles away.

The wind howled against the car and Nnedi's teeth chattered. She rummaged for her phone – it was vibrating. Claudia's name was on the screen.

'Oh Christ.' She cleared her throat before sliding the bar across. I couldn't believe the switch in her personality.

'Hi, yes, all sorted, she's in custody, locked down so you're completely safe . . . Yeah it worked perfectly . . . No, you don't need to do a thing just . . . actually this is going to hit the headlines within a couple of hours so you should vacate your house . . . Well yes, but the world's press are going to descend on your doorstep, and they will want a comment . . .'

I thought *I* was good at acting but Nnedi was something else. Oscar-worthy. Critics' Choice–worthy. BAFTA-hmm, I think Sarah Lancashire could have done it slightly better.

'It's best if you get out of here, ASAP,' she continued. 'Yes, that's perfect. Don't talk to anyone, and don't answer the door or the phone unless it's me.'

This conversation went on for a while and the basic upshot was she wanted Claudia to leave Bodkin House and, if possible, the country. She was still shaking but somehow managed to keep the tremble out of her voice.

'Tenerife sounds perfect. I'm very jealous too!' Cue fake laugh. 'I'll keep you posted but for now, it's all good. You're safe and so is Ivy. Take care.' She turned off her phone.

'Jesus, I thought *I* had a poker face.'

'Needs must,' she sniffed. 'She won't want any press coverage for this. They're going to stay with her parents in Tenerife until the dust settles.' She stared into the abyss surrounding us.

'It was never about finding me, was it?' I asked. 'It was about your dad.'

Her head bowed. I don't know if that made me feel better or worse. We both sat there, side by side, each bearing the bruises and cuts one another had inflicted, the battering wind outside pummelling the metal and whistling through the vents and cracks. I had absolutely no idea what to do.

I turned on my 5G and several messages pinged through from Billy, well into double figures. He was not happy at all. They got progressively more Irish in their slang and accusations. I called him back.

'You shouldn't turn your phone on, it's—' Nnedi said.

'I need to call Billy.'

'Who's Billy?'

'The twat supposed to be keeping an eye on me.' I clicked on his name. It barely rang before he answered.

'Oh thank fuck,' came the relieved Irish voice as I switched off the headlights and turned down the heater to hear him. 'Where the hell *are* you?'

'I'm at Dunraven Bay, in Wales. I haven't got time to explain—'

'What the fuck are you doing in Wales? I woke up and you'd vanished and I didn't know if—'

'I know, just listen a minute, will you?' I garbled a short, snippy expletive-ridden summary of the story so far, up to and including Seren's death, as Nnedi shivered beside me like the first kitten to leave the litter.

'And now we're on the run,' I finished.

'Tell me you didn't kidnap a cop. Tell me you don't have Ivy with you . . .'

'I didn't kidnap anyone. Géricault trapped us, brought us

to Wales to . . . It doesn't matter why she brought us here – fact is, she did and Seren tried to kill her and now Seren's dead.' I looked across at Nnedi who was staring straight ahead, eyes closed, tears streaming. 'It was self-defence.'

'Jesus, Mary and Joseph,' he said on a long-ass sigh. 'So are you under arrest then or what?'

'No. She's in as much shit as I am. Well, maybe slightly less. And now we're just sitting in a car park.'

'What for?'

'What for? We're waiting for the ice-cream parlour to open, what do you mean *what for*? We haven't got a fucking clue what to do, Billy!'

'Okay, listen, there's been a bit of a development here so whatever happens you can't go to the airport now. And you can't go back to San Diego either. Hang on, I'll send you a link.'

A *ping!* came through on my phone a few moments later – a WhatsApp message containing a web link to a CNN Breaking News story.

'Oh Jeeeee-zus,' I groaned, reading the headline:

BREAKING NEWS: BODY IN VERMONT GRAVE IS NOT SWEETPEA. SERIAL KILLER STILL AT LARGE

'Oh god,' said Nnedi, aka the woman who did everything in her power to have it exhumed in the first place.

The vomit finally rose its way up my throat and I heaved it straight outside the driver's door onto the car park.

'See what I mean?' said Billy. 'They've dug the damn grave.'

'I should have buried you next to Seren,' I spat at my passenger.

133

Billy continued. 'It's only a matter of time before somebody sees you on the US news and identifies you as Ophelia. Raf's family, colleagues. Multiple reports, it says. This changes the game. You can't go back.'

'But I don't look exactly the same as I did.'

'You don't look different *enough*, not for your family or your work colleagues not to recognise you; the people who've seen you up close recently. The people you've pissed off. And they must be legion.'

'What do I do then? I can't stay in this car park for the rest of my life.'

'Where's Seren's body?'

'In a field about a mile away from here.'

'How much cash you got?'

'A grand and a bit.'

'That'll tide you over for the time being.' There was silence on the line.

'BILLY!'

'I'm thinking, I'm thinking. Did you drug me? I haven't been able to get a decent train of thought going since I woke up.'

'A bit—'

'Rhiannon!'

'Yeah yeah, needs must, now what do I do?'

Big sigh. 'The only place I can think of right now . . . it's a long shot . . .'

'I'll take a long shot, a short shot, I'll take any shot you've got.'

'Okay, hang on . . .' In a minute or two another WhatsApp note pinged through. It was a map. 'Head for the Fishguard ferry port. There's a seven o'clock ferry. And avoid the M4 – too many cameras.'

'Why am I heading to Fishguard?'

'You're not – you're heading to Ireland.'

'*Ireland?*'

'Yes. Head back the way you came and go to the port. It's all A roads from where you are and there won't be much traffic around this time of the morning so it shouldn't take you more than three hours, according to Google.'

The rain pelted on the car roof. '*IRELAND?* That's ridiculous.'

'You can't come back here, can you, and you can't go to the airport. You're gonna have to go somewhere neutral and just lie low for a while. And I know somewhere you'll be safe.'

'How am I going to get past port authorities? What if someone IDs me? Will they search the car? What if—'

'You're just gonna have to risk it, aren't you? I'll text you the address of where you're heading . . .'

Silence gathered around us once again. The obvious question floated into the stale car air and Nnedi grabbed it. 'What do *I* do?'

I snorted. 'Not my fucking problem.'

'I have cash. Can your boyfriend get *me* a ferry ticket?'

'He's not my boyfriend – he's my husband's friend. And no, you can't come. Why the hell would you even want to?'

'I don't know what else to do.'

Our breaths fogged up the windscreen while I waited for the next message from Billy. 'Nope, not happening.'

She stared at me – I stared back. And from nowhere, I laughed. *Really* laughed. 'I've never heard anything so absurd in my already-absurd life.'

'How are you going to get to the ferry port without my car then?'

'I'll steal it. Chuck you out here.'

She shook her head. 'You know I'll fight back. And you know I'll best you. And if I don't—'

'We'll be back where we were.'

'I'll drive. I won't be in your way. I am in this too deeply to just go home. I need some time.'

'I don't owe you a thing.'

'I'm very aware of that. But I will—'

'You'll what? You'll bring my sister back from the dead? Call me in San Diego and tell me my daughter *doesn't* have cancer?'

'I will be in your debt. You know what will happen to me in jail. They'll tear me to shreds.'

'They'll put you in with the nonces, you'll be protected from the general pop.'

'I *can't* go to prison, Rhiannon.'

Pffft, I huffed, just as a *ping!* sounded. I couldn't decipher the word Billy had sent me to save my life. 'What the fuck does that say?'

'Ah shit, I spelt it wrong. It should be A.o.i.b.h.n.e.a.s,' said Billy. 'It's a village on the west coast. I've got family over there. You'll be safe.'

'I still don't know what it says.'

'It's pronounced Eve-ness. It's on the Corca Dhuibhne. You know it as the Dingle Peninsula.'

'Never heard of it.'

'Aoibhneas is a little village where I grew up. I haven't been back there for a while but it'll be safe. I'll wait until the coast is clear and come to you in the next couple of days and bring over the rest of your stuff. Go to the pub and ask for Fintan. I'll tell him to expect you.'

'This is *miles*, and a whole SEA away. I don't have any spare clothes—'

'My bag's in the back,' mewed Nnedi. 'You can borrow some of mine.'

'Your clothes won't fit my fat ass,' I snipped, before realising her offer was the only possibility of me getting out of my soaked clothes and possible early pneumonia anytime soon. 'All right.'

'If you have to stop on the way, there's a service station, about forty-five minutes from your current location,' said Billy. 'You can get what you need there, maybe a change of clothes, but don't linger. I'll book you a ferry ticket.'

'There's no way they're gonna let me into Ireland. They'll take one look at my passport, and it'll be Goodnight, Rhiannon.'

'You're out of options,' said Billy. 'Try and get to Aoibhneas and lie low as soon as you can until I can get to you. By then I should have come up with a plan.'

'Christ,' I muttered, seeing Nnedi's appealing face out of the corner of my eye. 'Quick Draw McGraw needs a ferry ticket as well.' I glared at her. 'If we get aboard that ferry without being collared, it'll be a fucking miracle.'

'You're gonna take a *detective* with you as you run from the police?'

'Looks like it. Well you know me, Billy – I like to make things as difficult for myself as possible.'

After a short lecture about the pros and cons of doing a road trip with a serving police officer, he left me with a warning: 'Keep your head down, Rhiannon. And be dog wide of that one. I don't care how much trouble she's in, she'll have something up her sleeve, cops always do.'

*

We needed to look respectable for the port authorities but at that point we were serving some seriously muddy and bloody lewks which was not going to cut any ice. So after a lightning-quick piss-and-wet-wipe session at the services, we chased the rising sun all the way to the ferry port and arrived just before 7 a.m. Snaking queues of coaches and hatchbacks lined the route all the way towards the prize – the hulking-great Stena Line ship that would, hopefully, take us to sanctuary.

Not that I bore much hope. After all, this was Passport Time again. And things almost went tits up and took on water at Heathrow. Now they could wholly capsize.

As the car crept further along the queue, it dawned on me again: my sister was dead. The girl who had once meant so much to me I'd begged her on bended knee not to move to the States. I'd got used to not seeing her; not hearing from her and her hating me – I'd sort of acclimatised to it – but I kept seeing her in my mind. Kept seeing her kids, waiting for her to come home. Waiting for her to ring them. I couldn't think about it too much – it made me feel weak, and I needed strength right now, so I parked them in that shadow of my mind where Rafael was – it was getting crowded back there.

Nnedi was in the driving seat, I was in the passenger seat and we both wore face masks.

'They're so gonna recognise me,' I sang as the car rolled ever closer to the inspection booths.

'They won't,' she snapped, flicking the wipers on to a higher speed to deal with the increasing drizzle. 'Keep your mask on; pretend you're asleep.'

'They're going to ask to see my passport, put it through the machine, it'll ping, red lights a-gogo and that'll be that – sack trucks and hockey masks the whole way down.'

'Stay calm,' she said, eyes fixed on the wet road ahead.

If it hadn't been happening to me, I'd have scoffed at how farfetched life had become in the last twelve hours. Here I was, in the most ironic of ironies, not only sitting alongside my deadliest enemy on a road trip to butt-fuck Ireland but wearing her clothes as well. Nnedi and I didn't like each other, in fact she despised me and made no secret of it, but at that moment in time, as we awaited our doom in that purgatory-esque line of cars, we had a mutual enemy neither of us wanted to face: the British police. And with the old adage of the enemy of my enemy being my friend, we clung on to the smallest shred of hope that there *may* be a way out of this.

And Aoibhneas was that shred.

Every time I lifted my hand to move my hair back from my face or fiddle with the sun visor, Nnedi would flinch, prepared for me to strike. Sometimes I'd do it just to test her and she'd always comply. That made me chuckle.

'Nothing about this is funny,' she muttered.

'It is a bit funny. You and me, like this.'

She could barely get the words out. 'I killed your sister.' But the words didn't land on me the way they did on her. 'You don't feel it?' she said. 'You don't feel sad about it? At all?'

'I don't feel things the way you do. The way *normal* people do.'

'Ain't that the truth.' She sighed, her breath clouding up her window. She wiped the fog away with her cuff. 'Besides, you had no choice. She was going to kill you ... I don't know why I don't feel it. I must have loved her once. I used to like playing Sylvanians with her when we were kids. And I begged her not to go to the States. And she was the first person I told when I found out I was having a girl. Once upon a time.'

'I suppose that proves you have *some* humanity.'

'I didn't kill *you*, did I?'

She turned to me. 'Why didn't you?'

I made her wait as I breathed the question in and out. 'Cos even though you're the itchiest haemorrhoid I've ever had up my arse, and even though you've ruined my life *and* killed my sister, you did it for the right reasons. And you *do* feel bad.'

Nnedi's eyes filled with water, but she seemed determined not to give vent to her sobs.

'Plus, as I learned with Craig, sometimes it's more fun to watch them suffer instead.'

The link to the tickets pinged through on my phone for the third time. *I got them the first time Billy. Thank you*, I sent back.

Just making sure, he texted. *Speak soon.*

I chucked my phone into Nnedi's lap.

'Thanks,' she said. 'For the ticket.'

'Don't count your hens just yet – I'm fully expecting this to go Pete Tong at any given.'

My lock screen flashed up – me and Raf at our wedding.

'Is that your husband?' Nnedi asked.

'Yes.'

'What's his name?'

'Rafael. With an F.'

'He's Latino?'

'Mexican.'

She was still looking at the picture. 'So you *did* go to Mexico.'

'Can you stop gawping at him please? Leave me one family member intact, why don't you?'

'I wasn't looking at him – I was looking at *you*. You look happy.'

'I *was*.'

'He's changed you.'

'No. I changed myself. There's always been more to me than killing people. Just took me a while to realise it, that's all.' I started tapping my collarbone – I'd seen a post on TikTok of this woman who talked about how much that helped her when she was anxious. I couldn't remember the exact spot she tapped on so I just went all around my neck, tapping. Every rotation of the wheels seemed to make my heart thump faster.

'You said he was in hospital?' Nnedi continued.

'He was shot. Some woman went postal at his work. He'll be okay. I think.'

'I've never shot anyone before last night,' Nnedi said. 'Never even pulled the trigger in a live situation.'

'Well, two more kills and *you're* a serial murderer just like me.'

'I am nothing like you. I'm a detective. And a bloody good one at that.'

'"Bloody good detectives" don't need to steal chloroform and handguns from police evidence lockers and kidnap their suspects.'

'They weren't going to catch you any other way.' She tapped the steering wheel in frustration, checking the queue behind. 'Look at it. It's miles long.'

After an age queuing behind a blue-and-white holiday coach that they were going through with fine-toothed combs, we came upon the checkpoint booths. As much as I was expecting it to be the finish line, I was praying to any god who was up at this time to hear me and spare us for just a bit longer.

My heart in my mouth, Nnedi buzzed down her window and presented the woman in the yellow hi-vis with my phone and both our passports. I stopped tapping my collarbone as she scanned the two QR codes, trying to look like just another tourist with nothing to worry about but a three-hour journey and the chance of there being any bacon left at the breakfast buffet. She took a good long look at Nnedi before glancing in at me, then turned to speak to a colleague who'd come into her booth.

I don't think either of us was taking breaths at this point.

The woman looked at Nnedi's passport and they exchanged pleasantries about the weather in Ireland and how stormy it had been recently. Nnedi said we were on holiday. The woman in the hi-vis did not look at my passport once.

'Pull in over there please, madam,' said Yellow Coat, pointing to a concrete hardstanding past the booths.

'Oh Christ,' I muttered as the car got going again.

'Could be nothing,' said Nnedi breathlessly. 'Just a spot check.'

'There's a dog,' I said as we came to a halt; a bouncy black labrador playing fetch with a couple of guys also in yellow hi-vis.

'He's heading for that coach, not us.'

Sure enough the dog and the men were ordered over to a touring coach in an opposite pull-in where he proceeded to sniff along the base of its locker.

Meanwhile, another yellow jacket with a large mirror on a stick came out of a Portacabin and swept it underneath the car, all the way around.

'What if she opens the boot?' I said through clenched teeth. 'The shovels are in there. And our muddy clothes.'

'She's not looking for human remains – she's looking for drugs or bombs,' Nnedi hissed back.

'Have we got any drugs or bombs?'

'I don't know.' She gulped.

People from other cars were getting out and having passports double-checked and body searches but amazingly, the mirror on a stick around the car was all we got.

'The bonnet's dented,' I remarked.

'It's not too bad.'

'Yeah but they might ask if we've been in an accident and why it's not fixed.'

'They won't.'

'It's gonna be us next.'

'It's not, stop panicking.'

'I know it is. We're toast, I'm telling you. They're going to ask us to step out. And it's all your fault.'

After an agonising wait where we watched every other car or van get pulled to one side and driver after driver getting out, a cheery ginger dude in green stuck his head through Nnedi's window and said: 'That'll be all, thank you, ma'am. Safe trip to you both. Hope the water's kind to yous today.'

'Much obliged,' Nnedi returned serenely as the Audi kangarooed away from the hardstanding to re-join the line of traffic headed up the gangplank.

I breathed out for the first time since we'd stopped. 'They didn't ask us to get out. They didn't check my passport.'

'They checked mine,' she replied.

'But they didn't check mine!' I said again because she wasn't grasping the full awesomeness of our situation. 'Don't you get it?'

'Yes I get it, *believe* me I get it.'

I shit you not, as we rolled all the way up the ramp and into Vehicle Deck 5, I kept expecting some hi-vis to come running up to the car or a police car to come speeding up in front of us, brakes a-screechin'. I stared through the rain-spattered windows and awaited whatever fate was definitely going to march up the gangplank towards us. But nobody came.

No. Body. Came.

We were guided into a parking space by a hi-vis official who then just walked away and guided another car in.

'I fucking love Ireland already,' I enthused.

No last minute 'Wait, stop there!' protests. No more security checks. No police. No sirens. We were on our own, on our way to sanctuary and even though it was cold and raining and the clouds covered every single morsel of sky, there was hope on the horizon. I could practically smell it.

Once we'd parked we followed all the other passengers up the snaking staircase and into the main passenger area on Deck 9, trying to keep as low a profile as the busy ship would allow. Here the ship unfolded into a series of open-plan seating areas, broken up by restaurants, bars, children's entertainment, cabins and suites. There was a large duty-free area and as we wandered around, the displays of overpriced bottles of vodka and perfume clinked and rattled on the shuddering engines. Even though it was the first crossing of the day, the place was a nightmare of large school trips, tired argumentative families, and old farts on coach trips cluttering the food lines and hogging the best chairs. When the ship was at sea, we found a bureau de change where we could change pounds for euros and headed into the restaurant. My anxiety having dissipated,

I got a full Irish brekkers – Nnedi obtained a cup of water and a delicious shade of green about her cheeks.

'I don't know how you can eat,' she said, sneering at my steaming plate.

'Like this,' I said, opening my mouth as wide as I could and folding in an entire hash brown loaded with bacon, egg, beans, sausage and chip.

She puffed out her cheeks.

'Are you gonna blow?'

'Trying not to,' she said with a tight mouth.

'There's a cinema on board showing the *Downton Abbey* movie. Fancy it?' She shook her head. 'No, me either. I never got into that when it was on TV. I liked the ep where the lord puked blood all over the dining table. Have you seen that one? Classic.'

She shook her head again, her cheeks slightly sucked in, staring out the window at the milky horizon. 'Have you got any Kwells?'

'No, funnily enough, I didn't factor seasickness into today's agenda. Might be a pharmacy on here somewhere.'

'There isn't,' she spat. 'There's a casino but no damn pharmacy.'

As though to rub sea salt into the wound, the ship lurched suddenly to one side on the strong winds.

'Deck 11's open if you need to hurl,' I said, scoffing down a forkful of bacon and egg and swilling it down with concentrated OJ that tasted like liquid hospital. I didn't see her for dust.

I did a full sweep of the duty free, ate half a Toblerone and read a discarded *Hello!* magazine from cover to cover and she still hadn't come back. Paranoia slowly settled on my shoulders like dandruff. What if she'd found a guard and spilled the beans as well as the contents of her stomach? Billy told me not to trust her and I didn't. But maybe she'd taken it upon herself to fog up the clear we were in?

I went on up to Deck 11.

But sure enough, Nnedi stood beside the railing, holding on for dear life against sprays of water and a howling wind. Her fur-hood was pulled up, so just her little head was poking out from within.

'You look like a clit,' I yelled.

'What?' she yelled back over the roaring wind and rain.

'Nothing. You been puking all this time?'

Her mouth was pursed shut and her eyes closed.

'I never get seasick. Lucky really. We've got two more hours of this.'

Bloody hell, her mouth said.

Two men stood in the sheltered smoking area, an older one and a twentysomething vaping, with about fifty zits too many to be wearing aviators. The older guy had Timberland boots on. If I didn't know better, from the back, I'd have said it was Dad and Craig. My stomach lurched.

Nnedi was still deep breathing like she was training to scuba. 'I just don't understand how you can just . . . wolf down a fry-up and talk about movies you want to see and . . .' She shouldn't have mentioned the fry-up. She chundered over the railing again, mostly bile. 'Maybe it hasn't hit you yet.'

'It generally doesn't hit me at all,' I said but I don't think she heard me over the battering wind.

'Go back downstairs,' she yelled when she resurfaced from another vom-a-thon. 'I won't be long. There can't be much more.'

'No, I'll wait.'

'Why?'

I answered with a shrug but she got it.

'You honestly think I'd hand us in *now*?'

I gripped the railing as the ferry climbed over another sea swell. 'I wouldn't put anything past you.'

'I don't owe the police anything.'

'Why? Cos they demoted you?'

She stared out into the rough, foamy-grey yonder and closed her eyes. 'It would be an almighty coup for them, if I took you in. All would be forgiven. They'd quash the thefts, the kidnap, everything. Even Seren's death. If I found an active serial killer, I'd be exonerated ten times over.'

'So? Why wouldn't you?'

'Because they'd take all the credit. And because I don't trust them.'

'Meaning?'

She spat over the side and breathed away another urge to purge. The two men in the smoking area had gone inside so she led me over there where it was more sheltered and we didn't have to yell.

'When I was working on the Sweetpea case, before you left the UK, I was digging into Tommy's files in order to link up some clues to find my dad. You know when I said there were rumours that Lyle Devaney had procured children for gentlemen's clubs in London?'

'My dad was nothing to do with all that.'

'No, I know he wasn't. But two Met police officers *were*. Commissioners no less. This was back in the Nineties but they were rampant. Between them they'd raped between thirty and forty young girls.'

'Serving *police*?'

'The highest ranks,' she said, nodding. 'Commissioner and deputy. One night, officers performed a midnight raid on one of these clubs in Mayfair and found four girls who'd been taken from care homes in Streatham and Tooting. And these two officials were arrested in the swoop. *Arrested* but never charged. The file was all but deleted.'

Another mighty urge came over her as the ship lurched again, but she managed to steady herself and deep-breathe it away.

'I found the reports in a long-forgotten strong box in the bowels of the evidence locker,' she continued, with a series of long, slow breaths. 'At the time, the squad who'd entered the club and made the arrests was ordered to hand over their evidence. Photos. Notebooks. Any and all statements. And the duty sergeant that night was told to release them both.'

She took a neatly folded tissue from her coat sleeve to delicately wipe her mouth.

'They were warned not to speak about it again under the Official Secrets Act. In short, they buried it. And these two commissioners carried on working until they retired on full pensions. Not a blemish to their records.'

'Ugh.'

'I forwent everything for my career in the police force – it was my one true love. I turned away from relationships, veered away from having children, knowing it would be harder to return. All to climb the greasy pole as high as I could. To prove something.'

'To who?'

'Everyone who would doubt a Black woman could rise above it all. But I did – and I kept climbing, no matter how many names I was called, or the passive aggressive interactions, or the myriad times I heard myself being spoken about while sitting in toilet cubicles . . .'

I recalled being at the *Gazette* and going through the exact same thing. But I guessed Nnedi had it far worse than I ever did.

'When I went to my chief about the redacted file and the two commissioners, I was told to forget it. And then I was demoted to cold cases. Told to take a break from active duty so I could ride the storm of the Sweetpea cock-up but keep my job, *and* my pension. I was so grateful to have been allowed to keep my precious job. And why? So high-ranking officials could keep their dirty secrets intact.' She shook her head, as though trying to shake the memory out of both ears. 'They wouldn't even put extra resources into finding my dad's body. They told me to "take extended leave". "You deserve it, Nnedi. You've worked so hard, Nnedi." Fucking bastards.'

It was weird hearing her swear. Like hearing Princess Anne swear.

'So you took your leave and decided to come after me on your own instead?'

'What would *you* have done?'

'The same, probably. But with a pinch more bloodshed. What happened to the girls from the care homes?'

She glanced at me. 'A few of them brought cases against the Met years later. A few started the judicial process but then stopped. One of them went over Tower Bridge. A couple more went off the radar. They'll never have justice for what those men did to them. Few ever do.'

'And the commissioners? Where are they now?'

Her smile was more forced this time. 'Died in their retirement years – one on the eighteenth hole; the other on his sun lounger in Puerto Banús. Natural causes – ale and good living.'

'Shoulda called me,' I said with a smile.

She didn't smile back. But she swung her leather backpack around to the front and unzipped the front pocket, pulling out a little green tin of mints. She opened the tin and offered me one. I took it.

'I went 834 days in the States without killing a single soul.'

'What happened on Day 834?'

'Raf's sister called me. She'd been raped by her estranged husband.'

She nodded, looking back to the sea like she were asking it a question. 'I don't know who I am outside of my job.'

'They might let you back.'

She snorted but added nothing else.

'What about the book you wrote? And all your TV interviews? Last I checked you were the self-designated Sweetpea Murders correspondent on any podcast that would have you.'

'The publisher didn't want another book. TV producers kept telling me I was just banging the same drum all the time with no new leads. I don't really care about either to be honest.'

'Liar. You wanted fame as much as I do – I could see it in your eyes.'

'It was fun, for a while. But it didn't mean anything. The only thing that's driven me for the past twenty-odd years is work and finding Dad. Now – I don't have either. I don't know why I'm running, to tell you the truth. You have something to run for. I don't. I don't have a family anymore. Even my flat's rented. Why am I doing this?' I stared at the gaps on her hand where her fingers should be – the fingers Dad took off. She saw me looking. 'What?'

'I think he's under the barn.'

Her eyes went wide. 'What?'

'Your dad. It triggered a memory when I saw the blue rope in his briefcase. I would have said something but Seren came up with that holiday home bullshit – just buying time, I guess.'

'You *saw* it?'

'No, but I remember the cement mixer going outside the barn. And Dad telling me not to go inside cos he'd just laid fresh concrete. I peeked my head around and he told me off. But I saw he'd roped off one end. It would have been roughly around the time your dad went missing.'

She waited. A single tear fell onto her cheek. 'Why should I believe you?'

'Because he shouldn't have tortured you, cut your fingers off. And he probably shouldn't have killed your dad. And this is me trying to make amends for it.' It felt like a back-rubby moment but I didn't imagine it would be welcomed so I stared at her instead.

Nnedi wiped the tear away. 'After everything you've done, all the pain you've caused. And then you say something like this.' She had pulled out a pair of cashmere grey mittens and her fingerless hand was now covered, whether through cold or shame I didn't know. She just looked at me, expecting more. So I gave it to her.

'I didn't realise how weird it was for a long time – that my dad was okay with me seeing him beat those men to death. Seeing him bleed one out over a trough. Teaching me how important it was to cut a body into sections and wrap each part so the smell didn't escape. And he kept doing it because I didn't show any fear or disgust. But I know it's wrong.'

Two chatty women in fake fur and Uggs came outside and attempted to enter the smoking area but the death glares we threw them made them both stand outside the shelter for their cigarettes. They couldn't get them lit anyway and quickly turned back inside.

'If he was a good dad, he'd have shielded me from that, wouldn't he? He would have looked after me better. He wouldn't have laughed whenever Craig made some comment about my weight or my inability to get a promotion. God, why was I so hung up on Craig? I don't get it now. It's weird thinking the lengths I went through to show him how mad I was with him for cheating. I couldn't give a shit now. It's not like he was much of a catch anyway. I've had bank statements cum through my slot slower than him.'

Nnedi stifled a laugh. 'What you said about Tommy though, you're right. He should have been your shield. It's not normal how he brought you up. Showing you his horrors. Making you like him.'

'Maybe he was brain damaged too, from boxing. He almost died in the ring once, before I was born. Bleed on the brain. Mum said it made him lose his temper much more easily.'

'That's possible.'

'I got the feeling he *liked* me seeing what he could do. Like he was proud he could destroy people. Like he wished he could destroy Antony Blackstone at Priory Gardens. He used to tell me what he'd have done to him if he'd got to him first. But he didn't. So he took it out on everyone else instead. "Be a warrior in a garden, Rhiannon, not a gardener in a war."'

Nnedi bit her lip. '*My* dad wouldn't even let me watch horror films.'

They hadn't found Seren's body by the time we docked at Rosslare just after 11 a.m. but regardless we still shot off that ferry like we'd robbed a bank. Nnedi drove the first leg, which was all motorway – a predicted four and a half hours of it. Grey roads, mist and rain – nothing of actual Ireland to see. And a Qashqai undertook us on the hard shoulder. I leant across intending to blow the horn at him but Nnedi balled me out.

'DO YOU WANT TO GET US BOTH KILLED?'

'No. I'm not quite at that stage yet,' I muttered.

It didn't even feel like we were in a different country for a while, then two hours in, we switched over so I could drive and hit the quieter roads. The clouds cleared and the sun peeked out and pretty soon we were encompassed by fields and skies so blue my eyes stung. My left wrist throbbed without my brace and my right palm stung from where my cut had got mud in it – I hadn't noticed when all the adrenaline had been pumping through me – and I was so tired. Nnedi was the most boring travel companion on earth which only compounded it. At least Billy chatted or sang or occasionally made semi-intelligent observation – Nnedi was dead silent and as a result, the journey time dragged like a stone coffin behind a donkey cart. She did three notable things during those two hours – cleared her throat, reached into her bag for a mint and changed the radio station from 'Hollaback Girl' to Handel's Passacaglia.

I thought about one of the last road trips Seren and I had taken before she'd gone to the States. She was going into town to do some shopping and I tagged along with her even though she didn't want me to . . .

Can we get hot chocolates and
eclairs in The Little Green Café
and play on the fruit machine,
like we used to?

> No. I've got too much shopping
> to get.

We can stop for a drink at least.
Bit of quality time before you leave.

> I had a coffee before we
> left home.

I'll pay.

> It's not about the money.

What is it about then?

> Never mind.

Say it. I'm not going to see you again after
today so you might as well.

> All right. I don't want to spend
> 'quality time' with you. Because our
> relationship is not of any quality.

You're my sister.

> I'm only taking you into town cos
> Dad told me to. You have made my
> life a misery the last few years – all
> our lives in fact. Your tantrums
> at school, the lying, the stealing,
> setting fire to my clothes, cutting
> my hair when I was asleep.

Julia cut my hair.

> Stabbing me with the scissors.

Julia stabbed me with her
fountain pen.

Mum was right – you did bring her
cancer on. I can't even look at you . . .

I tantrum because people don't listen to
me. I lie to make people like me. I steal
to make people notice me. The therapist
said that's why I do it. She said you
needed to support me more. My trauma
got worse because of you.

I don't give a shit why you do it.
I just don't want to be around
it anymore. I can't stand you,
Rhiannon. Nobody can.

I set fire to your clothes because you
didn't come to Sports Day.

What?

You said you'd come with Dad. I was in
the two hundred metres. It was my only
race. You knew I wanted you all there.
But you big fat weren't. None of you ever
turn up for me. I'm glad Mum's dead.
*And I **fucking wish you were too** . . .*

BEEEEEEEEEEEEEEEEEEEEEP!!!!

The steering wheel spun away from the car I was heading
towards as Nnedi yanked it her way and the car righted itself.
'What the hell are you doing?' she shrieked.
'Shit!' Between us we brought the car to a stop on one side
of the road and she pulled up the handbrake. 'You fell asleep!'
'I didn't, did I?'
'Yes!'

'Fuck.'

Once we'd both breathed in and out all the air in the car, she said, 'It's all right. No harm done. I did that on the way to the ferry when *you* were asleep.'

'I was thinking about Seren.'

'Were you?' she said, still breathless.

'I told her I wished she was dead once.' I looked across at her. 'You might have pulled the trigger but I loaded the gun.'

'We need to pull in somewhere and get some decent rest. I'd like to get to this Aoibhneas place in one piece.'

'We can't, can we? "Keep your head down," Billy said. If we go to a hotel, that's not keeping my head down and it's too late to book an Airbnb.'

'We'll sleep in the car then. Even if it's only for an hour or two. We're both exhausted.'

'I won't be able to lose myself,' I said.

'Well, you did just then and we were travelling at fifty miles an hour so I'm sure you can manage it.'

'You can sleep at such close quarters to a monster?' I said with more than my fair share of eyebrow.

'Right now, I could sleep on a clothesline.'

She'd already hit up Google and found us a spot in a fishing village called Ardmore. There was a beach front and a little café, and it was pissing rain so very few people were milling about, bar a few determined dog walkers with three excitable retrievers.

'Can we get hot chocolates?' I asked her.

'If we must,' she said.

*

When I woke up, the sky was dark and the damp street was silent. The lights were still on in the café overlooking the beach and Nnedi snored softly in the front seat. I sank the cold dregs of my takeaway hot chocolate and tried Rafael's number.

It has not been possible to connect your call.

'The fuck?'

I tried it again. Same message.

It has not been possible to connect your call.

I texted him – *Mi Tortuga, where are you? Please call me xxx*

Nothing. I tried Billy instead. It rang, briefly, and then cut out. I texted.

Again, nothing.

'Fuck's sake.' I stepped outside the car and tried both of them again. *Not been possible . . . *long beep* . . . not been possible . . . *long beep* . . . not been possible . . .* and then *the number you have dialled has not been recognised.*

'FUUUUUUUCKKK!' I screamed into the howling wind.

'What is it? What's the matter?' said a bleary-eyed Nnedi, stepping out of the passenger side with some difficulty.

'They're not answering. Neither of them is answering me, not Raf *or* Billy. It's not even connecting. Why won't they answer me? What's going on?'

'Calm down,' she said. 'What was the last thing Billy said to you?'

'I don't know, I can't remember.'

'Yes you can.'

'Something about lying low in Aoibhneas until he can come up with a new plan. Keeping my head down and not trusting you.'

'And Rafael?'

'He told me he loved me . . . and some *Last of the Mohicans* shit about how he'd find a way for us to be together . . . and I had to trust him.'

'There you go then.'

'But I trusted Dad, didn't I? And he let me down. And Seren and Craig and AJ and Marnie and Tenoch and—'

'But none of them are Rafael, are they?'

'No.'

'So you need to believe in him now. And forget everyone else.'

She stared at me long and hard before I nodded and she let go of my arms. She looked down at my bandaged hand. 'We should redress that, before it gets infected. I've got a first-aid kit in the boot. Get inside.'

Raf knew I hated uncertainty, so did Billy, and while I wasn't comfortable with the silence from both of them, Nnedi was right, as always: I needed to believe in something or else this whole exercise was pointless.

We stopped once at a Circle K to redress my hand and get petrol and switched over in Cloonbannin so Nnedi could drive the rest of the way. As the roads got narrower and the fields wider and the houses and shops fewer, we passed a number of signs for small tourist attractions – a prehistoric ring fort, beehive huts and somewhere called 'Pat the Pig', which was apparently a smallholding where you could help them pull vegetables and pat a pig. It made me think of Dicky. I missed him. I wondered if Ivy had hold of him in her little chub fist. Or if she'd thrown him in some bottomless toy box, never to be seen again. Why the fuck did I give him to her? I needed him. I reached into my pocket and found the little woollen gatita instead, holding that to my nose like I was trying to inhale the warmth of Mexico.

'You've been promoted,' I whispered, and tucked it inside my bra.

The further into Aoibhneas territory we drove, the more we were swallowed up by Ireland like an enormous green hug. The shops and buildings became even fewer, and the lumber yards, farms and fields of grazing sheep took over. Some of the houses had little Virgin Mary shrine boxes on their outer walls or statues in their gardens. This was a deeply devout place. Pious to the max.

I'm amazed I didn't burst into flames.

Daily Mail

With news that Brit serial killer Rhiannon Lewis is still at large, what are the Met police doing to capture her?

IN VERMONT, USA, this week an autopsy report on an exhumed corpse confirmed the body was *not* that of absconded British serial killer Rhiannon Lewis.

It had originally been thought Lewis's sister Seren Gibson had shot her dead when she broke into her four-acre estate in the upmarket Lawford Heights area, two years ago. Now, it appears, the woman Gibson identified was *not* Rhiannon but a doppelgänger – one of an army of so-called Bad Seeds – fans of the serial killer who have a growing presence on social media.

This means one troubling certainty: the murderess is *not* dead. So where is she? And what are the police doing to track her down? Can we sleep easy in our beds ever again?

In a statement last night, investigating officer Detective Sergeant Jai Amarkeeri, from the Met's Homicide and Major Crime Command, said Lewis was "wanted on an international arrest warrant. We have received information from a number of sources, including the National Crime Agency, and are certain she won't slip through the net for long. Our thoughts are, as ever, with her victims' families at this time."

Lewis was sentenced to life without parole in absentia in July 2019 after being convicted of murder in the first degree. She has been on the run ever since. Investigating officers have come under increasing pressure to locate her with commentators claiming "they don't want to find her because she only poses a threat to bad people."

Reports emerged today claiming that detectives failed to act on information that Lewis fled to the USA not long after leaving the UK. Claudia Silverton, adoptive mother of Lewis's little girl Ivy, now two, informed Met police officers at least six months ago that she knew Rhiannon was still alive as she had been in touch with her sister, Seren Gibson, with whom she has stayed in touch for Ivy's sake. Both Gibson and Silverton were unavailable for comment when this went to print.

The family of Dean Bishopston, the taxi driver murdered by Lewis in Birmingham in May 2018, would beg to differ. His wife Sarah said she was "extremely concerned" at the news Lewis is still on the run. "Dean never did anything wrong. It could be your husband next; your son, your brother. She's a very dangerous woman and she needs to be stopped. If you're one of these Bad Seeds who are saying you'd never grass on her, I dare you to look at the faces of my three fatherless little boys and say that."

*

While Nnedi drove, complaining about her bad back which 'isn't suited to sleeping in cars', I checked the news. Still nothing about Seren. I felt both happy and sad – on the one hand, there were no stories linking us to her death so we could carry on regardless, but on the other, she was still out there. Cold. Under a pile of leaves with her eyes half-open. I could see her in my mind's eye, all small and straggly like a just-hatched chick.

If that thought pinched at me, what the hell was it doing to her kids? At least I knew where she was. They had nothing.

Then I ventured into Bad Seeds territory to see if what Sarah Bishopston was saying about them protecting me was right, and lo and behold, it was. There were whole threads about it – I had my very own hashtag – #KeepHerBuried – and the vast majority of the messages were along the same lines: *Good for her. Keep going, Rhiannon. We love you.*

There were thousands of Sweetpea fans worldwide; maybe millions. Some host websites, others Facebook pages, but mainly it's all TikToks. Some of the Seeds have even formed tribes who go out and walk the streets at night – not to kill though, to *protect*.

A few American states have group members (mostly along the East Coast and Chicago) and while some of the sites only have about twelve subscribers (e.g., Secret Gardeners of Sydney and Die Wilden Blumen in Munich), some count over 20,000 'members' (e.g., Bud Union in London).

Most of the groups are UK-based. There's a Manchester gang called Root Cause, who are a little more hardcore and actually hunt predators down, posting videos of their confrontations and working with the police to get them jailed. There are similar crews in Cardiff (Di-Wreiddyn), Glasgow (Flowers of Scotland) and Leeds (The Bud Nippers). In Europe,

Les Fleurs Sauvages are the French contingent who go one step further and beat the living shit out of their quarries, as do the Wasps (Women Against Sexual Predators) of Montpelier.

The Feirdhris crew in Dublin stalk streets and trains at night, around forty people of all ages and genders, with the sole purpose of keeping women safe from opportunistic rapists. The Stems of Londonderry are their northern counterpart. They look after those who've been drinking or find themselves alone after dark, like the street angels or the Sally Army. Farther afield I've seen posts from collectives in Spain (Los Petalos), Morocco (Zuhur Qawia) and Greece (Syrriknoménes Violétes, The Shrinking Violets).

Time was I couldn't even make an impression on tracing paper – now, I had people protecting women and kids in my name. Whoda-thunk-it? From my semi-regular trawling of my fan sites, feeds, docus and vlogs, I've surmised there are three levels of Bad Seed. Starting with the lowest leaf on the stem:

The Fan
The Fan knows what I did, where I did it, has seen all the docus, read the biography and all the opinion pieces and endorses what I do whole-heartedly. They might wear a Bad Seeds badge or one of the T-shirts Sylvanian ears covered in blood if they're at a Halloween party. And if they recognised me on the street, they'd ask for a selfie and let me pass. Quite healthy.

Then we're into weirdo territory. At level two with:

The Freak
Now the freaky Bad Seeds are those who take their obsession a leap further. They'll have a standee of me in

their bedrooms. They'll pay full price for a Platinum ticket to MurderCon to meet one of the PICSOs or have a photo taken alongside some random from my *Gazette* days who's somehow forged a career just by their passing association with me. They will cosplay as me with a blood-spattered dildo in their hand or sleep with my action figure under their pillow. They'll turn up to my crime scenes – The Well House in Monk's Bay, Craig's old flat, the canal where Dickless Dan went fish-side. They'll send flowers to the *Gazette* offices, supposedly from me. They'll buy every book, every T-shirt and generally just adore me, but still from afar. A selfie wouldn't be enough for The Freak – they'd have to touch me or tear something off.

And by the fucking by, I don't see a penny of that MurderCon money. It all goes towards the PICSOs' hair extensions and veneers and Primarni.

But the far and away winner of Bad Seed Batshit Bingo is:

The Feral
These Bad Seeds comprise fans like Kacey Carmichael who take things to extremes because they have shit-all else to do. They'll have surgery to look like me, stalk family members, pretend to *be* me, steal from crime scenes, sell souvenirs on eBay, try and extract blood from the footwell of Elaine's Metro (it went up for auction at £70,000. Seventy grand for a Metro!). The Feral would even kill for me. I've read about date rapists stuck with knives, bus pervs attacked with acid, and vigilante justice meted out on known paedophiles, pimps and prowlers by running groups who 'take no prisoners' after dark.

These are my favourites, but don't tell them I said that, it only encourages them.

'You're looking at that Bad Seeds site again, aren't you?' said Nnedi, glancing at my screen. 'I saw you looking at it on the ferry.'

'So what if I am? God, you hate that I've got all these fans, buying my merch, doing my bidding, screaming *my* name, don't you?'

'I'd love to be loved by a lot of people, I admit it,' she replied, 'but *I'd* prefer to have done something more valiant to earn it, that's all.'

The Bad Seeds
Sweetpea fan forum
New thread: She's alllliiiiiiiive!

McNoodles1301 Date: Friday Oct 23

CRYSTELLE: OK you guys, deep breaths because this is a big one, and like we don't have this on the record as yet but it looks like the body in Vermont is NOT her. How INSANE is this?

FELIX: So the woman who allegedly broke into Seren's house was, like, a wannabe? Some chick who'd had a ton of surgery to *look* like Rhiannon and stalk Seren and her family but it like wasn't her at ALL!

CRYSTELLE: Yeah, she was like a doppelgänger but like a real batshit crazy one who'd had surgery and stuff. And she was stalking Seren for months before she showed up to break in and Seren shot her on her doorstep thinking it *was* Rhiannon. She actually identified her as Rhi and gave her a funeral and everything!

ALYSSA: Yeah which is crazy because, you'd recognise your own sister, right?

PAULA: I don't know, they hadn't seen each other for a few years, had they? Seren had moved away with her family and Rhiannon was left stuck in the UK with Creg [chorus of groans]. I don't think he's done any TV interviews this week, has he? Did anyone catch him on anything? [chorus of laughter]

CRYSTELLE: Paula, you always said it wasn't Rhiannon in that grave, didn't you? I think you were the only one of us who was just like from the start "That ain't her in that box, no frickin' way." Remember when we went and drank a toast to her at the graveside? Fun times.

PAULA: Yeah that was cool – I just didn't believe it when the story first broke and with what Rhiannon had said in the diaries about her sister and how they didn't get along, I thought maybe you know like it *could* have happened but there's been sightings everywhere, guys. It's tough to know what to believe.

FELIX: Yeah but there's always sightings. All over the world, in various places.

PAULA: Yeah but something about this just didn't ring true. And the fact she was buried so quickly and her family aren't even religious. Something stank.

ALYSSA: And now we have this body that's been found like half a mile from Honey Cottage, the place where Rhiannon and her sister grew up – they're saying it's Seren, guys. What do we think *that's* all about?

GEORGIA: Unrelated. I don't think that's Seren, or anything to do with Rhiannon. I think we're reaching. The woman they found in Wales was shot which ain't Rhiannon's MO at all. She never shot anyone before.

CRYSTELLE: As far as we know, right?

GEORGIA: Yeah, but it just doesn't seem like something she would do. And also, what would she be doing back in the UK? It's the last place she'd go. Kinda shittin' on her own doorstep.

FELIX: The description of the woman who was shot in Wales suggests she is older as well so it's definitely not our Sweetpea.

CRYSTELLE: But it doesn't prove Rhiannon *wasn't* there, does it?

ALYSSA: No but she's no reason to come back.

FELIX: Ivy's still here though.

GEORGIA: But she gave her away. You think she came back for *her*?

FELIX: I think it's possible. If she thought Ivy was in danger – especially as we now know of her stepfather's chequered past, shall we say . . .

CRYSTELLE: Yeah, him being a convict SO could be enough of a reason I guess. What would you guys do if you met her? Do you think about that kinda stuff? I know Felix has some choice ideas.

FELIX: Hell yeah. I always imagine writing to her in jail and one day she invites me in and I'm sitting across from her at the table and she leans in and grabs my balls and calls me a little bitch. That would be so hot.

GEORGIA: You are so sick and wrong, it's unbelievable! [giggles]

PAULA: Plus if they *did* catch her, she'd be in a Category A prison so she'd never be allowed that close to anyone on the outside.

CRYSTELLE: Ah bad luck bud!

FELIX: Don't mess with the fantasy. I know the reality. Having said that, I hope she *doesn't* get caught. I like imagining her out there, doing her thing.

CRYSTELLE: Oh totally. I would not say a word if I saw her in the street. God, imagine seeing her in the street, just walking by!

GEORGIA: That'd be INSANE. But yeah me too, I'm saying nothing until she's long gone. I might take a selfie though with her in the background.

ALYSSA: Me too!

PAULA: Me three! But think of all the promo, guys, if she *did* get caught! All the new pictures and standees we'd get of her in her boiler suit and handcuffs at the trial, being led into the van, waving to the cameras!

FELIX: Hell yeah, that'd be awesome!

CRYSTELLE: No guys, let's #keepsweetpeaburied, come on, be serious.

PAULA: #keepherburied.

ALYSSA: #keepherburied.

FELIX: #keepherburied.

GEORGIA: #keepherburied. Amen!

Part 2: Aoibhneas

We were two miles outside Aoibhneas filling up on petrol when I loaded the Wiki page and read up about the place, which didn't take long.

'There's fuck all to do here,' I said as Nnedi returned from paying. 'Like seriously, nothing.'

She threw me the keys and got in the passenger side. 'There must be something.'

'It says, "The settlement was established in the 1700s when a priest built a monastery there, later called Saint Aoibhneas for the joy he brought his flock when the plague ravished the Irish countryside." Thrillsville, so we're going to Plague Town.'

'*Settlement*,' Nnedi corrected. 'What else?'

'There's twenty-eight species of trees including Scots pine, Japanese larch, ugh god, there must be something remotely interesting about this place, other than some long-dead monk and a few trees.' I handed her my phone and she continued to read the page while I started the engine.

'Apparently there's a wind farm nearby. And some Mesolithic stones . . .'

'Ugh.'

'. . . and the ruins of the original monastery I think. No, just "a single wall remains".'

'Oh thank fuck, for a minute I thought there'd be nothing to do.'

'We're not here to "do", we're here to *hide*,' she reminded me. 'As long as we've four solid walls and no CCTV, we'll manage, I'm sure.'

'Well, it would be nice to have something to *do* while we hide. I might have to kill someone just to have something to pass the time.'

'Don't you dare.'

The sign for Aoibhneas emerged out of a light drizzly mist, splattered with cow shit as the dashboard clock ticked over to 4.29 p.m. As the car crested the horizon, we drove into a large, natural hug, a tiny village laid out in a semi-circle around the 'lough' or loch. Across the water stood the mountains, mist-topped and shadowy in the early afternoon light. As beautiful as it all was, the infrastructure was appalling – only one road in and out and thinner than my patience – but every driver we passed by or pulled in for waved hello.

'What a stunning place,' said Nnedi, leaning forward to stare at the blurry view over yonder. There was a caravan place with 'CLOSED FOR WINTER' scrawled across it, though it looked as though it hadn't been open for several winters. Down from that was a children's play area looking similarly rusty and abandoned. There was a garage, a church, sundry houses all set back from the road in decent-sized plots and at the bottom of a couple of the driveways on a wall sat a strange little basket.

'What are all the baskets for?'

'For travellers, I think,' said Nnedi. 'In case you're passing and you're hungry. I've known villagers do that sometimes, in close communities.'

'For free?'

'Yes, look.'

Nnedi pulled in at the end of one of the drives and got out to inspect the basket placed on the end of a low-lying cream-coloured wall, pulling out every item to show me. 'Courgettes. Potatoes. Fruit cake. Jam. Honey.'

'A whole fruit cake? Why?'

'I told you – for passers-by.'

I shook my head. 'Humans aren't like that. There must be some unwritten law around here – Thou Shalt Have a Basket

On the End of Your Drive and God forbid you if you don't put out bread for each other.'

Nnedi laughed, the first time I'd seen her laugh since . . . I had never seen her laugh. She took a jar of honey out of the basket and handed it to me as she got back in. 'Where I grew up, they used to do this. Things people had grown in their gardens. Jams. Loaves of bread. I like it. It's welcoming.'

'It's weird. You've just nicked their honey.'

She shook her head. 'No, I didn't. It's just what people do here. I like communities like this.'

'Where did you grow up? Quid pro quo, Clarice . . .'

She opened her mouth and closed it pretty quickly. 'You don't need to know that. I heard your friend Billy on the phone – "don't trust her, a cop is a cop". I get it. We're not friends after all.'

'You said I needed to trust Rafael. So I'll practise on you in the meantime.'

'Touché.'

I scanned the jar of honey. 'There could be cat hairs in it.' I held the jar up to the light. 'Or jizz.'

'Why would there be?' She sighed.

'You never know. These people might have a kink for doing things like that, dipping their dicks in free honey.' I unscrewed the lid, sniffing the top. I dipped my little finger in and sucked the tip. Begrudgingly I had to admit, it was the best honey I'd ever tasted. And no sign of hairs. Or jizz.

'I stand corrected. Maybe they're *not* dippers here.'

We rounded another corner into the village itself and pulled into the car park of the only pub, The White Horse, next door to which was a shop called Oifig an Phoist – I surmised that was the post office. Nnedi parked up underneath the swinging pub sign showing a hunter sat astride a white horse with a dead stag dangling over his shoulder, blood dripping along the path behind him.

'So they execute defenceless woodland animals around here but put out baskets of bread and honey for the tourists? What kind of contradiction *is* this place?'

'Don't start,' said Nnedi, switching off the engine. 'It'll be dark soon. We just need two beds and a roof.' She rubbed her eyes, looking every single one of her fifty-plus years.

I got out, stretching my limbs. The lough seemed to be pulling me towards it. For a moment my brain stopped rifling through folders of reasons why Billy had specifically sent us here and just drank it all in.

Aoibhneas looked like the little fishing village in that terrible Ted Danson film with the Loch Ness monster except we were in Ireland not Scotland, and there was no Ted Danson or annoying kid and the only monster here was me.

I stared out into the mist like the French Lieutenant's twat, taking in a great lungful of the clean air that smelled sweet, like the honey, and then I coughed, and the cough seemed to rebound back at me off the mountains all around. Four thousand kilometres of ocean and five thousand teeny miles of landmass were all that lay between me and Rafael. I remembered something that old woman Caro had said to me on the cruise, back before I'd met him. She said being alive wasn't enough unless there's something your heart aches for. I got it now. I got what she meant. It wasn't enough just to be free. If I couldn't get back to him . . . I didn't want to think about that right now.

'Are you coming or not?' Nnedi called, pulling up her mask.

'Do we need masks? There's nobody here.'

As we walked into the pub, it turned out there *were* quite

a few people here but they were all deep in conversation or glasses of ale. Nobody else was masked and when I went to pull mine down, Nnedi yanked it up and stepped in front of me to approach the bar.

'Hello, is Fintan around please?' said Nnedi to the short, sour-faced landlady with long black hair and a too-tight titty jumper.

She nodded and disappeared behind a red curtain.

The place looked like every other ye olde worlde pub I'd ever been in with added ruddy-cheeked Irishmen, sneaking the occasional glance. There were tankards a-gogo hanging from the eaves behind the bar, cobwebs in all corners, a couple of fruit machines and a jukebox playing The Corrs. Five farmer types in varying check-and-muddy-trouser combos leant on the counter, nursing ales, and dotted around the place seated at the tables, other locals tucked into bowls of stew, talking in another language. Talking *a lot*. I thought Billy was bad enough but these guys didn't come up for air.

'Fintan.' A chonky ginger guy with an easy smile appeared alongside Surly Barmaid with an armful of clean glasses. 'What can I do for you ladies?'

'Er, Billy sent us?' said Nnedi with a note of trepidation as old Sour Puss reappeared beside Fintan and continued to glower our way.

'*Our* Billy?'

Nnedi looked at me. 'Yes.'

'Billy O'Shea? Ah, céad míle fáilte!' said the landlady, her face morphing into something resembling happiness. 'Any friend of Bill's is a friend of ours. Come on in, get yourselves warm. The fire's lit. What can I get you, on the house, will it be a Guinness?'

'Or we have the finest Irish single malt whiskey straight from the cask?' added Fintan, showing us an array of bottles behind him. 'You know what they say about Irish whiskey, girls – the only drink that'll make you see double and feel single!'

The man looked a bit like Mad-Eye Moody but instead of the mad eye he had a lascivious glint and I made sure to give him the evils immediately – too happy. Dead giveaway for a wrong 'un.

Surly Barmaid – whose name was Mary – motioned towards a small round table with three upright wooden chairs by the hearth. The fire blazed with an enormous pile of neatly stacked logs on one side and a basket of rolled-up turf on the other. Mary turned out to be Billy's aunt.

'Sorry,' said Nnedi, taking a seat. 'Didn't Billy tell you we were coming?'

'No, we haven't heard from him in months,' she said, throwing a couple more rolls of turf on the fire and stoking it up before doing a double take at me. I pulled my mask up even higher, almost to my eyes.

Fintan brought over two small Guinnesses and set them down before Nnedi could mew the fatal words: 'I don't drink.'

Neither of them knew what to say to that. So I chimed in. 'Sláinte!' and I clinked my glass to hers. 'Oh I'm Rhia-Bria-*Brienne*, by the way. Like the tall blonde warrior chick in *Game of Thrones*. She's . . . N . . . Na*nette*.'

Nnedi threw me a look.

'Well, Brienne and Nanette, it's wonderful to have you here, welcome to Aoibhneas. You're not the two who robbed him in Ibiza, are you?'

'Erm, no,' said Nnedi.

'Left him there with no watch, no wallet and threw both

legs over the balcony. Stranded he was. Paid a heavy price for that threesome, so he did!'

'How awful.'

A couple of the lads at the bar tapped on their glasses to indicate they needed refills and Fintan hot-footed it back to the counter. When he reappeared, he was carrying a framed photo under his arm. It was a pic of a much younger Billy, uniformed up with his gun. He handed the photo to Nnedi and pulled up a bar stool to sit with us. 'Ah we're all so proud of him here.'

A tall, bulky guy who'd been sitting at a corner table alone sank half of his pint, got up and winked at us as he shrugged on a black overcoat. He had a face like God took one look at him and screwed him up and tossed him in the bin at the last minute. I didn't like the way he was staring at us.

'Where did Billy serve?' Nnedi asked.

'Mainly the Middle East,' said Mary. 'Afghanistan. Kabul. When he was injured out, we thought we might lose him. He came to live with us after he lost his parents in his teens, so we think of him like a son.'

'But he hasn't been in touch with you at all recently?'

'No,' she replied, 'we never know when we're gonna hear from Bill – one day he'll just pop up in a puff of smoke, so he will!'

'Nightmare,' I muttered, as Fintan stoked the fire in the inglenook. The smell was relaxing – barbecue smoke and old earth – surprisingly pleasant even if it meant I was going to die of carbon monoxide poisoning any second.

By this point, the huge galoot in the long black coat had started singing 'Zip-a-Dee-Doo-Dah' at high volume as he stood at the counter, glancing back at us and placing his three empty pint glasses on the bar.

'Two bowls of Irish stew coming up,' said Mary. 'Do you know, you look awful familiar.' She stared at me for a beat, which encouraged Fintan to do the same. I could see it in her eyes – she recognised me.

'Well, you might have seen me in Billy's photos or something,' I offered.

'Yeah, maybe,' she said, with a slow nod, continuing to stare as she turned back towards the kitchen to get our stew.

Thank fuck for the mask.

'You said he lost his parents?' asked Nnedi, still admiring Billy's photo.

Fintan took up the story. 'Well, his oul fella was a drinker and he caught the gaff alight one night. Billy tried to save them but sure, he was only a chiseller. He got his mother out – my sister, God rest her soul – but she died later in hospital. He's dodged death a couple of times, that boy. Someone's looking out for him up there for sure – he could have lost more than his legs that day in Kandahar.'

I didn't know what most facial expressions meant but I could tell by the way Nnedi kept looking at Billy's photo that she was a smitten kitten down to get bitten.

The huge galoot staggered over to our table and I can't report exactly what he said cos I don't speak drunk cunt, but I caught what I needed to.

'The fuck?'

Nnedi sipped her drink. Her face had contorted into the Nnedi I was used to – cold, rock solid, professional. 'Leave it.'

'Leave what?'

'We don't like your kind here,' continued the galoot. 'You should go back to where you came from.'

'What, Bristol?' I asked.

Fintan stepped forward, tucking the framed photo of Billy in the crook of his arm. 'Laddy, you've been warned before, leave the ladies to their drinks.'

'I'm just saying what needs to be said, Fintan,' said the aforementioned Laddy, one grubby palm up in surrender – the other clutching a half-drunk pint he'd liberated from one of the tables that had just left.

'That kind of talk you can keep to yourself, Laddy. Now, be on your way.'

But Laddy sat down in the third chair at our table before Fintan could stop him. I could not touch him. I knew from bitter experience that if I started I wouldn't stop, so I put down my drink and settled my hand on the arm of my chair instead, out of harm's way.

'So tell me, ladies, you a pair of dykes, are you?'

'As far as *you're* concerned, absolutely,' I replied.

His breath reeked of fish and the odd fleck of spit would soar out and land on the table or the lapel of Nnedi's coat as he spoke. She sat there serenely, sipping her drink and not making eye contact. It was a masterclass in grey rocking. I could learn a thing or two.

'Why didn't you choose one of your own kind then?' he asked me.

'Why didn't your mother swallow you instead?' I countered.

Laddy laughed, hacking another pall of filth mouth into the air, scratching his whiskery chin with two stubby fingernails. I grabbed the chair arm so tightly the wood started to crack beneath my grip.

I leant into him. 'If you don't leave us alone, I will kick your teeth through the back of your head until—'

'Until what, eh?' he cackled. 'What is the little dyke here

going to do to me, I wonder?' *Fish spit fish spit fish spit.* Ugh! My temper at boiling point, the chair arm snapped clean off in my hand but before I could stick him with it, Nnedi grabbed it and hoyed it behind her into the fire.

'Stop it, all right, just stop!' she seethed, slamming down her glass.

'Laddy, get out, now!' said Fintan.

Laddy went to move closer to Nnedi but before he could speak again, Fintan grabbed him by the collar.

Two other lads at the bar came over to see if he needed a hand and each man took Laddy by the arm and slung him bodily outside into the car park.

Nnedi turned round to stare at the broken chair arm catching fire, then back at me. She didn't seem cross though. 'You almost listened to me.'

'Yeah well. Growth, innit?' I knocked back the rest of my Guinness and slammed down my glass. I don't know if it was growth that had stopped me shanking that galoot with my hastily snapped off shiv but I do know the last time I intervened when a racist was giving it out, my husband ended up on life support. I was learning that my special brand of input was not always welcome in these situations.

Fintan returned, ruddy-cheeked and rubbing his hands as though they were covered in dirt. 'Sorry about that, ladies. He's just the local dose of shite, don't be worrying about him. Just stay dog wide.'

'Sorry about your chair,' I said, nodding to the absent arm beside me.

'Ah yer grand, that one was bockety anyways.'

I kept one eye out the window behind me – Laddy was

lingering outside the pub, puffing on a cigar. He seemed to be waiting for something.

'What's his problem anyway?'

Fintan ducked to see what I was pointing at. 'Well, we don't get too many visitors around here so you two are fresh meat. You'd do well to keep your distance from him. That's one bad apple. Anyway, never mind him, you're to come in here for all your meals, on the house, no arguments, all right? Any friends of Billy's don't pay.'

Nnedi gasped. 'Ahh you're too kind, but—'

Fintan smiled. 'It's no trouble at all, glad to do something to help Billy's pals.' I evilled Laddy through the window, mentally etching his name on a block of stone as he sauntered up the road.

'Will you be staying at Seamus's place or the Ryans's while you're here?'

'No,' said Nnedi. 'Actually, it was all a bit last minute. We don't have anywhere. We were hoping to find somewhere local, not too expensive . . .'

'Most people travelling through here, we send them to Old Meg's gaff.'

'What's Old Meg's?' I asked.

'It's a little cottage, just up the track, not ten minutes away. Meg left it to us when she died four years ago and we rent it out to travellers. Anyone passing through, needing shelter. Hikers, tourists, someone down on their luck. Billy's sent a few veterans in the past. How long are you staying?'

'We're not sure. Maybe a week or two? Just thought we'd do a bit of walking, sightseeing. See the . . . trees, the old . . . wall . . .'

'Old Meg's place will do you just grand. It's got good access to all the footpaths into the hills, and it's been empty for a while now. You can't drive down there though – track's not made for cars – but you can leave your car here and I'll run you down in the wagon. It'll be quite safe. There's no running water or electricity and you might be able to get some phone signal down there but it's a bit unreliable—'

'Oh is there anywhere else?' I said, throwing Nnedi a look.

'Old Meg lived there for ninety-five years, and she was very happy,' said Starey Mary, appearing beside the table with two huge bowls of piping-hot stew and two hunks of soda bread. 'Chopped her own wood, got her water from the spring. There's some paraffin lamps we can lend you if the candlelight isn't enough, and blankets and sheets for the beds.'

'Sounds perfect,' said Nnedi, still blowing on her first spoonful of stew. 'We'll take it, but we insist on paying.'

Fintan nodded, clearing our empty glasses. 'Right so you are. I can do you a good deal. Say, a hundred euros a week?'

'Great.' She put down her spoon and fished about in her handbag for her wallet, pulling out a crisp stack of notes. 'You're paying for next week's,' she said, giving me the evil eye.

'Hopefully I'll be dead of hypothermia by then.'

'I'll take you up there when you've finished your grub,' Fintan offered. 'It's just up the track.'

'Just up the track' turned out to be a twenty-minute amble along a muddy woodland lane well rutted by cartwheels and hooves. The horse pulling us was a brown Kerry Bog pony with mad hair and huge brown eyes and his name was Ben. Ben talked more than Fintan but using his arse.

'Don't mind him, he's got the farts,' Fintan said, cracking

the reins and spurring Ben into motion. 'He'll blow us all to hell one of these days! I call him Ben the Bungalow cos he's got nothing going on upstairs.'

The journey would have been shorter but Fintan kept stopping to give a history lesson and pointing out boring-ass flora and fauna and tales of a banshee who screams outside your house if someone's going to die soon.

'Ah you'll hear her before you see her, so you will.'

'Have *you* seen her?' Nnedi asked.

'No, but me mother did, just before my father had his stroke. Heard it keening outside the back window and when she looked she saw a hooded figure with long hair and when it looked up at her it had a veil over its face and glowing red eyes. Two days later, Father passed on.'

'Oh. Great. Can't wait for her to rock up for St Patrick's night then.'

The wagon rolled to a stop and the whitewashed stone-walled cottage, aka Old Meg's, came into view, almost hidden by long, rangy weeds in the garden and thick ivy covering some of the front wall. It was like a bloody witch's hovel. If there were any straggly-haired old crones in the area, I'd have put good money they hung around a shithole like this.

'Here y'are,' said Fintan brightly, helping us both alight with our lanterns. 'Here's a key – I've got a spare if you need it.' He handed it to Nnedi who was busy wresting her scarf out of Ben's chomping mouth. 'And don't forget what I said – you're welcome back at the pub any night for your dinner. Food's served until nine. We close at eleven unless there's a lock-in but I doubt there'll be one tomorrow as they're all out on a catch.'

I shone my lantern around the garden. There were four

raised beds, filled with winter veg, unperturbed by caterpillars and supported by canes.

'You can pick anything you want. Help yourself. I'll grab your blankets.'

'Thank you, you've been most kind,' said Nnedi as she grabbed her now horse-shredded scarf, and her bag from the cart and I followed on with mine.

All the matches and candles were in a handy wooden crate on the kitchen table. And the more candles we lit, the more the stark gloominess of the place came to light. It was one large room with a kitchen in the right-hand corner and a living room to the left.

Fintan handed us two bundles of blankets and towels wrapped in string and bin liners, courtesy of Mary, and set about making us a fire in the wood burner which sat between a shabby sofa and an old armchair with a sheepskin rug on it.

'There you are, that should keep you going. Anything else you need, you know where we are. You both take care now,' he said, 'and keep that door locked whether you're in or out.'

''Cos of the banshee?' I said.

Fintan shrugged. 'If you like. Goodnight, ladies.'

Before I knew it, he was back on the wagon, turning it around in the lane and shambling back along the track towards the pub.

And Nnedi and I were alone. Again.

'Why do we have to keep the door locked?' Nnedi asked.

'Well, there is an escaped murderer about,' I said. 'Two, if you think about it. Plus that weirdo in the black coat. We're "fresh meat", remember?'

She continued to light candles on the two deep window ledges as the fireplace roared to life. There was a basket of rolled-up turf next to it, like at the pub. Rows of well-thumbed paperback books sat haphazardly on shelves and there was a little stack of board games in the corner, all foxed and dogeared. Myriad animal traps were dotted about the whitewashed walls, and hung above the doorway was a large and slightly rusty axe.

'You're all right. I'm not in a Jack Torrance sort of mood today.'

Upstairs was a mezzanine and one queen-sized bed, only accessible by a rickety ladder, hewn from the same wood as the lintels and eaves. There was a porthole window carved into the wall behind the bed and on its sill sat an assortment of tchotchkes – a half-empty bottle of perfume, a well-thumbed book of Irish poetry and a little Mary figurine.

'A life just left. Nobody to carry it on,' yawned Nnedi, flinging her bag onto the bed and yawning unapologetically.

'Erm, hello?'

'I need it. I can't sleep on that sofa. You know I have a back.'

'Yeah, so do I – I want to go *back* home but *you* killed my sister so I'm stuck in this shithole.'

She stared me out. 'All right, I'll do you a deal – I'll chop all the wood and collect all the water if I can have the bed for the duration.'

I didn't have to think about it long. 'Yeah all right then.'

Friday, 22 October – Day 1
in Aoibhneas

1. *The designer of all the roads in Ireland.*
2. *People who wang on about whether there was enough space on Rose's door for Jack in Titanic – the boat sank a million years ago, the film was last century, let it GO already!*
3. *Emily Ratajkowski – yes, you're very beautiful, well done, piss off.*
4. *Jared Leto, Joaquin Phoenix et al. – yes, you're very method and clever, we get it. Have another Oscar and piss off.*
5. *Red Hot Chili Peppers – you're too old for that shit now, piss off.*
6. *Weird guy outside local shop with dirty fingernails.*

I woke up to the loud clattering of a bunch of logs dropping into the fireplace.

'FUCK ME SIDEWAYS!' I cried, jumping up off the sofa; a lightning-quick movement that my back did not thank me for.

'Sorry – thought you were awake,' said Nnedi, stacking the logs into a pile. 'Why didn't you make your bed properly?'

I looked down to find I'd just dumped the blankets and

sheets Fintan had given us on top of the sofa and fallen asleep on top of it all. 'Too knackered.' I nestled back in, wrapping myself in the blankets to doze again. 'I don't suppose any of that was a dream, was it?'

'Nope,' she said. The axe from above the door was shoved into her belt and bumped against her calves as she walked into the kitchen, filling the copper kettle with water from a large glass jug and bringing it back to the lit fireplace to hang on a metal stick thing above the flames.

'Have you been out to get water too?'

'Yes, from the spring down the track. It's not far. We've enough for a few cups of tea and two showers I think.'

'There's a *shower* in this shithole?'

'Of sorts,' she said. 'It's more a hose in a box affair. Fintan gave us fresh towels too – I've hung yours by the door. Tea?'

It was then I noticed she had washed, dressed and seemed to be sporting a sizeable Afro as well.

'Your hair looks nice,' I said.

'What does *that* mean?'

'I've never seen you with your hair down,' I said. 'It's always so slicked back and tight, ready for inspection. Now you look like a human being, rather than an automaton.'

'That serves as a compliment in your world, does it?'

'Yeah. You look . . . wonderful.'

Her eyebrows were raised but she didn't respond. She just said, 'It's a lovely day. Why don't you go out and stretch your legs? Better than being cooped up in here.'

'Bit too much fresh air around here for my liking.'

She swilled a handful of kale in a metal sieve at the sink. 'Reminds me of being a kid again, being here.'

'Quid pro quo,' I muttered, closing my eyes again.

'Doesn't seem like five minutes ago I was running around with my cousins, making dens, playing off-ground touch. Now I'm on HRT with a pension plan and varifocals. Where did the time go?'

'You're on HRT?' I said.

She ignored that. We were not friends. She didn't owe me an answer. 'Did we leave the gate open last night?'

'No, why?'

'It was open when I went out this morning. You didn't go out in the night at all, to the toilet or—'

'Why would I open the gate to use the bog? Anyway, I'm not in a hurry to use *that* thing again to be honest.'

'Yes, it is all a bit primitive, isn't it? Still, at least we're safe here.'

'Are we?'

Apart from the gate, there didn't seem to be anything else amiss with the place and about an hour later, the kettle spewed steam and Nnedi lifted it off with a manky tea towel to pour hot water into a chipped *ThunderCats* mug – more chip than mug. When she handed it to me I noticed it had a sprig of mint floating in it. It tasted like the crap I used to make when I was a kid playing dens in our shed.

'Just 'til we get some provisions – I noticed a shop along from the pub.'

'You seem to have adapted to this way of living rather easily.'

'What else can you do? Get busy living—'

'—or get busy getting caught.'

'Exactly.' She sat in Old Meg's armchair reading a magazine that was years out of date – Depp and Heard were happy as Larry, Bowie was touring, Orlando Bloom had his schlong out on a paddle board. I flicked some V's at her behind the magazine, but she didn't see.

'I can see what you're doing, by the way.'

'Oh.'

I couldn't bring myself to drink anymore twig tea and settled the mug on a stack of even older magazines on a roughly hewn table beside the couch.

'Christ I'm bored,' I groaned. 'I feel like when Dolores gets to the nunnery and realises how shit life is away from Reno. Except there's no jolly nun or a musical montage with brooms to cheer me up. Just cold and rain and chores and kale. And you.'

Nnedi threw me a look. 'I never understood that second film.'

'What?'

'Well, she's hiding out in the first movie, isn't she? The detective places her in the nunnery for safety because her mob boss boyfriend is going to kill her. It's temporary. So why does she go back there in the second film?'

'Because they're her friends and they ask her to run the school choir.'

'But she doesn't need to be a nun again. The mob boss is in jail, she's quite safe, why does she need to be a nun?'

'To help the school. The nuns ask for her help. They need her.'

'But why dress as a nun, is my point. She's not in hiding in the second film. Why can't she just wear her own clothes and be their music teacher? And how does saving the choir save the school anyway? The stakes are all wrong.'

I had absolutely no answer but at that moment, I think I hated her even more than when she'd just shot dead my sister. 'Oh fuck off.'

I could have sworn a flicker of a smile appeared as she picked up another magazine and tried to invest in out-of-date celeb gossip.

Just then, a buzz came through on her phone.

'Oh Jesus,' she said, scrolling. 'They've found Seren.'

'What? When?' I said, using my best pretends-to-be-shocked face when I knew damn well from the forum she'd already been found.

'Last night.'

'What does it say?'

She handed me her phone so I could see and after about five minutes, a short news clip had downloaded from Sky News:

Breaking News

Sky NEWS

'Fliss Foster here. We can go live now to south Wales, where Peter McIntyre has the latest on this breaking story. Peter . . .'

'Thanks, Chris, yes, I'm outside the Princess of Wales Hospital in Bridgend where the body of a thirty-five-year-old woman was brought in during the early hours of yesterday morning. The body was found in this woodland with a single gunshot wound to the head: we are just a mile from the cottage where serial killer Rhiannon Lewis grew up. Earlier this year, locals were reminded of that fact with the unearthing of two bodies in the back garden of the cottage, thought to be victims of serial killer Tommy Lewis, Rhiannon's father.'

'Is the body connected with Rhiannon Lewis, do we know, Peter?'

'Well, a formal identification takes place later today but we have learned that there is significant evidence to suggest that Rhiannon was involved in some way or at least that is what it looks like – police are being a little reticent to divulge any further information on that for the time being.

'We've also learned that Cody Gibson, Seren's husband, is over here with his kids having reported his wife missing several days ago so it's reasonable to assume the two events are linked. Police are appealing for witnesses – anyone who saw or heard anything at all within the last two days which could be deemed suspicious. They are looking at tyre tracks in the field where the body was found and they believe a car left the road though it's unclear why.

'This picturesque seaside village, popular with tourists, is getting an ever-darker reputation these days.'

'Peter – we know that Rhiannon Lewis is officially still at large – is there any hint that the body could be Rhiannon herself?'

'No word on that yet but police have said they're close to making an arrest. I'll keep on top of the story and bring you all the latest as I get it. Back to the studio . . .'

'Close to making an arrest,' I said. That was brand-new information I *hadn't* bargained on. 'Shit. They know it's us. How do they fucking know it's us?! We stayed off roads with cameras, they couldn't have traced your car... they didn't see the dent at the ferry port ... oh god not yet not *yet!*'

'Calm down,' said Nnedi. 'The investigating team will have fed that line to the press to put pressure on a culprit. They're trying to smoke us out.'

'Oh. I suppose you'd know about these things.'

'Yes, I do. They haven't got anything – *yet*.'

'Well, if they've got no witnesses, we're home and dry then, aren't we?'

'We are *not* home and dry,' she snipped, taking her phone back. 'They'll be looking at those tyre tracks and any paint that chipped off on the broken fence; they're bound to trace it to the Audi eventually.'

'Even if they do trace the car, they'll realise it belongs to a serving police detective and you'll be able to blag your way out of it.'

'I've never "blagged" my way out of anything,' she snapped, placing her mug down on Amber Heard's face.

'They'll blame it on me then; they're bound to.'

'There's nothing to tie you to it though!'

'Yeah, there is. I left a sweetpea with her.'

'You did what?'

'I left a dried sweetpea on Seren's body. A sort of calling card. So they'll either think it was me or a copycat. They won't be looking your way, trust me.'

'YOU BLOODY IDIOT!'

'That's not nice. I've got you to safety, haven't I? Nobody but Billy knows where we are, we've avoided the ANPR cameras as much as we could, and the car is hidden behind the pub. We just have to sit tight and wait for him.'

'And then what?' She batted her eyes so harshly I practically heard them slam. 'Why did you do that – leave evidence on her?'

'Accountability and all that.'

She stared at me for the longest time, then swigged the dregs of her mug and set it down on the magazine she'd been reading. 'You knowingly led them to you, rather than me?'

'Yes.'

Nnedi shook her head. 'As long as I live I will never understand how your mind works.'

'Me either, to be honest. So come on, are you gonna help me have a shower in this cave or do I wait until the mastodon arrives with a full trunk of water?'

The trick was to get everything washed in under four

minutes – that's how long the water lasted but first, one had to stand on a tree stump and pour it into a blue bag connected to a hose dangling inside a tall, rectangular 'shower' cubicle at the back of the house. The water was freezing, predictably, but mixing it with a little kettle water made it just about bearable and Nnedi had torn up a couple of clean tea towels for wash cloths and found a new bar of soap under the sink that stripped all the oils off my skin, so it would do. Admittedly, I felt as clean as a whistle afterwards and my skin tingled all over.

I wasn't telling Nnedi that though.

'Don't you feel better for that? Bathing in the freshest spring water, not a microplastic in sight?'

'Nope. And just for you, the next time I see a microplastic, I'm going to shove it right up my ass.'

But it was bloody hard work living at Old Meg's. *Everything* was hard.

Making a hot drink took over an hour, and that was only *if* there was any wood for the fire and water for the kettle and if there wasn't, you had to go out and gather or chop it.

Even going to the toilet was a chore, and not just because I was constipated – the 'toilet' was a plastic barrel with a wooden seat across the top and sawdust in the bottom, ensconced in another tiny wooden shed at the end of the path by the front gate. It had to be changed regularly or else it stank and so, ironically, even though I'd never given much of a shit about the environment before, I was now begrudgingly playing my part.

Nnedi had picked a load of kale for lunch from the raised beds and my stomach growled in protest at the truly diabolical sight on offer.

'Wow. That Grade C in Home Economics is really kicking

in now, isn't it?' I sneered at the bowl before me. 'Please tell me this isn't all there is.'

'This is all there is,' she replied, plucking a small green squirming thing out of her dish and setting it to one side.

'Seren used to make me the best cheese toasties. Cut into triangles, cheese top and bottom, flipped over in the pan so it was all burnt on, little blob of salad cream on the side. Sometimes she'd hide a slice of pickled onion in there and we'd play a game – first to taste the onion.'

Nnedi looked up at me. 'There's no bread. I told you, we need provisions.'

'Let's go to the shop then. We've got money. Just because we're forced to live like peasants doesn't mean we should have to eat like them as well.'

'Later.' She handed me a bowl of the washed kale shreds and beckoned me to sit down. I munched reluctantly through it like a depressed rabbit.

'Grim,' I muttered.

Nnedi paid it no mind. 'I heard a rumour that the shop has fresh fish delivered every morning so we could pick some up for supper. We could have fish, kale and potatoes. Get some butter for the potatoes.'

'You know society is just nine missed meals from collapsing? Well, I'm nine kale leaves from burning this entire village to the fucking ground.'

'Oh-kay, no kale then tonight.'

I watched her as she ate. Her eyes were rich and warm and her skin flawless, except for one frown line between her eyes – same place I had one. My stomach turned over at the thought of another mouthful of kale and I ate what I could and pushed my bowl away.

'You don't like it here much, do you?' she said.

'I've shed womb lining I'm more fond of than this place.'

'It's not that bad.'

'It *is* that bad. It smells and it's damp and, hello, not one plug socket. I can't stand being without Herbal Essences and tampons – and I'd kill *you* for a blueberry Pop Tart right now. I can't live on kale for the rest of my life. Christ – endless kale or endless jail. What a choice.'

'I like it. I like the quiet. My flat in Bristol is relentlessly noisy. If it's not the traffic, it's the neighbours. If it's not the neighbours, it's trains thundering past. I didn't used to mind it so much when I was working but . . .'

Her sentence petered out.

'Quid pro quo?' I said.

She carried on chewing her kale. 'As a child, I used to live in a place just like this. I mean, it was bigger and we had running water and electricity, but it was in deep countryside like this. So much space. Clean air. A proper garden. It's getting rarer to find this kind of space in the world. For me this is . . .' She struggled to find the word for ages, by which time I'd stopped listening anyway. But then she found it. 'Peace.'

'Piece of *shit*,' I snorted.

'You only think this is hard because you know what it's like to have a quick shower or a microwave meal or boil a kettle and have coffee in seconds.'

'Ohhh, coffeeeee,' I said, pining for a cup now she'd said the word.

'But when you have to work for something, it feels more of an achievement. To grow your own veg and harvest it. Gather your own water and wash in it. When things take time to create, it's often more worth it.'

This actually landed with me. It was something my mother-in-law would say about making segueza or chilaquiles the old-fashioned way – grinding the corn in a mortar rather than putting it in a blender, chopping everything by hand, and over open flame in our fire pit. She didn't have to – she chose to.

Nnedi went into a sort of trance as she continued to munch her kale. I knew that look – there weren't many looks I understood but that one I did. That was the look you get when you've been enjoying yourself and you suddenly remember something horrible. Then she snapped out of it.

'Who's "we"?' I asked. 'You said "we had running water and electricity". Quid pro quo.'

'Me and my parents.'

'Is your mum dead as well?'

'Same way as yours, oddly enough. Metastasized breast cancer. We'll go to the shop after *you've* washed up.'

'Okay.'

She got up and cleared our bowls away, glancing at my wrist. It was the first time my scar had been fully visible and in daylight. 'I haven't properly seen the scar before now. What happened?'

'It's a long story.'

'Quid pro quo, Dr Lecter. It's not like we don't have time.'

She was right about that. Without the distractions of TV or a strong wifi signal, talking was the main entertainment at Old Meg's. That and an unopened bottle of Irish whiskey stashed in a cupboard of which, amazingly, Nnedi partook. And the more she partook, the more she talked. And the more I partook, the more I talked. About everything. As I washed up, I told her about the Hacienda. About Tenoch, the ex-cartel hitman and his evil henchman Paco tying me to the fender and

199

threatening the kids if I didn't tell him where all the money was hidden. And the machete. And she just listened.

'Paco cut off your hand?' asked Nnedi, leaning back in her seat.

'No, *I* did,' I said, folding up the tea towel I'd been drying up with. 'I don't remember much about it – I remember waking up in the back of the car with my head rested on Rafael's lap and my severed hand in a bag of ice. And I remember just being so bloody happy to see Raf again that I passed out. I didn't feel any pain. I didn't even care if I was dead – if I *do* die, that's how I want to go. With Raf holding me.' My wrist was aching so much in lieu of my brace, I needed to squeeze it with my other hand.

Nnedi stared it. 'Until he cheats on you, like Craig did.'

'No,' I said. 'Raf's nothing like Craig. He's always complimenting me and boosting my confidence and whenever I'm sad, he won't leave me until I'm happy again. Biggest compliment Craig ever gave me was "With your calves, you'd make an amazing shot-putter". He couldn't understand why that made me angry. When he and Dad were together, I'd get it in stereo.

'"*You look like a bag of shit tied up ugly,*" Dad'd laugh and Craig would echo his laugh like a hyena.

'"*Why don't you treat yourself to a makeover in your lunchbreak?*"

'"*Debenhams closes at six, Tom!*" Ha ha ha.

'And of course, I'd laugh back. That was the rule of The Act after all – take a joke. Blend in. Be one of them. It wasn't just them – it was everyone. Everything my friends would say; every comment. The people at work. "*You don't mind, do you, sweetpea? You'll stay late and do that filing we fucked up in the first place, won't you, sweetpea? You won't mind if we don't promote you for the nth year running cos you're so easy going, aren't you, sweetpea? You never rock the boat."* All so I could fit in.'

Quid pro quo had become a full-blown convo. I was talking to Nnedi like a friend, not a whatever-the-hell this was. Amazingly, she was listening and nodding along.

'You get it?'

'Of course I get it,' replied Nnedi. 'Imagine how it was for me. If I didn't go along with the status quo, laugh off the misogyny, the casual othering, I had a chip on my shoulder. I'd be called "difficult" or told I had a "tone". "Fitting in", to me, is an insult. It means you put up with things you shouldn't. Because if you don't, you get a target on your back.'

'Yeah, I can see that. At least I had an outlet. Every plunge of that knife had an insult tied to the handle. Every stab, every cut. Rafael says if I'd had better care and support early on, I might never have . . . gone the way of the Pea. I don't know if I believe that. But it kinda makes sense.'

What Nnedi said next surprised me. 'I have to walk away from toxicity because if I don't – if I react – it comes back at me tenfold. So I never raised my voice, or my fists; or, God forbid, a weapon.' Her head bowed. 'The system would have chewed me up and spat me out if I'd even thought about it.'

'But I bet you'd like to though, sometimes. With people like those police commissioners. And that racist piece of shit in the pub?'

She didn't answer. It was all the answer I needed.

And it occurred to me then: we were like two sides of the same coin – the way I'd react to anything that angered me, Nnedi did the opposite. She had to. Where I stabbed or stalked or satisfied my blood lust, she divorced or diverted or just DNFd. She'd ghosted guys who'd hurt her; I'd maimed them. She'd turned the other cheek; I'd stabbed it. She'd steeled herself and walked on, head held high; I'd got myself some steel and taken their heads clean off.

We were just as angry as each other but she had more reason to be. I could get away with stuff more easily – she couldn't afford to. I wondered if the roles were reversed, she'd have behaved like me. Just let rip. Maybe, just maybe, we were the same.

But I wished I was more like *her*. Spitting the venom out rather than ingesting it and letting it infect me; infect everything. Maybe in that damn parallel universe – the one where my prefrontal cortex wasn't compromised – I *was* more like her. Serene. Focused. Self-sufficient.

But I wasn't. I always needed someone to mop me up. Be it Dad or Seren or the PICSOs or Craig's parents while I was gestating my baby, or Caro, that old broad who lived on the cruise ship where I literally lost my shit and she cleaned me up. Or Tenoch in Mexico. Raf and his family. And now Nnedi. On some level, that's probably the main reason I wanted her to come with me. I knew I couldn't survive on my own.

'Have I ever told you about when the PICSOs forgot to invite me to my own surprise birthday party?'

'Who are the PICSOs?'

'People I Can't Shake Off. College "friends". I mean I *have* shaken them off now but for a long time I kept them for The Act. Anyway, I eventually got a text from one of them and when I got to the restaurant half of them were pissed and the other half had bought me a load of presents I neither liked nor wanted – a foot spa, cheap wine, Baylis and Harding bath shit, sundry boxes of Hotel Choco-fuckin-Lah. I was supposed to get a taxi with Imelda afterwards but the bloke she was seeing collected her and drove off before I could get the door open. I killed an Austrian student that night. Tried to make conversation with me all the way from the bus stop and when he touched my shoulder, I freaked out. Stabbed him to death in the park. I was just so sick of being taken for granted. So sick of putting up with stuff, just for the sake of keeping the peace. Fuck the peace, I thought. Good old Sweetpea.'

'Have you heard that proverb about the oak tree seed?' said Nnedi.

'What's that got to do with the price of rice in China?'

'Sort of backs up what your husband said about you needing a better start. A seed will never become an oak tree if the pot it's in is too small. It needs a more nurturing space. I think that's what you did when you met Rafael – you planted yourself somewhere better and it helped you to grow. You met better people; made better friends. Found happiness. Maybe there is redemption out there for you; for what you've done.'

'It's always there though. It's got less over time but I can feel it building sometimes, like when I found out Ivy wasn't sick. I wanted to go over to that house and split Mitch Silverton in two. But I didn't.'

'Why take the risk? You could have gone back to San Diego and nobody would have known you were there.'

'Habit, I suppose. I went to Claudia's to kidnap Ivy and kill whoever got in my way, but I didn't do that either. Didn't feel right. A few years ago, I'd have killed Mitch and taken her and walked out wearing his intestines as a scarf. But I chose *not* to. Even though I'm a bad seed, I am trying to grow.'

She stared into the fire. 'Ivy didn't want you, did she? That's why she was screaming.'

'No. And do you know how I reacted? The same way my own mother would have. I called her a little shit and chucked her back in her bed. I took it personally. I took it the only way I knew how.'

'"I sat with my anger long enough until she told me her real name was grief,"' Nnedi replied.

'Huh?'

'CS Lewis.'

'*Narnia* bloke?'

'Yes.'

'I don't remember that bit in the film. Who said it, the stoned caterpillar?'

'No. Lewis just said it once, in one of his essays.' She rubbed her face over with one hand like an Etch A Sketch wipe of a bad drawing. 'Come on, let's go shopping.'

The only shop in Aoibhneas had a sign up saying 'Dúnta' meaning 'closed'. It adjoined the post office, separated by a glass partition. Nnedi and I stood outside like two Brits not knowing what to do unless somebody tells them, and sure enough Fintan drew up alongside us on his wagon, which was loaded with crates of what looked like bags of shopping – Ocado for the Amish.

'Arti's out for the afternoon, ladies. Yous two can just go in and help yourselves – leave your IOUs on the side.'

Sure enough, the door was unlocked so we moseyed on in and played *Supermarket Sweep*. The place was surprisingly well stocked for somewhere out in the sticks and if you wanted it, chances are they sold it – bread, pies, cheeses, meats, sweets, chocolate, INSTANT COFFEE, beer, medicines, fanny rags, even hella-dated DVDs – not that we had a DVD player in the hovel.

No damn clothes, sadly, unless you wanted unlimited pairs of old lady tights or embroidered hankies.

Nnedi checked out the fresh fish in the chilled cabinet while I checked out the magazines. It was all the same shit – celebs having breakdowns in their mansions and the latest on the sex life of Myleene Klass. There was one indirect mention of me in the form of Guy Majors, the journalist so wet for me he should be in a tank at Sea World. He was showing *Hello!* magazine around his beachfront Bahamas villa with the second wife he acquired not six months after the cancer death of his old one (got a bestselling book out of the grief though). He's asked why I was one of his fantasy dinner guests.

'Her story fascinates me,' he said, 'even after her death. I would have loved to sit down with Rhiannon and talk about her crimes; find out what made her tick. I covered a few of the stories that came out about her and she would have made for a truly insightful case study.' Prick.

The newspapers were all Irish-centric – *Irish Daily Mail*, *Irish Field*, *Irish Independent*, *The Kerryman* and magazines like the *RTÉ Guide* and *Ireland's Own*. No recent news on me. No recent news on Seren.

I reached for a box of fanny rags and some ibuprofen. And some Tayto crisps – I needed the salt. And some Jaffa Cakes. And a pack of KitKat Chunkys – I needed the sugar.

Nnedi totted it all up, placing the money and a note and Old Meg's address beside three other piles of little notes left that morning by the till.

'How come this place isn't constantly ramraided?' I said,

slamming down my wares onto the counter and fellating one of the KitKats.

'Everyone knows everyone here so you wouldn't dare steal. We used to have a similar system in Bodmin. Honesty boxes. Shops run by volunteers. I was listening to them in the pub. They're not just farmers or milkmen. They all do several different jobs. Some are volunteer firefighters and fishermen. The woman at the post office is a part-time nurse. Fintan and a few of the others help with the mountain rescue. It's a real community.'

I took from that little diatribe what I needed to. 'So you used to live in Cornwall,' I said. 'Are the lambs still screaming in Bodmin, Clarice?'

'We weren't farmers; we just lived there.'

'I just don't get how people can be so trusting. Unlocked, unmanned shops – baskets of free stuff on every wall. It's bizarre.'

'That's because you don't trust anyone.'

'Can you blame me? I trusted Seren and look where I am. I trusted Craig and look what he did to me. Do *you* trust everyone you meet? I'd think being a detective, trust would be impossible.'

'Doesn't mean I don't want to.'

I was still working that out when we stepped out into the milky daylight. I'd downed almost the entire sleeve of Jaffa Cakes by then. I was just chowing the last two when I noticed the tall, hunched figure beside the low-lying wall, straggly grey-streaked hair blowing on the breeze, one hand in his pocket, the other smoking a stubby cigar. Long black leather coat. Dirty fingernails. It was the guy we'd met on the first day – Laddy – except he didn't have too much to say for himself this time. He stared at us, unblinking, as we emerged with our bags.

Nnedi smiled at him. 'Good afternoon.'

Laddy didn't answer, just continued to stare at us as we walked past.

'Lovely day, isn't it?' I called out. The attempt at small talk tasted sour in my mouth but at least I was trying. Nnedi glanced at me, a small but distinct smile tearing into her mouth.

Saturday, 23 October – Day 2 in Aoibhneas

1. *People who refuse to adapt to modern methods and get decent broadband. Or electricity. Or running water.*
2. *Wags whose only claim to fame is getting their clam rammed by some footballer and suddenly they're influential.*
3. *Clean eaters. You're better than us, we get it. Move along.*
4. *Chris Puddimore, that insufferable funt who runs the YouTube channel It's All Gravy, where he visits the graves of famous murder victims, including mine. He always adds a bunch of garage carnations alongside the family tributes. 'Rest in peace, pal/sweetheart,' he says as he walks away. Not likely, with your fucking Timberlands tramping all over them. 'Thoughts, as always, are with his subscriber count.'*
5. *Laddy McVicker – racist piece of shit from the pub who seems to follow us around like a bad smell.*

It's still all pretty pass-the-noose here in Aoibhneas. There's nothing to do except walk to the shop or walk to the pub or walk into the fucking sea cos you're just so damn bored. I was up uncharacteristically early and Nnedi was already out doing her water-gathering bit so I scrolled the internet for a bit to feed my bored little mind a bit of dopamine. My signal was patchy at best and my burner phone's internet capacity was woefully inadequate, but I did manage to hop on to the Bad Seeds forum and find some posts to cheer my black heart. Like this one:

From 'The Bad Seeds' Tumblr

Dear Sweetpea,

Because of you, I roared tonight. I drew up to my full strength and I actually roared. I don't know where it came from – fear, I suppose – but when he ran off, I felt terrific.

So I met this guy on OkCupid two months back. It turned out he did the same degree course as me years earlier. I started to believe that he was someone I could trust. We met up, had a few nights out. We were sleeping together within a week. Nothing special. I had someone to send a Valentine's card to. Someone who cared whether I got home safely. People at work started talking to me like an equal, rather than an oddity without a bloke. Now I had another half, I was 'whole' in their eyes.

And then he got clingy. Constantly wanting to know where I was, who I was with, talking me out of nights out with my friends. Pretty soon, he became an irritant and I started doing that distant thing, not texting *him* back. One morning he showed up at my flat and demanded to know what I was playing at and I told him I'd had enough. I didn't want to see him no more. He walked off, hands in pockets.

Stupidly, I thought that was that. But then I started seeing him in places – the supermarket across the road from my flat. Parked outside my work. Following behind me and ducking into doorways when I was on a night out with the girls. It went on and on, until I got the police involved. They were great but they couldn't do much because he hadn't attacked me. I got scared. It was exactly what he wanted.

Tonight, as I was walking back to my car in Asda, I saw him standing beside his car, two spaces away from mine. I walked right up to him and I screamed in his face. I announced to that whole car park, which was full, what he'd been doing. I said he was a LOSER. I said I wasn't afraid no more and that if he ever comes near me again, I'd FUCKING RUN HIM OVER. He laughed as he got back into his car and drove off, but I don't care. I'd rather be angry than scared. I'd rather go to prison for killing him than be trapped in this headfuck any longer.

But Rhiannon – if you *are* out there and you're bored – please go after Ciaran Macuffey of 154 Clogheen Road, Clonakilty. He's a walking, talking waste of good pig fodder and I know you'd have fun with him. Cheers.

**from W in Clonakilty,
Republic of Ireland**

There's no danger of me paying young Ciaran a visit, by the way. I have no direct beef with him and besides, who am I, Rent-a-Psycho? Sorry, W from Clonakilty, that's one asshole you'll have to wipe yourself. Besides which, I had more pressing matters at hand, such as why neither my husband nor his idiot mate had contacted me in two days, which was only prolonging my purgatory in Hovelsville, Ireland. Each time my phone runs out of battery, I silently worry that one of them is trying to get through.

I'd just finished liking a few of the Bad Seeds' memes about Guy Majors when it did just that.

'Ah shit! Stupid piece-of-shit phone!'

So I made my sofa/bed and sat the little woollen gatita on my pillow to guard it for me and walked to the pub to juice it up. It was an ice-cold morning and I was glad of Nnedi's horse-bitten scarf as the freezing air bit at every section of uncovered skin.

'Good morning, *Brienne*,' Fintan called pointedly from the cellar doorway as I approached. He'd been inside tapping barrels. 'You wanting to charge your phone? Go right on inside – Mary's in the bar.'

'Great, thanks,' I called back.

'How's it going at Old Meg's place? Does it suit you?'

No, so far it sucks actual ass was what I wanted to say but it occurred to me that it would be rude and my phone was in desperate need of a charge so I just said, 'Yeah, it's fine, thanks. Nice and cosy.'

Fintan wasn't buying it. 'Ahh you don't fool me. What do you miss most, electricity is it?'

'Yeah. Electricity. A TV. Flush toilet. A general sense of happiness.'

Fintan belly-laughed. 'Ah yer one for your creature comforts, are you? I know, it's not for everyone.'

'Nned— Nanette has taken to it like a duck to water but, I don't know, the silence is just a bit maddening.'

'Ah well if it's a distraction you want . . .' He disappeared into the cellar and returned moments later with a small black plastic box with a handle on the side. 'Try this for starters. It charges via the handle there or you can leave it in the sunlight for a few hours and it uses solar energy. That'll give you your news, well, your Irish and world news, and a couple of music stations.'

I was oddly moved by this little gesture, even though I thought he might have gone to grab a generator and flat-screen TV and a Netflix subscription or something, but beggars can't be choosers, clearly, and perhaps the little radio would take the edge off my boredom. 'Thank you. That's . . . lovely.'

'No bother,' he said, handing it over.

Maybe I could get used to this small life, I thought as I waited in the pub, nursing a Guinness as my phone charged beside me. If Raf was here, maybe I could get used to the freezing showers and chopping logs to make a cup of tea and all that wilderness shit he's so good at. He'd resented spending all that money on our honeymoon hotel because he knew that to be happy, he didn't need much at all. Just me and a bed and maybe a change of clothes or two. That was enough for him. But without him, all I could think about was what I was lacking. What I couldn't have. And that sliver of discontent was where the rot began to set in.

The rot, in this case, being the man they called Laddy.

I watched him through the pub window, lingering outside the post office. Smoking a stubby cigar and trying to make conversation with anyone who came out – one of the Marys with her basketed bike; Eamon's wife Sheila in her mint gilet, putting her purse away quickly as he came closer. Arti, the woman who ran the post office, came out to change the advert on the A-frame and I could tell his proximity bothered her – at one point he touched her forearm, and she flinched, practically running back inside the shop.

He dropped his cigar to the ground and stamped it out, continuing to linger and eventually wandering in the direction of the pub car park.

'He's like a snake at a rabbit hole, isn't he?' I commented as Starey Mary stoked the fire beside me.

'Laddy McVicker? You should go and introduce yourself to him.' She smiled. 'I don't expect he's ever met anyone like you.'

This surprised me somewhat. 'Fintan said to stay clear of him.'

'Most people do. But you're not most people, are you?' she winked.

Oh fuck. She *had* recognised me then. I made to get up.

'It's all right – I know.' She beamed. 'I know who you are.'

'No, I'm not, I know I look like her and sound like her and—'

'No, it's all right, honest!' She glanced around the empty bar before sitting on the stool opposite me and pressing her hand to her mouth as though holding in giggles. 'Bless us and save us, I thought it was you when you first came in, I just wasn't sure! I'm so happy you're here!'

'It's not me – I'm *not* her.'

'I've got to tell you; I am a massive fan.' Her hand was trembling as she reached out to shake mine.

'Are you?'

'Oh yeah.' She unfurled the collar of her jumper to show the same black seed-shaped badge Billy wore, with a gold fissure. In the centre of the seed it said in German, 'ICH BIN EIN BAD SEED' in gold block caps.

'Oh-kay,' I said, not quite getting the joke.

'It says, "I'm a bad seed" in German.' I still couldn't catch whatever drift she was on. 'There weren't any Irish ones and they'd sold out of the English ones but I saw this one on Etsy and I snapped it up. Only thirty euros.'

'Right,' I said.

Mary did a face that I couldn't gauge. 'You do know what the Bad Seeds are, don't you?'

'Yeah.' I checked the battery on my phone – I could get by on thirty-three per cent for a day or so I figured so I unplugged. 'Well, I best be off . . .'

'Ah no, don't leave. I've scared you off, haven't I?'

'It's not that—'

'You're undercover, I know, but you're safe here. That's probably why Billy sent you here, isn't it? To hide out.'

'Yeah. The prick.'

'No no, I'm sure he meant well. I think you're marvellous, Rhiannon.' She whispered 'Rhiannon' like it was a bad swear she wasn't allowed to repeat. 'I read about what you did for that woman – the one who was raped by those men in the van.'

'Heather Wherryman. And she wasn't raped – I saved her.'

'Yeah, and your friend with the shite husband and that beast who hurt the dog, ahh honest to God, you're a modern-day saint, so you are.'

'I wouldn't go that far,' I scoffed. I *would* go that far but not out loud.

'Honestly, we need more women like you in the world. Ones like *him* just aren't listening but *you* make them listen.' She stared through the window at Laddy, lingering in the car park, chugging his cigar.

'I mostly just make them bleed; I don't really care if they listen.'

Mary laughed, prolonged and high-pitched, and it was

getting on my last tit. I was about to get up and find somewhere else to be miserable with my third-charged phone when she said something else. Something I wasn't expecting:

'You like doll's houses, don't you? I have a wonderful Victorian-era doll's house up in one of the back bedrooms.' She pointed behind her in the vague direction of the velvet curtain. 'Would you like to see it?'

'Um . . .'

'I'll make you a rasher sandwich. Extra crispy?'

'Yeah, all right then.'

As it turns out, it wouldn't take much to Fritzl me into a back room – promise me a play with your doll's house and a bacon sandwich, and I'm in. Not that this was the situation. Indeed, once Mary led me through the curtain, we ascended a back staircase up to the family quarters which were surprisingly light and airy for an old pub. The doll's house Mary mentioned – a *six*-storey one, complete with a lift-the-flap attic – sat in pride of place on the back wall of the second back bedroom, accessible through a short tunnel of cardboard boxes.

'Wow,' I said, as Mary flicked the single bulb light on in the cold gloom. 'It's a proper Victorian one.' It had maids and butlers and a pantry and one of those teeny tiny wooden-seat toilets with ye olde piss stains on it.

'My mammy passed it down to me and her mammy passed it onto her and I think it had been her mammy's too so it's pretty old. I've added bits and pieces to it over the years. I don't get much time to see to it now.'

'It's incredible. Why don't you have it on show anywhere? You could charge people to come and look at it.'

'It's too precious. I let one of Fintan's sister's grandchildren play with it a few years ago and they picked off all the wallpaper in the dining room and undressed both the maids. I felt like crying.'

'I used to have this old neighbour who helped herself to bits from mine – bags of flour, pots of jam, a whole kitchen unit once. Alzheimer's.'

Mary smiled. 'I remember reading about her in your book.'

There were eighteen rooms in the doll's house all lit by tiny lights hanging from the ceilings or wall sconces. I knelt before it and surveyed each and every room and all the tiny detailing throughout.

'I'd always dreamt of having lights in my doll's house. Craig said he'd do it for me one day but never got round to it. He was crap at electrics anyway.'

'Here,' she said, parking a padded pink dressing table stool behind me and lowering me down on it. 'Now you can see it all properly.'

'Thanks. You don't seem like the type who'd be into . . . well, me.'

'Oh I love true crime.' She smiled, eyes twinkling. 'And when I read about you, I don't know, it just ignited something. I think it did the same for a lot of people. All us Bad Seeds. Fintan's a big fan as well. Well, he is now I've told him who you are.'

'*Fintan* knows?' I said.

And as if by magic, the landlord himself appeared at the door with my bacon sandwich, cut neatly into triangles accompanied by a handful of crisps.

'Your sandwich, my good woman. The bird sings if you pull the switch down on the side of the cage.' He crouched down to do just that. 'Only problem with this thing is your hands are too big for it. It's meant for chiselers.'

Mary handed him a pair of tweezers and he used them to yank the switch on the birdcage. 'See?'

'Amazing,' I said as the little bird chirruped and warbled on its perch.

Fintan winked at me while I shoved the little tea tray in the maid's outstretched hands. I don't like men who wink, unless it's a reflex as they lie dying. He had his arm around Mary's shoulder.

'What?' I said, eyeballing them both.

'We're so glad you're here, Rhiannon. Stay as long as you want.'

'Thanks.' They both watched as I tucked into my sandwich.

'I suppose you're sick of all that rabbit food at Old Meg's aren't you? We'll have to see about fattening you up.'

'Thanks. Again,' I said, as the ominous weight of his hand lingered on my shoulder long after they'd both left the room.

What the fuck did *that* mean, "Fatten me up"? Was that just an off-the-cuff remark about a woman's weight that men of a certain age feel duty-bound to make or was there more to it? Were they such feral Bad Seeds that they planned to eat me or something? Was that why he'd showed me the bird cage?

But I wasn't locked in the back bedroom – they hadn't even closed the door – so I brushed off the comment and stayed there for two hours playing, removing furniture and putting it all back in carefully, piece by piece.

While I played, I caught sight of myself in the cracked full-length mirror, leant against the wall. I didn't see the little girl who loved Sylvanians. Or the little girl who jumped on beds with her sister in the dark and lay on hay bales watching the stars and practised French plaits and baked cakes to sell on the roadside. She had gone. And in her place was a grown woman playing with a doll's house. A grown woman with shitly conditioned hair, a bandaged right hand and a shit left one. And everything suddenly felt a bit stupid.

I closed up the doll's house and took my plate downstairs, placing it on the main bar.

'Thanks!' I called out as I left.

'Any time!' Mary called back, practically running in from the kitchen to greet me, a big smile strung between her two red-apple cheeks.

'Why do I feel like that policeman in *The Wicker Man*?' I said aloud as I walked back to Old Meg's. 'What's next – I'm going to come in and find them putting toads in their mouths or cavorting bollock-naked?'

There was no sign of the black-coated weirdo when I left, but back at the cottage, Nnedi had something strange to report. 'Did you leave the house unlocked?' she asked.

'Well yeah, you have the key. There's nothing to nick anyway, is there?'

Her face changed – a sort of wince. 'I think someone's been in here.'

'How do you know?'

'Things were moved – bowls, plates. Your bed was made.'

'Yeah I know, I made it.'

'And this . . .' she said, pointing to the seat cushion on the one armchair where there sat a small, fresh puddle of wet.

'Ugh, fuck's that?'

'I noticed it instantly because it wasn't there before I went out.'

'I didn't do it.'

'I know that. *He's* done it – to mark his territory.'

'Ugh. Today in Men.' I sighed. 'We'll have to burn it.'

'Leaving us with even fewer things to sit on, great.'

'Well, I ain't cleaning his spunk off.'

'I'll get some stuff from the shop.' Nnedi picked up the sheepskin rug and placed it on the back of the chair. 'We'll put that over it when it's dry.'

'Is your bed all right?'

'Yes, nothing untoward. I asked one of the locals what his name was, that woman who works at the post office – and I googled him. Laddy McVicker. I found this.' She showed me her phone screen – a news article about a court appearance years ago, accompanied by a grainy shot of a much younger McVicker coming out of the courthouse in Kilkenny. '"A school caretaker who took photos of young children and behaved indecently towards them has narrowly avoided a custodial sentence." Ugh, he would, wouldn't he?'

'It's notoriously difficult to prosecute if there's no physical abuse.'

I continued to read the article. '"It was suggested Mr McVicker would be 'manageable' within the community and could undertake a programme of rehabilitation . . . suspended sentence, rehab order . . . sexual harm prevention order." What a pile of crusty dicks.'

'It's the maximum they can impose for what he allegedly did.'

'There's no "allegedly" about it. The law is an asshole.'

'An ass.'

'I said what I said.'

'There are a couple of other articles too – one of the female teachers at the school brought a complaint against him for flashing and a receptionist accused him of attempted rape in the school grounds. Seems like his MO is very much what he can take, when he can take it. We should always keep this place locked. Who knows what he might do next.'

'Hmm,' I said. 'Unless I get to him first.'

'Let's not go rocking the boat here, all right?'

'Seems to me this McVicker prick has brought the quarrel boat to *our* shore, no?' I stared down at the wet patch on the chair and glanced up at the axe above the door. 'I'm sleeping with that tonight, just so you know.'

Later that day, after the chair had been thoroughly anti-bac'd and covered with the sheepskin, we ate a light supper of fried kale, courgettes and raw carrots in front of the fire as a storm raged outside, candles all a-flickering. The radio played on the table before us and for a long time we just sat listening to the crackling fire and the melodious violins coming from Ireland's answer to Classic FM.

'Do you ever think about your own death?' Nnedi asked suddenly, thoughtfully chewing on a raw cabbage leaf.

'All the time,' I replied, stroking the gatita against my upper lip.

'Does it scare you?'

'No. You?'

'Yes.'

'But you won't know about it. The *thought* of dying is the worst bit.'

'Like those men you dropped down the hole?'

'Exactly. They had the worst death of all. Some people get a quick dispatch – some feel when it's coming. But if you go suddenly, like an aneurysm, it's probably not that bad. It's just like the lights go out – *boof*!'

'You hounded Lana Rowntree to her death. Do you regret it?'

'What's that quote The Joker says in *The Dark Knight*? "Why should I apologise for the monster I've become? No one ever apologised for making me this way." Lana hurt me. And she knew she hurt me but she big fat did it anyway. Derek Scudd hurt those kids – he knew what he was doing, so I hurt him back. Patrick Whatever-His-Face-Is hurt that dog – so I pushed him down the well. I don't regret any of them because at the time, it felt like the right thing to do.'

'Even AJ?'

The sound of his name and the thought of Ivy's face and button nose and hair just like his stopped me in my tracks. 'Maybe AJ,' I said eventually, those two words tasting bitter on my tongue.

Nnedi smiled, one of her genuine ones before stuffing her mouth with another leaf of kale. Then she turned up the radio. 'Oh listen to this – it's stunning.'

I initially rolled my eyes and by around a minute in, the violins were starting to get on my wick.

'Concerto Number Four in F minor, RV 297, first movement. Allegro non molto by Vivaldi.'

'Gesundheit.'

I put the little woollen gatita down on the armrest and folded my arms in pathetic protest, figuring I could always go out and hide in the toilet until it was over. But then the violins kicked in – I recognised it from some commercial for bog roll. And it was like the sound picked me up and carried me away, like we were in a dance in my head, spiralling, twirling, running with me down dark corridors, wrenching me around, pulling me in and out of new rooms where the lights and sounds were all around me, and finally, finally, holding me in its arms and bringing me to an abrupt but satisfying stop. I had goose bumps popping up all over my back and forearms.

'I said do you want another coffee?' said Nnedi. The song had ended, and I hadn't even noticed.

'Uh yeah, thanks.'

By the time the programme was through, Nnedi had introduced me to Dvorak, 'The Planets' (Mars – absolute banger), La Campanella 'Nocturne in E minor' and *Samson et Dalila*'s 'Bacchanale' by Saint-Saens.

'Did you enjoy that?'

'No. Of course not,' I said. 'It was well boring. Give me "Wet Ass Pussy" by Cardi B any day of the week.' I leant forward and turned off the dreary presenter banging on. Nnedi smiled – another rare genuine one. It changed her whole face. Like when Roy Kent smiles – it feels like you've earned it.

'What was that?' she said, placing the mugs quietly on the table.

'What was what?'

'Turn the radio down.' She went to the window and looked out.

'I didn't hear anything.'

I joined her at the window, peering out at nothing untoward – a full moon glinting down upon the veg in the raised beds, all quietly growing away. A slight breeze rattling the door of the toilet shed. 'The door rattling do you mean?'

'No, not that. Something else.' She picked up one of the lanterns and turned it on, handing it to me while she picked up the other one and doing the same again. Carefully, she opened the cottage door and stood on the doorstep. I took down the axe from the wall above her.

She glanced back at me.

'Just in case.' I shrugged.

'Give it here,' she said, taking it from me. 'You stay here.'

'No, I want to come. What did you hear for fuck's sake?'

'A scream,' she said. 'Sounded like someone was in trouble.'

'Oh Christ,' I groaned. 'If it's that banshee, we're gonna need more than an axe. I'll get the Bible, maybe that'll spirit it back to Satan's arsehole or wherever it's from.'

'You won't need that – I'll look round the back, you take the lane.'

Apart from a few footprints in the mud which we'd probably made ourselves, there was nothing and no one about as I swished my lantern around the lane and the trees by the roadside, illuminating the blustery air.

I was about to shout 'Clear' to Nnedi when a terrible noise pierced through the darkness bringing me to a halt.

A loud, crisp wail, some distance away but echoing through the trees.

'Jesus Christ,' I muttered, going back inside the garden gate.

Nnedi emerged from the back of the house – wild-eyed, her lantern shaking in her hand. 'You heard that, right? Tell me you heard that.'

'Yeah, I heard it. It sounded close.'

'Come on, let's go back in. If it is a banshee, we're dead anyway.'

I didn't like that feeling of being scared. It was anathema to me usually but just of late, it wore a different effect. I felt weak with it. When Nnedi had asked me if I was afraid of dying I'd said no; force of habit. But the truth was hard to ignore – I *was* afraid of dying. Because I had something to live for now. And I was on fire to get back to it.

That sort of bonded me and Nnedi, that little sojourn into the windy night to find the source of the screaming, and together we barricaded the door with the heavy water jugs and found every sharp blade in the place to sit with until morning. Nnedi seemed scared – I could tell fear on a person's face now.

So I didn't mention the fact that when we got back inside the cottage, my little woollen gatita had vanished from the arm of my chair.

Sunday, 24 October – Day 3
in Aoibhneas

1. *Internet randoms who take it upon themselves to tell every single person in the world how loved and seen they are – I feel much better now. So good in fact that I'd love to see you with a cleaver through your skull.*
2. *Bill Cosby. Have I done him before? I feel like I've done him.*
3. *Prince Andrew. Feel like I've done him before too. Christ – think I'm running out.*
4. *People who don't eat until late – aka, Nnedi. Like, how do you not get hungry at 5 p.m., aka, teatime. What is this eating at 9 p.m. crap? She says some days she 'forgets to eat'. I truly think she is a robot.*
5. *People who can't make a decent cup of coffee – e.g., Nnedi.*

I had a dream about Raf last night that was so real, I woke up twiddling the tassel of the cushion by my head, thinking it was his ear. The disappointment of opening my eyes and realising I was still in the damp-earth-stinking-shit-in-a-barrel-shower-in-a-wooden-box fleapit was truly soul-crushing.

Worse still, as of this morning, there were rumours of a

new lockdown for Ireland later this month, possibly into December. Christmas was on the rocks, officially, again. Nobody knew for sure, even the Taoiseach or senior health officials – but the country's in its fourth wave and Mary and Fintan and Arti at the shop had already started doubling up on supplies. Some had booked flights out of the country for the holidays.

I still couldn't find the gatita and there was still no word from Billy or Raf. I'd been back to the pub a couple of times to try their numbers again with a full signal, but it was the same old story – one unrecognised and one *This number no longer exists*. The pinch of dread returned to my chest.

To compound my anxiety, I received the rude awakening of a blood-curdling scream and Nnedi bashing at the kitchen flagstones with the axe.

'That your idea of an alarm call, is it?' I croaked.

'It was a shrew!' she said, still all up in the air as her eyes never left the flagstones and she swept with the end of the broken broom under the counter and stove. 'Bloody thing – it scurried in as I was bringing in the logs.'

The freshly chopped logs had been dropped beside the open front door and had splintered all over the place.

'Oh right.' I yawned.

'It's a bloody shrew; will you help me!?'

'No, what's your problem? Shrews are tiny.'

'They carry disease!'

'No, they don't, look at where we are – we're surrounded by fields. It's probably a dormouse, looking for a crumb. I need a coffee.'

'We need a fire first if you want coffee,' she said, still scanning the place for our furry intruder.

'Oh yeah. I forgot we live in the fucking IRON AGE,' I sulked, stomping over to the wood basket and chucking it into the hearth. As I was packing it in and lighting the matches, I watched her, gingerly lifting tea towels, scanning the flagstones and sneak-opening cupboards.

'What are you going to do if you find it?' I asked her.

'What do you *think* I'm going to do? Kill it, of course.'

'Oh right,' I said. 'Seems oddly hypocritical.'

'Excuse *me*?' she said, looking up from the dustpan and brush.

'Killing an innocent creature for no good reason.'

'It could get into our food. Isn't that reason enough?'

I laughed. 'You're a little more like me than you care to think, aren't you? You had murder in your eyes when that horse was chomping on your Per Una.' She batted her eyes and scanned the room for small movements.

I noticed something on the draining board and reached out to her slowly for the dustpan. 'Gimme.'

I moved silently towards the bread board and tore off a chunk of wholemeal. I placed it in the dustpan and crept closer to the shrew washing its paws by the sink. In one swift movement, I bodged the rescue effort: the shrew got nowhere near the dustpan, I tripped over the axe and Nnedi screamed as we both watched the creature scurry across the draining board, drop to the flagstones and dash through the open door, his cheeks full of bread.

'Well, at least it's gone,' said Nnedi, breathless with laughter. We stood on the doorstep watching it disappear into the greenery. We spotted the man at the same time and took a step back in unison. He was outside the gate, stock still and smiling – Laddy McVicker.

'Can we help you?' called Nnedi, belligerently.

He said nothing, carried on puffing a stubby cigar and staring.

'What's the bet it was him screaming in the woods last night?' I muttered, looking back inside the cottage for the axe and grabbing it from where it was, leant against the doorframe. 'What do you want?' I hollered.

His cigar end flamed orange and he exhaled a big grey cloud into the air. Then, just when I thought he might continue on down the track, he reached over the gate and flicked up the catch and came inside our garden. But he didn't come towards us – he went left, straight into the toilet shed.

'He's using our toilet,' said Nnedi through gritted teeth.

'Urgh. One or two?'

She glared at me. 'Gimme that.' She snatched the axe from me but didn't move from the doorstep.

After a good five minutes, the creep crept out of the shed, zipping his trousers; coat brushing against the runner bean poles and kale leaves, and off he went, through the gate, puffing on his cigar and throwing us a brief smile as he started down the lane towards the village.

'The actual fuh—?' I started, marching with ill-judged confidence towards the bog. I could smell it before I saw it. He hadn't even had the decency to shovel sawdust on top of it. 'Ugh.'

He'd crept in, crapped and crept out again.

His cigar smoke hung in the air as I peered over the gate and watched his retreating black coat down the track.

'They do this, some men. Mark their territory. A mate of Craig's called Nigel was like this, every time he came round to watch the football. He'd save up his biggest shit of the day and park it in our loo.'

Nnedi took the axe from me. 'Come on. I'll put the kettle on.'

'Can we have the radio on again?' I said. 'You know, as we work?'

After cleaning the toilet and doing all the other daily chores the cottage demanded – wood chopping, water gathering – we made our way up the track to the pub for an early dinner and a charge of our phones. I was so starving I ordered the works – tempura prawns and chilli dip to start, a 10oz burger with triple-cooked chips and giant onion rings for mains, and sticky toffee pudding with custard for afters. And I was still hungry after that.

Cue the derisive glances from opposite, of course.

'That looks disgusting,' she'd sneered as I'd noshed on my dirty flame-grilled burger with extra cheese.

'"Presentation is there for thirty seconds – it's the flavour that holds the memory."' Gordon Ramsay. Sage of our times.

She set aside her half-finished no-dressing Caesar salad and glass of water to lean in. 'Fintan is treating us to our dinner here – you could have at least ordered something small.'

'God, you're like my mother. I'll pay him if it offends you so much.'

'That's not the point.'

'Look, I've had a trying day, I'm not in the mood for yet another lecture on How to Act Like a Lady, thanks. I just want to amuse my bouche, get shitfaced on Irish whiskey, go home and have a wank, all right? I've got chronic horn today. Have we got any of those courgettes left back at the ranch?'

'NO.'

'Killjoy.'

Mary brought out a big bowl of ice cream, which I hadn't

ordered but she thought I would like anyway (kiss ass), although I did eat it. And afterwards, Fintan brought over our coffees – a whacking great Americano bucket for me; small and dainty espresso for Nnedi – and set them down in front of us. He and Nnedi chit-chatted about the area and some local points of interest and just when the conversation descended to the level of boredom where I normally want to throw myself through a window, I interjected.

'Has Billy called yet?'

'No, haven't heard from him.'

I didn't think he had but Fintan's answer still frustrated me. I pushed my coffee away.

Nnedi cleared her throat. 'Fintan – that man in the long coat, we've had some trouble with him.'

His face instantly went all cliff-faced and hard. 'Oh, have you? What's he done now?'

'Well,' she began, avoiding his eyes, clearly struggling with how to relay the information daintily. So I helped her out.

'He curled one out in our bog.'

'Ugh, that man is a disgrace. Be dog wide of him, ladies. He's bad news.'

'Well yeah, we figured that much out for ourselves, but who is he?'

Fintan pulled up a padded beer keg serving as a bar stool and leant into us. 'He's lived here since the late Nineties and he's been done for . . . you know, bad behaviour with kids.'

'We know,' Nnedi groaned, glancing at me. 'I googled him.'

Fintan's eyes had got glassy. 'Ah right so you'll know all about it then. Then he moved out here to Colm's, his brother's place, just after the school court case. And I remember the date too – it was September 2001 when he moved in. The removals vans came the day before 9/11, that's why it sticks in my mind. Colm got cancer not long after and when he died, Laddy took the gaff over. I didn't like the fella from the moment I met him – shifty eyes. Not just cos he'd never stand his round or help out during bad weather. He didn't fit. Then word got around about what he did at the school . . .'

'Allegedly,' said Nnedi.

'Yes well, we didn't give him the benefit of the doubt anymore, once we knew about that. Since then he's been a pariah. The banshee's more welcome round here than him. You shouldn't have any more bother.'

Fintan's whole demeanour had changed – he'd come over to us with all the jollity of the happy fat ghost in *The Muppet Christmas Carol* but now, he looked like a tracing of that guy. 'Any more problems with him, ladies, you come up here and we'll make you some beds up in the back. There's a bit of damp up there but at least you'll be safe. He's barred from in here permanently after the way he spoke to you the other day.'

'Thank you, but I'm sure we'll be fine,' said Nnedi.

'Yeah, we've got an axe and we ain't afraid to use it,' said me.

Fintan winked and made his way behind the bar to deposit our empties. Nnedi was clearly heavy with thought.

'Penny for them,' I said. 'Unless they've gone up with the cozzy livs in which case, you can keep 'em.'

'Hmm?' she said. 'No, nothing. Come on, I'm ready for bed.'

We grabbed our now fully charged phones and walked back to Old Meg's aided by our torch lights. We found a working padlock and key in a messy drawer in Old Meg's dresser that affixed to the catch on the toilet and even though Nnedi kept yawning and saying how tired she was, she wasn't in any hurry to scurry up her ladder, preferring to linger in Old Meg's armchair, staring at the flickering candlelight on her breath, pondering.

A gentle storm blew up outside but not enough to rattle the roof tiles. Our dirt track was a proper wind tunnel and all manner of whistles and howls stirred around the cottage for hours. The candlelight illuminated corners of the large cottage room I hadn't noticed before – Old Meg's collection of Pampas grasses and decorative feathers in a large glass vase on the floor by the fire. Tiny driftwood ornaments she'd whittled, lined up all along the wooden eaves.

'What the fuck is Billy up to?' I barked to no one in particular. 'Why's he taking so long?'

'I imagine he's keeping his distance until he knows for sure he's not being followed.'

'Why would *he* be followed?'

'Because if the world now knows you are Ophelia White, aka Rhiannon Lewis, aka the Sweetpea Killer, the authorities will be checking your footprints – if they discover that Ophelia White left San Diego on a flight to Heathrow, first place they'll check is who you were flying with.'

'We didn't fly together. We did get stopped by security at Heathrow and claim we were eloping. We had to – my documents got flagged cos I had my married name on one and Ophelia White on another.'

'There you are then. He's probably waiting for the dust to settle.'

'How long's that going to take?'

'As long as it takes.' She sighed.

I sulked. Every now and again, one of us would get up and check behind the tea towels we'd pinned up at the windows for signs of McVicker, but there was nothing to be found and our padlock had firmly put the kibosh on any more of his visits to our bog.

'Maybe it's Laddy's night off,' I suggested. We still dragged the water jugs up against the bolted door and sat watching the fire in the hearth, sipping Meg's whiskey from jam jars and talking openly.

'I don't know what I'm more afraid of,' she said, taking a sip. 'What his intentions are if he comes back or what *yours* are if you get hold of him.'

I laughed. 'If he knows what's good for him, he *won't* come back.' I had the axe resting against my torso and craned my head to lick the blade just to disgust her. It did the trick.

She stood up and studied the shelves behind her, looking for a book.

'Far left, third one along.'

She pulled it out. '*The Wind in the Willows*?'

'Yeah. Read a bit to me. The bit about Badger. I think it's Chapter 4.'

And she did – she read out the whole chapter.

'". . . in the embracing light and warmth, warm and dry at last, with weary legs propped up in front of them . . . it seemed to the storm-driven animals, now in safe anchorage, that the cold and trackless Wild Wood just left outside was miles away, and all that they had suffered in it a half-forgotten dream . . ."'

'You've got the best voice for reading aloud,' I said dreamily, my eyes rolling. 'It's like Nytol.'

'Why did you want me to read that?'

'I like it,' I said. 'My friend Marnie – I always thought she was a bit like Mole, stuck underground, scared of the Wild Wood. Caro – she was this woman I met on my cruise around the Med when I was on the run – she reminded me of Badger. Hates society. Strict. Takes none of Toad's shit.'

'And you're Toad, I suppose?'

'A bloody idiot always getting himself into trouble? Yeah. I'm all Toad.'

'Terrible driver too.' Nnedi closed the book. 'I guess that makes me Ratty, does it?'

'Nah, you're way too routined. Ratty likes messing about on the river and writing poetry and stuff. But maybe if you let yourself go a bit.'

She leant forward. 'Listen, talking of animals, I checked our kitty today – we've got just over a thousand pounds left.'

'Where the hell's the rest gone?'

'Rent, food, the usual. It's not going to last forever.'

'Billy will be here soon, I know he will,' I said, trying to glance over the positive side of the fence for once. 'He *is* like Ratty – dependable, loyal, bit of a dreamer but we can rely on him. I think.'

Neither of us said anything for a while, just sipped our whiskey and stared into the fire.

'Why do you sleep with that?' she asked, looking at the TMNT shirt.

'It's Raf's.'

'There's blood on it.'

'It's my blood. I smashed a glass – that's how I hurt my palm. It doesn't smell of him anymore. It smells of woodsmoke.'

'I fell in love once. Nobody warns you how much it hurts – you crave it when you're young and when it comes, all of a sudden, you don't expect it to be so all-encompassing. To infect your life; to depend on it quite so much.'

'I had a friend who said it's like an open door that neither of you want to walk through.'

Nnedi nodded. 'Yes. I can see that. But in my case, it still had its restrictions. I would have had to give up my job for him. Luckily, he cheated before I got the chance.'

'Luckily?'

'At the time I thought that. I knew if we stayed together – if he had been true – I'd have given everything up for him. Career, prospects. I'd have moved to France where he wanted to go for his job, to be near *his* parents. I'd have gone there and lived a smaller life. In a way, his cheating saved me.'

'But you regret it now?'

She shook her head. 'No. I'd maybe have liked to live in France but he wasn't right for me. I haven't trusted a man since. Any man I would meet now has to contend with the peace I have found without him. I prefer being alone.'

'I'm no good on my own. I'll always need something. Someone. You're stronger than I am.'

'Had to be. You trust Rafael though?'

I twiddled the tassel on a cushion corner. 'You know that bit in the Bryan Adams song where he goes something something I'd walk the wire for you, I'd die for you, something something.'

'"Everything I Do, I Do It for You",' said Nnedi.

'Yeah, that's it. That's Raf. He's done all that for me, almost died for me. He took three bullets for me.'

'That's why he's in hospital?'

I nodded. My voice came out all wobbly. 'Despite knowing who I am, what I've done. Seren told me once that Priory

235

Gardens had smashed all the love out of me. But Raf found it again. I've never had that before. Unconditional love.'

'You still *have* that,' she reminded me.

I scoffed. 'Maybe in some parallel universe. Raf showed me this French movie once – *Amélie*?'

'Yeah, I've seen it.'

'He's always trying to get me to watch these boring-assed subtitled movies cos my taste in films is awful, but I couldn't stand most of them. *Belleville Rendezvous*. *À Bout de Souffle*. Some weird one about a dwarf and a brain in a vat. But *Amélie* I liked.'

'Me too,' she said.

'Do you remember the end, when Amélie gets her guy and she's on the back of his motorbike, and they're careening down these cobbled streets? And the camera's all shaky and they almost fall off, and he keeps taking his hands off the handlebars to scare her. Everything feels uncertain. Too fast. Too shaky. But she holds on to him and closes her eyes and none of it matters – as long as she's got him, she's okay. That's how I feel about Raf. Grown-up me is a monster – but six-year-old Rhiannon *wasn't*. She never got to live her life. She deserves to be happy. I always used to think there was a parallel universe where Other Me was living a better life sans brain damage, sans killing people. But there isn't one, is there? There's just this one.'

'As far as we know.'

'Did your husband want you to move to Paris?'

'No. Provence. God, why am I telling you all this?' She laughed. 'Must be the whiskey.' She set down her glass.

'Your prefrontal cortex is being shut down by alcohol. Mine was shut down by a hammer so I'm permanently loose-lipped.'

Nnedi smiled. 'We might have had a nice life over there, I don't know. I get the feeling I would have got bored with him eventually. Maybe Parallel Nnedi's sipping Châteauneuf du Pape and picking lavender, surrounded by babies.' Her face changed as she hugged her drink to her chest and stared into the fire.

'So what does the future hold for *this* universe's Nnedi then? You said you had nothing to go back to.'

'I don't.'

'Just cats and dildos the whole way down then, is it?'

Nnedi threw me the look everyone throws me when I've said something a bit too real.

'What makes you think I like cats?'

That made me laugh. It made her laugh too. It was a weird cosy moment between us before reality descended once again.

'I don't know,' she said, her face straightening out. 'At one point I was prepared to march down to the nearest egg-freezing clinic with my knickers in my handbag. But I didn't want to do it enough to do it alone. And I like my peace too much. Once you've found peace within yourself, it's very difficult to go along with the idea of inviting anyone else into your life.'

She chuckled but stopped herself, like someone had reminded her she was with a serial killer and there was nothing funny about that.

'Talking of France, me and Craig had a weekend in Paris once,' Some anniversary.

Went on the Eurostar. Saw the Venus de Milo. Ate horse. I didn't realise it was horse, of course I just saw "burger" on the menu. I thought *cheval* meant hair.'

'That's *cheveux*,' said Nnedi.

'Isn't that hat?'

'That's *chapeau*.'

'Oh.'

'You thought you were ordering a *hair* burger?'

'I don't know what I thought. I was starving and I saw "burger" and my fat ass ordered it.'

Nnedi laughed again, loud and true. I think it was the pent-up stress leaking out. She eased herself out of her chair. 'Do you want some tea?'

'Yeah, go on then.'

She went out to the toilet for a wee while the kettle was boiling and I stood at my post at the back door and watched out for her as she crept down the path with an oil lamp like Florence Nightingale (we were spotting each other in case Shitty McSneaksabout returned).

We'd forgotten ourselves for the last half an hour, chatting like two housemates. She wasn't so guarded or held in. I wasn't so sarcastic or wanting to lash out. It was comfortable. The raw ache in my chest from missing Raf had been dulled by whiskey, firelight and good company.

Then I heard a buzzing from the side of Old Meg's armchair: Nnedi's phone.

I didn't get there in time to answer it but she had three bars of signal and an unread voicemail message. From 'Jai A'.

Jai Amarkeeri. I remembered where I'd seen that name before. A news article – *Detective Sergeant Jai Amarkeeri* – the new CIO in charge of the Sweetpea case.

'*We have received information from a number of sources . . .*'

'*She won't slip through the net for long . . .*'

When Nnedi returned, I closed the cottage door and stood

by it with the axe at my side, watching her go back to her seat; waiting for her to take out the phone and look at the screen. But she didn't.

'"Memory, Agent Starling, is what I have instead of a view,"' I said, still in the doorway.

'What was that?' she said. The wind howled outside so it didn't surprise me that she hadn't heard me.

'"You fly to bed now, little Starling. Fly, fly, fly."'

'Don't you want your tea?' I shook my head. She moved the kettle away from the fire. 'Yes, I suppose it is a bit late.'

'Too late for you,' I said, and this time she didn't hear. Or maybe she was faking. With someone like Nnedi, you can never tell.

Monday, 25 October – Day 4 in Aoibhneas

1. *Tiny villages where every bastard you see, you HAVE to stop and have a bloody conversation. It's like, the law.*
2. *Séan who uses the word 'grand' in every sentence. 'Oh one of me sheep's having quads – so that'll be grand. Oh did you see there might be another lockdown coming? That'll be grand. I caught me feckin' leg in the mangle again, Mary, isn't that grand?'*
3. *Winston Churchill – apparently, he was a shit to the Irish. Can't remember what he did but they still hate him for it.*
4. *Nnedi Géricault, cos backstabbing Judas, obvs.*

Another night, another nightmare – this time, I was back arguing in the car with Seren, except this time it was the banshee in the passenger seat, covered in blood and Seren was in the back, holding a seatbelt to my neck, and screaming in my ear: *My kids! What about my kids!?*

I felt like that dude in *An American Werewolf in London* when his dead mate keeps popping up in various stages of decay, telling him to kill himself.

Was that the message Seren was trying to send me from

beyond the grave? Kill myself to atone for getting *her* killed? No way. That's her problem. But my chest did clench at the thought of Ashton and Mabli being in the UK and so excited to see their mum only to learn they'd never see her again. They didn't deserve that. And that was my fault.

When I awoke, it wasn't the banshee screaming but the kettle in the grate. Nnedi was making the coffee. I caught sight of myself in the mirror – hella sex hair and a Tayto stuck to my cheek. Stunning.

'Could you pick the kale for lunch please?' she asked, stirring the *ThunderCats* mug and handing it to me. 'My back's on the blink this morning.' She started doing some yoga poses in the hearth so I got out of her way.

I know it's stupid – *beyond* stupid that I had thought of Nnedi as anything other than a detective, not least one whom I had started to like – but the truth was, I had. I'd made the age-old mistake of thinking I could have a friend in her somewhere. I had ignored Billy's advice to be 'dog wide of her' and done what I always did – dared to believe she was different. Dared to see the shoots of friendship but they were just the shoots of betrayal.

I'd done the same thing with girls at school, like Julia Kidner, and look how *that* ended up. I'd done it with the PICSOs too initially, and people at work, like Daisy Chan. Craig. Marnie from The Pudding Club. One moment they're my friend; the next, they're abandoning me or letting me down from the highest height. I hated Nnedi that morning. Every word out of her mouth seemed dusted in lies and every answer I gave was short.

By the time she was up, I'd done all the chores and made the porridge. I left her bowl to cool and went out to pick the veg, wheeling the wheelbarrow towards the back door, full of kale leaves and muddy carrots.

'Did you harvest all that?' she asked, leaning on the frame, bleary-eyed and big-haired.

I barged past her, swishing on my coat. 'Yes.'

'Well done.'

'I don't need praise from you.'

'I know you don't. It's just not like you to do so much in the morning. You usually need about three coffees before you get your eyes open.'

'Yeah well. People change. I'm going out.'

'It's only 7 a.m.'

'So?'

'Where are you going?'

I glared at her, zipped up my coat and started off down the path.

'It's going to tip it down in a minute!' she called, glancing up at the sky.

'I'll get wet then, won't I?'

Outside the pub where the signal was best, I tried Raf's phone again but it was the same old story – wouldn't connect. My wrist was throbbing from my ill-advised wank with a courgette in the dead of night and I ached for my brace which would have eased the pressure loads.

'Where are you?' I said aloud. 'Fuck you, Billy, fuck you both!'

I immediately regretted incorporating Raf into that Fuck You but the frustration was real. I needed news; I needed someone to tell me something good was going to happen soon or I was going to go out of my mind. Again. I scrolled the Bad Seeds Tumblr page, fishing for anything to take the frustration away.

From 'The Bad Seeds' Tumblr

Dear Sweetpea,

I'm sick of being afraid. If I'm on a train, if I'm at a bar. If I'm walking across the parking lot at work. Why do we always have to be on our guard? It isn't fair! I seem to be surrounded by assholes! Catcalling, groping me as I pass. So so sick of it.

My boyfriend demands sex every night. Just lately, he's started choking me and getting real upset if I complain. He says his "marks on me look good and only he can see them." But I can feel them and I hate it! I've started using excuses for why I can't go around to his house, like my mum and dad have started getting really strict, but I'm running out of excuses!

The other reason I don't like going around there is his dad stares at my chest. I've been real well developed since I was, like, twelve so they're big but when he looks at me it's always at my chest, never my face and it's not like I wear slutty stuff. Like, just sweaters and T-shirts, but he always, *always* looks and it makes me so mad!

I wish I had your bravery. I feel like I'm trapped in this situation now cuz if I break up with him, I get the feeling he won't take no for an answer. I'm scared of what he might do. He's got these pictures of me that I only sent him because he kept calling me frigid. He's kept them all. I'm sure I only sent, like, five or something.

There's a guy in the local paper this week who's been caught touching up women on a bus route that I take sometimes. There are so many of these assholes out here. The first dick I ever saw was some guy's on a train who whipped it out to show me and my friends. Our teachers were like *Move along please, nothing to see here*, but it was traumatizing, man. How do we deal with this shit on a daily basis? There are creeps everywhere!

What do we do, Rhiannon? Well, I know exactly what you'd do. All those men you've murdered. All those assholes who aren't getting away with it anymore, because of you. I wish I were you, Sweetpea. I wish I could do that. Then maybe it would all just stop. And we could stop being afraid.

from E in Aurora, Colorado

You know you're fucked when you start asking me for advice. *What do we do, Rhiannon* – huh, as though I'm the go-to on how life should be lived. In my experience, you shank them in the ribs until they stop breathing and then go merrily on with your day but I guess old E from Aurora was not in the right frame of mind to reenact that when she reached out to vent on Tumblr. Unless you've got a broken head like mine, you're going to fear stuff, that's just the way it is, sadly, for most people. That hammer smashed the fear out of me so I couldn't really relate to E in Aurora. And society doesn't permit the kind of justice I'd want to mete out in this situation, so women have three choices: put up with it, stand your ground, or run.

It's not fair, is it?

I thought about this a lot as I walked, thinking how unfair it is that society is so skewed to the predator in these scenarios and how few rape cases go to trial and how many stalking cases end with murder/suicide. There's no solution to it all. While erections rule the world, there never will be. But I satisfied myself with the knowledge that E in Aurora's situation would never be mine. I would never be so stupid as to put myself in that situation. To put myself in any kind of risk when I couldn't get myself out of it.

And then it happened to me.

I don't know how long I walked for – long enough for the scenery to change from sheep-filled fields to empty fields, from potholed roads to flat, wide ones and for the dark grey sky to become blue. I thought about a thousand things as I wandered.

Nnedi's predictable betrayal.

Seren's body in a cold morgue drawer, speckled with frost.

Billy, somewhere between the Cotswolds and here.

Rafael in his hospital bed, wondering what the hell was happening.

Ivy, on a plane to Tenerife, in her little sheep slippers, kicking off because the air stewardess forgot to give her a colouring book. Maybe Richard E. Grunt was sat on her lap and she was feeding him nuts. He liked peanuts.

I went farther, through fields thick with mud until the blue sky turned grey again and the rain came down, and the more I walked, the more lost I became. The police were coming for me – that's what the call from Amarkeeri meant. What else could it mean? Nnedi was in cahoots with him and I was in the shit, once again. Any day now those sirens would ring out over the hill and the sky would fill with a dozen flashing blue lights. No wonder she was enjoying this bloody place so much.

There was only one thing for it if I wanted to get back to Raf: I'd have to kill her. Kill her, steal the car and . . . and what? I couldn't think straight while I was so lost. My head was as tangled as my unwashed hair.

I decided to turn back, making it back to the crossroads

where I had gone wrong. There was a sign in Irish that I couldn't read and one in English which I could – 'Aoibhneas Geolbhach [Aoibhneas Gill]'. 'Shortcut to Little Aoibhneas Lough', which fed the stream where we got our water. Finally, something I recognised. I followed the trail down a narrow tree-lined path – a 'holloway' that walkers had trodden through for many years. It sat lower than the land on either side of it, bordered by gnarled trees, some with their roots visible through the banks. There were deep animal holes too, probably home to foxes or badgers, but nobody was about except me. The trees provided some form of shelter from the elements at least, but the farther I walked, the narrower and darker the holloway grew.

I hadn't seen another soul about for the entire way around, but it never ceases to amaze me how anywhere you go – in any area of any country on God's earth – if you're a woman walking alone in a lonely area, at some point you will encounter a man walking on his own. I can almost guarantee it.

And of course, it was him. Old crusty peen himself, Laddy McVicker.

The looming shaggy-black-haired man who'd fired a load of racist abuse at Nnedi in the pub and who'd been lingering outside the shop and who'd helped himself to our toilet. Long black coat. Trilby hat. Not walking a dog or carrying a newspaper. No obvious reason why he was walking this way that early. And huge too, bigger than he was in my memory.

'Fuck's sake,' I huffed as the rain pelted down around me. I pulled my coat tighter and kept walking towards him. I had forgotten one of my cardinal rules: *Be prepared*.

I had no weapon, not so much as a credit card that could slice an eyeball. It was just me and him, walking towards each other, three hundred metres apart, in an incredibly narrow stretch of wooded wasteland bordering a stream. There was nowhere to run. And he wasn't turning back.

He was twice the size of me. I couldn't take him with my bare hands. He had me right where he wanted me. Alone. Unarmed. Afraid? Yeah, I had to admit it. Without a weapon – something to rely on – I was afraid. Weakened again. Just like E from Aurora.

I hated that.

And for the first time, I felt like your average woman, walking alone. Dry mouthed. Shaking. Every ounce of confidence dried up completely with the knowledge that if this man wanted me, there was nothing I could do. He outweighed me by at least five stone. It would be like a pebble trying to smash a boulder. However much anger I had; however much I screamed or kicked or went for the throat, he could do what he liked. But I still walked towards him.

Halfway along the gill, I bent down as though tying my shoelace and glanced up. He'd shortened the gap by fifty metres and was still walking.

'Bastard,' I muttered, standing upright and quickening my step; going further towards the danger, not away from it. Any right-minded woman would turn on her heel and walk the other way, but not this woman. Despite the obvious advantage Laddy held, I still somehow thought I could best him. Rhiannon Lewis does not walk away from danger – she marches towards it.

What a twat.

About another hundred metres to go and he was gaining on me all the time – his one stride easily matching my two. My breath came out in short bursts – I know! Me! Rhiannon

Lewis. Killer of twenty-seven whole-assed predators at last count. Or was it twenty-eight?

The woman who ripped off a man's penis and pushed him in a canal.

Who cut up her baby daddy in a bathtub.

The suffocater of paedophiles.

The axe *murderer*.

But without a knife, without any weapon, I was toast and I knew it. Another quick glance around gave me one idea – a short, thick tree branch which, when wielded correctly, could cause some damage. Not as much as a knife but it would have to do. I picked it up. It was rain-soaked and the underside was caked in mud but I brandished it before me.

Then I realised I had other weapons at my disposal – my voice, my anger and at least three working limbs that could lash out with the best of 'em. Whatever he wanted from me could not match the ardour I felt to kill him.

Except I didn't need my weapons. Before I could utter a damn word, another voice called out:

'OI. YOU!'

Laddy turned around and we both looked to see another figure walking behind him, about a hundred metres back. It was Nnedi.

Laddy stopped. I couldn't see his face for the rain and his trilby hat which hung low. I waited for him to react – to sprout wings and spring ten feet into the air and hover over me or something like The Creeper, but he just stared back at her. And then he turned to look at me.

'Any closer and I will smash your fucking brains out,' I warned him.

His hand reached into his coat. I expected a knife but he

pulled out a half-smoked cigar and a lighter. He shoved the cigar in his mouth and, shielded from the rain by his hat, he lit it – he was close enough that I could hear the click. He walked towards me again.

'YOU COME ANY CLOSER AND I WILL END YOU.'

And he laughed. 'I have to go somewhere, don't I?'

Nnedi rounded him, eyeballing him all the way – I could see the axe tucked into her belt under her coat, dangling beside her leg. She stood beside me and we both climbed a few feet up one side of the bank to let him pass.

'Sure I was only walking, you daft bitches,' he muttered, puffing his cigar and trundling on past, stinking of tobacco and body odour. 'It's a free country, isn't it?'

'Someone like you never walks anywhere without a very specific reason,' Nnedi hissed.

'Didn't I tell you to go back to where you came from?' he said, with an added grapeshot of vile names which seemed to push the button he'd been trying to get at since we arrived.

'You degenerate pervert,' she spat back at him.

He slowly turned back to face us. 'Aww, that hurts my feelings.'

I glanced at her, brandishing the thick branch like a baseball bat and readying myself to swing. 'Just one, *please*? There's no one about.'

'NO!' Nnedi barked.

Laddy smirked at me as he passed by, cigar shoved between his lips and both palms up in surrender.

'You're a fucking dead man,' I jeered.

He tutted and shook his head. 'Is minic a bhris béal duine a shrón.'

We watched him walk farther away before eventually

coming to the end of the gill and disappearing altogether. I'm ashamed to admit I was relieved.

'Did he just put a spell on us?'

'No idea. But he wasn't exactly contrite, was he?' said Nnedi.

I glanced at the axe. 'Would you have used that?'

She didn't answer directly. 'He used our toilet again. I followed him this time, to see where he went.' Her three-fingered hand was trembling.

'Thanks but I don't need you to save me,' I snipped, carrying on with my walk and yeeting the log into a hedge.

Neither of us said another word until we were at the back of the cottage.

'What's wrong with you today? You've woken up terribly grumpy, which isn't unusual I know . . .'

'Time of the month,' I spat, in no mood to look at her, let alone launch into the whole Jai Amarkeeri thing. I didn't want to sit down, I didn't want to make myself any more at home here. I wanted to go back outside and just keep walking – go down to the harbour and pay for a boat that would get me away – get me back out onto the water and sailing in Rafael's direction. But I couldn't, could I? I was stuck. Stuck in the middle of nowhere, thousands of miles from the one thing I wanted. Powerless.

Back there, in that holloway, I was that little girl watching *Fireman Sam* again. Sitting helpless as the man smashed his way through the patio doors with a hammer. Helpless. Hopeless. Human. Just a woman alone in the world with nothing to protect her. Except Nnedi. Begrudgingly, annoyingly, hatefully. I was glad she'd been there.

We were almost at a wide enough point in the hedge that we could climb through and take a short cut to the cottage rather than go all the way around to the front gate, when I stopped.

Nnedi almost walked into me. We looked down – there were cigar butts on the wet ground, opposite the shower bag on the metal gallows. He had a view of us whenever we showered.

'Ugh.' I glanced at her and she stared at the cigar butts and looked around as though to check his eyes weren't still on us somehow.

When we got back inside, I removed my coat to hang it up to dry on the back of the door and she started washing and peeling carrots at the sink. I chucked a few logs onto the dying fire, unnerved to see my hand was shaking. I wished I had my wrist brace to quell the ache in it at least but it was back in the UK with Billy. Everything I needed wasn't here and it was maddening.

She carried on picking vegetables and boiling water and was clearly not going to bring it up. Just before the kettle boiled, I did.

'You couldn't stop yourself, could you?'

'What?'

'I know this isn't exactly a fun road trip for old besties but I thought at the very least you were on the level now.'

'What are you talking about?'

'You're in as much shit as I am so why grass me up? Why now? What are you aiming for, eh? Getting your job back? Commendation medal? First prize for clever dicks at the next policeman's ball?'

'Rhiannon – will you please take a breath, calm down and tell me what on earth is your beef?'

'You and Amarkeeri. In cahoots. Plotting my downfall.'

A penny dropped behind her eyes. 'You read my phone.'

'Yeah, it fucking rang last night. Message from your old pal Jai Amarkeeri. The same Jai Amarkeeri spearheading the search for Sweetpea. The same Jai Amarkeeri who, if he found me, could lock me up for the rest of my life. So what time should I expect them? Have I got time to wash my hair? Guessing not with the length of time it takes to boil water here.'

'He was responding to an old message,' she said, patting her pockets for her iPhone and unlocking it. She shoved it on the table, unlocked, so I could see the screen and all her apps. 'I've nothing to hide, I assure you.'

'You play Tetris,' I noted.

'Read the messages I sent to him. They're all there. Look at the dates.'

I begrudgingly reached out and picked up the phone, then took a bloody good look through it. I opened the Messages app. Sure enough, there was a string of messages to Jai A – the first one dated Monday, 20 September, then Thursday 23, 29; 12, 13, 14 October and finally a whole batch of them on 20 October, the last one being – *we have a sighting. Silverton household. She's breaking in.*

'He hasn't responded to any of them,' I noted.

'I know,' she replied. 'He thinks I'm about as sane as you are. He's not coming. Nobody's coming. I have asked him in the past repeatedly to trust my judgement but he's such a little sycophant the only people he'll listen to are the ones above him. That's how he got the job.'

I had a sneaky look through her photos as well before I handed the phone back to her. I noted a small brown spaniel chewing a bone, and in another one, playing with wool. A black-and-white collie running through a field at dusk; the two of them on a beach, and curled up either side of her on the sofa.

She pushed the phone back towards me.

'Listen to last night's voicemail.'

'Hi Nnedi, it's Jai. Thanks for all your messages but this needs to stop now. I'm in no way suggesting you are lying but you have been under a lot of stress lately as we all know. It may well be that this woman you are following is Lewis – now the grave has been exhumed it certainly seems like she's still at large. And I do trust your instincts. But I need to be sure before I send reinforcements. If I allocate any resources and we don't get a result, it could look bad for us. And things already look bad. You're on leave at the moment and I suggest you relax and keep your wits about you. Call that therapist on the card I gave you – she can do wonders. I'll circle back with you soon.'

I clicked off her phone and slid it back across the table. '"Circle back." Ugh. Sounds like a right prick.'

'He is,' she said, pocketing the device. 'And that little "just keep your wits about you" at the end – do you know what that means? "If it *is* Rhiannon, try not to get yourself killed."' She almost-laughed. 'They don't care what happens to me. I am a difficult woman to manage, you see.'

'They're the best kind,' I said. Okay, so she *wasn't* a Judas. She had protected me in the gill not because she needed to take me in alive but because she wanted to. She was worried about me. As a person, not a prize.

'Who's looking after your dogs?' I asked.

'They're . . . not with me anymore. Nala got out onto the road chasing a squirrel. And I had to have Willow put to sleep last summer. She had tumours. I don't have anyone or anything waiting for me. My entire life for the past few years has been about finding my dad's body. I've let everything else go.'

'I told you where he might be buried.'

'I know and I believe you. But making *them* believe it is another matter.'

'Maybe if *I* told them where he was buried they'd believe *me*?'

'What are you saying?'

'I don't know. I don't know what I'm saying.'

I really didn't. But at that moment, I wanted to do something good for her. The little gatita in me was coming out, wanting to bring her a dead mouse to show my appreciation.

'So where do we go from here?' she replied, pulling out a dining chair and taking a seat.

I stared at her three-fingered hand. 'What if I wrote a confession? A full confession for everything that's happened since I got back to the UK?'

'Why would you do that?'

'Atonement,' I said, looking at her hand again.

She shook her head. 'That's not yours to atone for.'

'No, I know. But I'm the next best thing, aren't I? Or worst.'

'Why are you thinking about atonement all of a sudden?'

'I don't know. To get you off the hook I suppose. But I could confess, couldn't I? And still get away? I could say I strong-armed you at Claudia's, grabbed the gun, made you drive to Ogmore. I made you dig holes in the woods – your graves – and I was planning to kill you both.'

'Why would you take us all the way to Ogmore?'

'Cos I'm a psycho, aren't I? Roll with it. I was going to kill both of you in some symbolic way at my old childhood haunt as revenge for lying to me about Ivy being sick. I forced you to dig the holes at gunpoint – that's backed up by the shovels in the boot of the Audi. But you heroically tried to wrest the gun away from me and in the skirmish, Seren got shot. By *me*.'

'No, that's not right.'

'Then, gun still in hand, I forced you to drive somewhere,

and we ended up at Fishguard ferry port and maybe I'd heard Billy talk about Aoibhneas so we headed here. Nothing to do with Billy, nothing to do with you. All me.'

'This is beginning to smell of white saviour complex, Rhiannon.'

'Everything you've done, you've done for the right reasons. I've done it because I fucking wanted to. I want you to find your dad's body so you can bury him with decency because you deserve that. And I know I don't deserve to get back to Rafael. But it's *all* I want. And if there's a chance of me having that, I'll take it. But I could do without your hinderance as much as I could do with your help. So let me take this whole thing. You scratch my back, I'll scratch the fuck out of yours.'

The acid burned in my chest. Nnedi's lips trembled and her eyes blazed but she said nothing. I sat down dead opposite her.

'So you would want me to go along with whatever confession you put out?' she said. '*If* you somehow get away from here?'

'Yes. If I wrote out the full confession, sent it to Amarkeeri signed and sealed, they'd *have* to dig up your dad, wouldn't they? They wouldn't ignore that. And if I did that, all I'd want from you is to go along with it.'

I hadn't realised it until then, but I was gripping the handle of the carving knife beside the bread. I'd gouged a line in the tabletop.

Nnedi pressed her lips together as though they were ready to be sewn up, but eventually gave vent to the words she was trying to hold back. 'But if your friend Billy hasn't come up with a plan – what then?'

'He will.'

'But if not, maybe we should hand ourselves in . . . together.'

'What?'

'If you came quietly, with your confession; perhaps confessing to a few others if you felt like it—'

'No! I was only talking about sending a confession by *post*—'

'I could get you sent to a decent prison, more privileges—'

'Why are you even suggesting this?'

'Because I can't see another way out. We haven't heard from your friend in a while. Who's to say he hasn't been rounded up by the British police already? He could be being questioned as I speak.'

'No, he'd have got word to me somehow.'

'How do you know? How long have you known this Billy?'

'Long enough.'

'Sooner or later our money is going to run out and what then?' She looked me dead in the eye, unblinking. 'We need some sort of contingency plan. If Billy *doesn't* come through for you, we don't have any other options. Admit it, Rhiannon, defeat . . . is possible. *Probable*. And if it is, then we should get our stories straight and hand ourselves in. Do what's right. For once.'

I leant forward. 'If there is a *shred* of a chance of getting back to Rafael, I will take it. And nobody . . .' I held the knife in front of her face so the point of the blade was trained on her left eye, 'is going to stop me. Okay?'

She sat back in her chair. 'Okay. So for now, we wait for Billy.'

'Yes,' I said, slowly releasing my grip on the knife. 'We wait for Billy.'

Wednesday, 27 October – Day 6 in Aoibhneas

1. *Bastard dog walkers who find bodies it's not their business to find.*
2. *Guy Majors – the glow-up should not be making me this horny.*
3. *Any place in the modern world that has intermittent wifi connection these days. I'm sorry but get your act together, you troglodytes.*
4. *People who announce 'It's my balloon day!' on Twitter. Wet qweefs.*
5. *People who bang on about Android over iPhone, aka Nnedi.*
6. *Spotify – I feel like I'm in that episode of* Black Mirror *where he's forced to watch adverts unless he pays to not have to.*

Life had plateaued to bridge-jumping dullness, to such an extent I was helping Nnedi with the water gathering. I'd eaten so much kale I was ripping mad ass into the cushions and the cottage was beginning to smell like a compost heap.

Billy didn't come that day, nor the next day, so the limbo stretched into Day Six in Aoibhneas without a Bo Peep, kiss my ass from anyone. Our cash was running out, I missed Raf so much I was having sex fantasies about any man in the village (other than Laddy, obvs, I ain't *that* crazy), and Nnedi had barely said two words to me since our 'chat'. I spent most of Wednesday asleep, until I had the strangest dream . . .

Picture it: HM Prison, Haverfield, 2032: aesthetically pleasing shot of Guy Majors striding around the prison compound, gazing around himself, trying to pretend the camera isn't there. A 360-degree shot of him posing on a gravel hardstanding between two chicken wire fences – a clutch of mean-looking broads in orange boiler suits milling around behind him.

The voiceover's all deep and tense – *'This prison houses some of the most dangerous female criminals the world . . .'*

Cue close-ups of barbed wire and grizzled old hags scratching around the chicken coops in their Yeezy slides and glaring like they want to split you open and scrape you out. Majors smirks, doing the slow-mo swagger through the main doors to show how unafraid he is as long as they're caged.

'I'm about to meet the worst of them – Rhiannon Lewis, aka Sweetpea.'

This is Guy Majors. Hot-shot investigative journalist. True-crime expert. Fresh from a piece in *Architectural Digest* showing off his mansion in the Hollywood Hills and his second wife Virginia. Author of the bestselling books *Female Killers: Meet-Ups with Monsters* and *Majors on Murderers: Mamas Who Kill for Thrills*.

Through another set of doors he strides, cockhead of the walk, maybe Backstreet Boys's 'Larger Than Life' playing in the background. Then the song quiets and he flashes his leather-tanned smirk to camera.

'*Behind these purpose-built reinforced doors, you will find a variety of the worst female offenders in existence – they range from those who've committed larceny or drug offences right up to Category A prisoners who have killed or serial killed. And it is one of those prisoners who I will be meeting today – Sweetpea herself, Rhiannon Lewis.*'

He can barely keep the squee out of his voice, he's so excited. The trouser bulge in his Dolce and Gabbana skinny stretch jeans is unignorable.

There follows a musical montage, perhaps soundtracked by 'Boys' by Lizzo, as pictures of my victims flash up. Big boys. Itty bitty boys. Pretty boys, big beards, et cetera. And then we rewind to that '*dark day in our country's history when six-year-old cherub Rhiannon Lewis was viciously attacked by a hammer-wielding maniac and left for dead at 12 Priory Gardens . . .*'

Majors sits on one of the uncomfortable metal chairs in a large white room – blazer hanging over the back of the chair, shirt sleeves up, hair flopping teasingly over one side of his forehead, thanks to the transplant. He has a stack of notes in his lap and he's going through them professorially as I swagger in slo-mo to 'Bootylicious' by Destiny's Child – actually *not* slo-mo cos my ankles are tied and you can't slow-mo walk sexily when your gait is like an emperor penguin's trying to keep its egg warm.

'*Rhiannon, hi,*' says Majors, gesturing towards the only other chair in the enormous room. I shuffle over and sit down – we are an arm's-length apart but I can smell his aftershave. It's the same as the one Rafael wears – Tom Ford Venetian Bergamot – and his skin's more tanned than its usual gammon hue. He's lost some paunch – got a stylist. He looks – almost hot.

'So, Rhiannon, tell me, did you really kill all those people in your confession? Because looking at you now; you're a very beautiful woman, slim, charming, and I can't see this young lady before me – known as Sweetpea – killing someone, let alone chopping them up.'

'Yeah I did. I killed them all,' I say, doing the sexy lean back on my chair. Sometimes the chair falls backwards and the fantasy ends here but sometimes I just lean and leer at him, like I'm doing right now.

He flinches. 'Would you rather I said unalived instead? Is that triggering for you, saying what you did to them?'

'Call it what it is – I killed 'em. Rubbed 'em out. I trebuchet'd 'em back to God. Shoved them through the veil. Sang them a lullaby to their dirt nap.'

#DirtNap and #RubbedThemOut trend worldwide on Twitter. Demi Lovato calls me a monster on Instagram. Some influencer starts selling T-shirts with my face on and 'Sing Me a Lullaby' via the TikTok shop.

'Do you feel remorse for any of your victims?' Majors croons.

'No.'

'Why is that?'

'I don't know.'

He checks his notes. 'Before Priory Gardens, you were . . . normal, yes?'

'I was a child – mute, helpless, almost lifeless. Then I became an adult – and I entered the fight.'

'Your grandfather drowned in a river when you were eleven and you could have saved him, couldn't you? Any remorse there?'

'What, after he raped my sister? Yes, I am sorry for the

260

grandfather. I'm sorry the heart attack and the river got to him before I did.'

'You were eighteen when you killed Pete McMahon, your sister's boyfriend, and twenty-six when you killed Dan Wells. Eight years between. Did you kill anyone in that interim period?'

'That's for me to know and you to win another Costa Best Crime Award for, isn't it?'

He goes back to his notes. *'Gavin White, in Victory Park. Now you went after him, didn't you?'*

'Yes I was walking my dog and he grabbed me.'

'You wanted him to grab you though, didn't you? You went out with the express purpose of killing a guy who preys on lone women. You enjoyed it when he pounced on you, didn't you?'

'No. That's a common misconception. I've read your opinion pieces on what a piece of shit I am for "enjoying the thrill of being attacked". No woman enjoys that. No woman asks for that. I took my thrill from knowing that I was in control. That I can kill a man who wants to attack me. Sometimes I found I couldn't quite muster up the will to get stuck in, like with Gavin What's-His-Name in the park—'

'Gavin White?'

'Yes. I don't have a lot of self-esteem and on that night it took a while for the feeling to emerge.'

'The feeling of wanting to kill?'

'Yes. But then Gavin kicked my dog. And the red mist descended.'

'You cared more about your dog than you did for your own safety?'

'I don't like people who hurt animals.'

'Are you a vegetarian then?' he asked.

'No. Whoever heard of a vegetarian serial killer?'

'It turned you on though, didn't it, being grabbed like that? Women do like that. You were begging for it.'

'No, I wasn't. What I'm begging for is an opportunistic prick to come along at the right moment so I can show them what I'm made of: stainless steel, usually. The provocation is what turns me on. Knowing I can end this man's life if he tries his luck. Knowing that he doesn't know what's coming. That's what makes this little gatita roar.'

My voice goes all gravelly on that bit.

'What about Julia?'

'What about Julia?'

'You raped her.'

'Correction: I posted my cheating boyfriend's semen in and around her gammon hangers when she was a corpse. I got no pleasure out of that one, believe me. It was like staring at the back of a bin lorry after a carvery. That was a means to an end.'

'And Gwendolyn Pell, the fortune teller you battered to death with her crystal ball? How can you rationalise that one?'

'I'm not rationalising anything – you asked me if I felt remorse for any of my killings. And I don't. Anyone who died at my hand was meant to die at my hand. I don't regret a single one.'

'Even Lana, the poor girl you drove to suicide?'

'She was halfway there anyway. With some people all they need is a little push. I could have blown Lana over the edge; she was pretty close to it before she even met me. Or sucked off my boyfriend.'

'And Dean Bishopston – forty-one. Father of three, taxi driver, just doing his job when he picked you up in Birmingham.

His three little boys were devastated. You caused that. You left him to die in a car park in the middle of the night.'

That always comes up – even in my fantasies, those *three little boys*. Maybe I *did* feel guilty about that one. But not for long.

'What about AJ, your baby's father?'

My hackles were up again. *'Why do you want me to feel remorse? Why is that so important to you?'*

'I'm just curious,' says Majors, manspreading on his metal chair. *'It's difficult to imagine someone like you doing the things you've confessed to.'*

'That's because you are a misogynist,' I say. *'You constantly underestimate women and see us as delicate little Barbie dolls who can't do a thing without a man's permission. Well, maybe women were – once upon a time – but storytime's over, Guy.'*

#StorytimesOverGuy trends worldwide.

'Do you hate me, Rhiannon?'

'Why, what have you done?'

Majors blushes, checking his notes again. *'I'm just curious – why you did those things. What goes through your mind when you're killing? What drives that fury?'*

The longer I stare at his face, the more it changes – it morphs and remorphs until it's not him anymore. It's Rafael. Sitting opposite me in the blue suit he wore at our wedding – hair starting to curl at the neck because he doesn't shave it anymore since he met me. Brown eyes shining.

'Hey baby, you missed me?'

Before either of us know what's happening, he removes a pair of pliers and snips the chains at my hands and I jump into his lap, wrap my arms around his shoulders, and we kiss passionately and he sucks my tongue and bites my lip until there's blood.

'*You are such a good girl,*' Raf says in Majors's voice. '*God I want you.*'

'*Oh my god, I've missed you so much. Call me a good girl again,*' I pant, biting his neck and breathing into his ear which he loves.

'*Oh, that's my good girl. Tell me what that pretty mouth does.*'

'*Hurts your feelings, most probably.*'

'*What else?*'

'*Suck your dick.*'

'*Ooh yeah baby. Say more things like that . . .*'

'*No. Talk dirty to me. Tell me how you voted in the last election . . .*'

He growls into my neck. '*Conservative.*'

'*Ugh yeah, you filthy bastard! I need it in me. I need you in me, now.*'

He unzips his Dolce and Gabbanas and I bite his neck 'til it bleeds and then we're both bleeding and he's grinding against me and tearing chunks out of my neck and I'm so horny I want to ingest him completely. And he's wrenching apart the fasteners on my orange boiler suit to reveal my not-at-all-sagging breasts and he takes one of them in his mouth and I'm . . . breastfeeding him. Oh. My. God. This. Is. Hot.

'*Good girl, good girl, that's my good—*'

A tap on my shoulder wrestled me out of my sleep with a slurp of drool and a '. . . fuck yeah baby, go deeper'.

'I made you a cuppa,' said Nnedi, holding out the *ThunderCats* mug of steaming hot coffee. 'Sorry, did I wake you?'

'No, it's fine. It's really, *really* fine,' I said, taking the mug.

*

264

Later that evening, we had an early dinner at the pub. Mary cooked me fried chicken tacos (off menu – I think she'd have fricasseed Fintan if I'd requested it, such was her ardour for me) and she attempted champurrado like Bianca makes. I think she'd just melted a couple of Dairy Milks with some out-of-date cinnamon. Bless her for trying but it was nothing like home.

Nnedi's phone went as she was finishing her steak. 'Oh shit, it's Claudia.'

'Don't answer it.'

'I have to. She's probably heard about Seren.'

'What are you going to say?'

'I've no idea.' She slid her phone to Unlock and got up to take the call outside.

I sat there waiting for the phone call to end, watching through the window to see if I could gauge how the conversation was going from the changing expressions on Nnedi's face – I couldn't. And as she was talking, a figure emerged out of the darkness and walked towards her.

Laddy McVicker.

'Ugh,' I muttered. 'Here we go again.'

I watched as Nnedi finished her call and pocketed her phone, standing her ground outside the pub as Laddy came up and spoke to her. To all intents and purposes, it was a man having a pleasant conversation with a woman but if you looked closer, you could see the woman wasn't saying anything. Wasn't doing anything. Just standing there, staring into his soul.

'No good?' asked Mary as she despondently picked up my still-full mug of steaming whatever-the-fuck-it-was.

'I'm just a bit full,' I said. 'But thank you anyway.'

'No problem at all.'

I was still distracted by the goings-on outside as Mary went back to the counter and it was when Laddy started poking Nnedi's shoulder that I got up and went out myself.

'You all right?' I asked, standing beside her.

'Oh here she is,' Laddy slurred. 'You dykes owe me an apology. She called me a weirdo and YOU called me a pervert.'

'You even managed to fuck *that* up,' I said. '*I* called you a *fucking* weirdo and *she* called you a pervert, get it right.'

'That's not very nice, is it?' he said, scuffing towards me. I was around three metres from him, but I could smell him even in the cold still air – tobacco and fish. Like a pirate. *Blaghfuckin-blagh-not-very-nice-blagh-blagh-fishhhh-fissssh-pervert-fucking-fish-fuckin-blaggghhh.*

Then I caught a whole sentence.

'I ain't taking it from you and I ain't taking it from the likes of *this* bitch.'

Nnedi just stood there as he continued to fire a host of unoriginal racist insults at her, and sexist ones at me like a poor imitation gatling gun.

'What do you want me to do?' I asked her.

'Nothing,' she muttered, face full of thunder and lightning; her teeth gritted almost to powder.

'I can finish him now,' I offered, slinking the steak knife I'd stolen from her plate down my sleeve.

'Do. Nothing,' she stated, all low and slow, continuing to stand firm. So I just stood next to her, gripping the knife handle loosely in my palm and together we stared him down, right down the barrel, not rising to any of his weak-ass challenges.

And eventually, he got bored. 'Ah fuck off, ya pair of dykes.' He laughed, stubbing his filthy cigar butt out on the pub wall and wandering back up the road from whence he'd come. I went to follow him, but Nnedi grabbed my coat collar and pulled me back. 'You should have let me stab him.'

'What good would that do? Despite what you've been taught, Rhiannon, no matter what the question is, violence is never the answer. Anyway, I'm armour-plated when it comes to those names. I've had to be.'

'And you don't need me to save you, right?'

'Touché.' She blew out her cheeks and the air came out steamy. 'Come on. Let's go home.'

I got a very small buzzy feeling in my stomach when she said that, just a brief one, like a bumblebee had flown in but then straight out. Home. I longed for a home somewhere. Took me straight back to Raf again. I shook the feeling away.

'What did Claudia say?'

'Oh,' she said, patting her pocket where her phone was. 'Yes, it's all okay – ish. She said Ivy keeps asking about the woman with the blood but she's okay.'

'Do they know about Seren?'

'Yes. They saw it online. I said it was all in hand – that there had been an accident and you had killed her but that I had . . . apprehended you and taken you in.'

'Hero of the hour. So why so sheepish?'

'Because I just lied through my teeth. Again.' She sighed. 'What the hell have I become?'

'You get used to it.'

Thursday, 28 October – Day 7
in Aoibhneas

1. *That celeb medium guy, Tyler Henry – what a load of old bollocks.*
2. *Leprechauns.*
3. *Men who call her The Wife.*
4. *Women who call him The Hubs.*
5. *The Bad Seeds on the #CutForRhiannon Challenge – grow the fuck up.*
6. *Billy.*

I was shredding kale at the sink when a tapping sound at the window almost made me jump out of my skeleton. I grabbed a carving knife from the block and marched over to fling open the door expecting McVicker and his trilby and dirty fingernails. But to my delight, it was somebody I *wanted* to see.

'OH MY GOD YOU MASSIVE CUNT!' I cried, as the door swept open and Billy was standing there in his usual denim jacket and green cargo trousers with his bag on one shoulder, and mine on the other. 'You utter UTTER bellend!' I dropped the knife to the floor and we hugged like old friends.

'Good to see you too, Rhiannon!' He laughed, drawing me in as I nearly knocked him off his titanium pins, and showing no signs of the anger he'd briefly shown on the phone when I'd admitted I'd drugged him to get away. 'Make your mind up, am I a cunt or a bellend?'

'BOTH!' I hugged him again. I felt like crying I was so happy. And also a bit horny. He was wearing Boss aftershave, like Raf sometimes wore. I closed my eyes and breathed him in. 'Oh my god, where have you been? Is Raf okay? Why didn't you answer your phone? What's going on?'

'Steady on, can I get me fake feet through the door first? I've had a long journey and I'm gagging for a cuppa.'

'We don't have any water yet – Nnedi's gone out to get it.'

'Oh your new detective friend, is it?' he said, swinging his bag onto the back of a kitchen chair and dumping my rucksack on my sofa/bed. I immediately tore into it and found my wrist brace – the ache left my arm the second I strapped it on. What a relief!

'I wouldn't call her a friend but she's the nearest thing to one I've had for the last week or so. Thank GOD for clean clothes – thank God for *my* clothes.' I held my hoodies and my long-sleeve clean tops to my nose and breathed them in. 'So tell me about Raf, is he all right? Is he better? Is he here?'

'No, of course he's not here. Look, I'll tell you everything you need to know but is there a toilet where I can drain the lizard first?'

God, he was getting right up my bunghole and not in a good way – for a man who didn't stop talking he was being infuriatingly slow to give me any useful information. It didn't matter though, as minutes later Nnedi returned with the water jugs and we could get the tea on to lubricate him so all the news could start flowing.

'Billy, this is Nnedi; Nnedi, this is Billy O'Shea – the biggest

269

slag in Ireland, been passed around more times than a Netflix password, no legs below the knee, small cock, big army pension.'

'Hey!' Billy laughed. 'It's not *that* big, my pension!' He shook Nnedi's hand and the second he did I saw the blush in both of his cheeks. And Nnedi smiled with full teeth, which I hadn't known her do before.

'Hello, Billy.'

'So what's the craic here then? You're the great detective? How did this all come about?'

Nnedi smiled wanly. 'I wonder that hourly.'

'It's all a bit of a mess, isn't it?'

'You can say that again.'

We got Billy up to speed on everything as I put the kettle on and he scrummaged around in his bag for three smaller, white paper bags with greasy specks on the outside. 'Nice gaff here, isn't it? Me and the cousins used to build our dens at the back of this place, in the woods. Every summer. Spent hours out there. Meg used to make us bread pudding.'

He threw Nnedi a look I couldn't read and placed the white bags on the tabletop. 'Mary sent you over some lunch – a few spice bags. Thought you'd be sick of the kale by now.'

'I am – very sick,' I said, launching into one of the lukewarm bags and knocking back the battered chicken as they continued to chitchat about the 'charm' of the place.

'How's your hand?' he asked, reaching out to take it and inspect the fresh bandage Nnedi had dressed it in that morning.

'All right thanks,' I said. 'But what about—'

'Did you hear they've found Seren's body?' said Billy, taking a seat at the dining table and serving up our spice bags on three clean plates.

Nnedi said nothing.

'Yeah we know about that – just tell us something we *don't* know.'

'What do you want first – the good news, the really excellent news, the bad news or the dog-shite news?'

Nnedi threaded her remaining fingers through the handle of her *Dogtanian* mug and sipped her coffee. 'Something good would be . . . good.'

'So the *good* news is Rafael is on the mend and he's left the hospital.'

'He's *left*?' I said. 'When?'

'Four days ago. He said he was going to be in touch with me when he's got a new phone but he didn't know how long that would take. But as I said, that was four days ago.'

'Okaaay, so where is he now?'

'That's the bad news – I haven't got a fucking clue.'

'What are you talking about?'

'I called Nico yesterday and again first thing this morning – it was the middle of the night over there – and he said Raf had discharged himself, went home, took his bag, shaved his head and left. Nobody's heard from him since.'

'Oh my god, what's he doing? Why did he shave his head?'

Billy was the only one eating, tearing into his chicken and chips with all the daintiness of a hippo attacking a boatload of tourists. 'Nico doesn't know. He says he talked about going to Mexico to stay with his aunt Salomé and waiting it out there until we could safely get you to him but he's gone off the radar so he might have gone somewhere else. Or . . . he might not have gone at all. The interview dropped two nights ago.'

'What interview?' Nnedi and I said, in perfect unison.

Billy scrolled his phone until he found the desired page he'd bookmarked. A news report:

KILLER HERO – WICHITA WONDER KID IDs HIS RESCUER

River Dade Goffey, the boy dubbed the Wichita Wonder Kid, who was found alive in San Francisco last month after being held captive by paedophile Elliot Mansur for three years, has identified the woman who saved him as British serial killer Rhiannon Lewis.

'Oh. Fuck. No,' I said.

Lewis was declared dead in January 2020 when she turned up at her sister's house in Vermont having fled the UK. She was supposedly shot by Seren Gibson on her doorstep. Gibson had positively identified her sister as the woman who'd been stalking her for months in revenge for informing on her to the British police. Now evidence has come to light that this deceased woman was not Lewis but an imposter, meaning the woman dubbed the Sweetpea Killer is still at large and possibly in the San Francisco area.

'Fuck my fucking life.' I sighed.

'Your picture flashed up on the news from a Starbucks in San Francisco and you were positively identified as Ophelia White.'

'Someone from work, I bet,' I seethed.

'And so now the word is spreading that you are Ophelia Jane White, formerly Rhiannon Lewis. Which means . . .'

' . . . which means Raf is under suspicion as well.'

'Yeah. And that he's the one who killed Elliot Mansur while you were saving the kid.'

'SODDING SODDING SODDING FUCK!'

'Quite,' said Billy, his lips shiny from his continued grease onslaught. 'But I did say there's some really excellent news – you're heroes!'

'Who *me?*' said Nnedi, face brightening.

'No, Raf and Rhiannon. The Bad Seeds have gone *crazy* for you guys.'

Nnedi's expression returned to its usual cliff-face aesthetic. 'They were already crazy.'

'No, but now they've stepped up the campaign to keep you hidden, Rhiannon. Nobody's in a hurry to find you at all – apart from the police of course. You saved that kid's life – you two are like Batman and Robin: news outlets are creaming their jeans over yous.'

Nnedi stirred her tea and handed a mug of it to Billy. 'Who is River Goffey? I've heard you mention him but I still don't know who that is.'

Billy handed Nnedi his phone so she could read the full story.

'That's part of the dogshit news though, Rhiannon: you can't go back.'

'To the States?'

He shook his head. 'No. The California Justice Department has put out a warrant for your arrest. They know about Roadrunner too.'

'What's Roadrunner?' asked Nnedi, still scrolling the article. I mouthed to Billy to keep his trap shut on that one.

'So what am I supposed to do? Where do I go? How the hell does Rafael get out of the States if *his* passport's now flagged too?'

'You can't go anywhere – your Ophelia White cover's been blown. And it'll take months to get a new passport.'

'What about Mexico? Or South America? He's got another—'

This time Billy eyeballed me and mouthed for me to stop talking and I did. 'For what it's worth, I am sorry I'm not bringing you better news.'

Nnedi was still reading the article about River Goffey. She looked at me. '*You* did this? You saved this boy?'

'Yeah. Well, me and Raf.'

Billy scoffed the rest of his spice bag and sank his tea. 'This is a grand cuppa tea, by the way, fair play to you.'

Nnedi smiled, briefly, scrolling further down the same article.

'If you two start shagging, I'm sleeping in the car,' I griped, which sent both of them into an awkward silent meltdown, to my brief delight.

Nnedi changed the subject back to River Goffey. 'This is unbelievable. This boy – he was missing for three *years*.'

'They moved around a bit,' I said.

'And get this,' said Billy. 'I bet she hasn't told you this: the guy they killed who'd abducted this boy, had molested *Rafael* when he was a kid. So she tracks him down – takes her a year, right? – to an apartment in San Francisco and persuades Rafael to go there *on their honeymoon*. She goes to his apartment, intending to slay him on his doorstep, but Rafael gets there first so she doesn't have to. They didn't find the boy 'til after. Poor kid.'

'It was a fluke,' I said. 'We didn't know he was there.'

Billy chuckled. 'I bet *River* wouldn't say that. You saved his life! You saved Liv's life too. Her sister-in-law. She had this asshole husband, Edouardo. Raf told me about him. Rhiannon killed Edo for her—'

274

'No, Liv saved *herself*. I just disposed of his body. Not that she thanked me for it. Or reimbursed me for the Uber when I ditched his car.'

Nnedi's face did a thing – I couldn't read it.

'Whatever. You've come through for a lot of people, Rhiannon.' Billy turned to Nnedi. 'She doesn't deserve jail.'

Nnedi's face changed again. And again, unreadable. But there was a distinct show of bottom teeth when Billy had said 'you're heroes' and meant me and Raf. Was she jealous?

'She's saved God knows how many kids from God knows how many creeps. Don't brush this under the carpet. And yeah, all right, uneasy lies the head that wears the crown, but you wear it well. And a lot of people adore you. Probably *millions*.'

'Yeah, people adored Ramirez until they smelt him.'

I didn't give a crap about anything anymore. Without Rafael it was all meaningless.

'It'll be all right, Rhiannon,' said Billy, cupping my hand with his own. And he gave me the Billy wink – not a fuck-wink this time. A something-else wink. But as with all facial expressions, I couldn't quite read it so I just assumed it was a fuck-wink and moved my hand out from underneath his.

'Of course it's not going to be all right. What's the point of running – where am I running to? You were supposed to come here with a plan.'

'Look, it's just gonna take a bit longer that's all. You're just gonna have to trust me – this is a safe haven while we work things out.'

'You're *already* supposed to have worked things out!' I yelled. 'What's the point of me being here if there isn't an escape plan? I might as well just let her take me in now.'

Nnedi looked up at Billy, threading what was left of her

fingers through each other. 'I've made up my mind to hand myself in, tell them what happened with Seren. She can live with the guilt; I can't. But if Rhiannon comes quietly too, I can make sure she is treated well, given special privileges—'

'We've been through this, I'm not giving myself up.'

'Yes, but you said that if there was a chance of getting back to Rafael – now there's no chance. Is there?'

Billy looked at her and shook his head, slowly, almost imperceptibly and continued playing with the leftover chips on his plate.

'There has to be,' I said. 'There *has* to be.'

'You're not going to be able to get access to your money for a new passport now,' said Billy. 'You'll be flagged as Ophelia White everywhere you go. I'm sorry, Rhiannon. I thought Raf would'a called me by now. Something musta happened. He did say it was risky.'

'Are you serious? This can't just be it. It can't be. I'm not going to jail.'

'What other options are there?'

The silence was almost ear-splitting. Nnedi cleared her plate and mine but Billy put his hand over his as he still had a few chips left. When her back was turned at the sink, he span the plate towards me, briefly – he'd spelt out 'TRUST' with his chips. Then he scraped them together and shoved a handful in his gob as she turned back round and he handed her the empty plate.

'Thanks, darlin',' he said with a flourish. 'That's set me up for the day.'

She took his plate, and he wiped his hands on a tea towel, and as her back was turned, he threw me the briefest of winks.

Friday, 29 October – Day 8
in Aoibhneas

1. *Chris Pratt – I've just remembered how much I hate him.*
2. *People who get all offended when you remark how losing weight has aged them (e.g., Billy, when I said he looked fitter on his army photos).*
3. *Nokia – for not designing a smartphone that can hold a charge for more than eight hours. All right, so it's a cheap-ass phone but still.*
4. *That Chicken Shop Date woman. Ugh. Fuck off already.*
5. *People still wearing real fur but not living in caves – you unutterable cunt swabs. Kill yourself. Before I do it for you.*
6. *Laddy McVicker.*

Billy came to fetch us just after nine this morning and offered to accompany us to the pub for a 'slap-up breakfast'.

'No, thanks,' said Nnedi. 'I find I'm sluggish all day if I have a big meal to begin with.'

'Well, a piece of toast or some muesli or something at least.'

'Does the pub even do breakfasts?' I asked.

'They will for you two. Come on, I'm starving.'

I hadn't noticed how itchy-anus Billy was about getting us

to the pub that morning. If I had, we wouldn't have walked straight into an ambush. The moment we stepped across the threshold, the pub doors were slammed behind us, bolts slid across, and we were forced to sit on barstools while two shotguns pointed at our faces.

I glanced straight across at Billy, who was already ensconced safely behind the counter. 'Nothing to do with me, I swear,' he said.

Fintan's shotgun was trained on me – Eamon's, the curly-haired farmer with the holes in his checked shirt, was on Nnedi.

'Easy now,' said Eamon. 'No sudden movements. No messin'.'

There were fifteen other people in the main bar, I counted – mainly men, mainly farmers in similarly holey shirts or thick jumpers and shit-splattered wellies – all of them silent but standing, some with broken shotguns over their arms, others with sticks or pickaxes.

'Nobody's going to hurt you, Rhiannon,' said Fintan.

'The two guns pointed at our faces beg to differ,' I said, heart pounding, full Sahara gob, counting the number of exits in my line of vision – two doors. Both blocked and bolted.

Nnedi had her hands up. 'Cover seems to be blown then.'

Both sets of eyes continued to glare at us behind their guns.

'We all know who you are,' said Grahame, a bald guy who seemed to have all thirty-two teeth on the top set and wore dungarees like he meant it. 'We've taken Billy at his word that you mean us no harm, you and your lover . . .'

'Her *lover*?' said Nnedi, dropping her hands, until Eamon nudged her and they rose up again. 'We are *not* lovers.' Nnedi swallowed and side-eyed me, presumably realising that it wouldn't be the best idea to announce she was a cop right now. 'Yes, all right, we're *lovers*.'

'We just want to talk to you – there's no need to be afraid of the weapons, they're just insurance.'

Fintan's Irish lilt wasn't nearly as soothing as it had been when he was serving us dinner. There was a jagged edge to it now and I was ready to launch into the mother of all tantrums with added flying barstool. He motioned for everyone in the room to sit, and they did, weapons on laps or lying across tabletops.

Starey Mary smiled at me from behind the beer pumps, like a proud auntie on recital night. I wanted to strangle her with her own peach polo neck.

There came a loud *rat-a-tat-tatt* on the locked doors and Grahame strode across begrudgingly to slide the bolts across to let Séan in, a younger guy I'd seen about delivering milk from the farms. He was quite fit for a yokel. If I lived here permanently and wasn't married and drastically lowered my standards, I'd probably, at a push, give him a ride. He apologised for his tardiness, stank of cow shit and took his place on a red-velvet banquette.

Starey Mary came out from behind the bar and stood beside Fintan. 'We are sorry to do this to you, Rhiannon – to both of you – but you being here, it seemed like a gift from the gods.'

'Yeah, you're our Bé Chuille,' said a beefy guy called Dean.

'Be what?'

'Bé Chuille, the great sorceress who bested Carman the witch, and stopped her invasion of Ireland.'

'I'm not a sorceress – I'm an admin assistant!'

'No, you're not,' said Starey Mary, 'you're far more than that. And we believe you've been sent here for a reason.'

'No, I was sent here cos *he* told me it'd be safe,' I said, pointing at Billy.

'I swear, Rhiannon, I sent you here with the best intentions – to get you away, to keep you free. To look after you, just like Raf wants me to. I didn't know they were going to do this, honest.'

'Bullshit!'

'God's honest! Mary recognised you and told Fintan and he and she started telling the others; what could I do?'

'We need your help,' added Starey Mary. 'In return for our silence.'

Nnedi glanced across at me, and then a grey-looking fuck with a portable oxygen tank and two see-through pipes up her nose cleared her throat to speak. She was called Moira. 'That bastard's been a shroud over this village the past twenty years, Rhiannon, and we can't take no more of it. My late husband, Malcolm, God rest his soul, he worried about him coming to the house in the dead of night until he took his last breath. He spied on me – he spies on all the women round here . . .'

Moira had a wedding ring on, squished so tight so I don't think she could take it off if she'd wanted to. If *I* didn't kill her, the hypertension would.

'I haven't got long,' she continued, on shallow breaths, 'but I want to go to me grave knowing people round here are safe from him. Please help, Rhiannon.' Moira sat back down on her banquette, even greyer than when she'd started. If she thought a dying woman would have any effect on me, she had another think coming. I barely cared about people I knew who died, let alone randoms I'd just met.

'I want to walk out on my own again,' called out Arti, the brunette hippy-type with the droopy earrings, who ran the post office. There were two miniature Dachshunds beneath her table, curled up under her skirts inside her long floral scarf like two large baked potatoes. 'I'm afraid to walk my dogs. This used to be a nice place to live, Rhiannon – before he came here. I've been afraid for twenty years.'

'I want to bring our grandchildren to stay here,' added Starey Mary behind the pumps. 'But there's no way, not with him around. Our daughter Gracie never visits us anymore, we always have to go to her in Kerry – she won't take the risk with her chiselers.'

Fintan cleared his throat. 'You've both had problems with him, haven't you, and you've only been here a week. We've all had *twenty years* of it. Laddy McVicker is evil, Rhiannon.'

A guy called Brian Ryan (yes, really) with a Habsburg jaw and wearing a holey green jumper took up the story.

'He lives on the outskirts of my farm and he only ever seems to appear when there are women about, on their own, or kids,' continued Brian Ryan. 'He sits in that gaff of his like a *bodach*. God knows what he gets up to because he doesn't do a lick of work. But every day he will come down to the village to pick up his provisions or just hang around, taunting the womenfolk or stalking people. *None* of us want him here in all fairness.'

'Yeah we want *you* to kill him, Rhiannon,' added Séan the latecomer.

'Séan!' Fintan shouted across the room, followed by a load more Irish that I did not understand a single word of.

'What? You were going to ask her to do it anyways!'

Fintan sighed, seemingly rearranging his thoughts. 'We were going to ask for your help, knowing you've . . . sorted out men like him previously.'

I stared down the barrel of the one remaining shotgun still trained on me. 'Am I missing something here? This is supposed to be a God-fearing community, established by monks. Most of you have got the Virgin Mother in a shrine on the outside of your houses. Or is that just for the tourists?'

'No, of course not,' said Fintan. 'But you're the one who knows how to deal with his type.'

'And *you're* the ones with the guns and ammo. Why don't you do it yourselves?'

'These are good men,' said Starey Mary. 'We all have our skeletons in the closets, but none of us are killers.'

'You can't expect Rhiannon to do this,' said Nnedi. 'You can't honestly think this is the right thing to do.'

'It's all we can do,' said Fintan, summoning Starey Mary over from the bar with a box she'd kept hidden behind the counter. 'We've kept all the clippings about Laddy over the years – all the court appearances, all the interviews he's given to the press. Some of the offences were done under his real name – Lawrence Michael Purcell. Others done under the name he's got now – Laddy McVicker. He tried to hide using his mother's maiden name.' Fintan handed me the box. 'There's over fifty offences detailed in those articles and for not one of them did he receive a prison sentence. He always manages to fly under the radar. Until now.'

'What do you want me to do with all this?' I asked, rattling the box. Nnedi reached for it and I handed it to her.

'I want you both to have a look through it. See what kind of man he is. It's all there – what he did in Cork, what he's into. Little girls, little boys, women alone. The more vulnerable the better.'

'He'll never stop,' added Grahame. 'There's no cure for men like him.'

'I found a pretty good cure,' I sniffed. 'But why should *I* do this? I get that I'm probably the most qualified in the room but why not Billy? He's a killer. He snuffed people out in the army, in Syria and Afghanistan.'

'I was medical support,' said Billy. 'I dressed wounds, I rigged up IV drips. I'm more used to *saving* lives than taking 'em.'

'You carried weapons and were taught how to use them, same as Raf.'

'I'm not a killer. But *you* are.'

'No shit, Hurt Locker.' I looked around the room. 'You hunt stags, you catch and gut fish. You strangle chickens on your farms. What's the difference with one random perv?'

'Not *people*, Rhiannon,' said Fintan, giving it the sad smile. 'And this is one person who's got to go.'

'Can't you just call the guards every time he hurts someone or—'

'That's just it,' said a blond middle-aged bob called Sinead beside the shove halfpenny table. 'He doesn't hurt people in the usual sense of the word. He just stalks. He stalks and he watches and he terrifies. Nothing the guards can do about that. Someone has to physically suffer before they lock him up. We have a nice community here. No ripples on the pond, except him.'

'Arti, tell them,' Fintan ordered.

Arti stood up at her table, careful to avoid waking up her two snoozing hounds. 'He followed me home once, Rhiannon, about five years ago. He didn't do anything, just followed, along the gill at the back of the village. When I shouted at him to go away, he laughed at me. He knew how afraid I was walking home in the dark. I've been on tablets ever since – can't catch a wink. He stares through the shop windows sometimes. Weeks can go by and I think he might have stopped and I pray he's died of a heart attack at home or something and we're not going to see him again. But then he'll reappear, at the window, all of a sudden, and . . . I'm so frightened.'

Starey Mary took up the baton.

'I've been in here a few times, polishing the tables before we open on the lunchtime and he's been at the window, staring in at me too. Doing something to himself. He always does it when he knows Fintan's in the cellar or out on a delivery. Some others in the village, Mary O'Rourke and Sheila Kenny, were too scared to come here today but they'll tell you the same – we're all afraid of him. We're afraid of what he might do.'

'He's a fox in a hen house,' said Fintan. 'We want our hen house back.'

The room erupted in applause and cheers.

'Hang on, hang on,' Nnedi called out, in her usual bucket of cold water tone. She put down the articles she'd been sifting through and stood up. 'If he hasn't touched any of you, hasn't caused any physical harm to anyone in this village in the time he's been here—'

'No physical harm?' said Fintan. 'What do you call *that?*' He pointed through the pub window at something just outside in the car park. It was Ben's horse cart, burned to a cinder.

'When did that happen?' I asked.

'Last night, just after you two went home. Had words with him, didn't you? He marched in here, steaming angry, necked Eamon's pint and then went straight outside and did that.'

'Is Ben okay?'

Fintan stared at me hard and in that silent moment, I was ready to set fire to Laddy myself and toast marshmallows on him if necessary. 'Ben's fine, he was in the stable at the time. But that's what I mean, Rhiannon. Nobody saw him do it – we can't do anything. And he feckin' *knows* we can't do anything. It's always our word against his.'

'He's got to go, girls,' Séan interjected, manspreading on the banquette in his washed-out jeans with a sizeable package I couldn't take my eyes off. My mind went straight back to Rafael. I couldn't even enjoy lusting after men anymore since him. He'd ruined me for all others. I glanced at Nnedi. 'What do you think?'

'No,' she said. 'Just no.'

'You know as well as I do that all those things he's been tried for – the flashing, masturbating, taking pics – they all lead to stuff like kidnapping or murder. They're . . . what-do-you-call-its . . .'

'Escalating behaviours,' she finished, chewing the corner of her perfectly manicured thumbnail. 'Even so – you can't just *kill* him.'

'But she's killed loads of people; what's one more?' called out Séan.

Starey Mary took up the baton again. 'Okay, Rhiannon, we'll give you another reason to do this: if you kill McVicker for us, we'll keep you here, safe, as long as you need. And when the day comes when you have new passports or whatever, we'll get you away. We'll buy tickets to wherever it is you want to go in the world and we'll make sure you have safe passage back to your husband. We know lads who work at the airports and a couple at the ferry port at Rosslare. They're fierce sound and they can get you as far as continental Europe or West Africa for sure, no danger. They're die-hard Bad Seeds, don't worry.' She winked when she'd said it and Billy cupped her hand on the countertop.

'I can pay for my own tickets,' I snipped. 'And anyway, my passport's flagged now. I can't go anywhere on that thing.'

'We can sort you a new one, like they said,' said Billy. 'It might take a few months but I know some people. The point is we can keep you safe here until it's ready. No one'll come looking for you.'

I didn't know if it was the sudden heat in the room as Fintan had chucked a new log on the fire, or the proximity of so many living, breathing BO-smelling bodies, but I needed fresh air. I got up off the barstool, but two meaty hands sat me down again.

Nnedi'd had enough, waving away Eamon's gun barrel. 'This is ridiculously short-sighted. You think her killing McVicker is the answer to all your problems? It'll be just the start. His blood will be on *your* hands. Forever. She doesn't have a conscience so someone's bound to pay.'

They all looked at me. 'She's right; I don't.'

Nnedi continued. 'Can you live with the guilt of knowing what she will do to him? Because *I* couldn't.'

The glances flew about the room for a bit and then every single person there looked straight at her again.

I glanced up at Nnedi. 'I think they've made their peace with it.' She sat back down, shaking her head and muttering all the while.

'How do you want it done?' I asked the room.

'Any way you want,' said Starey Mary. 'We'll leave that up to you.'

'When?'

'As soon as possible,' said Moira.

'What about Sunday?' suggested Eamon. 'It's old Cormac's funeral – we'll all have an alibi.'

'Brilliant!' cried Arti and everyone else echoed the sentiment, almost to a round of applause.

'Hang on, hang on – what happens once he's dead? Once I've slashed his throat, cut off his dick, what *then*?'

'I've some hydrochloric acid on me farm,' said Eamon. 'Bury him out in his back field and dissolve the corpse.'

'Or we could let the pigs have him?' suggested Séan. 'He won't be missed, the filthy article – not like he has family beating a path to his door.'

'There must be someone,' said Nnedi. They all looked blank again, which isn't unusual because most faces look blank to me. 'Distant relatives? A social worker? A probation officer he still speaks to? He has an SHP order on his card – there must be someone keeping an eye on him.'

Fintan sucked his breath in over his teeth. 'There *was* but I think it's run out. It was only for a limited time. But there was that short, bespectacled fella who came in here once or twice on a lunchtime – a supervision lad from the probation service. Haven't seen him for a while now. I don't think he comes anymore. McVicker must be keeping his nose clean.'

'You said he comes up to the village to collect provisions?' said Nnedi. 'He's of pensionable age – does he collect that too?'

Everyone looked at Arti.

'No, that gets paid directly into his bank,' she said. 'But I guess they might get suspicious when he doesn't make any withdrawals. The service may investigate then.'

'One of us could collect it for him.' Séan shrugged. 'Result!'

'Making you an accessory if they do checks,' Nnedi added. Everyone glanced at Séan like he'd just said the world's stupidest thing.

'Once someone knows he's missing, they will come here and interview every single one of you. How are you going to persuade them you know nothing about this man's untimely disappearance? How will you persuade them, Eamon, that you know nothing about the disappearance of a barrel of your hydrochloric acid?'

Silence from the throng. Ice cubes clinked in a glass on the counter.

Nnedi sniffed. 'Do any of you have dash cams? CCTV? Camera doorbells?' They all shook their heads. 'Does *he*?'

Nothing.

'What about smartphones? Where's the nearest phone mast?'

'Ballymanly,' said Arti. – 'It's a beach about half an hour away or so.'

'This is the kind of thing police will investigate when someone goes missing, right? And if they find a body, they'll look at every message that pinged off that mast.'

'How do you know all this?' asked Eamon.

'I've studied law,' said Nnedi, without a beat of hesitation. I was impressed. What a beautiful liar she'd turned out to be.

'We could all turn our phones off on the night you kill him?' said a white-haired woman at the back – also called Mary but bearing no striking differences to Starey Mary. I'll just call her Blarey Mary because her voice was uncharacteristically loud for the room size.

'Yeah,' said Eamon. 'We could say it was out of respect.'

'Okay, let's say you all have an alibi for the night of the murder but they still can't trace him and they believe foul play – they'll bring cadaver dogs to the scene. They'll follow the breadcrumbs that lead from whatever jumper you were wearing at the time you picked his body up at his house and dumped him at the deposition site on your farm.' Nnedi stared at Eamon. 'Even if it's months later. Something will give you away. Are you ready for that? I don't think you've thought this through.'

'Yeah but we won't be guilty,' said Billy. 'The finger of suspicion will fall on Rhiannon.'

'. . . whom you'll have been harbouring here for months,' Nnedi cut back.

The whole room went silent again but for the sucking sounds from Moira's oxygen tank.

And then Grahame piped up. 'You need to start coming up with solutions, ladies, cos all we're hearing are problems.'

'This is one big problem you're going to have to sort out yourselves,' said Nnedi, folding her arms. 'I'm having nothing to do with this, killing an unarmed man in his own home. It's barbaric.'

She may as well have fired a toy gun that said 'BANG' on a little flag. They were practically laughing at her – they were practically laughing at *both* of us. But then Fintan piped up again – the lone voice in the awkward stillness. He held aloft Nnedi's phone.

'How did you get that?' she shouted.

'Yer coat pocket,' he replied, glancing at Eamon who'd managed to get it out without her noticing and pass it all across the bar, through the hands of several villagers on the way. 'You will go along to McVicker's house with Rhiannon, and you will keep a lookout while she does the business. Or else I will take this phone to the house and get you flagged as an accessory for murder as well.'

'No, this isn't right. This is entrapment, it's—'

'Your only hope,' said Fintan.

'Hashtag Keep Them Buried,' I scoffed.

'You're doing this,' said Fintan, 'on Sunday, while we're all at Cormac's funeral. And that's the end of it. Now, who wants a drink?'

Billy walked us back to Old Meg's that lunchtime, feeling like it was 'his duty' but the second he got inside the cottage and his back was turned, I tore down one of the gin traps from the wall, snapped open the teeth until it hinged and shoved him backwards into a chair.

'What are you doing?' he shrieked.

'Sit!' I ordered Billy, which he did with a thump. I forced his knees open and shoved the lower jaw of the trap under his balls. 'One pull of this chain and I'll tear it all off; cock, balls and whatever else you've got down there.'

'Rhiannon, please, listen to me—'

'No, I've done all the listening I want to do today. You fucking planned this, didn't you? Admit it!'

'I didn't! I swear!' He glanced across at Nnedi for clemency, but she stood beside the table, arms folded, evidently in no mood to help either of us.

'I swear to God when I sent you both here it was because it's a safe place – a sanctuary, like you needed. I knew Mary was a Bad Seed so I knew she wouldn't rat on you. I don't even know the feller they're on about!'

'Liar.'

'I don't! All I'd heard about him was that he was a bit of a gobshite – a few drunken outbursts in the pub and he'd been seen nicking veg from people's gardens but that was all. I didn't have a clue they'd conscript you into killing the feller. But I guess they're desperate.'

'When did they plan all this?' I asked. 'They all seemed to sing from exactly the same hymn sheet in the pub just now – when did they get together and decide to ask me?'

'Last night – they had a lock-in after hours to discuss you, just after you left. The burning of Ben's wagon was the final straw I think. We all leant a hand putting it out, then the next round was on the house and Mary came up with the plan: "we ask Rhiannon to finish him, once and for all". And then Fintan – he was pretty pissed by this point – just said, "No, we don't ask her – we *tell* her." That's what he said – and we all drank a toast to seal the deal.'

'What do you mean, you all drank a toast? You were there, last night?'

'Yeah, me and Séan were playing pool out the back – I'm staying with him while I'm here. We go way back, primary school actually . . .'

'I don't give a damn dingleberry about your school days with Séan! You arrived *yesterday*? And you waited 'til this morning to tell me about Raf? Knowing I'm going out of my mind in this shithole?'

'Well, there was no news!' he cried. 'If there was some concrete news to tell you, I'd have come straight here but there didn't seem any point in rushing to you. And me and Séan . . . kinda started smoking some joints and we lost track of time.'

'Fucking idiot,' I snarled.

'Rhiannon, I swear I argued me point with Fintan. I said

what you said in the pub, Nnedi – that it wouldn't make anyone's lives any easier if you killed Laddy but they all shot me down, one by one. They want him gone and they think you've been sent here by some supernatural force to do it.'

I squeezed the trap down a little more over his balls.

'NO! I COULDN'T! PLEASE! AAAGGGHHH!'

'Rhiannon!' cried Nnedi. 'It's not his fault, take it off him! Let him explain, for God's sake!'

'He *has* just explained, and I didn't like the answer.' I shoved the gin trap further back in the chair under his arse. 'Why did you write TRUST with your chips?'

'WHAT?'

'Why did you spell out "trust" with your chips?'

'I didn't want to get your hopes up . . . but I think Raf's left the USA.'

'What? He's left? When?'

'About four days ago, roughly. That's when I last heard from him.'

'Musta ditched his phone.' I tightened my grip on the trap. Billy's watering eyes looked to Nnedi then straight back to me, and again, and back. And again, and back.

I felt Nnedi's soft fingertips on my forearm. 'He's telling the truth.'

I moved the trap away from him but kept hold of it. Billy deflated somewhat and eased forwards in his chair, catching his breath, a definite new sheen of sweat about his brow. I sneered down at him.

'I knew Raf had some sort of plan up his sleeve to get somewhere and then send for you . . .'

'Get where?'

'He wouldn't tell me a thing – he just said, "Wait for a call"

292

and then he went off comms but he said to trust him. "Tell her to trust me." That's what he said, exactly. He's keeping us out of the loop in case the cops are onto him.'

I could feel Nnedi take an enormous breath beside me and swallow hard. Outside, the gate clinked and she went to the window to see, stepping outside and coming back moments later with a carrier bag bulging with what looked like internal organs.

'Blackberries,' she announced. 'The note says they're from Mary O'Rourke "with grateful thanks".'

'Gifts from appreciative villagers,' sniffed Billy.

'Bribes, more like,' I scoffed.

'Let's get back to the main story,' said Nnedi, dumping the bag on the table. 'We're supposed to kill McVicker, or else the village will hand us in to the Gardai, right?'

Billy nodded; a sheepish sort of agreement. 'But in return, they'll do whatever you want. They'll look after you here, keep you buried as the hashtag says, for as long as it takes and get you wherever you want to go. And new passports. Money. I mean, it's worth it, isn't it? He's just an old pedo.'

'But it'll take months to get a new passport,' I said.

He nodded. 'Yeah, probably. But you'll be hidden.'

'This is coercion,' said Nnedi. 'They can't do this.'

'We've got even fewer legs to stand on than him,' I reminded her. 'We don't have a choice.'

'Yes, we do – we hand ourselves in, right now, and then we don't have to do any of this. That was the plan, right? If Rafael couldn't get here nor you to him, we would turn ourselves in.'

'I never agreed to that. And we still don't know where Raf is, do we?'

Billy shook his head. 'Last time I spoke to him he said he

needs to get clear before he calls either one of us. But that was four days ago. I thought he'd have been in touch by now. Until he is, you've just got to sit tight.'

A silence fell over the place – the only intermittent sound was the crackling of the dying fire in the hearth. I stared at Billy without blinking.

'I'll do it on my own. There's no need for her to come.'

'McVicker's huge,' said Nnedi. 'You can't take him down on your own.'

'I'd have done fine in the woods the other day if I'd had a weapon. If I'd had that.' I pointed up the wall towards the axe. Unfortunately I was pointing at it with my duff hand – the one with the wrist brace which did nothing to help my argument. 'I can take care of myself.'

'I know you can, but you don't have to. I'm coming with you,' said Nnedi, the fire back in her eyes – the same fire that was there when she'd been questioning me at the police station about stalking Lana. The same fire she had in her TV interviews and the same fire as the night we went digging for Daddy Géricault. I quietly glowed with her offer. It reminded me of when Seren stopped a bigger kid picking on me in the hospital ward. He was laughing at my bald head and she stepped in and tipped up his Lego castle.

'Besides which, I want a look around, see if there are any clues.'

'Clues to what?'

'Other things he may have done while he's lived in Aoibhneas. Like this . . .' She went to the sofa where I'd dropped the box of articles Fintan had given us. She sifted through the ones on the top of the pile, eventually pulling out one with the headline:

CAISLEÁN DEARG HOUSEWIFE
ATTACK REMAINS UNSOLVED

'We passed this place on the way in, about three miles from here,' said Nnedi. 'If Fintan's right about dates, this happened the same month McVicker moved to his brother's farm – September 2001. Fintan clearly thinks he had something to do with it. And don't you remember – he said Laddy moved in on 10 September – this rape occurred on the fifteenth. I'm wondering if there are other unsolved attacks in the area which occurred after 2001.'

'Why didn't they catch someone for the rape?' asked Billy. 'They had DNA testing back in 2001, didn't they?'

'He made the woman take a bath, it says here,' she said, tapping the article. 'And she noted the man's fingerless gloves and "tobacco-stained fingernails". She said he stank of the stuff.'

'No unsolved cases round here,' Billy began but Nnedi cut him short.

'That you know of. It's okay, I'll do my own digging. But I need McVicker to be out of the way, ideally. When's he most likely to go out? I mean, *out* out – rather than just down to the village to stalk lone women.'

'I told you, I know nothing about the guy, but I can find out from Fintan. I do know he'll likely have a shotgun – most of the homesteads do around here, especially the farms, for ducks and deer and stuff.'

'That doesn't matter,' I said, reaching up to remove the axe from the wall. 'With a bit of careful planning, he won't know what's hit him.'

Saturday, 30 October – Day 9
in Aoibhneas

1. *Fintan*
2. *Eamon*
3. *Séan*
4. *Grahame*
5. *Malcolm*
6. *Darragh*
7. *Seamus*
8. *And anyone called Mary*

From 'The Bad Seeds' Tumblr

Dear Sweetpea,

You are not a bad woman. All those men you killed deserved it. All men deserve it. I have been raped and mauled and pawed by men my entire life – my father, brother, first two husbands. But you did not go far enough with your punishments. Women rarely do. I did. When a woman has been treated as poorly as I have, there comes a point when enough is enough.

It was when my third husband raped me that I snapped. I bit his cheek which made him angry. He smashed my head against the bed knob and I went unconscious. When I woke up, I felt drunk and he was sitting down watching TV like nothing had happened. He said that if I hurt him again, he would strangle my dog. I got a hammer from the tool box and smashed him over the head with it.

I had not felt my heart beating so fast in years. I still had the taste of his blood in my mouth and it was not unpleasant. We are poor and I do not buy meat often because it is expensive but this was free! I cut off the parts of him that I could and fried them. His brain and his buttocks, with a little salt, and potatoes and fresh peas from the garden. That was all they needed. Other parts of him, I froze and what I couldn't use, I threw to my pigs. They demolished parts of him that I could not!

The police have no evidence. They think he has frozen to death while out on one of his hikes. The problem is now that I have a taste for it. The meat is so tender – like pork. But I would not eat my pigs again. And he is running out, so soon I will need to replenish my freezer.

from G in Svetlogorsk, Russia [translated]

I dreamt about the banshee again last night. Either that or she was screaming outside in the lane again. Screaming and clawing her own face off. This time the screaming was different though – she was screaming 'TRUST'. Over and over and over again. TRUST. TRUST. TRUUUUST. And I dreamt I went outside with my lantern to find her and she was standing at the end of the lane and when I got up close to her it was my mum. Her face being torn off. Her screaming. And then she screamed herself inside out and became Seren instead.

Fuck knows what it all means. Well, I know what the mum bit means – I'd been thinking of her before I went to bed as 31 October is her anniversary. And I know why Seren kept showing up. But the banshee? No clue.

In the old days, I'd need to kill something to get rid of the dreams. Derek Scudd's murder had put paid to my nagging nightmares about Dad. Maybe offing McVicker would see off the banshee. I don't know. I'm too tired to think clearly this morning.

I opened my eyes to see Nnedi's phone screen in front of my face – a small article in the *Irish Mirror* about Claudia, Mitch and Ivy being spotted in Tenerife where Claudia's retired parents now lived:

SERIAL KILLER BABY SEEN WITH STRESSED-OUT ADOPTED MUM IN CANARY ISLANDS

My eyes creaked open to see the picture of Claudia pushing a Bugaboo outside a supermercado near the beach in Los Cristianos – her shouting, crosspatch face aimed squarely at the photographer trying to get a pic inside the pram, but Ivy couldn't be seen. Once my eyes had fully cracked open, I'll tell you what *could* be seen:

Richard E. Grunt! Jammed tightly inside Ivy's fist! He was there, I could see him so clearly – blue dungarees, green neckerchief. Cheeky face. That wily little pig was looking after her now, that was for sure. Trust him to get a piece of the limelight. And you know something: it sounds silly but I *knew* she was going to be okay then. Claudia must have known that pig came from me – Ivy didn't have any other Sylvanian stuff in that house. Claudia probably intentionally didn't buy her any because of me, but Ivy had woken up with Richard and refused to let go of him, I was sure of it. Probably threw a massive strop so Claudia had to let her keep him. I couldn't stop smiling.

'Anything else interesting going on in the world?' I yawned.

Nnedi sat down on the opposite sofa. 'Nothing about you. Some MP scandal about cash for honours; Covid cases on the rise again – they're expecting another lockdown here; farmers and hauliers staging a protest about fuel prices; Russian invasion of Ukraine "imminent" . . . and they're looking for me. They've linked me with Seren's death now.'

'The bullet?'

'Probably.'

'Well, that's all right – doesn't change the plan.'

She clicked off her phone and shoved it on the coffee table. 'I know. It just feels wrong. Well, it *is* wrong.'

'But I'm all about doing the wrong thing for the right reasons so let the confession take care of it, all right?'

'Okay, so what's in this one?' Arti asked as I posted my two heavily taped parcels underneath the glass screen.

'Just papers.'

'Papers?' she said, tapping on her keyboard. 'Sorry, I can't quite read that second name . . .'

'Cheney,' I replied. 'Freddie Litton-*Cheney*.' There were some slices of complimentary barmbrack on the counter. I helped myself. It was fresh.

Arti affixed the postage to Freddie's parcel, placing the second smaller one onto the weighing scale. 'And what's in this one?'

'Uh . . . a key,' I said.

'Great stuff,' she said. 'Cody Gibson, 1185 Hell's Peak Road, Lawford Heights, Vermont . . .' she typed. She didn't even ask what the key was for. 'Won't be a tic. This one's going to be a little more because it needs to go air mail, okay? But I can get that one tracked for you.'

'Fine,' I said, gazing around the room while I was waiting, like nothing in those parcels mattered one iota. 'Just some early Christmas presents.'

Arti smiled but didn't question the oddity of 'papers' and 'a key' as Christmas gifts. 'I read about what you did for that woman – that solicitor woman who was taken by the men in the van. I think you're marvellous.'

'Oh right. Thanks.'

Arti switched back to her day job as post mistress. 'Very wise sending them now. They're expecting shortages in the sorting offices over the holidays. And there's talk of a strike as well. There you go, that's International Tracked and Signed For at the other end. So that's those two plus the envelopes and parcel tape . . . twenty-four eighty-five.'

She handed me my receipt and shoved the parcel in one of the bulging sacks behind her, tying it up with a yellow cable tie. Two more bridges burned.

I looked at the plate of barmbrack again.

'Tóg píosa eile cáca, ná bí cúthail.'

'What?'

She shook her head. 'Sorry. I keep forgetting you're a blow-in. It's like you've been here years! Take another piece.' She pointed to the plate.

'Thanks.'

I could sense her still looking at me, even as I was looking down at her two dogs, miniature Dachshunds who had the run of the shop floor and a joint bed secreted under the greeting cards shelf. One of the dogs was stomping about the shop like Mick Jagger with a wad of parcel tape stuck to his paw. I helped him out.

'They're cute,' I said, picking the smaller one up for a smush. 'I miss having a dog.'

'Ah they're the best. They're miniature. They cost a fortune but they're my babies; I wouldn't be without them.'

'I had a chihuahua, called Tink. She was my baby for a long time. Went everywhere with me. But I had to leave her behind.' I smoothed my cheek against the dog's velvet ear and she licked the end of my nose.

'I know.' She smiled. 'I read about her in the papers. She's such a cutie. I read that she was going on *Britain's Got Talent* next year.'

'Doing what?' I said. 'Tink doesn't *have* any talents – took me about a year to teach her to do 'paw'. And even then she was shit.'

'Ah I think she's only on there because she's your dog.'

'*Was*,' I emphasised.

Arti unlocked the Perspex partition and headed for the keyring carousel on the counter. She unhooked one of the keyrings and handed it to me personally – a small, rectangular one with a shamrock on the front with 'Go n-éirí leat' above it for good luck. On the back it read:

May God grant you always
a sunbeam to warm you,
a moonbeam to charm you,
and a sheltering angel,
so nothing can harm you.

'Here. Something for your trouble. It's not much but . . .'

'Thank you.'

'We won't forget this, Rhiannon. You'll always find sanctuary in Aoibhneas. Oh before I forget, I've ordered that lad's book about you on Amazon. It should be coming tomorrow. Would you sign it for me?'

'Yeah. Sure, why not?'

'Hashtag Keep Her Buried!'

'What?'

'The Bad Seeds's motto. I've joined the fan club.'

'Ah. Great. Cheers. Thanks a lot.'

'Will you be in the pub later? Fintan's given up the back room for old Cormac's coffin.'

'Who's old Cormac?'

'The old lad from the village. His funeral's tomorrow.'

'Oh yeah. The alibi funeral. Got it. Yeah, I might pop along. Cheers.'

And then I did this sort of weird hand gesture which I've never done in my entire life. No idea what was going through my mind – it just struck me that if this was going to be the kind of Bad Seeds interaction I was going to have hence forwards, I'd need a 'thing' – a gesture to go along with #KeepHerBuried. I now know that I can't carry off a hand gesture – I'm too British. I walked out of there feeling like a complete cunt.

The wake for old Cormac initially seemed like any other night at The White Horse. A bit of singing, a cluster of people playing instruments in the corner, Fintan and Mary pulling pints, and a bit of dancing on the hearth rug.

The only difference seemed to be the corpse in the back room.

But on closer inspection, there were a number of rituals that had been carried out for the occasion. The mirrors had been covered with torn sheets, the wall clock had been stopped at 5.48 – the time of Cormac's death – and the back function room where they usually held darts tournaments was now a makeshift chapel of rest with a wailing old woman under the dartboard who 'keened' as people came in to pay their respects.

Nobody seemed unhappy about Cormac going and I wondered if he'd been as loathed as much as Laddy but apparently not – this was just the way people dealt with death here. Once they'd seen the coffin and said their prayers for him, they went into the main bar, toasted his passing, shared stories about him and talked about the 'better place' he'd gone to.

The sound of the old keening woman drew me into the coffin room though I didn't know why – I'd never even met Cormac. I think I just wanted to see his body. See if it elicited the same erotic charge as it had in the past whenever I had killed someone.

But it didn't.

It didn't stir anything in me at all.

It was just a body; waxy, still and smelling slightly of BO and mouldy vegetables, lying in a box lined with white satin in the middle of a function room. He wore a suit and his hands were clasped on his stomach and wrapped with rosary beads. His eyes were stitched shut like Grandad's had been. The keening woman glanced at me, mid-wail, and I thought I might burst into flames or something. Then she closed her eyes, carried on, and continued to howl her plaintive notes through the window.

'It's freezing in here,' said a voice beside me.

'Fintan said they have to keep a window open in case his soul hasn't left yet.'

'Ah right.' Nnedi crossed herself and stared at Cormac's waxy face, the same way I had done. The top window was on the latch. 'Why are you in here?'

'Just wanted to see if it had any effect on me, like it does everyone else who's come out of here dabbing their cheeks.'

'And does it?'

'Nope. No reaffirming character arc for me. I barely give a shit when people I *know* die. Why would I care about this old trout?'

I sort-of laughed and Nnedi looked at me and sort-of laughed back. 'What's happening in there, anything?'

'The bald man – Seamus? – he's just arrived with a concertina. He was moaning about his "shower of bastards" sheep that got out on the road. He'd only just finished rounding them up. Billy and Séan have just got here too.'

'You fancy Billy, don't you?'

'I do not,' she scoffed.

'Yeah you do. Why don't you ask him out?'

'Hardly the time or the place.'

'Oh just do it, Nnedi – don't wait. Grind on that bulge 'til it falls off.'

Nnedi laughed and the keening woman stopped and glared at her, as wild-eyed as the banshee. Nnedi went back to piety by the death bed.

'I can't stand enforced socialising. I'd rather be with the corpse.'

'Me neither actually,' she said. 'Oh and we've about a dozen free drinks apiece at the bar, Mary said. Courtesy of various regulars.'

'More bribes,' I scoffed, looking at old Cormac's blank face. 'I remember seeing Grandad like this when they brought him to Honey Cottage before his funeral. My nan insisted on it. She locked me in the kitchen with him. She said, "You should see what you've done, you little psychopath." True story.'

'That's terrible.'

'It didn't have the desired effect. She wanted me to bang on the door screaming and crying to be let out. When they unlocked it, they found me playing Tiddlywinks with him. I made up this game – if a wink landed on his face, that was ten points, on his eye fifteen . . .'

'Yeah I get the picture,' said Nnedi. I couldn't read her expression but it was the usual one people had on their face when I'd said something weird, so I left it at that. But then she said: 'For what it's worth, I don't think you're a psychopath.'

'No?'

'I've known psychopaths and there is no empathy whatsoever. You do have empathy.'

'What's wrong with me then? What am I?'

'I don't know,' said Nnedi. 'You're a confusion of lots of different things. There's some lack of empathy but not entirely. There's some narcissism but there's kindness as well. There's a great deal of love there, but it gets buried sometimes underneath bitterness and the need for revenge.'

'Maybe.'

After a long time she said: 'But I think mainly, you've always wanted power because at an early age that was taken from you. And you've spent a long time proving to yourself, and the world, that you do have the ultimate power. You can take a life without giving it a second thought. And for a disenfranchised person, a bullied person, a cheated person, a put-upon person, being able to do that is a very appealing prospect.'

'Oh right.'

'And you do have a lot of power still. You are holding all the cards here. Even over them.' She nodded towards the main bar and the cacophonous Cranberries sing-along that had just started up. 'You don't have to kill again – you could subvert all their expectations and just . . . hand yourself in, if you wanted to.'

'No way. I'm looking forward to tomorrow. The Marshmallow Man has been summoned and that is fucking that.'

She nodded, imperceptibly, as we continued to listen to the old woman wailing and stare at the waxy old Cormac in his box. I kept wondering if some sad feelings about Seren would bubble up from somewhere as I stared. But it wasn't there. It just wasn't there.

Neither of us said much else. We didn't talk, we didn't sing, and when we were done at the coffin-side, we sat in our usual corner by the fire (specially reserved) and listened as the fast songs melted into a slow air on the concertina, with various Marys taking it in turns to sing plaintive sean-nós songs. The turf fire beside our table crackled and Fintan would come over now and again to stoke it up or chuck on a couple of rolls of turf.

'Are you enjoying yourself, girls?' he called out over the music.

We both nodded but neither of us answered. Mary brought over another tray of drinks, courtesy of Arti from the post office, and we sláinte'd her from across the bar. Everyone looked happy – big smiles, ruddy cheeks, terrible teeth. I wished I could have felt what they were feeling. It was a safe and warm place to live, but without Raf it was just a place. Everywhere was nowhere without him. I couldn't even fake the act for once; that night, I just couldn't be bothered.

I needed something to bring me back to life again and before Raf it had been killing. Maybe killing McVicker would bring me back to myself – the self I'd come to know. The self who could solve all her problems, remove her anxiety and clear up her acne with a couple of axe blows to the back of a neck.

The trouble was, that's not what I really wanted. I wanted Raf to walk through that door right now. Pathetic, I know, that I was pinning all my hopes on my Mexican knight in shining armour to come striding through that door to save me. But I was. I couldn't think of anything else beyond that. Without him, I may as well give myself up like I know Nnedi wanted me to. But I had to keep believing. I knew Raf wouldn't let me down. I stared at my phone, continuing to wait for a miracle text that wouldn't come.

Then I remembered – someone like me doesn't deserve miracles.

Sunday, 31 October – Day 10 in Aoibhneas

Laddy's house was nearly a mile away from the village itself, down a quiet side road which turned into a winding lane too narrow for two vehicles to pass simultaneously. Fintan's intel told us McVicker always attended a big record fair in Dingle, about half an hour away, and so our best bet was to break into the house, Nnedi could search for clues to unsolved cases, and we could surprise him when he came back, Gordon Ramsay clap – done. Billy showed us on the map a copse one field away from his place where we could park up. On the other side of the field was a hedge leafy enough to hide behind where we'd have a perfect view of him leaving.

'It's a traditional Irish long house,' Nnedi informed me.

'What does that mean?'

'People and animals used to cohabit in them under the same roof – animals at one end, living space at the other – and they called them long houses. He's got a fair bit of land at the back by the looks.'

'His car's still there – Billy said the record fair was at ten, didn't he?'

'Yes. It's almost ten now.'

'What if he didn't take the bait?'

'He will. Believe me.' Nnedi took a deep breath.

'What?'

'I don't know. This is uncharted territory for me, staking out a house of an alleged sex offender with a murderer of alleged sex offenders.'

'Every day's a school day,' I muttered, scanning the house. 'And there's no "alleged" about it – this guy's like a stick of paedo rock. I noticed a load of steam coming out around the back – he must have a tumble dryer on. That'll be the best place to check for an open window.'

We waited another twenty minutes and my knees were going to sleep, crouched down behind that hedge. 'I've had enough of this.'

'NO WAIT!' urged Nnedi, pulling me back down.

'It's nearly eleven o'clock – an hour we've been here now and we haven't seen sight nor sound of him – he's not going, the plan failed. I'll just go in there and shank him.'

'I just saw something. Someone walked past that window. I swear it was him. Hold your horses.'

True enough, no sooner had Nnedi seen him than the front door opened and out he lumbered – the big galoot in the long black coat and trilby; shaggy hair like a Halloween wig, heavy boots – heading towards a clumsily parked green Volvo on the front gravel. He clambered inside his car, waiting an age while he lit another stubby cigar, then finally the engine started and he reversed out of the driveway. We edged around the side of the hedge so he wouldn't see us when his car backed out and eventually disappeared up the road.

'Okay, let's go,' I said, but Nnedi pulled me back down.

'Give it a minute – in case he has to come back for something.'

We gave it fifteen minutes, to be precise, before we moved from behind that hedge, by which point one of my knees had locked and Nnedi had pins and needles in both feet. By the time we made it around the back of the house, we were reanimated and ready for action.

The house itself was dead ugly – all pebbledash render and windows that hadn't seen a washcloth or a lick of paint in decades. There were a number of weather-beaten sheds dotted around the back yard, the wooden walls half rotten away at the bottom. The odd algae-spattered water bowl or chewed dog toy lay scattered about along with sundry other pieces of debris of no fixed abode – a hosepipe kinkier than an Amsterdam brothel. Cracked flower pots a-gogo. Stinking, overflowing bins. Scummy drain covers. Broken paving slabs. Old bald tyres stacked up. And a patch of grass with a large black scorch in the middle of it, clearly reserved for bonfires. He'd had one recently too – pallets and rusty mattress springs were all that remained.

One of the back windows was on the latch and there was indeed a tumble dryer hose wedged in the opening and the steam was still billowing out. 'There you go, told you.'

With Old Meg's axe safely tucked in my belt, I reached inside and undid the catch on the larger window with my right, but the bugger wouldn't open – painted shut by the looks.

'Oh ball sacks.'

'Hang on a sec,' said Nnedi, trying the back door. It was unlocked.

'Why would he leave it unlocked?' I said, still with one leg up on the sill.

'Who's he got to be afraid of around here? Everyone's afraid of *him*.'

'Good point.'

Nnedi went on in ahead of me, walking almost on tiptoes and keeping her back firmly against the wall at all times.

'Why are you walking like that?'

'Like what?'

'Like you're on *Line of Duty*. We just saw him leave.'

'Force of habit,' she said.

The first room was a dingy utility area with the aforementioned tumble dryer and washing machine under the window, a Belfast sink where some grey long-johns were soaking, and cupboard of cleaning equipment – mop bucket, rubber gloves, tubs of Swarfega, and a family-size box of Daz.

'No tied-up hostages or vats of hydrochloric acid,' I remarked, pulling on my gloves. 'Yet.'

We entered the kitchen via a flagstone floor like the one at Old Meg's – just as dingy as the utility and occupied by unkempt piles of random objects – tins of paint, rusty gardening equipment, tools, household appliances mid-repair, candles in dishes, old newspapers, books, VHS tapes (mostly porn) and rolls of chicken wire, presumably acquired for the purposes of mending the broken perimeter fence. In a corner of the ceiling hung dozens of fly papers, all rammed with long-dead flies.

'That's never a good sign,' I said.

Nnedi was studying a plate of what looked like mouldy cheese lying out on the draining board. 'He doesn't seem particularly fond of food hygiene so there's any number of reasons he'd have flies.'

'What about these?' I said, picking up a video from the VHS porn pile.

'Not illegal,' she noted. 'They've all been on general release; all at least twenty years old or more.'

'What are you looking for exactly?'

'Evidence. Clues. Trophies. I'll know it when I see it. But I'm going to start with his computer. I'm going to check upstairs.'

There was a green curtain hanging on the wall opposite, leading to a doorway. She flicked on a grimy wall light to ignite a dim, winding staircase.

'Place stinks of sweat and regret. Take this,' I said, handing her a hammer from a metal toolbox on top of the fridge. 'Better to have it and not need it, eh, Nnedi McPhee?'

'I can't,' she said, as she'd said just before we'd left.

'Just in case he comes back,' I reaffirmed.

She took it but I knew she was about as keen on not using violence as I was of using it. I continued to look half-heartedly through his stuff, rooting through boxes and bags and finding nothing more interesting than a cracked Beyoncé CD and a glass box containing a taxidermy bird with no head.

'Okay, now you're just being creepy for creepy's sake. I'm not impressed,' I muttered, throwing it back in its box. Just off the kitchen on the opposite side to the utility was a pantry and the door was ajar.

'Holy Armageddon preppers, Batman!' I gasped, pulling on the light. It wasn't so dirty in there – in fact, it was immaculately clean and stocked better than the village shop. Cases of bottled water on the floor, all wrapped in plastic; myriad cans of soup, beans, fruit, chopped tomatoes; unopened boxes of cereal bars, bottled oils, jams, pasta, rice; sacks of potatoes and carrots; and a sort of washboard thing hanging from the ceiling, on which he appeared to be drying out various strips of meat and fish.

I sniffed them in turn, picking the nearest one down to ensure it *was* just meat and fish and not disembodied peen or vadge. After the headless bird art, I wouldn't put it past the creep to have home-smoked female vajoodles.

In a large upright box in the pantry he had a stash of weapons – three shotguns, several boxes of ammunition and a crude-looking pellet gun with a knife strapped to the barrel. If I'd had more time, I'd have gone at that cupboard like the fat guy finding the hatch on *Lost*, but only one item in there shone brighter than the rest: around five boxes of Pop Tarts.

'Hallelujah sang the angels! Oh yes, hello my pretty babies!' My mouth filled with saliva. 'Gotta be done.'

I pocketed a box inside my hoodie and placed the rest of them back on the shelf, arranging the boxes back like I'd found them before realising that the guy would be dead by sundown anyway, so what did it matter how much of his stash I ate? So I took all of them – every last box – and piled them all up on the kitchen table. I located a toaster, fairly clean, in a cupboard and plugged it in to roast two tarts. Perks of the job and all that.

There was still no sign of any movement outside – no Laddy bombing back up the lane in his green Volvo, no Gardai coming to take me away *ha ha*, so I ventured up the stairs Nnedi had taken to the first floor. Low ceilings abounded like the place was achingly collapsing in on itself and the floorboards creaked like a thousand moaning corpses so I moved slowly, careful not to alarm the hostage he had tied to his king size.

But he was clean. Well, not clean, but clean of hostages, corpses and bedpost skulls anyway.

'Oi Oi! You about?' I called.

'In here,' came the somewhat muted reply. As I followed her sound, I walked into a second bedroom that had been set up as part sleeping quarters, part office with a laptop open on an old writing desk covered in battered green leather. The walls were edged with heaving bookcases and the desk overlooked the front garden. Nnedi sat at the laptop, staring at the screen.

'You got into his computer?' I said.

'Yes. It was just hibernating.'

'Anything juicy?'

She almost did an *Exorcist* 360-degree tun of the head to look at me. 'Yes, unfortunately. He seems to frequent the dark web. I'm just sifting through a few tabs to see what he's been looking at. Or buying.'

'Obvs,' I said. 'Oh my god!' I cried, storming across the room to his tallboy where my little woollen gatita was perched.

'Ugh,' said Nnedi. 'He *did* break in then.'

'The fucker.' I smelled the little woollen cat. 'I hope he hasn't done anything on it. Or to it.' I checked the stitches on the back and placed it back down on the tallboy. It had lost its comforting presence in my life somehow.

'What's that smell?' asked Nnedi, still engrossed in all things digital.

'Pop Tarts. I found some in his pantry. Just toasting some off.'

She afforded me another glare. 'You're cooking *Pop Tarts*?'

'Yeah. Do you want one? He's got loads – he won't miss 'em.'

She turned back to the computer muttering, 'Unbelievable' under her breath. I glanced around the room at the myriad stacks of boxes, bags, piles of clothing and cupboards beside the bed.

'Any clues to the housewife rape yet?'

'No, he's cleared his browsers fairly recently, so if he keeps tabs on the investigation we wouldn't know just from a search.

He's got a lot of files and folders on here, short stories and a lot of poetry, all doggerel . . . there's some diaries as well but I'd have to do some more digging to link any of the entries with unsolved cases in the area . . . if he's guilty there's bound to be something though. He's written some children's books as well, of all things.'

'Ugh god, let's have a look . . .'

Nnedi clicked open a series of folders containing Word docs titled things like 'The Elf Who Crapped Out Christmas' and 'The Fairy Who Shat Glitter' and things like that – I've embellished slightly, I ain't advertising his shite.

While Nnedi continued sifting through the man's digital rubbish, I wandered next door to a room full of shelves containing all his twelve-inch records. It seemed to contain every single album ever made – you name it – and they were all pristine, some still in the plastic wrapper, some in faded, flattened Our Price or Woolworths bags and some scratched up to oblivion. There was a record player in the corner, plugged in, overlooking the back field with the broken chicken wire fence.

'There's another bonfire patch at the back,' I called out.

'What?'

'*Two* bonfire patches actually. Is that significant?'

She sounded distracted. 'Not sure – go and check it out maybe?'

'Shall I go practise my axe swing while I'm out there?' I said, popping my face back around the door of the second bedroom. She shooed me away, still glued to the computer screen.

I went back downstairs on the pop of the toaster and reeled off five sheets of kitchen roll to eat my Pop Tarts on. I had a cursory look in some of the cupboards as I practised swiping my axe through the air, forming a half-assed plan in my head as I chewed – stand behind the back door, wait until he comes in, then twat him when his back's turned. He drops to his knees, I hack him again, across the neck if I get a clear shot, but my aim wasn't so great anymore with my shitty wrist. I did have one extra tool in my arsenal though – the element of surprise. That was always the clincher.

I'd read an entire copy of *The Irish Post* and eaten four Pop Tarts while I waited for Nnedi to come down. I practised my stance behind the back door – swinging the axe through the air where it made a satisfying **Thwip!** I wandered about the place, rooting through more cupboards and drawers, drawling my outdated *Through the Keyhole* impression – Loyd Grossman era.

'What kind of a paedophile lives in a house like this? This fine Irish long house, where cows used to shit up the walls, now boasts the best in unkempt and unfashionable furnishings. The store cupboard is prepped with more tins of Scotch broth and mulligatawny than I've seen in my entire life, which tells me the owner of this house is ready for anything – mainly soup.

'If we go into the living quarters, we see these moth-eaten sofas and armchairs sporting hairs of wolfhounds long dead. Now you'd expect a house like this to contain maybe a little mould and damp but here we have an entire ceiling full of it . . .'

I unclicked a latch to a little store cupboard off the living room containing a Henry vacuum cleaner, gathering more dust than it had ever sucked up.

'Henry clearly doesn't see much action around here. And if we go into the first of two ground-floor store rooms we'll find . . . shite. And in the second of the two ground-floor rooms, even more shite. This householder is really going for it with the whole . . . pile-of-shite aesthetic—'

I nearly jumped out of my skin when Nnedi appeared behind me, without warning; hammer raised in her fist. No creaks on the stairs to herald her arrival, no talk, nothing. She was just there, like a ghoul.

'You have to kill him.'

'You've changed your tune.' I laughed. She didn't.

'Do it,' she said.

There was a noise outside. The green Volvo pulled into the driveway, covered in fresh mud spatters. The digital wall clock ticked over to 12.14 p.m.

'Why? What have you found?'

'Fuck!' she said, as we both ran towards the kitchen. I silently hoped he'd come through the front door into the lounge, rather than the back. Nnedi Homer-Simpsoned herself into the wall behind the open pantry door as outside footsteps crunched across the gravel towards the back of the house.

'Typical.'

I ran across into the utility room and made for the dark corner behind the door. I could still see Nnedi diagonally across the kitchen from me – she made no effort to move from her spot behind the open pantry door, still gripping the hammer.

'Finish him, now,' she hissed.

'Why?' I mouthed. 'Tell me what you found!'

She didn't blink. She didn't answer either.

There was no time for her to elaborate anyway. I could hear his boots crunching across the gravel, coming ever closer to the back door. I hadn't covered my tracks in the kitchen at all – the pantry light was still on and the door wide open, there were boxes of Pop Tarts all over the cluttered kitchen table and the countertop was covered in toast crumbs.

Goldilocks was about to be rumbled by the biggest of all the bears. But the worst part was I realised I'd left my axe on the table. Aka nowhere near me. Aka I was going to have to face down this creep *again* without a weapon. Blimey, was *I* out of practice at all this.

'Can you pass me my axe?' I whispered to Nnedi across two rooms.

'*What*?' she mouthed.

I needed it. So I legged it out from behind the door and ran to the kitchen, just as the latch went on the back door.

No time to do anything else, not even hide as the creep crept in, a stack of vinyl records tucked under one arm, and lumbered into his house on a waft of tobacco and a string of wet coughs.

He set down the records on the tumble dryer and wrenched off his hat and coat, hanging them on the pegs on the back door. And then he saw me.

'What the Jesus . . . YOU AGAIN!'

'Surprise!' I said, standing there with my axe dangling by my side.

'GET OUT OF MY HOUSE, YOU CAN'T BREAK IN HERE. How feckin' DARE YOU!' his voice boomed, shaking the foundations. 'I have rights. Where's your bitch friend? Is she here as well?'

'No,' I said.

'I been watching you wash your tits. Very nice.'

'Well, that's as close to them as *you'll* ever get.'

I watched as he flipped the kitchen table right over in a

show of strength designed to scare me. I glanced past him at Nnedi, wide-eyed and stock still, cowering in the shadows. I willed her with my eyes but she just continued to stare.

He stepped closer. 'What you gonna do then? Cut my head off, Little Red Riding Hood? Go on then.'

I didn't move.

'GO ON THEN! DO IT! KILL ME!' he roared.

'Nah.'

'Why did you bring the axe with you then?'

'For a laugh.'

'Liar. You came here to finish me off, didn't you? You and your slave girl. Well, come on then – finish me. Where is she, out picking cotton? Go on, finish me off. I dare you.'

'No.'

'DO IT!'

I glanced again at Nnedi, then back at him. I said it slowly and purposely this time. 'No.'

With no further monologing, his arm thrust out before him and he grabbed my throat in his meaty fist, squeezing as hard as he could muster. I couldn't breathe at all – in or out; I was stuck in stasis as he tightened his grip; teeth bared, bloodshot, sweaty-eyed and wild, his jowly neck quivering with the force of his exertion. He forced me down, down, down to the kitchen floor, onto my knees. I searched for Nnedi but she was blocked behind the great stinking whiskery bulk of McVicker and his meaty fist.

I gasped as he squeezed me tighter.

'Not so clever-tongued now, are you, bitch?' he spat, his voice all wobbly with the effort of his squeezing. 'Yeah, you just shut that clever mouth. I feckin' dare you to say something smart to me now.'

But I couldn't. I grabbed at him but couldn't reach; I couldn't see the axe anywhere – my head was stuck facing him as my neck sang with pain. He'd beaten me. The lights were dimming as I tried again to gasp but caught nothing; no release – just the vice-like grip on my throat that wouldn't ease. My world darkened before my eyes – the start of a tunnel appeared, and I started the long walk down it.

'I'm going to kill the pair of you!' I heard him yell, and just as I could feel myself falling into the abyss, I saw her; saw the mighty sweep of her arm, as Nnedi thumped the hammer down hard on the back of his head with a satisfying *CRAAAAACK!*

His grip released on my throat and I stumbled away, towards the wall, panting and gasping back to full wakefulness.

When I looked back at her, Nnedi was tearing into Laddy's skull with the hammer like she was in a rage room. The only time I'd ever seen anyone go in harder than that, it had been me. It was like all my rage had been sucked out of me and slid into her. She smashed and bashed and screamed as that hammer went in and in and in, turning Laddy McVicker's once perfectly normal-sized head into a slit-open watermelon with added pulp.

' F U U U U U U U U U U U U U C C C C K K K K K K YOOOOOOUUUUUU!' she yelled.

It was fucking beautiful.

'ARRRGGHHH! DIIIEEEE YOU FUCKING BASTAAARRRDDDDD!'

And then it was me stopping her – holding her wrist just as she was about to launch in for the hundredth time. The hammer stood aloft in her quivering fist, the anvil covered in a hairy, bloody pulp formerly serving as Laddy McVicker's brain, scalp and cerebrospinal fluid.

'It's done,' I breathed with her. 'He's gone.'

When she met my stare, her eyes were watery and unblinking, fierce and furious. Her grip released on the hammer and it fell to the floor with a metallic clank. She stood before me, shivering, slamming her shaking hands to her face, looking down at what she'd done with what I can only assume was abject horror.

Without warning, she burst into tears.

'What did you find? On his computer?'

'The . . . motherlode,' she whispered, like the word hurt her to say it. She hid her face in her hands. 'He's a monster. Women, girls, babies . . .'

I looked down at the person formerly known as Laddy and caught sight of the axe lying a few feet away by the upturned table. I could have lain into him myself, cut his head off his shoulders, and drop kicked it into the bin. But I didn't. There was no need. Instead, I moved closer to Nnedi and held onto her, expecting a shove backwards. But she didn't. And moments later, I felt her arms around me too and we hugged.

Nnedi had killed TWO whole-assed people since I'd been with her. My kill count was still on ZERO. See? That's growth. I was the goody-two-shoes saint for once and *she* was the maniac.

Who'da thunk it?!

It was around 5 p.m. by the time a can of petrol had nicely got Laddy burning like a hog roast beneath a pile of gathered logs, pallets and planks. The night sky blanketed us with a cold, starry chill. Nnedi was too quiet for my liking, sitting out beside the fire, watching Laddy burn and keeping her thoughts to herself. I made us hot chocolates – thought it might cheer her up.

'TA-DA!' I said, greeting her at the bonfire with a plate of Pop Tarts and the two hot drinks. 'Get that down you – I put two sugars in.'

'I don't want it.'

I set the tray down on the ground in front of us and sat back on my tyre stack, sinking a mouthful of warming sweetness and gasping out the steam into the cold night air. 'You did good in there.'

'Did I?'

'Yeah. You went to town on the fucker.'

'You don't get it, do you?'

'What's to get? He was a paedophile. Now he's an *ex*-paedophile. One down, seven hundred and ninety-nine million, nine hundred and ninety-nine thousand, nine hundred and ninety-nine more to go.' I removed the long black bundle from my pocket and opened it up on the ground before the fire.

'What's that?'

'Barbecue set. Sabatier too, of all makes. I found it on the top shelf in his pantry.' The set included a fork, knife, spatula, and pair of tongs, all held in place by elastic hoops. 'Choose your weapon.'

'You want to toast marshmallows over his burning corpse?'

'No, Pop Tarts. Take one or I'll skewer you with it.' She stared up at me. 'I'm kidding, just take one.'

Nnedi took the knife; I took the fork and we sat there, almost like two mates around a campfire. Except we weren't telling stories or reminiscing and she wasn't eating or drinking. She seemed lost, deep inside her own mind.

'Why didn't you fight back?'

'I was waiting for you to.'

'Why?'

'Cos I wanted you to save me.'

'But *why*?'

'Cos you needed to. You bottle everything up. You need to let it out once in a while, just for once.'

'You *made* me kill him? Are you insane?'

'Have you only just figured that out?'

I got up and handed her the hot chocolate again. 'Here, drink it while it's warm.' This time she took it. And she drank, blinking into the flames.

'Men like him are not worth a second of your sympathy. As far as I'm concerned, you just put down a rabid fox that was causing nothing but harm.'

'I know,' she said.

'Then why are you being all sulky and shit?'

'Because I don't understand myself anymore.'

'Cos you killed a paedophile?'

'No. Because I don't feel anything. I killed a human being with my own hands and I don't feel sad. I feel . . . scared. I don't recognise what I did as me.'

'You get over it. I was the same with my first. It gets easier.'

'I don't *want* it to get easier. I don't *want* to be a killer.'

'Bit late for that, innit?'

'I don't know who I am when I'm with you. I find myself rooting for you. And I know I shouldn't. But what I saw on his computer . . . brought something out in me.'

'This is the kid porn, right?'

Her eyes flashed. 'Don't call it porn – it is online child exploitation. More like a gateway to hell.'

'What do you mean?'

She sipped her drink and exhaled steam into the night air. 'He has all these folders titled strange things . . . a word that doesn't make sense or a word with numbers and letters, like he'd just ran his hand across the keyboard when saving them. There are pictures of girls in them. Girls in toilets. Changing rooms. Supermarkets. Pushchairs.'

We both stared into the flames.

'There's worse too. Pictures other people have taken which he's saved. That's what he uses the dark web for, amongst other things. McVicker is – *was* – a member of a site called Ganymede, a forum where mostly men exchange conversations and imagery. And videos. Of children. Some newborn.'

A pinch in my chest. 'Can't say I'm surprised.'

'There's one man on there, in Thailand, goes by the name AsianPhil101. But he's not Asian – he's a white man in his sixties by the looks. Seems to be one of the main procurers of the children in his posts. He must pay their mothers, I don't know. I couldn't look for long. And there are three other men, all of whom seem to run this forum. Four admins – thousands of subscribers.'

'You found out all this in a quick search of his laptop?'

'It didn't feel quick. The thread McVicker had most recently posted on was him sharing photos of a child on a bus. Talking about what he'd do to this . . . toddler. And there were others. Pictures he'd made. Appointments he was setting up with other men to abuse their little girls.' She stared into the fire, watching him burn.

'Your breathing's levelled off,' I noted.

She paid it no mind. 'There are children being abused, *right now*,' she continued, like she'd only just realised these things went on. 'Somewhere in Thailand by AsianPhil101. By the *dozen*.' She looked across at me, face lit on one side by the flames. 'I want to bring them down, Rhiannon. All of them.'

'Then let's do it,' I said. 'You can track these admins, right?'

'Their posts are encrypted, as is the whole site, but I think their IP addresses are traceable via their avatars.'

'Well then.'

'Well, *what* then?'

'These other admins don't know Laddy's dead, do they?' I said, pointing at the fire. 'You can trap them. Get them to reveal their exact locations. *All* of them.' I chucked my remaining Pop Tart on the pyre. 'We both have our ways of dealing with these cunts. I do *this* . . . you "do the right thing". We don't have to be the same. But my god are we on the same side.'

She nodded, almost imperceptibly.

I continued, finally seeing what she couldn't. 'You tracked *me* down – lured me to Claudia's, knowing I'd do anything for Ivy. You knew Laddy was going to follow me the other day. You knew Billy was telling the truth. And you knew how to navigate that computer. You can track *them* down. You can save those kids. *You* can do that.'

'How?'

'What do you mean "how"? You're a detective. This is literally what you're trained to do. And you do it fucking well.'

'These men are all over the world. There are thousands of them.' But Nnedi being Nnedi knew there was always a way. She got to thinking. 'I mean if I connected with other agencies . . . formed a taskforce, maybe . . .'

'There you go! And if the man at the top won't take you seriously, I'll give you the number of a journalist who *will*.' I pointed back towards the house. 'You've got the means right there on that laptop.'

The flames illuminated her features as new shoots of

possibility seemed to sprout in her mind. 'You really think they're going to let me be a detective again, after this?'

'They don't know about this, do they? As far as Jai Amarkeeri knows, you're going up a blind alley following leads about me anyway. They don't even know you're here.'

'Yet. When they trace the Audi—'

'Forget that. I told you, I can take the blame for most of this. And when you're back in work, you can set up your own taskforce – and if they don't let you, set up as a *private* dick instead. Fuck the Met, like they fucked you.'

'I *can* track them down,' she said, with more confidence. 'I noted there was one in Berlin. Another in Toulouse. Two in London, and this AsianPhil101 somewhere in Thailand. I got as far as his Facebook page and a note of his car reg. I'm pretty sure, with the right equipment, I can extract his geolocation data from the video of him abusing one of the girls.'

'What you've got up there is Pandora's Box,' I told her. 'That laptop will lead you to all the others. And the best part is – they won't know it's you.'

But she shook her head. 'I'm good but I'm not *that* good. I could pass it on to someone. Maybe, I don't know.'

'Let someone else take all the credit? Don't you want to help those kids?'

She stood up straighter. 'Of course I do!'

'You didn't help those girls at the care homes much, did you? You buried all that to save your job.'

'FUCK YOU!' she yelled. 'How dare you say that to me!'

'It's true, isn't it? You were told to bury it and you did. You did what you had to do to keep your job.'

'They'd have had me killed! And I have been in HELL since I found out about that – there was nothing I could do to help those girls. They *can't* be avenged – it was too long ago! Don't you dare say I sent them down the river – I am in torment for them.'

'What good does torment do?' I spat back at her. *'Aww no, little Nnedi feels so bad for those kiddies but her hands are tied, soz* – WHAT ABOUT THEM? How do you think they've felt every day remembering what those bastards did to them? How do you think those kids feel on those webcams? I've done some pretty bad things, I admit. But one thing I've *never* done is allow a predator to get away with it when I knew I could do something.'

She stayed quiet for a long time. Then, much quieter, she said:

'I'd have to be careful not to give my identity away. I'd need to study all his posts. Ugh, I'm not trained in this.'

'Trained schmained,' I flapped. 'You're the bravest, smartest, most devious bitch I've ever met. You fronted out Laddy McVicker with a rusty hammer. You fronted out my dad when he was cutting off your fingers. You came after *me*. Alone. You're their worst nightmare. Apart from me, of course.'

She threw me a look which I couldn't read – I didn't know if she was going to kiss me or confess something. Turned out to be neither. But she did do one thing which was fairly shocking – she smiled. She liked this plan. The fire was in her eyes again.

I smiled back at her. 'I knew there was a reason I couldn't kill you.'

'What about the untouchable ones?' she said.

'What do you mean?'

'This Asian Phil – looks as though he's got money. Could

be a top businessman in Thailand. The ones at the top are always hardest to trap.'

'Send them to me. I'll deal with them. Good and evil can be two sides of the same coin, you know. Just depends how you flip it.'

She held out her mug – I held out mine. 'To flipping the coin,' she said.

I clinked my mug with hers. 'Always.'

It was just before 9 p.m. when we'd cleaned the kitchen, burned all the evidence we could find and left the bonfire as glowing embers having slung what was left of Laddy McVicker down his own cess pit.

When we got back to Old Meg's, there was a bottle of homemade blackberry whiskey on the doorstep. I read the note on the neck:

'Courtesy of the McLaggans up at Teer Farm' whoever they are and wherever that is.

'Good idea,' said Nnedi, taking the bottle from me and unlocking the door. I went around lighting candles and brought two jam jars over for us to drink out of but Nnedi was already sitting before the fire, necking the bottle.

'Jesus, get a room.'

She came up for air, squinting from the glug. 'My GOD that's good. Who are the McLaggans and do any of them have single sons?'

I took the bottle from her and tried it for myself. 'Fuck me. After that first hit that makes you feel like you've been punched in the throat, you get a splash of fruit and then it slips like a . . . like a . . . sword. But a nice sword. A rubber sword.'

'Don't become a wine taster whatever you do.' She laughed,

reaching for the bottle again. The fire in the hearth crackled before us.

'So what do we do now?' I said. 'Now we've done the deed?'

She shrugged. 'Wait it out, I suppose. However long it takes.'

I stared down at the side of her armchair where she'd dumped Laddy's laptop and a bunch of cables. 'You going to make a start on that lot?'

She shook her head. 'Not tonight. I just want to get pissed.'

I took the bottle. 'Your eyes are already rolling and you've only had about three sips.'

'Good,' she said. 'The sooner I'm comatose the better. But I don't want to dream tonight. I don't want to dream ever again.'

'Thank you,' I said. And she didn't ask me what for, just reached for the whiskey so she could take another glug. 'You did good tonight.'

'I know.' She grinned.

She had passed out in the armchair before the bottle was finished and she did indeed drink the lion's share of it. I showered and changed for bed and as I was brushing my hair out in front of the fire and listening to Nnedi's plaintive snores, there came a loud *rat-a-tat-tat* at the door.

It was Billy.

'Hey, you good? All done, is it?' he asked on the doorstep.

'Yeah, all done.'

'Ahh you been on the old McLaggans moonshine, have you?' he remarked, spying the empty bottle on the table and the snoozing detective in the chair. 'She'll be out for days.'

'It was tough today. Well, she found it tough. I found it all rather enjoyable. Like being back in the saddle.'

'What have you done with him?'

'Burned. Did some of his clothes too to make it look like he'd gone on holiday. Even filled it in on his little wall calendar. Ashes went down the drain and any bones went in the cess pit. It's dealt with, it's fine, don't worry. If the cops come knocking, it'll look like he's on a trip.'

'Good. Then we can go.'

'Go where? It's nearly ten o'clock; the pub'll be shut.'

'We're not going to the pub. Grab your things, come on.'

'No. What's happening?'

From his back pocket, Billy produced a small white envelope. 'Everyone had a whip-round – there's about four grand in there in euros. You can change it up at the airport.'

'Airport? We're going to the airport? Have you heard from Raf?'

'Yeah, this morning. He emailed me your ticket and told me to get you to the airport by midnight tonight, that's all I know.'

'But—'

'No buts, c'mon, hurry or you'll miss your flight.'

I looked back at Nnedi snoozing away and the roaring fire before her. I took down one of Old Meg's paperback books, tore off the cover and wrote her a note on it. Once I was packed up – which didn't take long – I left the note folded up on her chest and, I don't know why, but I kissed her cheek as well. I didn't want to leave her. It was all too sudden; no plan, no information. It felt wrong.

Billy had borrowed Séan's wagon to collect me with Ben – his car was parked at the pub with ours. I smoothed Ben's snout and clambered up on the seat as he backed up out of the lane.

'Yer grand, we're making good time, stop worrying.'

I clutched my bag to my chest. 'It's not *that* I'm worried about.'

'What is it then?'

'Where am I going?'

'I told you, the airport.'

'Which airport?'

'Shannon.'

'So where am I going from Shannon?'

'Well, your plane ticket is for Faro so I presume he'll meet you there?'

'Faro? Where the fuck's Faro?'

'Portugal. I doubt that's the final destination; knowing Raf, he'll have cooked up something a bit farther afield maybe.'

'I can't live on maybes, Billy.'

'Look, I'm just doing as I'm told, all right? Don't shoot the driver.'

'What the fuck's he playing at? His number's still out of service; he hasn't told me anything.'

'He will. Trust him,' said Billy as we alighted the cart and he pressed the fob on his keyring to unlock his car. I watched him load my bags in the back seat and hugged Ben goodbye, smoothing my cheek against his fur.

'I don't want to go, Ben. I really don't want to go.' Ben farted in response, a real buttock-flapper, which I took to mean he wasn't listening to me either.

My breath fogged up the window as Billy drove. My god it seemed such a long time since I'd last sat in a car with Billy driving – the journey from Heathrow to Coddleford-on-the-Fosse. Inhaling the fumes of his faded coconut Sex Wax air freshener dangling from his mirror. Ten days ago – it seemed like two lifetimes ago.

I suddenly felt so tired at the thought of a two-and-a-half hour journey to Shannon but Billy was the one doing all the work I suppose. My work was done. I just had to sit tight, again, and pray Raf had sorted something out.

'What if something goes wrong, Billy?' I murmured, smoothing over the front of the white envelope.

'What if *what* goes wrong?'

'The ticket, the . . . Oh my god, what about a passport? I can't use the Ophelia White one anymore I'll be flagged – how the hell—'

'It's all right don't sweat it,' he said. 'We know some lads who work at Shannon – they've been told to keep an eye out for you. They'll wave you through.'

'It's not gonna work. It might be a small airport but they're not just going to not check me.'

'They will, don't sweat it.'

He did his usual shit-eating grin and the oncoming headlights actually twinkled off his teeth.

'And what happens at Faro? They'll check me there. Oh Jesus.'

I thought about Nnedi, tucked up back at Laddy's in front of the fire. Waking up in an empty house, wondering where I was. 'Do you think she'll be all right on her own at Old Meg's?'

'Yeah, she'll be grand. When I was tucking Ben up for the night, I told Fintan to keep an eye on her. Mary cooked a ham today so she's gonna take her round a hock and some homemade bread. They'll look after her.'

'But what if—'

'No more what-ifs, Rhiannon. Look, I know you don't like not-having-a-plan but you got to trust Raf has sorted something out for you. Believe in him. He's got you and you've got this. Now, you've got a long journey ahead of you, so why don't you snuggle down and get some shut-eye, eh?'

I gripped the keyring Arti had given me in the shop and read over the message engraved on it in the light of passing cars:

May God Grant you always
a sunbeam to warm you,
a moonbeam to charm you,
and a sheltering angel,
so nothing can harm you.

I stared ahead at the long, unlit road, determined to stay awake and stew the whole way. I had to take this in small chunks or I'd get overwhelmed and then lash out. We just had to get to Shannon, that was all. That was the first step on a staircase that seemed too endless to comprehend.

I felt the car slowing as I woke to the sound of the indicator clicking. I blinked myself awake to see the clock had ticked over to 23:41 p.m. It was pissing with rain and the windscreen wipers silently flicked away water so I could home in on the large floodlit building at the back of the car park we'd just turned in to. A white sign loomed into view with a big gold K emblazoned on it.

'Welcome to Shannon Airport'. The anxiety gremlin began trampolining on my chest. I didn't want to move. I wanted to stay on the heated seat for another hour. I didn't want to step out into the cold and wet and uncertainty, homeless again. I wanted to be back in front of the fire with Nnedi; where I knew I'd be safe. I reached behind me for my bag and scuffled around for Richard E. Grunt before I remembered with dread that he was gone. In my head I was straight back to 2019 and getting aboard that cruise ship.

'Welcome to Shannon, Rhiannon,' announced Billy as the car slowed.

'I've never liked travelling. I still don't. Take me back to the cottage – please. I can't do this.'

'Yeah you can, come on.'

'No, no, I can't. I don't want to wander around the world again, aimless and homeless, I can't go. Please, take me back. I haven't signed Arti's book – she said it was coming soon. I need to sign it for her.'

Billy ignored me and pulled into the short-stay car park underneath one of the orange streetlights, yanked on the handbrake and switched off the engine. The silence in the car was deafening. The main airport building was tiny in comparison to some of the others I'd visited in my time.

'Look at the place – it's titchy. I'll be recognised!'

'You'll be grand. You've got your mask, your ticket. And the cousins'll keep an eye out for you – one works on the check-in – head for the red-haired guy who calls everyone darling, and his husband works in security. He's got a death stare a bit like yours. They'll see you right. They're Bad Seeds too.'

Billy winked and that wink seemed to assuage my anxiety somewhat but I couldn't help thinking this tiny, prying place, which could be very well lit at this time of the evening, was going to be my undoing. *Trust*, I reminded myself. I have to trust this will be okay. I had no other options.

'I can't.'

'I'm not taking you back, Rhiannon. Now come on, out.'

I did as I was told and pulled my coat around me to save

my body from the biting wind and rain. We stepped out of the car and Billy grabbed my bag from the back seat and handed it to me, settling the straps on my shoulders and raising my hood to keep me dry.

'Well, this is where you and I say goodbye, my dear.' He reached out and flung an arm around my back but I didn't hug him back. 'We'll give you a couple days to get clear and then we'll call it all in, all right?'

'Okay.'

'You'll be all right. You're Rhiannon Fucking Lewis.'

'Yeah.'

'You two look after yourselves, all right? And try and send me word you're okay every so often, would ya?'

I squeezed Billy's hand. 'You've been a good friend.'

'Ahh, get out – yer making me blush. Go on, you'll miss your flight.'

'Can't you come with me? Like before?'

'No, Rhiannon. It's not my turn.'

I nodded and turned away from him, before realising with dread. 'Hang on, you haven't emailed me my ticket.'

Billy patted his pockets all over with a blank expression. 'Ah shit, I lost me phone . . .'

'Oh for fuck's sake—'

'Ah yer grand,' he said, with a flap of his hand, leaning back against the car. 'We'll just ask that guy if he's got it instead . . .'

'What guy?'

I followed Billy's line of sight towards the next orange streetlight along. Underneath it stood a lone figure, bundled up in a coat and black-and-yellow Padres baseball cap, a sports bag on the ground beside him. I could see his breath on the freezing air.

I turned back to Billy whose eyebrows jumped. 'Don't kill me – he made me do it.'

'No, it's not,' I said, looking back towards the figure under the streetlight. 'I'm still asleep, aren't I?' I realised with an ache. But I felt the ache – I wasn't dreaming. For once, it *was* him. My beautiful Rafael. And he *was* real.

'Hola, mi cielo,' said the voice; the voice I'd been dreaming about, waiting for, craving, praying and crying for all this time. I couldn't move. He had to come towards me and step into the next orange light along before I could believe it and even then I couldn't see him; there were too many tears.

'What the fuh—' was all I could get out before he scooped me up in his arms and picked me fully off the ground.

'Ay Güey, baby, I've missed you so much,' Raf said, cry-laughing. I wrapped my arms around him and breathed him in – the smell I'd missed – and he wrapped his arms so tightly around me, it was like he was cursing himself for not having enough arms to hold me with. I wilted like a flower in his arms but he held me up and I never wanted him to let go. We pulled back and I held his face in my hands and looked him all over and we kissed hungrily and desperately, like he was kissing every single break and fracture, every bad word, every bad thought away.

'You're shaking.'

I was in shock. I've had hugs before – not often – but this one was something else. Nobody looking at us on the outside would be able to feel the emotions that passed through it but we could feel them, just us two. Almost like a last hug and a first hug, at the same time. Like the last one you ever give someone you love who you know is dying, but the first hug you ever give someone who's come to mean everything to you.

I don't know what the fuck that even means but that's how it felt – important. Everlasting. Almost holy. Like his wings were wrapped around me – my sheltering angel.

'Jesus kids, all right, get a room, would ya?' Billy chuckled behind us.

'I can't believe it—' I sobbed, squeezing him again until Raf *ouched*. 'Oh my god, I'm sorry! Did I hurt you?'

He smiled. 'No, just take it easy – my stitches are only just healing.'

I wiped his cheeks dry and took off his baseball cap to run my hand over his shaved head. 'Oh my god. Your hair!'

'It'll grow back. It's just like you say about your flowers. Doesn't matter how hard you cut them back, they will return to you, every single time.'

We bumped foreheads. 'You came for me. You're alive.'

'I would die for you,' he said. 'Again.' And even though we seemed to have stumbled headlong into the script for *Robin Hood: Prince of Thieves*, it was beautiful. I'd never felt as happy as I did at that moment. Just knowing that someone, finally, was there for me. Had waited for me. Had believed in me. Wanted me. Risked it all for me. That someone truly loved me.

'I haven't killed anyone,' I told him. 'While I've been away, I mean – not a single person. I promised the Man in the Moon I wouldn't if you lived.'

'That's my girl.' He smiled and I rubbed his cheeks again to make sure he was real. 'I've missed you so much.'

'Billy said you were meeting me in Faro?'

'Billy's a liar.' He smiled as the two liars embraced and patted each other on the backs like the sneaks they were. 'I knew you'd hate travelling on your own so I decided to get to you first before you had to. I didn't want to get your hopes up though in case I couldn't make it. Thanks, buddy.' They hugged again and laughed at their own audacity.

'They didn't try and stop you? Nobody recognised you? I mean, how?'

He shook his head and took a deep breath. 'Uh, San Diego to Dallas–Fort Worth, then onto Charleston, North Carolina. Layover to Newark then a slow boat to Halifax, onto Reykjavik and finally Belfast to Dublin. Billy picked me up in Dublin yesterday. I've been sleeping in a youth hostel for the last two nights.'

'And you brought the Slovakian passports Max did for you, didn't you? I completely forgot about them! Oh god, I love being married to you!'

He smiled and slid our new documents briefly out of his pocket as I threw my arms around him again. 'Ditto.'

Billy laughed. 'Yeah the cousins are grand and all but neither of them work in passport control so it's probably best to have backups there.'

I turned to Billy and gave him a proper hug. 'Thank you. You sneaky little fucker. I'm sorry I shouted at you.'

'No bother.'

'Look after Nnedi, won't you?'

'Course. Hey, you know her better than I do – do you think she'd be up for dinner with me sometime?'

'Try it. Maybe not when she wakes up though cos she's going to have the mother of all hangovers.'

'Good thinking.' He swung his car keys around his finger and made his way back to his car. 'Don't be strangers now. Love yous!'

Raf took my hand and one of my bags and we walked towards the airport building as the rain pelted down.

'I can't believe you came all that way for me,' I said. 'You went through all that for me.'

'I'd do anything for you.' He stroked my face and kissed me again. 'Haven't you realised that yet, you fucking maniac?'

'*You're* the one who loves a fucking maniac. What does that make *you*?'

'Guess I must be a fucking maniac too then.'

Yay yay, I got my way. Well, for a bit anyway.

We had three imaginary wingmen as we traversed the separate continents over the next few days – Covid, crowds and a Karen. The first allowed us to keep our masks up and our distance from the next human along. The second ensured nobody gave much of a shit about yours truly when the real endgame was getting out of somewhere before it locked down again.

And the third, the Karen, helped us out a lot when we were waiting an age in the queue for boarding. With her shrieking and throwing sandwiches and coffee cups around like a jacked-up baboon, nobody's eyes were on us and the security staff were on her like a hot pocket, pulling her to one side so they could continue checking passports. We shuffled along, gawping, like the good little non-obstructive holidaymakers we were.

We must have walked past hundreds of police officers in those three airports, fully expecting at least one of them to notice me at any second but for some strange reason, nobody did. Or if they *did*, they ignored me, too busy answering questions about masks on flights or directing someone to customer complaints or looking for smoking foot soles.

There was one hairy moment at Zurich when there was a

gasp behind me and we looked to see two holidaymakers – a couple; one short and brunette (the dude) and one tall and blonde, covered in tattoos (the woman).

'Try and get a pic. Don't be obvious,' he muttered – a British mutter.

But between my mask and my hastily bought 'I ♥ the UAE' baseball cap at Hamad International Airport, there was no way a decent picture could be taken anyway. It happened again at Hyderabad, and again at Changi – a sly picture here, a muttering there. How many 'Bad Seeds' were keeping the secret, I wondered? Did everyone recognise me and were just choosing to hashtag KeepMeBuried? Two days we spent here and there and nowhere at all and the uncertainty – of not knowing if the next check-in desk was going to be the one to end them all – was almost too much to bear.

But I had Raf, and Raf had me. And the check-in desk of doom never came. Our new identities had done the trick. We sailed through every checkpoint like two ordinary tourists; a couple of boring-assed, normal-assed holiday makers with nothing to declare. And the anxiety and the stress and the frustration and the endless, *endless* journeys had all been worth it.

Worth the guy berating his wife for losing their boarding passes.

Worth the woman in security who used five trays for her carry-ons but didn't get the 'no aerosols' memo.

Worth the family of twelve who walked twelve abreast on the travelators and stopped dead randomly in front of me, tripping me up.

Worth Loud Headphones Man, Obvious Fart Woman, Another Loud Karen Who's Had Too Much Wine, Quiet

Mike Who Smells of Beef, Yet Another Shoes-Off Hippy, the Gate Crowders, the Big Baggers, the Aisle Hogs, the Gate Lurkers, the Baggage Carousel Crowds, the Screaming Kids, the Nagging Mums, the Shouting Dads, the Seat Hogs, the Needlessly Officious Airport Staff and every single smelly, whiney, self-important, patronising, contemptuous, haughty, infantile, vapid-ass motherfucker in between.

Because I was with the one person who stayed. He with the dazzling brown eyes, the jawline for days; who wanted to live life alongside me; he with the broken heart tattoo that matched mine, and a face carved by the gods, his black hair shaved to the scalp. Back in army mode again.

'We made it, sweetpea,' he said, scooping me into his arms as we walked through Arrivals at our final destination. 'Can you fucking believe it?'

'Yes,' I said as the blazing sunshine of the day greeted us with open arms. 'I can believe anything now.'

NEW THREAD: Seren's funeral – Bad Seeds Representin'

KatieDaynes6663537: Anyone going to Seren's funeral? If you want to be in on my flower drop, hit me up on PayPal and I'll sign your name on the card.

BTSInMyWardrobe: Yessss meeeee! I plan to get there the day before and stay over in case train's late/delayed/blows up etc.

JonesyShawns77: Yes I'm going. I was wondering what to wear too. Are you guys taking gifts? Cards etc?

Flipper222: I'm taking toys for her kids. I'm gonna catch the train from Grand Central at like lunchtime so I could be there early pm? Do we go colour/black? I don't wanna be disrespectful.

TomHollandsTampon29: Be a lot more respectful if you didn't, like, turn up at all?

KatieDaynes6663537: I won't tolerate abuse on my thread.

TomHollandsTampon29: I'm just saying it'd be a lot more respectful if you *didn't* go to the funeral at all seeing as, like, you didn't know her and don't care that she's dead?

JonesyShawns77: Cody said he appreciated the support.

TomHollandsTampon29: I'm sure he'd rather you stayed away tbh.

[Reported to moderator]

TomHollandsTampon29: You're only going cos you love her sister who, hello, is a SERIAL KILLER.

KatieDaynes6663537: Why are you even on this thread if you don't approve of us? Take a hike, bozo.

TomHollandsTampon29: You're grief vampires. You're like the eejits who turned up to watch Bundy. If you were in a room with Rhiannon, you'd piss your pants like the rest of us.

[User has been removed]

Flipper222: So as I was saying, do we go colour or black?

JokeyMissCumberbatch: I'm going! I'm soooo excited to see you all in the flesh! Do you think it would be okay if I brought her kids some toys? I got some Jellycat bears I wanna give them.

BTSInMyWardrobe: OMG I so wanna do that too!!! Please try and cry though guys, okay? We owe it to her kids.

KatieDaynes6663537: Yeah, well I'm going to be giving flowers and the scrapbook I made. Did you see her husband Cody on Live with Chase and Schuyler? OMG he was soooo cute when he cried!

Flipper222: Cody reeeally hates Rhiannon, doesn't he? He was hella sexy when he got all riled up. *dies of cute*

BTSInMyWardrobe: Stella was SO flirting with him though, old bitch *angry face emoji* *face with steam from nose emoji*

JokeyMissCumberbatch: Cody's much cuter than Craig. OK so I'm gonna bring the Jellycats in case – I can always leave them outside the house if I can't get close at the church. What are we doing after, does everyone wanna do lunch?

PenelopeCruisinForaBruisin: I'm wearing black and taking flowers. When he was on Live w/ Kelly and Ryan he said he was grateful for the cards and gifts. Mine was one of them *squee*

Flipper222: I wish he'd do more promo.

PenelopeCruisinForaBruisin: Maybe he'll do MurderCon next year – if he does I am SO there. She hated the cameras. Prolly cos she was an ugly bitch.

KatieDaynes6663537: She was hella rude when we said hello to her son when he came out of school. We'd travelled over 300 miles.

Flipper222: I know. Such a rude bitch!

BTSInMyWardrobe: I hate her. I hope Rhiannon *did* kill her.

KatieDaynes6663537: I like to think she knows how much we love her. We know she lurks on forums. I wonder if she'll show up????

JokeyMissCumberbatch: OMG wouldn't that be UH-mazing!?!?!?! Like, I'd *seriously* die. Just bury me right next to her sister.

Flipper222: The husband will be there though, that's enough for me *licky tongue emoji*

PenelopeCruisinForaBruisin: LOL
JokeyMissCumberbatch: ROFLMAO
BTSInMyWardrobe: ROFLMAOPMPL

Epilogue

16 May 2024

Johnno Howe is the worst presenter on daytime TV in Australia but he has the best ratings and always trends on social media when he makes a faux pas, which is every day, and is a straight menace when it comes to interviewing young women. He wears a mid-temp fade he's sixty-two years too old for and a double-breasted navy Armani suit he's three stone too heavy for. Whenever he's on TV you can't take your eyes off him, waiting to see where the next cringe is coming from.

Today, that cringe comes courtesy of his interview with Nnedi Géricault, former police detective, now bestselling author.

The hour-long talk and current affairs show he hosts – *Howe's It Hanging?* – is largely people laughing at him and sharing memes on Aussie social media. He poses himself as an expert on all true-crime cases, even though he's not done a lick of study of the area, and he will talk over criminologists and scholars on any given subject.

I feel a bit sorry for him, as he's always talking about this memoir that he's writing that no one wants to publish. He's hella bitter about it all and mentions it regularly. He'll also drop in uninvited titbits about his personal life at any given interval – the time he got mugged in an underpass in Brisbane, the time he went skinny dipping and 'definitely saw a mermaid' and how his first wife shit herself twice in labour.

He has a wing-woman on his show – Patsy Wirrapunda – who actually studied journalism and had an illustrious career as a radio broadcaster and award-winning documentary maker before she got the job on the channel's flagship show. Now she spends her mornings propping up Howe's ego and backing him up when he forgets his cues (a lot) and his lines (a lot more). His nickname for her is 'the glamour'.

'Welcome back to *Howe's It Hanging* with me Johnno Howe and the incomparable, the effervescent, the indescribable—'

'—Patsy Wirrapunda, hello, welcome back. For our next segment, we're talking to the detective-turned-author whose second book *Breaking Bud: Unearthing the Sweetpea Killer* has stormed into the Australian top-10 bestsellers list. It's also been a *New York Times* and *Sunday Times* bestseller in recent months and the author, Nnedi Géricault, joins us live today.'

'Nnedi, a warm welcome to Sydney,' cuts in Johnno. 'You're smelling especially fragrant this morning. I smelled you in the green room. Is that J'ardin dAmalfi or Van Cleef and Arpels?'

'Thank you for having me. Uh, I've no idea actually. One I was given for my birthday, I think.' She's serving some serious cunt in her grey power suit, high-neck burgundy knit, her full Afro held back by a classy gold Alice band.

'I've got my Dior Sauvage on today,' Johnno adds. 'Hopefully things won't get too *sav-age* between us, heh heh . . .'

Nnedi patiently waits for him to get it out of his system. Patsy's got a little drum beating in the side of her mouth.

'Let's go back to the start, well, not the start, *nearly* the start or else we'd be here all day – heh heh – we all know that Rhiannon Lewis, terrible, awful serial killer, fled the UK, the police couldn't catch her, she went on the run around the world for a couple of years. She was seen in various places from Indonesia to Kathmandu, America, you name it, but she'd gone completely undetected. Then she came *back* to the UK under an assumed name in October 2021, didn't she, and that was because of an extraordinary scheme that *you* cooked up with her sister, wasn't it?'

'Yes. I got some information which I pursued in my own

time to track down Rhiannon, who I knew was still alive, and I went rogue to get her back to the UK and arrest her.'

'Only things didn't quite go according to plan, did they?'

'No. To cut a long story short, soon after the kidnap, Rhiannon wrested the gun away from me and an innocent woman ended up being killed.'

'This was Rhiannon's sister Seren?' adds Patsy.

'Yes. Rhiannon and her . . . got into an altercation and the gun went off.'

'So Rhiannon killed her sister?'

'Yes.' She looked straight down the lens – a look that was meant for me.

'She then kidnapped me and drove me to Ireland where she held me captive for ten days.'

'She tied you up?'

'Yes.'

'For ten days?'

' . . . yes.'

'And the idea was to get free and arrest her once her guard was down?'

'Yes.'

'But she slipped through your fingers again, didn't she?' says Howe, who has been staring at Nnedi's somewhat fingerless hand.

'She is a very clever woman. Highly manipulative. She's had to be to get away with what she's done all this time.'

'What is she like, up close and personal?' asks Howe, flashing his Rolex to the camera, 'because you lived with her for ten days so you must have seen her red in tooth and claw.'

'She is normal, to all intents. Quite boring actually, for the most part.'

'Were you scared for your life when you were with her?' asks Patsy.

Nnedi ponders this question, looking around, the studio lights catching her eyes and dazzling her. She looks back at Patsy, then at Howe. 'I was wary but I never thought she was going to harm me, no.'

Patsy shuffles her papers. 'It says in *Breaking Bud* . . . that you stayed at a cottage in Ireland which you've since *bought*, isn't that right?'

'Yes, I moved there permanently almost a year ago now.'

Howe's incredulous. 'You bought the house a *serial killer* almost killed you in?'

'It's a beautiful little house and I've made it my own now. But yes, to answer your question, I live in the place where she held me captive.'

'Is it true she introduced you to your boyfriend?' says Patsy, face resting on her hands like she's asked Sandy how summer shagging went with Danny.

'I'd prefer not to talk about my private life, thank you.'

Patsy continues. 'So you're at the cottage, tied up, scared for your life, and then this guy comes on the scene whom Rhiannon had catfished and he was a suspected child sex attacker, right?'

'Yes, Lawrence McVicker lived in the village and I knew nothing about him, but Rhiannon knew he was predatory and she saw an opportunity to enact bloody revenge on him, as is her wont.'

'Revenge for being a member of a certain site on the dark web, yes?'

'Yes, Rhiannon . . . took me to the man's house, and forced me to watch as . . . she killed him. With a hammer.'

'And you witnessed this didn't you?'

Nnedi nods. 'Yes. And while she was disposing of the body, I discovered the laptop with the evidence on about these sites.'

Howe is silent for once. So Nnedi continues unchecked.

'We're working with the families of other potential victims of McVicker to see if we can get them some resolution. There may be more unsolved cases with which to connect him, including a number of rapes in the west of Ireland since 2001, and we're actively working on those.'

'And this McVicker, did she chop him up in the tub?' Howe chuckles.

'No. She just cut his head off,' Nnedi replies coolly.

Howe bares his veneers and scrolls his iPad. 'You got a suspended sentence for perverting the course of justice, didn't you, Nnedi – that was for stealing a police-issue handgun, wasn't it?'

'Yes, but I was shown mercy by the CPS who did not think it was in the public interest to incarcerate me when the real villain was Rhiannon.'

'And because of the massive breakthrough you made while you were at McVicker's house, wasn't it?' Patsy smiles. 'And it involves this forum he was a member of on the dark web?'

'Yes,' says Nnedi. 'Eventually, we were able to identify the four main site contributors, crack their locations, obtain information about most of the other members and along with colleagues in Germany, Denmark, the USA, Australia and Thailand, we worked with victim ID specialists and were able to form one of the world's biggest taskforces to take them down, one at a time.'

'You smashed the paedophile ring to pieces, let's be fair,' says Patsy, beaming.

'Sounds painful!' Howe laughs.

Patsy bats her eyes. 'And how many were arrested, Nnedi?'

'At last count, eight-hundred-and-seventy-six, men and women, so just over a quarter of the contributors. We have multiple leads to more offenders and are actively tracing them right now so we can protect their victims from more abuse. A lot of children are safe now because we've dismantled this site.'

'There are many more sites of this nature though, aren't there?' says Howe, with his metaphorical bucket of cold water.

'Yes, but with the help of our increasingly sophisticated technology, we're coming for them, have no fear. And we will not stop.'

'This is what you do now, isn't it?' asks Patsy.

'Yes. If I can save one child from being abused, I will consider it a life well lived. But I would like to save all of them, and I would like to bring the full force of the law down on the perpetrators. And anyone who is hiding them. And they will all see my face through that cell door, make no mistake.'

'You sound like that guy in *Pulp Fiction*,' notes Howe, straining his Botox to think. 'You know, the *Pulp Fiction* guy – "I will bring down upon thee great vengeance and . . ."' He can't think of the rest of the quote. Patsy and Nnedi ain't helping. They're waiting, patiently, for him to grow some self-awareness. That ain't happening either.

'And if you don't arrest 'em, Rhiannon's gonna kill 'em?' Howe laughs.

Nnedi's face changes; a Mona Lisa smile. 'Last time I saw her she was tying me up and fleeing into the night. I don't know what she's doing now.'

'Where do you think she is?'

'I have no clue.'

Howe glances at the camera, then back to his iPad. 'Her dad chopped up *your* dad, didn't he? Tommy Lewis?'

'Tommy killed my father, yes.'

'And Rhiannon told you where to find his body, that's what you allude to in the book, don't you?'

'Owing to a tip-off, we were permitted to dig under the barn at Honey Cottage where Rhiannon grew up. And we excavated my father's remains.'

'And your book, which is your second one on the subject, is selling brilliantly at the moment too, isn't it?' asks Patty.

'It's doing very well indeed. I'm very proud of it. And the first one has gone back into the charts as well, which is great.'

'Any plans to write more?'

Nnedi smiles, another fake. 'No. I just want to concentrate on my job which I can do pretty much remotely now we have decent broadband. Sadly, this type of work is everlasting. They will not stop so neither can I.'

'No more books or TV then?'

'When it's necessary,' she replies. 'The books have set me up to live the life I want and that's enough.' There's a glimpse at Howe's limited-edition diamond-encrusted Rolex ($128,000's worth). She fake-smiles again. 'Enough is plenty for anyone.'

'Well, thanks so much for coming in today, Ngozi,' says Howe, seemingly having his first Adele Dazeem moment of the day. 'My wife is a massive Bad Seed so I'm gonna pass on my copy of *Breaking Bud* to her for bedtime reading – don't have much else to do at bedtime these days, do we darl? – and we're gonna take a break but come back after cos we've got a *killer* competition for you. You could win a signed copy of Ngozi's extraordinary new book about her road trip with Sweetpea, we've got it right here, show it to the camera, Pats, that's a good girl, and all the details are coming up for you next—'

'Loughlin Talbot will be here as well after the break,' adds Patsy, 'fresh from a sell-out stint at the Edinburgh Festival—'

'—in your neck of the woods, Ngozi, Scotland,' cuts in Howe.

'I live in Ireland and my name is Nnedi.'

'Oh right, yeah sorry, that's the other one we've got coming in next week to talk about her artwork, isn't it? Sorry about that, love, anyway, Loughlin's going to be here talking about his wife's long, lingering death from brain cancer six months ago and how he's come through to the other side with a new book, a new stand-up show – *Don't Throw Yourself Off the Bridge Just Yet* – and a brand-new *wife*, twenty years younger too, the lucky bugger. So we look forward to seeing him. You like jokes, don't you, Nnedi?'

'Not as much as your wife, clearly,' she snips, to great guffaws of laughter in the studio. Patsy is pissing herself as professionally as possible.

'Oof!' says Howe. 'Why don't you give me a paper cut and pour salt on it while you're here?'

'Pass the salt.' She winks and again the studio erupts.

'We'll see you after these messages!' Howe nervous-laughs as the camera pulls back and he shuffles his papers and grooves along to the programme's theme tune – 'Hangin' Tough' by New Kids on the Block.

December 2024

Tuesday, 31 December – Place unknown

Well, my New Year's Eve has certainly gone off with a bang, I don't know about yours. I woke up around nine as the sun seared its way through our thin-assed bedroom curtains and through one bleary eye I could see a baby monkey on the windowsill, drinking our wine from last night. Both glasses, the little lush.

Then I felt this weight on my chest: a warm, spongey sort of weight. I opened the other eye to see my baby son lying on my chest. We lay there together, me and him, as Raf left us to go make the coffee.

'Morning, sunshine,' I whispered, kissing that addictive little head. His fluffy hairs tickled my chin. There's no denying that smile of his or the big brown eyes or that same tuft of hair Raf has at the base of his neck. They even have the same eyebrows. Sweet peas in a pod, the pair of them.

'Can you stop looking so much like your daddy today please? Jesus – did my genes even put up a fight? I carried you for nine months. The least you could do is take after me in some way. But not *every* way.'

I kissed him again. He wriggled and snarfed and even though it's been three months since we met him, every movement he makes is still fascinating. First time he sneezed, Raf and I cried. It would be pathetic if I were watching someone else's life. But I'm not – I'm watching mine. And I can't believe it.

I keep thinking how happy twenty-seven-year-old Rhiannon would be if she knew this was where things were heading. I felt like giving up so many times. Made so many wrong turns. But now here we are. He is bliss. I've found him, finally. I've found *them*.

And I don't wanna hear about how I've let the sisterhood down by being reliant on two men either. You've got to be reliant on something in this world. I've tried to live life on my own – it doesn't work. I will always need something to live for. Someone to kill for. That's just who I am. And they are my someones.

I only have one secret from Raf – the key I sent to Cody, Seren's husband. He doesn't need to know about that. He never knew about the other $900k that Tenoch had left me in the New York deposit box. I only brought back what I could carry. I can't ever remove the pain I've caused Cody, or Seren's kids, Ashton and Mabli, but it's something, if they want it. Apart from Ivy and the baby, they're the only two people in the world whose blood ran in my veins too. Just felt I needed to do something for them. Guilt? Shame? Yeah, maybe both.

Raf came in with the coffee and set mine down on the side table and re-joined us in bed. The baby yawned and went back to sleep. Every yawn is delightful. His little fists. His nose. He's like a painting. Sometimes we watch him for hours, lying between us, two goons in love with our boy.

'He doesn't look anything like me,' I said again, twiddling Raf's ear. 'Was I even in the room?'

'Yeah he does,' said Raf, studying him closely. 'His ... ears are like yours.'

'You think so?'

'Definitely.'

'Do you think he's happy?'

'Of course he is.'

'But we don't have a permanent home or a garden for him or many toys.'

'He doesn't care. He's got us and we give him what we can. He doesn't know any different.'

I nodded and sighed against Raf's neck. There's a vase of fresh orchids on the window that kicked out a smell now and again, from yesterday's trip to the market. The room usually smelled divine. But today's idyll lasted five minutes. Another smell permeated, and then I felt this little explosion against my hand, and a brown wetness appeared up the back of the baby's onesie.

'Shit.'

'Shit!'

'Grab the wipes.'

We sprang up and set to finding the changing bag and nappies and because neither of us was in that super-organised phase of parenting yet; nothing's where it should be, our place was a mess and we're tripping over shoes and bags to find things and the shit was dripping on the bed but it's . . . funny. *Really* funny.

I should be mad; I should be railing about having baby shit up my forearm. I should be moaning about how messy everything is cos we haven't properly settled in yet and not only that but we don't know how long we're going to be here.

We never settle anywhere – we're always moving on. We have to. But it's okay. As long as I have them, it's fine.

Because nothing bad will happen while we're a three. We're solid. And we know what we would both do to protect this portable idyll we've created.

The horrible stuff is still there, outside. We'll see a market vendor kicking a dog. Or a sex-tourist touching up a waitress. Or a white-haired gammon called 'Asian Phil' miming a blow job to a boy young enough to be his grandson.

Raf gets it now. He gets why I kill. He tells me so when he's gazing into the bassinette, or he's got the baby on his chest while we're watching TV. He says I've 'reawakened his hyper vigilance from his army days'. His soldier's bearing never left him really, but he's much more soldier-like now than he was in San Diego. He's left his art behind too – hasn't sketched or painted as much as a still life in six months – and he keeps his head shaved and his walk purposeful, eyes always on lookout. His protectiveness is a heady mixture of horny and scary (like a Mexican John Wick). And that's always been my bag.

Maybe it's dangerous to trust Rafael as much as I do – the thought is always there, in the background, lurking, that he might get bored of this life or that he might see a woman he fancies who is offering herself up to him on a plate, but as long as it doesn't become real, it's all right. *I'm* all right. When he's walking through the market with the papoose on, you should see the women descend on him like a flock of horny seagulls. But I don't think he carries him because of that. He takes every subtle opportunity to introduce me, his wife, and flash his wedding ring, and they back off.

If it wasn't for him, life would be a lie again. An act. He

got rid of his Ophelia tattoo – we found a place in Bangkok that put lasers on it, turned it into just a bunch of flowers – sweetpeas with a skull in the centre and no name at all. I like that one better.

'Still at the top spot,' said Raf, fiddling with his phone – he showed me the screen. The headline read:

KILLER BIOGRAPHY RECLAIMS TOP SPOT AFTER NINE WEEKS

Freddie Litton-Cheney's latest bestseller *Dead Head: When the Petals Came Off* comprises everything from Ivy's birth up until I left Ireland. It's a beast of a book but that's his lot now – he ain't getting any more. The Bad Seeds have more than enough Rhiannon fodder to be going on with and they're spreading, all over the world, on every forum and message board and thread; growing more and more Sweetpea vines, stronger all the time, teaching younger generations what I did and why we must root out the rotten ones, wherever they may grow.

Nico is hoping to fly out to see us in a few weeks but we're still being cautious on that score. I don't know if Liv and Bianca have decided to come with him yet. Once they see how happy Raf is and meet the newest member of their family, maybe they'll soften. I choose to live in hope.

'Have you fed The Fish today?' I asked when we'd all cleaned up, strapping the baby's papoose against me.

'No. Is there any point if we're moving out today?'

'I guess not.'

'I'll take this one. You can lay down your armour today, baby.'

'You sure?'

'Yeah. I could do with the workout.'

I looked at him and there was a pang in my chest which I've come to realise is guilt. And Raf can sense it – my face must change or something.

'I've turned you into the criminal you tried so hard not to be, haven't I?'

Raf stroked the baby's back as he drifted back off to sleep. Lines that were there on his face before disappeared. Then he said, 'If what we're doing is wrong, maybe it's criminal to be right.' And he leant across and kissed me.

I looked down at the bub and stroked his toe beans. I craned my head to listen as though the baby's talking to me. 'Wha was that? Oh. Your son says Go Daddy.' And I shake his little fist like it's a pom pom.

Once we'd dressed and packed our stuff, I set the bags down on the doorstep and we accompanied Raf down to the basement. He slid the door across. There's a shuffling noise at the shadows at the back and a rattling of chains as The Fish cowered down, shielding his eyes from the light.

'Morning, Phil,' I called out.

There's a whimper and more begging, more waterworks. More of the 'Please please please!' with added prayer stance and stumps for fingers.

'Nah, it's too late, we've got to move on now, sorry. My husband will take care of you today. You'll find him more hospitable to guests than me – he won't keep you dangling for so long.'

His grey hair's lost its bouffant now – it's greasy and hangs in strands at his neck. His permanent smirk has been replaced by a puffy, bruised expression with a starkness about the eyes – a little like Laddy's eyes looked when I last saw him. Like that guy whose cock I severed before pushing him in the canal. They all bleed into one another after a while.

'Please no! I have money, I can give you money, as much as you want!'

'Oof! The algo is rhythmin today, isn't it? I knew you were gonna say that. Again. And again.'

'Please . . .'

'Well, you've asked me very nicely but no can do, I'm afraid. See, I'm not on duty this morning. He is.' I handed Raf the machete. Phil's fingerless hand raised to his face to cover a gasp.

'Take the baby outside,' said Raf, kissing our boy's fluffy head and ushering me through the door.

'Thanks, Daddy,' I said with a kiss on his lips.

Raf doesn't like the baby being anywhere near it. But he needs to do this. He needs it like I did – it's his therapy. He keeps seeing that image of Phil in the market with a little boy no older than six. It haunts him.

And without hesitation, he strode across the floor. I turned my son's face away and pulled the door across and we went back upstairs to the hallway to collect our bags and take them out to the garden.

'Hey, Mali.' The dog got up from her sun patch to join us on our walk. Raf reckons she's part Malinois, so we call her Mali or The Maligator. She's the same colour as Tink but with a darker face and twice the size. Raf fed her a hotdog one day and we cleaned her up and de-flead and -wormed her and she comes with us everywhere now. He used to work with Malinois during drills in his army days, practising controlled aggression, so he knows what to do to keep her in check. She's hyper-protective of us so she fits right in. That's all she needed – someone to notice her and take pity on her, give her some training and a lot of love.

Just like me.

She'd do anything we tell her to do. Raf's training her like Brad Pitt's dog in that film – to attack and cease on command. Her first success was Asian Phil. Ripped his scrotum clean off following one click of Raf's fingers.

Girl after my own heart.

I stopped to smell the jasmine and frangipani bushes on the path. Sometimes I wish we stayed somewhere long enough to grow our own flowers, but for now ones planted by other people will make do.

The screams began from inside and we walked further into the gardens until we couldn't hear it anymore, buffeted by the mango trees and palms. We sat down on the low wall to wait for him – he wouldn't be long, he never was. He doesn't keep them waiting like I do. It's nice to have someone else do the admin for once so I can just relax. Mali rested her chin on my knee and licked the baby's foot – he wriggled in delight. I stroked her sun-warmed head and sent my text: *AsianPhil101 – Gordon Ramsay Clap – done XX*

Within minutes, a text came back from the unknown number and it's always the same emoji – a Black woman's face smiling and two kisses.

Not all men are evil, I know that. But as they say, not all viruses can kill you but we still wash our hands after crapping, don't we? Well, I do. I've probably walked past thousands of good, honest, decent men as they go about their business, push their children in buggies, working jobs to feed their families. Men in my *own* family. Trustworthy men who wouldn't hurt you. I'm going to teach my little boy how to be good and he has Raf too for a comparison study of course. Good men are everywhere, and it gives me hope that the world is worth saving somehow. Not all men hurt kids or animals or follow women down alleys at night. Not all men lack the understanding of no. Not all men bring out the 'bad seed' in us.

But some of them *do*. Some of them *are*. Some women are too. And it's those some I have to stick around for. Because the problem is much bigger than I am, so I must be much bigger than it. Silence is violence.

But *my* violence is worse.

One day I *will* get caught. There's a golden rule that Raf and I have agreed on – if I get caught, I go alone, no questions asked. He takes the baby and I go quietly without any fuss. It's a fair cop and all that. We'll keep dodging it until then, shielded by the Bad Seeds and their agenda to #KeepHerBuried, but when it comes, that's what we will do. The world is only so big and we can only move around so many times. However many Bad Seeds want me free and growing as nature intended, there are still those determined to cut me down.

So wait for it. It's going to happen. I sowed this field, and I have to reap what comes of it, weeds and all.

You might be sitting in your office one day and they'll burst in shouting, pointing guns and arresting that woman who sits at the desk opposite you.

Or you'll be in your garden with the kids and you'll hear the battering ram on the next house along.

Or you'll be on a train or a plane and they won't let you off until the police have cuffed me and led me down the steps first.

That lone woman with the busted tyre on the side of the road.

That lone woman you pushed past in the line.

That lone woman you touched up on the bus, on the train, in the lift, on the stairs, bending over the supermarket freezer.

That lone woman you followed home.

That lone woman standing over your body with an axe in one hand and your head in the other.

I am that woman, but you won't hear me roar. With any luck, you won't hear me coming at all.

Acknowledgements

Jenny Savill and Silé Edwards at Andrew Nurnberg Agency for keeping the faith, my editors Cat Camacho (Bad Seeds), Katie Seaman (Thorn + Dead Head), Clio Cornish (In Bloom), Anna Baggeley (Sweetpea), copyeditor Eldes Tran, Paola Gómez, Penny Skuse for all the 'Bristol Airport Faces' that keep me on the right track, Maggie Snead for being my Bilge wrangler, Matthew Snead for always being First Reader, and all my students at BSU who enthuse about my books and spread the word of The Pea.

I'd also like to thank the bloggers, booksellers, book pushers and Bad Seeds who are STILL shouting Rhiannon's name from the rooftops and forcing it upon unsuspecting readers, namely:

Adrian O'Leary, Amy Jeavons, Amy Whittaker, Ann C. Howard, Bec @Bowden Aesthetic, Catherine Gauden, Cherie Brook-Smith, Chloe Lynch @DalmatianPongo, Chris Scotland, Christine Guest @christybookish, Claire Allen, Claire @Books By Claire, Claire Louise Deeley, Colin and Sarah Rees, Colette Hunter, Dani Collings @dani_collings7, Corpse Girl, Danielle Lanae, Debby Donnelly-Addison @TheBohoBaker, Dominique @reading_untamed, Ellie Jones, Emily Healey @what_ems_ reading, Emma @emmasbibliotreasures, Emma @scousepie,

Emma Y @emzamy, Emmie Fletcher @emf_books, Gem @zeroshelfcontrol, Hannah B, Hannah Elizabeth, Janet Emson, Jannah @TheBookWorm20, Jessie @poodlenoodlecanoodle, Jo @onlyifIcanbringabook, Izzy Wheeler, Jeni Scott @jenifun, Karen Marie Diyar, Karen JK Hart, Kate Forsman @Date With a Thriller, Kayleigh @Kayleigh'sReadingCorner, Kirsten Ranf, Lauren Blight, Lauren Canino and Shae Hawkins @ Book Bitches, Leann@books_green_tea, Lesley at Bridge Books, Dromore, Liv @oliviasbookcorner, Lucy Lawson, Melanie Campbell, Michael Bartowski @bartowskibookclub, Morren Aconite, Mrs Gloss, Owen Williams, Penny Feather, Philippa Lord @titanium_pip, Rebecca de Winter, Rhiannon-Elizabeth Williamson, Sara @my.bookworm.life, Sarah Patterson, Sasha @Booky Weirdo, Sean Caddell, Tara Clover, Martin French and Lord Timothy Sheldrake, Toni Mae Leckie, Tracy Fenton @ TBC, Vicky @BaileysBear, Victoria @booksbyyourbedside, Victoria Warby.

I'm sorry if I've missed anyone - it's either perimenopausal brain fog or you did fuck all to help.

Cheers anyway.

CJx

P.S. And it you want to read Ivy's story, keep pestering and maybe one day it'll get finished 12

Can't get enough of everyone's favourite serial-killer-next-door, Rhiannon Lewis?

Don't miss the rest of the Sweetpea series

SWEETPEA

Although her childhood was haunted by a famous crime, Rhiannon's life is normal now that her celebrity has dwindled. By day her job as an editorial assistant is demeaning and unsatisfying. By evening she dutifully listens to her friend's plans for marriage and babies whilst secretly making a list.

A kill list.

From the man on the Lidl checkout who always mishandles her apples, to the driver who cuts her off on her way to work, to the people who have got it coming, Rhiannon's ready to get her revenge.

Because the girl everyone overlooks might be able to get away with murder…

IN BLOOM

Rhiannon's back and killing for two . . .

Rhiannon Lewis has successfully fooled the world and framed her cheating fiancé Craig for the depraved and bloody killing spree she committed. She should be ecstatic that she's free.

Except for one small problem. She's pregnant with her ex-lover's child. The ex-lover she only recently chopped up and buried in her in-laws garden. And as much as Rhiannon wants to continue making her way through her kill lists, a small voice inside is trying to make her stop.

But can a killer's urges ever really be curbed?

**Victim. Murderer. Serial Killer.
What next?**

DEAD HEAD

Can a serial killer ever lose their taste for murder?

Since confessing to her bloody murder spree Rhiannon
Lewis, the now-notorious Sweetpea killer, has been feeling
out-of-sorts.

Having fled the UK on a cruise ship to start her new life,
Rhiannon should be feeling happy. But it's hard to turn over
a new leaf when she's stuck in an oversized floating tin can
with the Gammonati and screaming kids. Especially when
they remind her of Ivy – the baby she gave up for a life
carrying on killing.

Rhiannon is all at sea. She's lost her taste for blood but is
it really gone for good? Maybe Rhiannon is realising that
there's more to life than death . . .

THORN IN MY SIDE

Sometimes, you can be your own worst enemy . . .

Rhiannon Lewis thought she finally had it all:
thanks to the pandemic she's had to keep a much
lower profile but has found happiness with her
fiancé Rafael and his family. For once, she is
surrounded by people who love her for who
she is (or who they think she is).

**After over 800 days without murdering anyone,
the woman formerly known as the Sweetpea Killer
thinks she might have finally turned over a new leaf.**

That is until her soon-to-be sister-in-law has a run in
with her abusive ex, and Rhiannon rediscovers her
taste for revenge. This time, with a loving family in tow,
the stakes are much higher. Wedded bliss and life
as a normal person are finally within Rhiannon's reach,
but you can never keep a good serial killer down.

ONE PLACE. MANY STORIES

Bold, innovative and
empowering publishing.

FOLLOW US ON:

@HQStories